Imaro the forsaken ...

Growing up among the Ilyassai, a fierce tribe of warrior-herdsmen who despise his origins, the young Imaro struggles for acceptance after the breaking of a taboo forces his mother to leave him behind.

Imaro the outcast ...

The boy becomes a man, unlike any other the Ilyassai have ever seen. His quest for acceptance and identity continues. Yet he learns he has powerful enemies, human and inhuman. Prevailing over foes who desire nothing more than to see him dead, Imaro finds that in victory, there can be loss.

Imaro the warrior ...

Departing from the Ilyassai, Imaro roams afar, wandering across the vast continent of Nyumbani, pitting his prodigious strength and courage against men, beasts and demons. Hunted by relentless foes, Imaro becomes the hunter. Eventually, he finds friendship and love among people who are, like him, exiles and outlaws.

Yet forces beyond Imaro's comprehension are aligned against him. As he rises to prominence, events preordained before Imaro's birth begin to unfold.

Powers are stirring in Nyumbani, the Africa of a world that is beyond the one we know. And Imaro learns that some of those powers are aligned against him. As he struggled to hold on to his hard-won acceptance, the warrior seeks the answer to the question that has haunted him all his life:

Who am I?

Charles R. Saunders was born and grew up in Pennsylvania. He earned a degree in psychology from Lincoln University. Saunders moved to Canada in 1969. After appearing in many small-press magazines, he published three novels based on African myths and legends, featuring the warrior-hero Imaro. Saunders has also written short stories, screenplays, radio plays, opinion columns and non-fiction books. He passed away in May 2020.

IMARO

IMARO

CHARLES SAUNDERS

FEATURING AN INTRODUCTION BY
CHARLES DE LINT

NIGHT SHADE BOOKS
New York

Night Shade books may be purchased in bulk at special discounts for sales promotion, corporate gifts, fund-raising, or educational purposes. Special editions can also be created to specifications. For details, contact the Special Sales Department, Night Shade Books, 307 West 36th Street, 11th Floor, New York, NY 10018 or info@skyhorsepublishing.com.

Night Shade Books™ is a trademark of Skyhorse Publishing, Inc. ®, a Delaware corporation.

Visit our website at www.nightshadebooks.com.

10 9 8 7 6 5 4 3

Library of Congress Cataloging-in-Publication Data is available on file.

ISBN: 978-1-59780-036-5

Jacket art © 2006 by Vince Evans
Jacket design by Claudia Noble
Interior layout and design by Jeremy Lassen

Printed in the United States of America

INTRODUCTION
BY CHARLES DE LINT

It's hard to believe that it's been twenty-four years since DAW Books published the first Imaro novel (though of course, Imaro stories had already been appearing in small-press magazines for at least a decade before that). What I find even harder to believe is that, in all that time, there have been so few fantasy novels based on the rich and fascinating cultures and mythic matter of Africa.

But I'm not surprised that no one has yet come close to bringing it to life so well as Charles R. Saunders.

* * *

Like many of us working in the small press at the time, Charles was inspired by the work of Robert E. Howard when he first began to write. But while Howard was, and Charles is, a born storyteller, that's pretty much where the similarities end.

"The trouble," he used to tell me in those days, "is that there are so few black characters in fantasy or sf who actually *matter*."

So Charles started creating them—not so much to provide character identification for other black readers, as that this was a way he could "read" these kinds of stories himself. And in the process he discovered an abiding love for the cultures, traditions, and mythological matter of Africa that continues to this day.

The first thing he understood was that there is no single "African" culture. Like the tribes of the North American Indian (who are also lumped together in many people's minds as having only one culture), the peoples of Africa are part of a wide spectrum of cultural identities as rich and diverse as those of any of the world's other continents. From Yoruba creation myths to Anansi trickster tales, from the Dogon temples of Mali to the palaces of sultans on the

Swahili coast, from the Masai tribes of the Serengeti to the pygmy bushmen of the Kalahari—Africa has enough cultural, historical, and mythological wealth to fuel the stories of a thousand writers.

Charles delved into this material, mixed it with a brew distilled from what he learned reading the heroic fantasies of Howard, Fritz Leiber, and other classic masters of the field, then put his own inimitable stamp upon it all to create the world of Imaro and the characters who inhabit it. Bandits and warriors, priests and strange monsters, loyal retainers and back-stabbing traitors.

And towering above them all is the character of Imaro himself—still a youth when we meet him in the book you're about to read, headstrong, and certainly out of his depth at times, but already a man, willing to grow and learn. A warrior who seeks peace. An outsider who has been denied the companionship of family and tribe, and so has to create his own.

I've never understood why these books have languished out of print for so many years. For me they rank at the very top of the heroic fantasy field, not simply because the storytelling is so immediate and absorbing, but for the fresh wealth of culture and myth to be found in their pages, and the sharp insights into the human spirit that Charles brings to each character.

I know why the initial DAW sales stalled and died—that's simply the vagaries of the publishing field. By the time the second book came out, the first was no longer in print, so any reader who wasn't there at the beginning (snatching up a copy from that initial small print run), could either enter Imaro's world in what felt like the middle of the story, or turn to some other series where they were able to buy the first book.

Unfortunately, most people don't like missing the beginning, and so the series floundered.

Their loss, you might say to those folks. But it was our loss, too, because Imaro's full story was never completed at DAW, and to all intents and purposes, Charles vanished from the fantasy field.

But he never stopped writing. He simply turned to writing about other things.

Moving from Ottawa, Ontario, to Halifax, Nova Scotia, in the eighties, he wrote copy, columns, and op-ed pieces for the local newspapers there. He published a number of nonfiction books: *Africville: A Spirit That Lives On* (1989) to accompany an exhibition relating the history of an indomitable black Halifax community, leveled by the local government under the guise of "progress"; *Share and Care: The Story of the Nova Scotia Home for Colored Children* (1994), a superb history of the neglected and unwanted children of Nova Scotia's black community; and *Black and Bluenose: The Contemporary History of a Community* (1999), an insightful and passionate collection of his columns and op-ed pieces.

And he continued to write fantasy.

Besides preparing these new editions of the Imaro books, and also working up a Dossouye novel (she was the lead character in another story-cycle from his small-press days), for many years Charles has been working on a stunning series of high fantasy novels combining Celtic and African mythology. I've read portions of them in manuscript form, and they easily rank among my very favorite novels, period.

It's my fervent hope that the book in hand will be a rousing success. First, because it, and Charles, deserve that success.

But I also hope that it will provide the impetus for our finally getting the whole story of Imaro out in book form. And then, that it will also pave the way for the publication of these new books he's been working on. Lord knows, the field needs the fresh and discerning insights that only Charles R. Saunders can bring to it.

* * *

I'm speaking sincerely here, but I'll also admit a certain bias—and privilege. Charles and I have been pals since the mid-seventies—his moving to Halifax didn't change that. We published our own small-press magazine together, inspired by other great little zines like the late Gene Day's *Dark Fantasy*. We shared our stories with each other—a process from which I learned a lot more than I think he did, since he was already a far more accomplished writer than I was in those days. We helped each other move (and there's a true sign of friendship: helping to move another bibliophile's library) and spent a lot of time just hanging out, talking about this love we had for the field. This love we still have.

Since those early years, his level of craftsmanship has certainly risen, but the power and intensity of his stories remains unchanged. And the rich tapestry of his settings and characters has only deepened.

That doesn't surprise me.

Because Charles remains that born storyteller he was when he first set pen to paper all those years ago. He's one of those gifted writers who can tackle any subject, in fiction or nonfiction, and make it engrossing. At times, even inspiring.

I, and the few others lucky enough to read his manuscripts, already know this. But it's high time the rest of the world has the pleasure to discover this as well.

—Charles de Lint
Ottawa, summer 2005

REVISITING IMARO

BY CHARLES R. SAUNDERS

"You can never go home again ..."
"If only I could go back and do it over ..."
"If I knew then what I know now ..."

Such are the laments of the lost past. The truism states that the past is gone, finished, done and cannot be undone. For a writer, however, the iron in which that truism is clad is not unbreakable. A writer can go home again, do it over again and apply the experience of the present to the circumstances of the past. On the blank page, all things are possible.

But sometimes, a writer can forget that basic tenet of the craft. And a catalyst is needed to rediscover it.

During the summer of 2003, I received an e-mail from a young Australian named Benjamin Szumskyj. Unbeknownst to me, Ben had discovered my long-out-of-print Imaro novels, and they had made a favorable impression on him. He wanted to see the entire Imaro saga—the three published novels, the published short stories, and the unpublished Imaro material, including a complete fourth novel and an uncompleted fifth one—in print, rather than have them continue to languish in used bookstores and my trunk.

There was a time when my own desire to reach that goal was no less fervent than Ben's. But by the summer of 2003, that desire had long since ebbed. And I didn't think either Imaro or I could go home again.

A little background music, Maestro ...

Imaro and his milieu came into being during the early 1970s, a time when the fantasy genre was on a feverish roll, fueled by the popularity of Robert E. Howard's Conan stories and J. R. R. Tolkien's *Lord of the Rings* trilogy. Fantasy paperbacks filled the shelves in bookstores, and I read as many of them as my money could buy. Back then, I was more attracted to Howard's sword-and-sorcery subgenre than I was to Tolkien's high fantasy.

Inside most, if not all, fantasy readers, a fantasy writer lurks, waiting to be unleashed. I was no different. However, the fantasy I wanted to write was, indeed, different.

Of course, that's what they all say. But my ideas really *were* different. And "they all" say *that*, too, right?

Fantasy was not my only consuming interest at that time. I was also very much absorbed in African history, culture, and mythology. I can't remember the exact, "eureka" moment, but sometime in 1970, the Imaro character emerged from the depths of my subconscious, and his story demanded to be told.

Imaro would be the anti-Tarzan, and the setting in which his story unfolded would be an alternate-world Africa rather than an imaginary prehistoric era of the Earth we know, as was the case in Howard's Hyborian Age and Tolkien's Middle Earth. Imaro's Africa, which I named Nyumbani, would serve as an antidote to the negative stereotypes about the so-called "Dark Continent" that crept—advertently and inadvertently—into the fantasy world of far too many other writers.

In 1971, I began to write Imaro stories, and other African-oriented fantasy tales as well. During the mid-1970s, my stories appeared in various small-press magazines, and eventually they made it into mass-market anthologies such as *The Year's Best Fantasy Stories* and *Swords against Darkness*.

By the early 1980s, I had stitched some of the previously published stories together to create two novels—*Imaro* and *Imaro II: The Quest for Cush*, which were published by DAW Books in 1981 and 1984, respectively. DAW published the third novel in the series, *Imaro III: The Trail of Bohu*, in 1985. The third one was all original, with none of its content adapted from previously published stories.

However, Imaro's shelf life ended with the publication of the third novel, even though I had completed a fourth volume of the Ilyassai's adventures, and was partway through a fifth one. The books did not sell well, and DAW declined to publish the fourth Imaro novel.

Looking back, I can attribute that outcome to the vagaries of the publishing industry, and the "vagueries" of my life.

First, the vagaries. DAW had attempted to market the first Imaro volume as "The Epic Novel of a Black Tarzan"—much to my chagrin, as that gambit was antithetical to the message I was trying to convey. And I wasn't the only one dismayed. A threat of legal action from the estate of Tarzan's creator, Edgar Rice Burroughs, put an end to DAW's plans to include the "Black Tarzan" blurb on the cover of the first Imaro novel. The need to redo the cover so that the blurb read "The Epic Novel of a Jungle Hero" delayed the release of the book by a month, which led to subsequent distribution problems.

As for the "vagueries," because of personal problems and a lack of discipline, it took me far too long to produce the second Imaro novel, so it reached the stands three years after the first book, which had more or less disappeared. I finished the third book much faster, and it came out only a year after the second one. But for DAW, the die was cast: the sales numbers simply did not add up, and they declined to publish the fourth novel. Other publishers weren't interested in picking up the series.

And that looked like the end of Imaro. Obviously, that was a turning point in my life as a writer. I branched out into other areas of the field, ranging from screenplays to journalism, with varying degrees of success. Imaro drifted farther and farther away, until he became what I thought would be permanently unfinished business.

And that's where matters stood with Imaro when Ben's e-mail appeared on my computer screen.

As I read the e-mail, Ben's genuine enthusiasm for Imaro rekindled a spark in me that had long lain dormant, deep in the part of my subconscious from which Imaro had come. Yet even as that spark flickered back into life, I was preparing to send Ben a reply that would say that Imaro was retired, and part of my past, and I did not want to bring him into the present.

The reason for my reluctance was that during the years between the writing of the fourth and part of the fifth Imaro novels in the mid-1980s, and the arrival of Ben's e-mail in the summer of 2003, the real world had crashed headlong into the world of my imagination, leaving me caught on the horns of a moral dilemma.

More background music …

As I was developing the alternate-Africa Nyumbani setting for Imaro's adventures, I followed the Robert E. Howard recipe for world-making: take one part of real-life history and mythology, including names; and one part of purely imaginary elements, including names. Mix these ingredients well in the imagination; then serve on the printed page.

Many factors figured in the creation of Imaro's milieu. I had already done extensive reading in African lore, sampling everything from Basil Davidson's *The Lost Cities of Africa* and W.E.B. Du Bois's *The World and Africa* to the back issues of *National Geographic*, which used bookstores once sold for a quarter apiece. I found there was enough information available to imagine several alternate Africas. The task of winnowing it down to what was needed for one such world wasn't easy.

That world, Nyumbani (which means "home" in Swahili), took shape as an amalgam of the real, the semi-real and the unreal. As my imaginary continent, and Imaro's place in it, developed, I included altered versions of some of the real Africa's most iconic ethnic groups and historic kingdoms and civilizations. For example, Imaro's people, the Ilyassai, are a thinly disguised version of the Masai, of lion-slaying renown. Cush is Kush, an ancient black civilization that was contemporaneous to Egypt. Both spellings of the kingdom's name can be found in history books. Howard included Kush, spelled with a "K," in his Hyborian Age, and I placed Cush, spelled with a

"C," in Nyumbani.

And then there were the Watusi. Before the 1994 genocide that occurred in Rwanda, the Watusi, more correctly known as the Tutsi, were an almost mythical people even in the real world: a regal tribe of people who averaged seven feet in height, lording it over a normal-sized people called the Hutu in the twin Central African states of Rwanda and Burundi.

A movie adaptation of H. Rider Haggard's novel *King Solomon's Mines* had further embedded the "Watusi" image in North American popular culture. There was even a hit rhythm-and-blues song and dance craze during the early 1960s called the "Watusi."

At the time I was beginning to draw my mental map of Nyumbani—the early 1970s—a Hutu rebellion had overthrown Tutsi rule in Rwanda, but not Burundi. The romanticized image of the "Watusi" remained, but events in other parts of post-colonial Africa pushed the Hutu-Tutsi conflict into the background.

I incorporated the "Watusi" into Imaro's world because I wanted to reinterpret the legend in a way different from the Haggard version of the people, just as Nyumbani itself was, in part, a reaction against the way Africa was depicted in Burroughs' Tarzan novels, which turned the continent into a gigantic jungle theme park full of ferocious beasts, savage black tribes, and lost white civilizations.

In the Nyumbani setting, the Tutsi/ "Watusi" became the "Mwambututsi," the Hutu the "Kahutu," and their kingdom Ruanda, which is the French spelling of Rwanda. The story in which Imaro encountered the Mwambututsi was called "Slaves of the Giant-Kings," and it appeared in a small-press publication during the mid-1970s, and was later included in the first Imaro novel. In the story, Imaro leads a rebellion of Kahutu slaves against their Mwambututsi masters in a gold mine that did not belong to King Solomon. He also meets the love of his life—a Kahutu woman named Tanisha. At the end of the story, the Mwambututsi are massacred—but only at the gold mine, not throughout their entire kingdom.

When I wrote "Slaves of the Giant-Kings" in the 1970s, and when its modified version appeared in the first Imaro novel in the 1980s, I had no way of foretelling the horror that was to come in 1994, when 800,000 Tutsi and moderate Hutu were slaughtered by Hutu extremists. The reality of that genocide was worse than anything I, or any other writer of fiction, could have imagined. As I read the horrific stories and saw the gruesome pictures of the unfolding tragedy, my shock, horror, and sadness were profound.

At the time of the Rwanda genocide, the three published Imaro novels were out of print. I had entertained sporadic thoughts of reviving them, but those considerations ended as the impact of the events in Rwanda hit home. My fiction had inadvertently crossed the border into reality, and there was no way I could allow "Slaves of the Giant-Kings" to go into print again. To do so would have given the impression that I was trying to exploit the Rwanda genocide, even though the story was first written nearly twenty years before the event.

I was, of course, loath to leave Imaro's saga unfinished. But the beginning was, in my mind, fatally flawed because reality had superseded fantasy.

As the years passed, several solutions to the "Slaves of the Giant-Kings" dilemma crossed my mind. But I discarded each one as inappropriate.

Perhaps an author's note explaining that "Slaves of the Giant-Kings" had been written well before the real-life Rwanda genocide, and was in no way intended to exploit that tragic event?

No. The story makes me uncomfortable now; it cannot be explained away so glibly.

Change the names of the "Mwambututsi" and "Kahutu" ethnic groups, and the "Ruanda" kingdom that was the setting for the story?

No. That would be too much of a cop-out.

Dispense with the height disparity between the overlords and their subjects, which would eliminate the Hutu-Tutsi identification?

Tempting, but no. The height difference was a key dynamic underlying the original story. Without it, the tale would fall as flat as a tire that had spring a leak.

Delete "Slaves of the Giant-Kings" from the narrative altogether?

Impossible. "Slaves of the Giant-Kings" was the story in which Imaro and Tanisha met. Without that background, she simply pops up in the narrative, with no context to explain her presence.

There was another option that I overlooked, perhaps because I was thinking inside the box instead of thinking creatively. It was an alternative that did not occur to me until my fingers were poised on the keyboard, about to write Benjamin Szumskyj an e-mail thanking him for his interest in Imaro, but also telling him, regretfully, that the Ilyassai had to remain in retirement, for the above-stated reasons.

At that moment, a stray neuron fired in my brain. And the e-mail Ben received that day was not the one I originally planned to write.

Sometimes, the simplest solution to a problem is also the most elusive. That flash of a neuron told me that the way out of my dilemma was to eliminate "Slaves of the Giant-Kings" from the first Imaro novel—and replace it with a new story, in which Imaro and Tanisha meet under different circumstances.

In my e-mail to Ben, I explained my dilemma, and informed him of my plan to write a substitute story—for which not even the glimmer of an idea had yet occurred. Ben wrote back, saying he understood my problem with "Slaves of the Giant-Kings," and that he agreed with my proposal to write a replacement story. His enthusiasm to get the entire Imaro saga, published and unpublished, into print remained strong, and it rubbed off on me.

So now, the ball was in my court. I had not written a word of new Imaro material in eighteen years, and I had become resigned to the probability that I would never write about him again. I had buried him in my subconscious, and I wasn't certain that I could bring him back to life.

However, my Ilyassai friend proved to be tenacious. Slowly, then more quickly, the substitute story took shape, germinating from elements of "Slaves of the Giant-Kings" that were not directly related to the Hutu-Tutsi conflict. Imaro had not lain totally fallow all those years, and it turned out I had more to say about him. Before I knew it, the substitute story had grown into a novella, which I decided to call "The Afua."

Thus, the Imaro saga had changed. But that course of action opens the door to controversy of a different, and definitely milder, sort from anything that might have arisen from leaving "Slaves of the Giant-Kings" in the novel.

To revise, or not to revise? Is it acceptable for a fiction writer to alter an already-published piece of work? There are conflicting answers to that question. On the one hand, there is the argument that once a work is published, it should not be touched because it embodies what the author had to say at that point in time, and it should remain as it was—untouched, and not second-guessed later in life.

Then there's the other side of the argument, which holds that freedom of expression and creativity does not come to an end once a work is published; and if the writer decides to revise, rewrite, or revisit previously published material, that is his or her prerogative.

When I decided to write "The Afua," I placed myself irrevocably in the latter camp. You can't get much more revisionist than substituting a new story for one that was previously published. And that isn't all that has changed in this revisitation of the first Imaro novel.

The insertion of "The Afua" created a ripple effect that necessitated changes in the rest of the first novel's narrative flow. As well, because of the altering of the circumstances under which she and Imaro met, Tanisha's character has changed substantially. Although her name and her physical appearance remain the same, Tanisha is a completely different person now. The way Imaro interacts with her is different, as well.

Imaro's character has changed, too. Not to worry—he's still the "Baddest Man on the Planet." However, his experiences in "The Afua" affect him in a way that is not quite the same as the events and aftermath of "Slaves of the Giant-Kings." Unlike Tanisha, Imaro remains essentially the same person. He is a little more mature now than he was when I first wrote about him—hopefully, a reflection of his creator's own character development.

And there was more development to come.

After "The Afua," my work on Imaro wasn't yet done, though I didn't know it. In the original novel, and the revisit as well, I gave short shrift to a pivotal part of Imaro's life—the betrayal and defeat of the bandit army Imaro led, and the survivors' subsequent repudiation of him. Jeremy Lassen, the editor at Night Shade, suggested that this story needed to be told in full. After reflecting for about two seconds, I agreed, and wondered why I hadn't seen that gap in the narrative myself.

Now, that story has, indeed, been told, in a new segment of the novel titled "Betrayal in Blood."

Jeremy had another insight, which was a bit further outside the box. The events in "Betrayal" constitute the end of the first phase of Imaro's life. Jeremy suggested that "City of Madness," the last segment of the original novel, is really the beginning of his next phase. Therefore, "City of Madness" is now the start of the second Imaro novel, *The Quest for Cush*, rather than the end of the first one.

In the end, the revisit of Imaro involved more than a matter of copyediting my work decades later, although that has been part of the process, especially in the sections leading up to "The Afua." It's more a matter of applying what I know now to what I created then.

The ripple effects of "The Afua" and "Betrayal in Blood" will be evident in the subsequent Imaro novels. As a whole, this revisit is not a matter of pouring old wine into new bottles; it's a matter of improving the vintage that's already there.

If Ben had not sent that momentous e-mail, the wine of the Imaro novels would have remained the same, and the bottles would have stayed in the cellar. This revisit owes a great deal to Ben; without his initiative, it would never have happened.

As I survey the three-decade gap between the creation of Imaro and this revisit, I see changes great and small—starting with me. The fires of righteous indignation that motivated me during the early 1970s have been banked by the passage of time, but they have not been extinguished. My reasons for writing the Imaro stories remain the same. Essentially, I am writing the stories I wish I could have read back in the days when I first encountered fantasy and science fiction.

However, the social and cultural context has changed immensely since the 1970s, and so has the genre. The grievances I had then are, for the most part, gone now. Following in the large footsteps of pioneer Samuel R. Delany, writers such as Octavia Butler, Steven Barnes, Tananarive Due, and Nalo Hopkinson have ensconced the African, African-American and Caribbean experiences firmly into the science fiction/fantasy genre. And in her *Dark Matter* anthologies, Sheree Renee Thomas has unveiled a plethora of new writers of African descent.

Also, in the works of writers of other ethnic backgrounds, nonstereotyped black characters appear with varying degrees of frequency. In one interesting twist, Joe Lansdale wrote a Tarzan novel in which the ape-man encounters a lost African civilization that is black, not white.

In this more diverse literary landscape, I believe there is still room for a revisited Imaro to roam.

As I mentioned earlier, I have always considered Imaro to be unfinished business, and as the years passed, it seemed that he always would be. Now, thanks to Benjamin Szumskyj and Night Shade Books, I can, indeed, go home again and finish Imaro's journey.

PART I
THE ILYASSAI

'I LEAVE A WARRIOR BEHIND'

Among them will come
The Child of Wonder
And they will
Know him not.
—Prophecy

A warm rain misted down on a small boy standing motionless in the tall, yellow grass. Although he enjoyed the sensation of rain on his skin, the boy's expression remained solemn—too solemn for a child who had seen only five rains wash through the Tamburure. His height and breadth would have been envied by a boy of seven rains' passing.

His mother stood a short distance behind him. She was a tall, slender woman with iron in her backbone and fire in her eyes. She wore a brief garment of tanned antelope hide draped over one shoulder. A large leather sack stuffed with dried journey-food was slung over the other.

A long spear rested lightly in her hands. It was an *arem*, the spear of the Ilyassai. Half its length consisted of razor-sharp iron. With such spears, the Ilyassai ruled the vast yellow reaches of the Tamburure plain.

The woman's mahogany-brown skin reflected a sheen of beaded raindrops. Her face bore an expression that was as solemn as her son's. They both knew that before this day was done, they would not see each other again. The woman, who was called Katisa, allowed her mind to drift in memory....

Once before, Katisa had departed the Tamburure. Darkness had cloaked her passage then, eight long rains ago. Katisa was fleeing a forced marriage to Chitendu, who was her clan's *oibonok*—sorcerer and shaman to Ajunge, Spear God of the Ilyassai. Three rains later, she had returned, bearing a boy-child in her arms. Upon her return, she had exposed Chitendu for what he was: a servant of the Mashataan, the Demon Gods. The Ilyassai had nearly slain the *oibonok* before he finally fled. Only his sorcerous skills had saved him from death; since his departure, no trace of him had been uncovered in all the Tamburure.

Katisa's face clouded as her memories grew darker. The Ilyassai had not hailed her as a heroine for her deed. Far from that—the infant she nursed bore mute witness to Katisa's violation of the strictest of Ilyassai taboos. She had given birth to a child by a man who was not Ilyassai, a man she consistently refused to name. The Ilyassai were as proud as they were fierce; death was the fate of a woman who yielded to the touch of a man who was not of their tribe, and death to the child as well.

Katisa had known this well when she returned. But she knew her return was necessary nonetheless, for the evil influence of Chitendu had to be forestalled. She knew her deed could balance her transgression of taboo. That she could still never dwell among her people again she was well aware. But her son must. Only the Ilyassai could impart the war-skills he would one day need....

She had offered her clan of the Ilyassai, the Kitoko, an alternative. For the first five years of their lives, Ilyassai boys were cared for by their mothers. In the fifth rain, they were taken from their mothers to begin *mafundishu-ya-muran*, the arduous training that made Ilyassai warriors feared by man and beast alike across the Tamburure. Katisa proposed to remain with her son for the five rains all Ilyassai mothers were allowed. When the fifth rain came, she would again exile herself from her people—this time, forever.

In return, she had asked that the Kitoko clan allow her son to undergo *mafundishu-ya-muran*; and, when he came of age, *olmaiyo*. *Olmaiyo* was the final rite of manhood, in which warriors-to-be proved their courage and skill by single-handedly slaying Ngatun the lion.

The elders of the clan had weighed her request. Her violation of taboo could not be forgotten. Neither could her courage in confronting Chitendu, who had subtly steered them along a path contrary to the Way of Ajunge. The elders decided in favor of Katisa. Not all the clan agreed with that decision....

The far-off roar of Ngatun brought Katisa's mind back to the present. She shook her head sadly, reflecting on how swiftly the rains had passed since her return to the Tamburure. She shut off the memories. To pursue them further would be to play the lioness chasing the impala that bounded disdainfully just beyond her claws.

She looked at her son. Already his body was hard and powerful beyond its years. She had seen to that. She had told him what was to come. He had accepted it with sullen stoicism.

It is time, she decided.

"Imaro. Come," she said.

Slowly Imaro turned. He tilted his head upward to meet his mother's gaze. As always, Katisa interposed a barrier of lovelessness like a shield between herself and the son she had always known she must leave. Thus, there was no warmth in Katisa's eyes when she looked at him....

Then something changed in her gaze—a sudden flicker of emotion swift as the beat of a bird's wing against the sky.

She held out her hand to her son.

Imaro hesitated. Gestures like this had been all too rare, for his mother had deliberately withheld her affection to prepare him—and herself—for this day. Still, young though he was, Imaro understood why Katisa reached out to him now. Stepping forward, he placed his small hand in hers.

She held his hand tightly, but did not look at him while she led him from the site of the *manyatta* they shared. As the dome-shaped leather dwelling dwindled slowly in the rain-misted distance, Katisa reflected bitterly on how far the elders had demanded she live from the clustered *manyattas* of the rest of the Ilyassai. She seldom took part in the activities of the tribe. Even rarer were the times she brought Imaro among them. This would be the last time she would see any of them. Her only regret at that inevitable turn of events was walking beside her.

The whisper of the rain subsided as they came within sight of the *manyattas*, gray-brown domes rising like the backs of elephants resting in the grass. Even through the warm, rain-damp air, the smell of *ngombe*—cattle—reached their nostrils in a pungent caress. The woman and boy could see the great herds of *ngombe*, the meaning of the lives of the Ilyassai, grazing placidly in their endless yellow forage, safe from all predators.

Coming closer, they heard the sounds of the *manyattas*: the metallic rasp of spear points being sharpened by warriors; the crackling hiss of cooking fires newly started now that the rain had passed; the shrill sound of children's laughter; the subdued murmur of men and women in close conversation....

Katisa knew why the people were keeping their voices low. They were talking about her and Imaro. She released her son's hand. His face became a set mask, as did hers.

Together they strode past the outlying *manyattas* toward the open space of stamped-down grass at the center of the ragged, concentric circles of leather dwellings. Tall, whip-lean men and women of red-brown hue watched mother and son go by. The faces and bodies of the men were daubed in crimson ocher, and their hair hung in thick plaits plastered with orange clay. The heads of the women were shaved bald.

Katisa's thatch of wooly black hair set her apart from the others as little else could. The women turned their faces from her in open disdain.

Standing alone in the center of the open space, a warrior of middle years awaited the two outcasts. He held his lean, corded arms folded forbiddingly across his chest. A *shingona*, the tall headgear formed from the mane of the lion he had slain long ago on his *olmaiyo*, complemented a face set in a stern, stony expression. This was Mubaku, *ol-arem*, or First Spear, of the Kitoko clan.

Tall enough to overbear Katisa, Mubaku gave her a fierce glare. Calmly, she met the scorn that was naked in the *ol-arem*'s eyes. Not looking up, Imaro stood impassively at his mother's side. The rest of the clan began to gather in the open area: warriors and women, children and elders. The tension that gathered with them was as palpable as the rainbeads gleaming on their skin.

"You know why I've come," Katisa said, clear-voiced.

Mubaku nodded curtly, saying nothing.

"You will keep your word? My son will undergo *mafundishu-ya-muran* and be given the same opportunity to reach *olmaiyo* as any Ilyassai boy-child?"

"We will keep our word," the *ol-arem* replied. "Now, keep yours. Go."

The rebuke stung. Katisa displayed no reaction. Ignoring the silent onlookers, she turned to Imaro. She gazed at him long and intently, striving to convey a message beyond words, beyond touching—an expression of love held painfully in abeyance.

Finally, at the very moment Imaro feared he would lose control and fling himself tearfully into his mother's arms, she spoke, as much to the gathered Kitoko clan as to him.

"I go … but I leave a warrior behind."

Then she turned and strode stiff-backed from the central area; walking away from the *manyattas* and the *ngombe* and the *arems* and the uncompromising obstinacy of her people; walking away from her son. Imaro watched her tall, straight form dwindle in the distance.…

A vicious blow cracked solidly against his back. Crying out at the abrupt pain, Imaro sailed headlong through the air. Even as he hurtled toward the ground, the long hours of lessons he had absorbed from Katisa came to the fore. He rolled on impact with the ground and sprang quickly to his feet.

The laughter of the onlookers burned his ears; tears stung at the corners of his eyes. He carefully composed his face, then looked up.

Masadu, the warrior who had struck him with the butt of an *arem*, stood scowling beside Mubaku. The fearsomeness of Masadu's appearance was heightened by the hideous row of scars that disfigured the left side of his face—a legacy left by Ngatun during Masadu's *olmaiyo*. He had slain Ngatun, but the lion had exacted a price. It was Masadu who guided the clan's youths along the demanding course of *mafundishu-ya-muran*.

"We'll soon learn what kind of 'warrior' that woman left behind," Masadu sneered. "Follow me, son-of-no-father."

Imaro's young eyes turned hard. His face showed nothing of his struggle to master the pain knifing through his back. Holding his body stiffly erect—like Katisa—the boy hurried after the scarred warrior. But his thoughts followed his mother.

Why, why, why couldn't you take me with you? This was his unspoken cry, echoing silent sobs.

The weapon was in the crucible....

TURKHANA KNIVES

The language of the Ilyassai
Is the language of the spear.
— Tamburure saying

Imaro scowled at the tall, lean figure approaching him through the yellow grass. He glanced quickly toward Kulu, the *ngombe* that had been entrusted to his care. The large, long-horned cow did not look up from the sun-scorched fodder upon which she grazed.

Far across the golden sweep of the Tamburure, the herd-boys of the Kitoko clan tended scattered clusters of *ngombe*. The size of the youths' sub-herds varied according to their ages and their progress in *mafundishu-ya-muran*. A few, close to readiness for *olmaiyo*, had twenty or more *ngombe* in their charge. The youngest, thin brown sticks of boy-children who had just begun warrior-training, were entrusted with no more than one of the precious cows.

Imaro, now well beyond his fourteenth rain, still tended only Kulu. Kanoko, the youth who was approaching him, was of an age with Imaro, yet he had eleven *ngombe* in his care. He seldom allowed Imaro to forget that, or any other indication of Imaro's low status among the Kitoko.

Kanoko strode insolently across the unseen boundary that marked the range past which only an Ilyassai could approach. From the beginning of *mafundishu-ya-muran*, Ilyassai youths were taught that anyone, or anything else—warrior, beast, or demon—that came within a spear-cast of a *ngombe* must be slain.

Unconsciously, Imaro curled his fingers around the hilt of his *simi*, the short, iron sword sheathed at his side. He reluctantly uncurled his fingers and raised the tip of his *arem* skyward in a gesture of acknowledgment. Often were the times he wished Kanoko were not Ilyassai....

The two youths glared at each other in long-established mutual enmity. Already, Kanoko was approaching the height of a full-grown warrior. Wiry, catlike thews danced along his lean frame as he walked. Red-brown skin, bare except for a single leather garment knotted over one shoulder and dropping to midthigh, gleamed slickly in the light of Jua the sun. His hair, braided and plastered with red clay, clung like a barbaric helmet to his narrow skull.

Yet tall as Kanoko was, Imaro was half a head taller. His physique boasted a brawn that was still only a promise of what were bound to be massive adult proportions. His sheer physical impact overshadowed the tattered state of his antelope-hide garment and the sullen expression on his face. The dark, earth-colored undertone of his complexion and the broadness of his nose, cheekbones, and mouth suggested a parentage different from that of Kanoko and the rest of the Ilyassai—a parentage for which Imaro had been made to suffer more times than he could count.

"Kulu looks hungry, Imaro," Kanoko observed. "That is strange. She has so much grass to herself here."

There was no mistaking the condescending curve of the youth's lips or the derision glinting in his eyes. Imaro did not reply to the gibe. He had long since learned not to allow himself to be goaded by Kanoko's sharp tongue.

Once, several rains past, he had responded to the other youth's taunts. In the ensuing battle, he had come close to beating the life out of his tormentor. Kanoko had told Masadu that Imaro had started the fight, and the dour warrior-trainer had taken Kanoko's words for truth. It was Imaro who had endured the ensuing beating with a stick thick as a spear shaft. He had borne the punishment in silence—the day Katisa departed was the last time he had cried out in the presence of an Ilyassai—and thereafter, he had fought hard to suppress the anger Kanoko all too often succeeded in provoking.

In mock seriousness, Kanoko said, "Silence in the presence of a gift, Imaro?"

"I see no gift," Imaro replied shortly.

Kanoko reached inside his garment and produced a bundle of sweet grass wrapped in a leaf of the plant called elephant's-ear. It was a *kutendea*, a gift Ilyassai herders presented to the cattle of their friends. Imaro's eyes narrowed in suspicion, for in no way was Kanoko a friend of his.

"Why do you do this?" he demanded. His bluntness concealed the sudden hope that the low regard in which his clan held him had suddenly changed.

For reply, Kanoko thrust the *kutendea* into the snout of Imaro's *ngombe*. Kulu's teeth tore eagerly into the green bundle; to a *ngombe*, elephant's-ear was a rare delight. Kulu chewed—then bellowed in pain as scores of red-six-legged dots burst from their leafy prison and swarmed into her nose, eyes, and mouth. Whipping her horned head from side to side, Kulu spat the false gift onto the ground and bolted. She dashed past the startled *ngombe* of the other herd-boys and stampeded beyond the grazing-range the Ilyassai had wrested from the beasts that roamed the Tamburure.

Flame ants, Imaro realized the moment he saw them. Flame ants—insects with a bite that burned like fire! Somehow, Kanoko had contrived to capture enough of them to drive any beast mad with pain. Furiously, he turned on Kanoko.

"Why did you do that to Kulu?" Imaro demanded. "*Why?*"

"*Why?*" Kanoko mocked. "*You* know why! You are the son-of-no-father. Your mother was driven from the clan before she brought *you* back from her wanderings. You have no father, and your mother's kin won't even let you know who they are. You are not fit to be an Ilyassai! Wait till Masadu finds out you lost your miserable *ngombe*! You *do* know what happens when you lose your *ngombe*, don't you, you—"

Kanoko said no more. Swift as lightning, Imaro's balled fist hammered into Kanoko's sneering face. The other youth's reflexes were cat-quick, but he could not pull his jaw away in time to avoid the full force of Imaro's blow. The impact lifted him off his feet and left him sprawled semiconscious in the grass.

Murderous rage glinting in his eyes, Imaro stood over Kanoko, *arem* upraised in his hand. Then, realizing that Kulu was fleeing farther into the wild part of the Tamburure, he turned and raced through the grass after his stricken charge.

Ignoring the pain spreading through his jaw, Kanoko threw back his head and laughed as only a malicious boy on the brink of manhood can. Of all the youths undergoing *mafundishu-ya-muran*, only Imaro surpassed him in the skills of hunting and war. Now—Imaro was finished. When the time came to pen the *ngombe* herd in its thornbush *boma* for the night, Imaro and Kulu would not be there. For that, Masadu would surely kill the son-of-no-father, if the beasts of the Tamburure did not do so. And Kanoko's prowess would stand alone among the warriors-to-be.

Kanoko laughed louder, sending a scornful echo racing in pursuit of Imaro's dwindling form.

***

Freedom. The concept held little meaning for Imaro, except during times such as this, when he ran alone in the Tamburure, dry grass swishing against his bare legs. It was then that he felt that he truly belonged in the savanna, at one with the vast herds of impala, zebra, kudu, gazelle, and countless other hoofed creatures that, along with Tembo, the mighty elephant, roamed wherever their will guided them. Even more did the youth identify with the Tamburure's deadliest predators: Ngatun the lion, Chui the leopard, Matisho the hunting-hyena. These creatures hunted the grass-eaters as it pleased them, without regard to the strictures imposed by clan or tribe. If he were Ngatun or Chui or Matisho, Imaro sometimes supposed, he might then be free.

But now there was no time for such musings. The longer it took to reach

Kulu, Imaro knew, the less chance he would have to return his *ngombe* to the *boma* before nightfall. He applied himself to the chase, running at a steady, loping pace. He strove to remain at least within earshot of Kulu, whose bellowing cries of torment stabbed at his heart.

Imaro knew that when he finally caught up with his *ngombe*, he would have to immobilize her, then scrape the flame ants out of her snout and eyes. The task would not be easy, for in her pain, Kulu would be dangerous; she might not even realize who Imaro was.

When he had first seen Kulu, the *ngombe* had been only a sickly calf, not expected to survive more than a single rain. That, perhaps, was why Masadu had chosen Imaro to care for her. With painstaking effort, the boy had nurtured the *ngombe* to health. He remembered the naming-day, when he drank blood tapped from the *ngombe*'s veins and they had become part of one another, as were all Ilyassai with their cattle. He had given her the name "Kulu," meaning "friend."

And Kulu was indeed his friend, the only one he had in all the huge reach of the Tamburure, the plain that seemed the entire world to him. But that bond would be tested before the day was done. He had once seen a *ngombe* bull outduel Mboa the buffalo for a spot at a waterhole during the dry season. Kulu would be no less formidable if she were maddened by pain.

Thinking sorrowfully of the pain his friend was enduring, Imaro inadvertently allowed the resulting hatred for Kanoko to seethe like a fire-coal in his mind. Momentarily, he lost his *kufahuma*—the attunement of his senses, the melding of all his faculties into one, making his awareness at one with the Tamburure. This awareness was one of the first skills Masadu had taught him. Now, he was allowing his rage to rob him of the gift of *kufahuma*.

Thus, he remained unaware of the menace hidden in the yellow grass, pacing him easily, stride for stride....

The leopard had but recently wandered into the Tamburure from the lands beyond. Man had driven him here; he knew the hated smell of humankind only too well. But humans were easy prey when they were alone. This leopard had not yet learned to fear the smell of the Ilyassai. It knew only that the rasp of grass stems against the moving legs of the human it stalked was loud enough to mask its stealthy approach. Baring its fangs, Chui the leopard moved closer to the running youth, and prepared to spring....

Then a ground-squirrel, panicked by the scent of Chui so close to its burrow, darted in a brown blur across Imaro's path. A warning. Screeching in frustration, the leopard sprang toward Imaro, raking its deadly claws like curved knives through the air, striking—nothing!

Imaro had reacted instantly to the ground-squirrel's flight. With a twist of his body, he sidestepped the leopard's claws. Then he crouched, gripping his *arem* tightly, facing the baffled and enraged leopard.

"Chui," Imaro called to the spotted cat. "Go your way, Chui. Ilyassai meat is not for the likes of you."

Without so much as a growl of warning, the leopard sprang forward. Its paws moved faster than the eye could follow—yet the shaft of Imaro's *arem* was there to deflect Chui's talons.

Snarling in fury, the leopard half reared on its hind legs and again struck at Imaro with its forepaws, blows flickering like black-flecked lightning. Imaro, wielding his *arem* as though it were light as a wand, parried Chui's paws. The sharp impact of wood and iron against cat-flesh resounded across the plain.

Not once had Imaro used the point of his weapon. Not once had Chui's talons touched his flesh. Even though the great cat retreated now, half limping on bruised forepaws, Imaro knew that Chui would not abandon the fight. The leopard was feigning retreat; the lashing of its tail revealed its true intentions....

Again, Chui sprang. Imaro evaded its claws. But this time, when the leopard landed on the ground, Imaro lunged forward with his *arem*. The iron point of the spear plunged through Chui's spotted hide; deeper, ever deeper; not halting its momentum until the leopard was pinned to the soil of the Tamburure.

Impaled by the awesome force of Imaro's thrust, Chui shrieked a death cry. Its limbs thrashed in a paroxysm of reflexes out of control. Releasing his grip on the spear shaft, Imaro jumped out of the reach of slashes that, undirected though they were, could still wound him seriously if they chanced to land.

Finally, Chui's spasms ceased, and the great cat fell silent, its blood crimsoning the yellow grass. Imaro's heart soared in triumph. *If only Masadu were here*, he thought. *Even he would find no fault with this kill!*

Concealed in the grass, keen eyes had witnessed the young warrior's feat. Those eyes did not belong to Masadu, or any other Ilyassai....

***

The watchers crouched like shadows in the cover of the grass. They numbered a dozen: warriors all, armed with long spears, short swords, and knob-ended throwing-clubs. On their left wrists, they wore bracelets with raised, sharpened edges of iron. Circular sleeves of leather sheathed the edges to prevent the blades from accidentally damaging their wielders when the weapons were not in use.

Coils of woven grass circled the waists of some of the strange warriors. To a man, their heads were shaved except for a topknot thick with feathers. Attracted by the noise of the conflict between Imaro and the leopard, the intruders had seen the youth transfix the beast to the plain.

Hand signs denoting excitement and purpose passed swiftly among them while Imaro set his foot to the carcass and bent to wrench his *arem* free. *Alive,* the hand signals said. *We must capture this one alive.* The intruders crept closer, unslinging the knobbed clubs from their belts....

Imaro was thinking of Kulu when a whir of wood through the air alerted him to new danger. He jerked his head aside, averting the full impact of the throwing club. Still, the knobbed end glanced from his temple. Pain jolted through his skull.

He staggered three steps away from his *arem.* His hand reached toward the hilt of his *simi.* But he was stunned; his motion was a fraction of a second too slow, giving his attackers time to swarm like a pack of wild dogs through the grass.

Hands clutched at Imaro's limbs. Bodies pressed heavily upon his, forcing him to the ground. The intruders kept their wrist-knives sheathed; they sought not to slay but to restrain the Ilyassai youth long enough to loop their grass ropes around him.

Imaro's head cleared, and he responded to the assault with as much fury as would the leopard he had just slain. Bellowing the Ilyassai war cry, he uncoiled his body and surged to his feet, hurling his surprised attackers from him as if they were children.

The intruders looked at each other in confusion as they regained their balance. This was only a youth, but he had the strength of a man, and perhaps more. How was that possible?

For their moment of uncertainty, they paid dearly. Again, Imaro's hand sought his *simi.* This time, the hilt smacked solidly into his palm. The iron blade sang from its sheath and buried itself in the abdomen of Imaro's nearest foe. The warrior shrieked once, then sank to the ground.

Imaro now knew who his attackers were. A quick glance had taken in the topknots and wrist-knives, and identified their wearers. These warriors were of the Turkhana, the only tribe that dared to dispute Ilyassai dominance of the Tamburure. They had come from the same direction in which Kulu had fled. And Imaro could no longer hear her cries....

He knew then that the Turkhana had taken his *ngombe.* He snarled a curse at the warriors. If they wanted Kulu, they would have to pay for her in blood.

The Turkhana surrounded Imaro warily. They had seen him slay Chui; they had seen the swiftness with which he had cut down one of their own; they had felt the strength in his youthful thews. But the Turkhana were brave men: warriors, as much so as the Ilyassai. And they had a mission they dared not fail to accomplish. As one, they leaped toward Imaro.

The first Turkhana to reach him was spitted on the young warrior's blade. The *simi* caught in the Turkhana's rib cage; while Imaro struggled to tear the blade free, a knob-club smashed viciously against the side of his skull. He fought the explosion of pain, but his fingers still loosened. The Turkhana he had struck threw himself backward in a dying act of defiance, tearing the hilt of the *simi* out of Imaro's hand as he fell.

Imaro was now weaponless, and the Turkhana lashed at him with their knob-clubs. Red *arems* of pain lanced through the youth's brain, and a black curtain folded over the yellow glare of the sun. Still, in a phenomenal display of tenacity, Imaro's hands found the throat of one of the Turkhana. Only when he felt the bones of the Turkhana's neck snap in his grasp did Imaro finally succumb to the scarlet hammers that pounded consciousness from him.

***

When he awakened, Imaro was walking. It was an unusual transition—from blank oblivion to instant awareness, with no gray state of semiconsciousness intervening.

Pain was a drummer, pounding a steady rhythm behind his eyes. None of the beatings Masadu had given him had been as severe as this one, but Masadu had, unknowingly, prepared him well for the Turkhana's assault.

He blinked eyes that were already open. The lowering of Jua toward the flat Tamburure horizon told him that many hours had passed since the Turkhana had ambushed him. He flicked his gaze from left to right. Two Turkhana flanked him, gripping his arms tightly just beneath his shoulders. His forearms were bound with so many coils of grass, he couldn't see his own skin. Dried blood—not his own—caked his hands and feet.

His ankles were hobbled with a length of rope that allowed him to walk with only an awkward, shortened stride.

He heard the sound of hooves shuffling in the grass. *Kulu!* he thought. He turned his head to the sound and saw his *ngombe*. Like Imaro, Kulu was hobbled; she walked with an ungainly, hopping gait. A length of tanned leather torn from a Turkhana's garment had been wrapped her head, covering her eyes. Only such blinding could render an Ilyassai *ngombe* tractable to an outsider.

What the Turkhana had done to relieve Kulu from the pain of the flame ants' bites, Imaro did not know. But whatever it was, they had paid a price to subdue her. Blood reddened her horns, and one of the Turkhana walked with one arm dangling uselessly at his side. For a moment, pride surged through Imaro's heart. He knew what other tribes of the Tamburure said about the Ilyassai: *Even their cattle are warriors.*

Then Imaro's thoughts became clouded with confusion. For the second time that day, the word "why" whirled through his mind. Why was he still alive?

That Kulu still lived, Imaro readily understood. The Turkhana stole Ilyassai cattle whenever they could; on the Tamburure, stealing the cattle of other tribes was simply another form of warfare. But from the Ilyassai themselves, the Turkhana valued only their clay-caked braids of hair, flayed fresh from the scalp. The wrist-knives of the Turkhana had equal value for the Ilyassai, preferably still attached to the severed hands of their wearers.

Rarely did the Turkhana dare to venture so deeply into Ilyassai territory. And never had the Turkhana taken captives in their conflicts with the Ilyassai—a practice the Ilyassai reciprocated.

Why had that changed now?

Imaro knew he would learn little from his captors, who exchanged a few words in their dialect of the root-tongue of the Tamburure. Although Imaro understood what the Turkhana were saying, their sparse conversation told him little. He knew better than to question the warriors, for the Ilyassai and Turkhana spoke to each other only with weapons and curses.

Bitterness festered in the youth's dark eyes. Ajunge, Spear God of the Ilyassai, had truly turned his back on him—as, in any case, Imaro had ample reason to suspect the god had done long ago. However harsh his existence among the Ilyassai had been, he could expect only worse—far worse—from the Turkhana.

Despair, an emotion against which he had always struggled fiercely, whispered subtly in his soul. Masadu, Kanoko, and all the others … perhaps they had not been mistaken in their scorn for him. He had failed Kulu; failed Katisa….

Then, before the youth's morose broodings claimed him entirely, a scene born of memory long suppressed suddenly appeared, superimposing itself with sharp clarity over the vista of the Tamburure. Again, he was a boy of five rains; again he stood in the midst of the Kitoko clan's *manyattas*, gazing upward into the proud face of Katisa. Again, he heard his mother's final words to him: *I go … but I leave a warrior behind.*

Those words had sustained Imaro as memories of lost love never could have done through rain after cheerless rain of striving to earn the respect of a people who despised him.

I leave a warrior behind…. The vision faded with the last echo of Katisa's words. Imaro shook himself like a lion bestriding a new kill. Startled, his captors tightened their grip on his arms. One Turkhana unslung his knob-club and shook it menacingly under Imaro's nose.

The youth smiled. It was a smile totally devoid of anything resembling human mirth, frightening on the face of one who had seen so few rains.

Imaro could not guess what fate the Turkhana planned for Kulu and him. But he knew that whatever the outcome, the Turkhana would learn the truth of Katisa's promise.

***

Sunset spread like a bloodstain across the sky as Imaro's captors reached their destination. Thick herds of grass-eaters huddled nervously, knowing that when Jua finally disappeared from the sky, the night would belong to the predators. Already, Ngatun's roar and Chui's cough and the eerie, laughing bark of Matisho rolled across the plain.

Imaro knew he was now in The Land of No One, a wild, uninhabited stretch of territory that served as a borderland between the realms claimed by the Turkhana and the Ilyassai. It was not uninhabited now. A band of Turkhana had set up a small encampment, consisting of a fresh-dug firepit and a circular barrier of spiky thornbush. It was the encampment of a hunting party or a war band, quickly erected and easy to dismantle.

Warriors, numbering perhaps twice those who had captured Imaro and Kulu, rushed out to greet their returning comrades. Fierce joy lit their faces at the sight of the Ilyassai youth and the *ngombe*. Imaro paid scant heed to the warriors' hot-eyed glares, though. Something else had claimed his attention.

Outside the thornbush barrier stood a cage fashioned from heavy poles lashed together with resilient vines. A lion was imprisoned within the cage, which was actually a trap into which live bait had been placed to lure Ngatun into tripping a rope mechanism that dropped the door of the trap behind him.

Aroused by the scent of Kulu, Ngatun rose and lunged at the bars of his prison. The construction of the trap seemed so fragile the sound of the lion's roar could shatter it. But the poles held firm as the lion strove to break through to attack the *ngombe*. Though she was blinded by the wrappings around her eyes, and her nose was deadened by the bites of the flame ants, Kulu heard Ngatun's roar and bellowed a challenge of her own, tossing her horned head from side to side. Several Turkhana held on to her head, struggling to prevent her from bolting.

The leader of Imaro's captors pointed to a thick stake driven deep into the ground on the far side of the encampment.

"Tie the *ngombe* there, and let N'tu-mwaa know we've returned with what he wants," he said.

Imaro stood freely now, with Turkhana warriors stationed close by. Their spears were poised to strike instantly if need be. Because the young Ilyassai was hobbled, they reasoned that he would not attempt to escape. But they also remembered what his capture had cost them, and they remained alert.

As Kulu was led away to the pole, Imaro's mind was occupied by more than his dim prospects for escape. The sight of Ngatun in a cage angered him; the Ilyassai believed that the souls of their dead occupied the bodies of lions before returning to animate a human of a succeeding generation. Thus was Ngatun the most honored of foes; only by slaying a lion and freeing an Ilyassai soul to become human again could an Ilyassai youth gain full status as a man and a warrior.

To cage Ngatun like a hare or a ground-squirrel … That was as disconcerting to Imaro as his own capture.

A figure emerged from an opening in the thornbush. The warriors stepped aside deferentially, almost fearfully, as the man approached.

To Imaro, the man was obviously an *n'tu-mchawi*—a magic man, like the *oibonok* of his own clan. Warriors did not don such elaborate accouterments as the buffalo skull that fitted the newcomer's head like a helmet, or the long streamers of monkey hair that hung from copper bands encircling his arms and legs, or the mantle made from the spotted skins of hyenas that swathed his shoulders.

Besides the ubiquitous wrist-knife, the *n'tu-mchawi* had a heavy, curved dagger hanging from a thong looped around his neck. Its blade was stained brown with old blood. Nearly a giant in height, the Turkhana was nonetheless so lank in build that the youthful Imaro easily outweighed him.

When the Turkhana came closer to Imaro, the Ilyassai suddenly saw the thing that distinguished this man from all others. Most of his body was revealed by the open mantle: from head to foot, his skin was splotched with patches of a pale, almost white hue, as though it had been daubed with kaolin clay. But even in the muted light of sunset, Imaro saw clearly that the Turkhana's markings were not decoration—they were as real as the color of his own skin.

And he realized this was the "N'tu-mwaa" the Turkhana leader had mentioned earlier, for in the language of the Tamburure, those words meant "Blemished Man."

Imaro had never forgotten that a *n'tu-mchawi* had been the cause of his mother's exile from the Ilyassai. For that reason, he hated sorcerers, including Muburi, the *oibonok* who had taken the place of Chitendu, the one Katisa had overcome many rains ago. Imaro's eyes hardened in response to the intense stare he now received from N'tu-mwaa.

"A lion, a *ngombe*, and an Ilyassai," the Turkhana crooned, breaking the silence. His voice was high, singsong, as though he were speaking to children rather than an assemblage of warriors.

"And I," he continued. "I—a man apart from all others. I, who will become all three."

He smiled at Imaro before continuing.

"Ilyassai, hear my words: Through you, and your *ngombe*, and the lion in the cage, our god, Kupigana, will triumph over your Spear God, and the Turkhana will become the masters of the Tamburure!"

Imaro did not speak. He glared at the *n'tu-mchawi* with eyes that mirrored the frustrated fury in the eyes of the caged lion. Then N'tu-mwaa bent to peer more closely at Imaro. He gazed searchingly. Then his face twisted with wrath.

Turning on the startled Turkhana war-leader, he cried: "Fool! Did I not tell you to capture an Ilyassai? This is no Ilyassai!"

Dismay and disbelief swept through the band that had ambushed Imaro.

"Not an Ilyassai?" the leader protested. "If this is not an Ilyassai, why are three of my best warriors now food for Mbweha the jackal?"

"He broke Wagulembe's neck even as we broke our clubs on his skull," cried another.

"We saw him *play* with Chui the leopard before slaying him with one thrust of his spear," added a third.

"And he was chasing an Ilyassai *ngombe*," said the warrior whose arm still bled from Kulu's goring.

"He fights like a lion, and that's what makes an Ilyassai," the leader said flatly. "He has Ilyassai hair; he wears Ilyassai clothes; he bore Ilyassai weapons. How can you say he is not an Ilyassai, N'tu-mwaa?"

The sorcerer had remained unperturbed during these protestations. At his insistence, the warriors inspected Imaro with eyes more appraising than they had been during the heat of battle. Now, the disparities between their captive and the other Ilyassai they had known were unmistakable: the broader features, the bulkier physique, the darker skin—all marks of a legacy alien to the Tamburure.

"N'tu-mwaa, you are right," the war leader finally agreed. "Whatever this young one is, he is not Ilyassai."

"Whatever he is, this whelp is of no use to me," N'tu-mwaa said venomously. "Kupigana demands three hearts … the three hearts of the Ilyassai: the *ngombe* that are their life; the lions that give them their manhood; the men themselves, who rule the Tamburure and keep the best grazing land for their cattle.

"Kupigana wants a heart from each. And I, a man apart from any other … only these three things can bring forth the power of our god to rest in *me*. Then, I will make *us* the masters of the Tamburure, not the Ilyassai.

"But this one you have brought me—he is useless! He must have stolen the *ngombe* you say he was chasing—"

Imaro leaped without warning. Though the hobble prevented him from running, the muscles in his thighs possessed more than enough spring to propel him toward the *n'tu-mchawi*.

No longer did Imaro seek to learn the reason for his mysterious captivity. Rage shattered the restraints of caution. He had not spent years absorbing the abuse meted out by the Ilyassai only to hear the same insults, and worse, spill from the mouth of a Turkhana.

His arms strained against his bonds even as he crashed full into the startled N'tu-mwaa. The impact hurled them both to the ground. Imaro landed on top of the sorcerer. He clutched at the dagger bouncing against the Turkhana's bare chest.

N'tu-mwaa's body was as supple as a serpent's; he twisted and writhed while Imaro fought to get a grip on the dagger's hilt. Before Imaro's hands could find full purchase on the weapon, N'tu-mwaa slid from beneath him.

The initial surprise of Imaro's unexpected attack was gone. Now, other Turkhana leaped into the fray. Somehow, Imaro managed to find firm footing while five warriors dragged him from N'tu-mwaa. With a violent, wrenching motion, he shook off the Turkhana's grasp.

But his freedom was only momentary. His arms and ankles were still tied; he was almost helpless. Two warriors rushed him from the front. Others dove at his back and sides. Imaro levered his bound arms upward. His fists landed solidly against the chin of an onrushing Turkhana. The warrior spun backward, crashing onto the ground.

Imaro's bound arms clubbed against the side of another Turkhana's head. He pivoted to strike at another assailant—but the hobble betrayed him. Jerked off balance by the rope connecting his ankles, Imaro sprawled headlong onto the grass. Half a dozen Turkhana buried him beneath a pile of heaving flesh.

Had they removed the sheaths of their wrist-knives, the warriors would have slashed Imaro to ribbons. But they remembered N'tu-mwaa's admonition, even though they no longer believed their foe was a true Ilyassai. They kept their weapons sheathed—with the exception of one, whose razor-sharp edge drove downward toward Imaro's snarling face.

Before the circular blade could strike, a white-blotched hand fastened about the wrist of its wielder. The descent of the blade was abruptly halted. With a strength surprising for one of his gaunt appearance, N'tu-mwaa tightened his grip until the warrior cried out in pain and dropped his weapon. The disarmed warrior trembled as N'tu-mwaa fixed him with a baleful stare.

"This whelp is for *me* to slay as I will, in the way that I wish," the *n'tu-mchawi* grated. "And my wish is that he be left outside the encampment tonight, for the jackals to devour, even as they devour the warriors you say he killed."

"Must we then return to the Ilyassai country to capture another warrior?" the Turkhana war-leader asked. His lack of enthusiasm for such a venture was plain.

"No," N'tu-mwaa replied. "They will come to us. Some of them are bound to be on the trail of the missing *ngombe*. We will wait for them; then I will have a true Ilyassai to join lion and *ngombe*."

The warriors exchanged uncertain glances, which angered N'tu-mwaa.

"Do not stand there, gaping like children!" he snapped. "Get this whelp out of here—*now*!"

The warriors hastened to drag Imaro to his feet. Then the young warrior spoke for the first time since he had been captured.

"Spotted man … your life is mine," he said quietly.

N'tu-mwaa looked at him. The temptation to laugh at those futile words passed before he could act on it. For there was something disconcerting in the stubborn set of the strange youth's features, the defiance smoldering in his night-dark eyes….

N'tu-mwaa turned away. Half a dozen Turkhana moved to carry out the sorcerer's command. They expected fierce resistance from the young warrior, but it did not come. As they knotted grass cords around his legs and carried him from the enclosure, the warriors reasoned that the false Ilyassai had resigned himself to his fate.

Their reasoning was wrong.

***

The pale light of Mwesu the moon picked out the various shapes of the Tamburure night: moving of nocturnal prowlers and their terrified prey; immobile clumps of flat-topped acacia trees scattered across the plain; and a lone figure, human, struggling mightily to free itself from tenacious bonds.

Hours had passed since the Turkhana had unceremoniously discarded Imaro in the grass. Despite the hunger that was beginning to gnaw deep in his stomach, Imaro strained continuously against his bonds. His efforts seemed of little avail; not only was the grass fiber of the ropes much more resistant than it looked, but the Turkhana had bound him with such cunning that he could not raise his arms high enough to reach his teeth, making it impossible to chew his way free.

In time, Imaro knew, he would slacken the ropes sufficiently to wriggle loose. But he also knew he would have little time once the predators and scavengers became aware of his helplessness.

Only moments before, a pair of jackals had skulked cautiously toward him. Imaro roared at them with all the fury of Ngatun himself; the display of bravado had frightened the carrion-eaters, and they had fled. But he knew that before the night was done, braver beasts than Mbweha would confront him.

He suppressed an impulse to scream in frustration. His limbs were bound in a way that prevented the full use of his strength. If the Turkhana had only thrown him near some protrusion of rock against which he could abrade the ropes…. There were many such outcrops on the plain, but Imaro knew that the rustling of the grass he would cause by searching for one, then rolling toward it, would surely attract the attention of a lion or leopard.

Instead, Imaro continued to apply pressure against the ropes. A core of determination burned deep within him. He *must* break his bonds; he *must* free Kulu before it was too late for her; there *must* be a reckoning with N'tu-mwaa....

Suddenly, a wild uproar broke out in the direction of the Turkhana encampment. Although the warriors had left him some distance from the thornbush barrier, he could hear a keening wail of feline agony. A shudder passed involuntarily through the youth's frame. Never before had he heard such a cry torn from the throat of a lion. Uneasily, he wondered what N'tu-mwaa had done to the captive Ngatun.

Then he heard the bellow of a mortally wounded *ngombe*.

Kulu!

Anguish was a knife point, twisting in Imaro's heart. He barely heard the howls of human horror that followed the death cry of his *ngombe*. Nor did he heed the shrill, awful laughter that could only have come from N'tu-mwaa.

"Kulu! Kulu! Kulu!"

Imaro shouted his *ngombe*'s name as he rolled frantically through the grass, searching for a hard surface to rub against his bonds. No longer did he concern himself with attracting predators; the chaos from the encampment would claim the attention of every beast in this part of the Tamburure. And it would obscure whatever noise he made in his efforts to free himself.

Desperately, he rolled and twisted in the grass. A cry of exultation escaped his lips when something hard and rough scraped against the small of his back.

Turning onto his stomach, Imaro ground the ropes binding his arms against the low surface of rock pushing through the soil. The grass fibers that had resisted the force of his muscles for so long shredded easily against the stone. Imaro could feel the ropes beginning to part....

Then the tumult in the encampment ceased. And behind him, Imaro heard a rumbling growl. He turned ... and stared into the face of Matisho, the hunting-hyena.

Matisho was twice the size of its carrion-eating cousin, Fisi, and possessed none of Fisi's well-deserved reputation for cowardice. Teeth capable of crushing the bones of elephants lined Matisho's gaping jaws, and its eyes were twin pools of malignance, reflecting Mwesu's light.

Another youth might have been frightened into near-paralysis at the sight of Matisho so near. Imaro, drawing upon reserves of strength he never before knew he possessed, wrenched his arms in a final effort to break his bonds. As he did so, Matisho leaped onto his chest. Lethal jaws darted toward Imaro's face just as the ropes on the Ilyassai youth's arms snapped and fell away.

Before Matisho's teeth could reach him, Imaro stabbed stiffened fingers into the beast's eyes. Matisho yelped in agony, and its slavering jaws veered away from Imaro's head.

With a lightning-quick twist, Imaro levered his body onto Matisho's back. For a moment, his weight, equal to that of the beast, pinned Matisho to the ground. Imaro clamped his arms around Matisho's hairy throat. The youth's legs were still bound; they dangled uselessly along the hunting-hyena's spine while Imaro exerted all the power in his arms against the beast's throat, blocking the flow of air into its lungs.

The youth's advantage lasted only a moment. Uttering strangled, wheezing howls that were nothing like the yipping laugh of Fisi, Matisho hurled its body in lunge after frenzied lunge, seeking to dislodge the death-dealer riding on its back. The beast flung Imaro about as though he weighed nothing. Imaro clung persistently, the pressure exerted by his arms inexorably constricting the giant hyena's windpipe.

Had Matisho possessed the agile, taloned forefeet of the great cats, it could have reached backward and slashed Imaro's arms and shoulders to the bone. But the hyena's limbs were doglike, adapted for chasing rather than seizing its prey. The huge beast could only attempt to fling Imaro from its back, then grasp an arm or leg in its crushing jaws.

Its struggles grew weaker. Then, abruptly, Matisho fell. The hunting-hyena's breath came in ragged, choking gasps; its paws waved feebly, uselessly. Only when even those movements stopped did Imaro release his hold. Matisho lay lifeless, its throat crushed by Imaro's unfettered strength.

His triumph over Matisho gave him no joy. Only Kulu was in his thoughts.

Kulu is dead, he lamented silently. There was a stinging behind his closed eyelids as he bowed his head and panted from his exertions.

Then he stiffened. His *kufahuma*, distracted during his battle with Matisho, was screaming a warning. His eyes snapped open—and a gout of flame swept directly toward his face!

Imaro hurled himself backward, just barely eluding the searing fire. Legs still bound, he sprawled awkwardly in the grass. Half blinded by the glare of the flame, he was as vulnerable now as he had ever been in his life.

N'tu-mwaa did not press his advantage. He plunged the unlit end of the spear-tall torch he carried into the earth. And he glared down at the supine Imaro.

The *n'tu-mchawi* had dispensed with his cloak; his gaunt, blemished body was naked save for a strip of hide around his loins. Imaro blinked in the flickering orange firelight. Surely, he thought, his eyes were still dazzled by the flames that had nearly blinded him. Surely, the hideous apparition the Turkhana had become was not real.... N'tu-mwaa's face had not really become the face of Ngatun the lion, and it could not be the horns of a *ngombe* that sprouted from the thick-maned skull—the horns of Kulu, still crusted with the blood of the Turkhana warrior she had wounded....

Imaro tore his eyes from the grotesque sight of N'tu-mwaa's face. He looked farther down, only to confront a sight that was even more appalling. On

N'tu-mwaa's chest, where his sacrificial dagger had dangled from a thong, blood rilled in sickening scarlet streams from the raggedly severed valves of two hearts suspended from a length of beast-gut.

Bile rose in Imaro's throat as he was forced to realize that the grotesque thing looming over him was no more an illusion than the flame sputtering atop the torch in the ground.

Heart of lion, heart of ngombe, N'tu-mwaa had raved. And now...

As if he were reading Imaro's thoughts, N'tu-mwaa spoke, whispering eerily from the lion's mouth that had replaced his own.

"I have come to claim my final bounty, boy-child," he said. "Kupigana showed me what the others did not see. They are blind; I have Kupigana's sight, and I would not let them know what I know. You are not Ilyassai; you are more. *More!* You have killed Matisho with only your hands. What youth of your rains could have done the same? It does not matter that you are not Ilyassai...."

He tossed his horned, maned head. Beast-madness shone in his eyes. He waved the dagger he had removed from his neck. It still dripped with the blood of Ngatun and Kulu.

"I'll have your heart, boy-child. Kupigana says you are the one who will become the greatest of all warriors. Heart of the lion, heart of *ngombe*, heart of the one who is to be mightiest of all—now, *I* will be mightiest of all, not you. I will lead the Turkhana to victory over the Ilyassai! All of the Tamburure will be mine! Give me your heart, boy-child! Give it to me, *now*!"

N'tu-mwaa's voice had risen to an inhuman screech. His curved dagger drove toward Imaro's chest. The point bit deep into flesh—but not the flesh of Imaro.

It was the flesh of Matisho, whose body Imaro had interposed between himself and N'tu-mwaa's blade. Hissing like a maddened cat, the Turkhana struggled to pull his blade free from Matisho's carcass. At the same time, his unsheathed wrist-knife struck at Imaro's face. The youth shifted aside; N'tu-mwaa's deadly forearm whipped harmlessly past Imaro's head.

With one hand, Imaro caught the Turkhana's arm, just above the arm of the wrist-knife. And he dragged N'tu-mwaa to his knees.

For all the horror of his altered appearance, the Turkhana had not completed his conjuring. He was still only N'tu-mwaa, and even maddened as he was, he could not match Imaro's strength. He looked upon the features of the not-Ilyassai. Those features had twisted into a terrifying mask of vengeance and hatred.

For a moment, the derangement that drove N'tu-mwaa subsided. And he knew, then, that he faced his doom.

His lion-mouth cried out inarticulately, and his *ngombe* horns tossed wildly as he fought to free himself from Imaro's iron grasp. Blood from the beast-hearts splashed across the youth's face. Imaro fastened his free hand around the wrist of the hand that held the curved dagger. He forced the blade out of the body of Matisho, even as N'tu-mwaa maintained a desperate grip on the hilt.

Then the dagger dropped to the ground, and N'tu-mwaa shrieked in pain, for the bones in his wrist were beginning to splinter. Imaro was unconscious of the force he was exerting; with the killer of Kulu in his hands, he had become implacable, inhuman....

"It's not over yet," N'tu-mwaa snarled.

Jerking his head forward, the Turkhana sorcerer seized Imaro's shoulder in his lion-jaws. Fangs tore through the young warrior's flesh. Biting back a cry of pain, Imaro snatched N'tu-mwaa's dagger from the ground and plunged it into the Turkhana's chest, in the space between the two hearts that dangled there. Instantly, the lion-jaws relaxed and fell away.

N'tu-mwaa shuddered, then sank backward onto the grass. He gurgled, blood bubbling from his gaping mouth. He seemed to be trying to speak....

For a reason he could not name, Imaro leaned over N'tu-mwaa to hear his dying words. The lion-eyes were dimming, but the Turkhana's voice was still clear.

"I ... cannot die now ...," he rasped. "I still have to *show* them.... I am better than they.... I am better, even though *they* say I am not...."

N'tu-mwaa said no more.

***

Two corpses—N'tu-mwaa and Matisho—lay in the blood-dewed grass. Their slayer used N'tu-mwaa's curved dagger to cut the ropes away from his legs. Then Imaro sprang to his feet, free for the first time in many hours from Turkhana restraints.

He glared down at the *n'tu-mchawi.* N'tu-mwaa's lion-eyes were still open, reflecting the glare of the torch. Imaro shook his head angrily, as if to rid himself of the inexplicable sense of ... *kinship* ... he felt with his dead foe. They were, each of them, different from the others in their tribes. Each, in his own way, had striven to gain the acceptance and respect of those who despised them for their differentness. N'tu-mwaa's weapon in that struggle was sorcery; Imaro's, strength.

Strength ... long had he known that he was far stronger than other boys of his rains, as well as many who were older. But his strength had never before been tested as it had this day. He recalled N'tu-mwaa's words: *The one Kupigana says will be the greatest warrior of all....*

Imaro spat into the grass. He would not be duped by the lies of a madman, or of another tribe's god. He was who he was: Imaro, the son-of-no-father.

Yet the words lingered, despite the harsh inner voice that reminded him that he had done nothing more than slay one who meant to slay him. It was the same voice that told him he had lost Kulu....

Eyes still on N'tu-mwaa, Imaro murmured, "I told you, Turkhana, your life is mine."

Now, he became aware that he was ravenous, not having eaten since the rising of the sun. With no other food available, he used N'tu-mwaa's dagger to cut strips of flesh from the carcass of Matisho. Then he burned the strips in the flame of N'tu-mwaa's torch, and began to eat. As he chewed on the rank meat of the hunting-hyena, Imaro looked toward the encampment of the Turkhana. Its night-fire blazed like a beacon against the night sky.

Despite the slaying of N'tu-mwaa, Imaro still needed a reckoning with the Turkhana who remained. Kulu's death demanded more than one life in return....

Imaro was well aware that death was the fate of an Ilyassai who lost his *ngombe*. Yet he also knew he could turn his back on his mother's clan now. In this vast, uninhabited stretch of the Tamburure, he could live alone and free, a predator among predators, battling Ngatun and Chui and Matisho for better meat than the half-charred hyena flesh he forced down his throat.

Freedom from the ongoing ordeal of life among the Ilyassai—it could be his, once he exacted final retribution from the Turkhana.

He thrust that notion from his mind. He could not—would not—run away. His only thoughts now were for Kulu.

Kulu was dead. Yet in the pitiless code of the Ilyassai, there was a way to balance that death, even to the satisfaction of Masadu. He would still face a flogging at the scarred warrior's hands for having allowed Kulu to die. He had endured floggings before, though, and he knew the pain would pass. And he knew why he chose to bear this and any other torments the Ilyassai could inflict.

I leave a warrior behind, Katisa had said. But only by the slaying of Ngatun on *olmaiyo* would the Kitoko clan be forced to accept the truth of those words. And only then would Imaro himself believe it.

The promise of fulfilling Katisa's prophecy was the only link that remained between Imaro and the fading memories that were all he had left of his long-departed mother. Those memories could sustain him no longer. His own determination would. The day he slew Ngatun would be the day of his freedom.

He swallowed another hunk of Matisho's flesh. Then he rose to his feet. Gripping the torch in one hand and N'tu-mwaa's dagger in the other, he stalked toward the encampment like a blood-spattered harbinger of destruction.

***

Spotting a bobbing point of fire approaching in the night, the Turkhana sentries assumed that N'tu-mwaa was returning to them. Unnerved, as were all the war band following N'tu-mwaa's frenzied slaughter of the lion and the *ngombe*, the entries were slow to notice that the silhouette of the figure bearing the brand was not the horned, maned apparition N'tu-mwaa had become.

The figure halted. The fire-point drew back—then streaked like a comet toward the thornbush barrier!

Caught completely off guard, the sentries could only stare blankly while the flaming missile struck the dry thornbush, scattering sparks like drops of fiery rain. Immediately, the barrier ignited.

Shrill cries of alarm rose from the throats of the sentries. Rushing from the interior of the thornbush circle, the other warriors helped the sentries beat madly at the flames with long strips of cured leather. If the flames spread to the grass surrounding the encampment, the entire plain could become a burning maelstrom, cutting them off from their own country.

Then the dreaded war cry of the Ilyassai smote their ears. And a fear even greater than that caused by what N'tu-mwaa had done was realized.

"It's an attack!" the war leader cried. "The Ilyassai have found us! See to your weapons! And *get that fire out!*"

Brave men were the Turkhana: warriors second only to the Ilyassai. But on this night, they had witnessed horrors that had shaken the souls of even the most fearless among them. When N'tu-mwaa had *changed*, brave men had wept like infants....

Imaro hurdled the flaming thornbush, and drove his blade into the throat of the war-leader. As blood spewed from the Turkhana's neck, the iron hand of panic crushed the courage from the rest of the warriors. To their terror-stricken minds, Imaro was a ghost returned for vengeance, for they could not believe that a bound man or boy could have survived the Tamburure at night. Shrieking prayers to their gods and ancestors, the Tamburure broke and fled. And Imaro ravened among them like Ngatun himself.

In the crimson glare of the blazing thornbush, the dagger of N'tu-mwaa flashed again and again in Imaro's hand. It was as if the blade were still thirsty for sacrificial blood, regardless of its source.

Had the Turkhana retained sufficient presence of mind to retaliate, their sheer advantage in numbers would have enabled them to cut Imaro down. But they believed he was only the first of a horde of vengeful Ilyassai demons, and they fled like a herd of impala, leaving weapons, mortally wounded comrades, and the burning encampment behind them. Five Turkhana lay motionless in widening pools of gore.

Blood madness still lit Imaro's eyes as he watched the surviving Turkhana disappear into the darkness. He did not pursue them. His arms were becoming heavy, and his breath burned inside his aching chest. His body was beginning to beg for relief from the demands he had placed on it this day.

Yet he lifted his arms high, threw back his head, and shouted in exultation. The shout had nothing of the Ilyassai in it—it was a cry of personal triumph, and he did not care that no one else heard it.

The flush of victory was short-lived. For in the flickering glow of the fire, Imaro saw the butchered carcass of Kulu. And he knew then that his tasks were not yet completed.

***

The morning sun painted the Tamburure in tints of saffron and gold. Ten Ilyassai of the Kitoko clan, fully armed, marched purposefully across the plain. At dawn, they had left the *manyattas* to search for Imaro and his *ngombe*. The Ilyassai always allowed a herd-boy the opportunity to recover a lost *ngombe* himself—or to slay whatever had caused the *ngombe*'s death, and return with evidence of the deed. Imaro had not returned, so the hunt for him and his *ngombe* had begun. Kanoko was among the searchers. So was Masadu.

The trail left by the fleeing Kulu was still easy to follow; the story told by broken grass easily read. They came to the site of Imaro's first encounter with the intruders. A fallen feather resting between strands of grass caught their attention. *Turkhana*, it all but shouted.

Dark hands tightened on spear shafts; *simis* were loosened in their sheaths. Masadu sent a runner back to the *manyattas* to summon more fighting men. The warriors seethed with indignation, Imaro and Kulu momentarily forgotten. The Turkhana had dared to venture past the Land of No One. For that, the befeathered wrist-knife wielders must be punished....

Kanoko's spirits soared. His ploy had turned out better than he had ever hoped. He fought to suppress the outward expression of glee the prospect of Imaro's having fallen into Turkhana hands roused in his soul.

Then he saw Imaro, striding through the grass toward him and the others. He came to them like a conqueror: in appearance, still a boy, but in reality, much more than that.

And not even Kanoko could deny that Imaro had done what Ilyassai tradition demanded. That Kulu was dead, they would soon learn. But the loss was well atoned. For with him, Imaro carried half a dozen wrist-knives—still attached to the stumps of hands skewered on the blade of a captured spear. On the topmost hand, pale blotches showed through blood smears.

The weapon was still in the crucible, and was not found wanting....

THE PLACE OF STONES

Where the Ilyassai walk,
Ngatun roars softly.
—Tamburure proverb

Jua's light danced across the points of twenty Ilyassai *arems*. Twenty Ilyassai warriors of the Kitoko clan stalked soundlessly through the yellow grass. Besides their spears, they carried painted oval shields made from the hide of Kifaru, the rhinoceros. Their faces were grim and alert—the faces of men who knew they were masters of the Tamburure.

With the bright ocher that bedaubed their limbs, the warriors looked like crimson spectres of death. Zebra, gazelle, and even the rhinoceros and Tembo, the elephant, raised their heads sharply at the scent of Ilyassai iron reaching their nostrils. For the Ilyassai were predators no less fearsome than Chui or Ngatun or Matisho. The grass-eaters observed the warriors closely, their muscles tensed for instant flight should the Ilyassai come too near to them.

But the warriors paid the grass-eaters no heed. For on this day, they were not hunting for food. This was the day of *olmaiyo*, the end of *mafundishu-ya-muran* for an Ilyassai youth about to enter manhood. For *olmaiyo*, the prey was Ngatun, the lion.

A sudden break in the flatness of the plain signaled the end of the warriors' march. Fanning out in a long, straight rank, the Ilyassai gazed down into a shallow, cuplike depression, the bed of an ancient lake that had long ago been dried out by the heat of Jua.

While the rest of the warriors stood still as statues carved from mahogany, two broke the rank and strode down the grassy slope to the bottom of the lake-bed. Along with his weapons, one of them carried the long, spiraled horn of an oryx. This was Muburi, the *oibonok* who had succeeded the disgraced Chitendu. The other, the only one who did not wear a *shingona*—headgear made from Ngatun's mane—was Imaro. The *olmaiyo* was his; on this day, he would earn a *shingona* of his own—or die.

In the four rains that had passed since the death of Kulu, Imaro had fulfilled his promise of physical splendor. There were other Ilyassai who equalled his height of six and a half feet, but none of them could match the formidable thews that rolled across his lionlike frame. Yet for all his massive musculature, the young warrior moved with a loose, feline litheness.

Fierce determination was stamped in his heavy features, and a sullen defiance stoked by a lifetime of mistreatment burned in his eyes. Still, a flicker of hope half hid beneath the interplay of suppressed resentment and mounting anticipation of the battle to come.

Imaro knew his deeds over the past few rains had earned him a measure of reluctant respect within the clan, for all that they continued to look askance at his ambiguous parentage and scorn the memory of his mother. Imaro's was the *arem* that had brought down a maddened bush-pig that had threatened the wife of the *ol-arem* of a neighboring clan, the Enyoka. And he had washed his *simi* in the blood of battle against the Zamburu, a tribe whose hunters had dared to encroach on Ilyassai territory.

Deep into the land of the Zamburu the Kitoko clan had raided: burning, killing, and taking cattle and women. Imaro acquired five new cattle for his small herd during that raid, along with a young Zamburu named Keteke.

Although his mother's mating with a man who was not Ilyassai was the cause of Imaro's persecution, Ilyassai men were free to mate with, and even take as wives, women they stole during raids and wars. The irony of that inconsistent standard was not lost on Imaro. But he did not vent his anger on Keteke. To her, he had finally opened a heart that had remained inviolate since the slaying of Kulu. And Keteke had responded in kind.

But since Imaro had not yet fulfilled the obligation of *olmaiyo*, Keteke was still a captive, belonging to the clan as a whole. Once Imaro slew Ngatun, she would belong to him alone, and they would be able to wed.

Imaro and Muburi reached the bottom of the depression. The unpleasant smile on Muburi's lips reminded Imaro that for all the grudging acceptance some of the Ilyassai now accorded him, there were others who still spurned him. Muburi was one. Masadu, who stood with the others, high up on the slope, was another.

Kanoko was there too, his eyes staring spitefully from beneath the *shingona* he had recently earned. Imaro had told no one about Kanoko's part in the fate of Kulu, but Kanoko had shown no gratitude. The animosity between the two young warriors had increased over the ensuing rains.

"You are prepared?" Muburi demanded gruffly.

A curt nod was Imaro's reply. His opinion of sorcerers had not changed since he had slain N'tu-mwaa; he spoke to the *oibonok* only as necessity dictated.

Muburi raised the oryx horn to his lips and puffed into a small opening at its point. A startling sound resulted: more like the growl of a beast than a musical tone. Its challenge echoed across the dry lake-bottom—and was answered by a deep, rumbling roar. Then Muburi climbed back up the slope, leaving Imaro to face the ultimate trial of an Ilyassai warrior.

From the opposite side of the depression, the roars rumbled like rainy-season thunder. Imaro could feel their vibrations rising through the shaft of his *arem*. He remembered the elders' stories about how Ajunge himself had placed an oryx horn in the hands of the first *oibonok* of the Ilyassai, to summon Ngatun to test the valor of the warriors. He knew that if he slew Ngatun, he would be freeing an ancestor's soul to be human again. He wondered if this ancestor would disdain him as much as his contemporaries did....

The roaring grew louder. A huge, tawny, black-maned shape appeared on the lip of the far side of the lake-bed. With an easy bound, Ngatun entered the natural arena. As much a giant of his own kind as Imaro was of his, the lion padded purposefully toward the waiting warrior. Its tufted tail twitched in anticipation of the bloodshed to come.

Imaro relaxed into a fighting stance: *arem* point outthrust, shield held closely to his body, protecting him from neck to ankle. He knew Ngatun could cover the distance remaining between them swifter than the eye could follow.

The long years in *mafundishu-ya-muran* had drilled into him the things he must do to meet that deadly charge. When Ngatun made his final leap, Imaro must hurl his *arem* into the great cat's breast. At no other time would Ngatun be so vulnerable. Then Imaro would fall under his shield even as Ngatun's weight pressed onto him. Beneath the shield's protection, he would draw his *simi* and stab it into Ngatun's body until the beast died.

If Ngatun survived long enough to rip through the thick rhinoceros hide of the shield ... At that moment in his teaching of *mafundishu-ya-muran*, Masadu would point silently at his own scarred face.

Suddenly, there was no more time for reflection. With an earthshaking roar, Ngatun sprang at Imaro.

The young warrior's reaction was instantaneous. His *arem* shot with arrow-like speed from his hand. Its point, and half its long blade, burrowed deep into Ngatun's chest; Imaro crouched, then fell backward beneath his shield.

Ngatun crashed full into the barrier of rhinoceros hide. Squalling in pain, the spear embedded in its body, Ngatun still tore large strips of hide from the shield that was Imaro's only defense. Blood pumped from the mortal wound the *arem* had inflicted. But Ngatun was always slow to die.

Now was the time for Imaro to draw his *simi*. But he had something different in mind—something he had practiced by himself, away from the ever-watchful eyes of Masadu.

He did not draw his short sword. And for a single, terrifying instant, with Ngatun's tremendous weight crushing down on him, doubt penetrated his mind. Then he saw the white gleam of a claw punching through the hide of the shield.

And he acted.

With all the power of his massive arms and legs, Imaro heaved upward against Ngatun's weight. And the thrust hurled both lion and shield away from him. The lion toppled onto its back, claws still embedded in the shield. At that moment, Ngatun lay helpless.

With a speed rivaling that of the great cat itself, Imaro sprang to his feet, *simi* drawn and gripped tightly in both hands. Before the lion could tear its talons away from the rhinoceros hide, Imaro swing his *simi* downward. A lifetime's frustration powered that stroke. Through Ngatun's shaggy mane and thick-muscled throat Imaro's blade sheared, not stopping until the bones of the lion's spine were severed.

Blood gushed from Ngatun's gaping throat. A strangled wail; a pumping of clawed limbs in a final fury; then Ngatun lay still.

Straddling the huge carcass, Imaro hacked viciously at the lion's neck. Triumph coursed fiercely through his veins. He knew he had only narrowly escaped death himself; with only an eyeblink more time without the protection of his shield, his would have been the gore that now leaked onto the Tamburure.

But he had won his gamble, and he had triumphed over Ngatun in a way no Ilyassai had ever done before. *Ilyassai*—so many times, he had cursed the very syllables of that name. Yet he was proud now, for he had won his *olmaiyo*, and his mother's people would have to accept him now, whether they liked it or not. And they would, indeed, accept him. The Ilyassai were merciless, but they were also honorable.

Finally, the *simi* cut completely through Ngatun's neck. Imaro dropped the weapon and hooked strong, dark fingers into the lion's mane. Effortlessly, he raised the huge, heavy head of the lion above his own. Blood from the stump of its neck showered like hot, salty rain onto his shoulders and upraised face. The taste of Ngatun's blood was the taste of vindication....

Then he heard a rustle in the grass.

Imaro lowered his head, blinked the lion's blood out of his eyes, and saw that the warriors had descended the slope. Now, they surrounded him. And the cry of joy with which he had meant to greet them curdled in his throat.

The warriors remained silent, their red-daubed faces set like stone. Imaro's euphoria faded like dawn mist at the first touch of Jua, the sun.

Where were the shouts, the chants, the leaps of ecstasy that marked the victorious end of a warrior's *olmaiyo*? Why weren't the others cutting out Ngatun's heart and slicing it into portions to be eaten raw by all the warriors, marking the final freeing of the soul the lion's body had contained?

There was no celebration. Masadu, Kanoko, and the others tightened their circle around Imaro. They moved forward stiffly, as if they were no longer in control of their own bodies. Only one was not affected by the mysterious torpor: Muburi. The *oibonok* smiled, malice plain in his narrowed eyes.

With a sudden, sick sensation, Imaro realized he had been betrayed.

In his mind, his life had been a contest: his will against that of the Ilyassai. They had set the conditions for the contest; he had fulfilled them. Now—they had reneged on their own rules.

With a strangled sound that was half sob, half scream of hatred, Imaro hurled the head of Ngatun toward the advancing warriors. Trailing blood, the grisly missile crashed full into the nearest man's shield, sending him sprawling backward. Then Imaro lunged for his *simi*, which was still lying in the grass by the carcass of his kill. He no longer thought; his only desire was to repay the Ilyassai's deceit with blood, even though they were his mother's people.

He never reached his *simi*. Before his fingers could touch the hilt of the weapon, half a dozen spear butts smashed against his head. Bolts of pain exploded in his skull, and he sank to the blood-spattered grass. Unconsciousness awaited, but before the world blinked out, a single thought whirled in the chaotic confusion that overwhelmed him: why had the Ilyassai waited until *now* to destroy him, if they had meant to do so all along?

***

He awakened hanging from a pole supported on the shoulders of two warriors. His wrists and ankles were lashed securely to its ends. Despite the jolts of pain each step of the warriors' quick pace sent through his skull, Imaro instantly realized the significance of the manner in which he was trussed.

Warriors who were victorious in *olmaiyo* marched proudly back to the *manyattas*, carrying the mane of the lion they had slain in their hands. The tuft of its tail would decorate their spears. Those who suffered serious wounds in their victory—like Masadu—were carried with honor on the remnants of their shields. Those who died beneath Ngatun's fangs were left on the plain for the scavengers to devour, as were all other Ilyassai dead.

Only an *ilmonek*—an un-man, one who fled in terror before Ngatun's charge—was returned to the *manyattas* bound to a pole like the quarry in a hunt for game. And when an *ilmonek* came within sight of a clan's *manyattas*....

When that thought entered his mind, the true depth of the betrayal become clear to Imaro. He struggled against his bonds, nearly toppling the pole from the warriors' shoulders.

"Why are you disgracing yourselves with this *lie*?" Imaro shouted. "Do you hate me more than you love your honor?"

"Who are you, *ilmonek*, to speak to men about honor?" Masadu replied scathingly.

The scarred warrior spat on Imaro's shadow. The others glared at him, contemptuous curses and epithets spewing from their mouths. The glazed, unseeing expressions their faces had worn when they struck Imaro down were gone now. And Imaro realized then that the warriors truly believed he had fled from Ngatun.

But why?

His gaze turned to Muburi. The *oibonok*'s features were a mask of scorn. Yet in Muburi's eyes, Imaro recognized the same cold amusement he had seen just before the warriors' spear butts collided with his head.

In a sudden insight, Imaro knew the answer to his question. Somehow, the *n'tu-mchawi* had used his sorcery to induce the warriors into believing they had seen Imaro throw down his weapons and run from Ngatun, rather than what had actually happened. They had slain the lion themselves, they believed, in order to spare Imaro for the Shaming.

The warriors marched in forbidding silence. Imaro knew there was no use in further conversation. Despair and a sense of futility threatened to overcome the young warrior as no weapons ever could. Muburi had used *mchawi*—sorcery of the foulest kind; the same sorcery that N'tu-mwaa of the Turkhana had practiced; the same kind that had brought about the downfall of Chitendu, who was the clan's *oibonok* before Muburi.

But Chitendu had long since vanished. And Muburi had no reason to wish Imaro any harm—at least, no more than any other Ilyassai. And why the elaborate deception? If Muburi had desired Imaro's death, an *arem* in the back would have been much simpler. But what if it was not his death Muburi wanted? What if it was his disgrace?

Imaro's thoughts deepened and darkened as the warriors continued to carry him across the Tamburure.

***

Jua was touching the western horizon when the cheerless procession finally reached the *manyattas* of the Kitoko clan. Men, women, and children gathered in the open space at the center of the concentric circles of dwellings. From afar, they had seen the manner of Imaro's return—*ilmonek*.

The warriors carrying Imaro shrugged the pole from their shoulders. Imaro landed on the ground with a jarring thud. Before he could catch the breath driven from his body, the jeering began.

It was through other tribes' fear of Ilyassai courage and prowess that the warrior-herdsmen dominated the Tamburure. Only the truly valiant could use fear as a weapon—this, the Ilyassai well knew. *Mafundishu-ya-muran* and *olmaiyo* were the ways the Ilyassai expunged fear from the hearts of their warriors.

For the *ilmonek*—those who failed to conquer their fears in the face of

Ngatun's wrath—the Shaming awaited. The abuse the Ilyassai shouted into Imaro's ears was but the beginning of the Shaming. *A lie,* he cried, without opening his mouth.

A harsh shout rose over the din of taunts and curses. Mubaku, the *ol-arem,* had arrived. The tumult quickly subsided, and the throng of people parted to allow Mubaku to pass.

Nearly sixty rains had washed through Mubaku's life now. The lines their passage had left were clearly visible even beneath the ocher daubed on his face. His limbs were leaner than they had been the day Katisa left the clan's *manyattas.* Still, the *ol-arem* stood straight as the shaft of the spear from which his title was derived. In battle, his skill and ferocity were equal to that of warriors a score or more rains younger.

Mubaku looked down at the bound Imaro. Imaro thought he saw a shadow of disappointment pass through the *ol-arem*'s eyes—but only briefly.

"Cut him free," Mubaku said.

The two warriors who had borne Imaro from the plain bent down and used their *simis* to sever the thongs that bound Imaro to the pole. Imaro rose to his feet. He refused to allow the effects of the clubbing or the uncomfortable trek back from the *olmaiyo* to show. Erect, unwavering, he faced the *ol-arem.* The warriors who had cut him free stood close by, their *simis* still drawn.

"This is a lie," Imaro said quietly.

"Silence, son-of-no-father," Mubaku growled.

Inwardly, Imaro winced. Rains had passed since Mubaku had last referred to him in that way.

"Let Muburi and Masadu speak first," the *ol-arem* said. "Then the son-of-no-father. Then we will decide who speaks the truth. Such is the Way of Ajunge."

"Such is the Way," the others intoned.

The *oibonok* and the master of *mafundishu-ya-muran* recounted the tale of Imaro's supposed cowardice. To Imaro, those words were like venom dripping from the fangs of a serpent. *Lies, all lies,* he thought. *Why can't they realize they are lying?*

But the other warriors who had witnessed the *olmaiyo* nodded their agreement. Kanoko had cut in with words of his own, stating that his was the spear that had slain Ngatun, just as the lion was about to bring the falling Imaro down from behind. The warriors' eyes mirrored their scorn for Imaro.

And the judgment of the other warriors who had not participated in the *olmaiyo* was obvious. For many rains, they had resented Imaro's strength, speed, and skill; hated the reality that the son-of-no-father, who was only half Ilyassai, could surpass the greatest physical feats the full-blooded Ilyassai could accomplish. Now, with the evidence of the warriors who had been part of the *olmaiyo* that Imaro had fled from Ngatun and had failed the final test of a warrior, their grudging respect for Imaro's prowess disappeared.

The swift erosion of the acceptance he had striven so long to gain was clear to Imaro; he could see it falling from the Ilyassai's faces like the cast-off skin of a shedding lizard. He knew that none of them would believe the truth about his *olmaiyo*.

Yet when Mubaku bade him to speak in his own defense, Imaro told his tale with quiet dignity, ignoring the open disbelief that greeted its telling. He did not mention his suspicions about Muburi, for he had no way of proving the *oibonok* had used *mchawi* against him. Before the people spoke in response when Mubaku asked them which story they believed, he knew what they would say.

"The son-of-no father lies!"

"No one has the strength to throw Ngatun from his shield!"

"Not only is the son-of-no-father *ilmonek*, he is a liar as well!"

"Shame him! Shame him!"

"The Ilyassai have judged," Mubaku said after the tumult died down. "You, son-of-no-father, are *ilmonek*—un-man. You must suffer the Shaming. You will be stripped of weapons and clothing, and cast out of the lands of the Ilyassai clans. Every tribe in the Tamburure will know you for what you are, for your head will be shaved smooth as a woman's."

Mubaku's words beat against Imaro's ears like the measured cadence of a funeral drum. His lifelong goal—to attain full warrior status among his mother's people—was dead. It lay at his feet like the scattered, yellow bones of an old kill.

"It is a lie," Imaro murmured. The word referred to more than just the fabricated story the warriors who had accompanied him on *olmaiyo* had told.

Kanoko stepped in front of Imaro then.

"An *ilmonek* dares to call true warriors liars!" he shouted before smashing the butt of his *arem* full into Imaro's mouth.

Blood spurting from his lips, Imaro's head snapped back and a fresh jolt of pain lanced through his skull. And sheer madness swept through him like a burning, crimson wave.

Before the sneering Kanoko could move, Imaro was upon him. A tremendous blow of his balled fist lifted Kanoko from his feet and sent him crashing into the leather wall of a nearby *manyatta*. Blood pouring from his lacerated lips, Imaro sprang toward the supine body of his lifelong tormentor.

His path was quickly blocked by a horde of lean, strong warriors. Imaro charged into them like a buffalo attacking a pride of lions. With macelike blows of his fists, he sent his tribesmen sprawling. Closer he surged to the dazed Kanoko, murder blazing in his eyes.

But even Imaro could not prevail for long against so many Ilyassai. Despite the punishment the maddened warrior dealt, the others swarmed over him, striking heavy blows of their own. They used only their hands, for they knew Imaro must be kept alive for the Shaming.

Yet Imaro refused to fall … until Mubaku tripped him with the shaft of his *arem*. Imaro fell then, and for the second time that day, his head was the target of a shower of spear butts.

Before blackness enveloped him, Imaro saw the warriors gaze at each other in wonderment. Through clouding eyes, he saw the doubt that was in their minds revealed on their faces: how could such prodigious strength and ferocity be housed in the body of one who was *ilmonek*?

Then he heard Muburi's voice.

"That's enough, damn you!" the *oibonok* shouted. "Would you have him die before the Shaming ends?"

Even as he sank again into unconsciousness, Imaro saw the doubt recede from the warriors' eyes. It was as though he could hear their thoughts: *He is not truly Ilyassai.... His courage now is that of the cornered rat.... Nineteen Ilyassai warriors would never lie.... We saw what we saw....*

Then oblivion claimed him, mercifully.

***

A foul smell hung almost palpably in the dark *manyatta*. From the round entrance of the leather dwelling, a circle of dim light vied vainly against the deep shadows inside. The wan flickering of the Ilyassai night-fires meant little to the figure lying bound on the bare dirt floor. Imaro savored the darkness, for night signaled surcease from the ordeal of his days.

Though he seemed only a motionless shadow in the black confines of the *manyatta*, the warrior was far from quiescent. He strained with dogged persistence against the grass ropes binding his limbs. At times, it seemed he was back in the Land of No One, held captive by the Turkhana. He had been bound in the open plain then, but it was all the same, he thought bitterly.

He continued to extend his arms and legs outward, pushing against the fibrous bonds. The ropes had been tied in a way that caused them to grip him more tightly the more he fought them. Yet he continued to fight them.

During the two days and three nights that had passed since his *olmaiyo*, Imaro had pitted his strength against ropes normally used to restrain *ngombe* bulls that had become unruly during mating time. There was nothing against which these fibers could be abraded, as had been the case in the Tamburure during that long-ago night when he thought the worst had already happened to him. Yet resistant though the fibers were, he knew they would eventually yield to his unrelenting pressure. *They must....*

The toll exacted by his lack of food since the Shaming started was a harsh one. But the molten core of hatred deep within him sustained him as no amount of food ever could. The final humiliation of the three days of Shaming would greet him with the morning rise of Jua unless he overcame his bonds this night. And if the pain of the ropes cutting deep into his skin threatened to hinder him, he needed only to allow his memory to dwell on the events of the past days to goad him into greater effort....

He had remained motionless and silent when Masadu tore away his clothing and cut the clay-caked braids from his head. He had not resisted when Muburi bound him. In what seemed to be resigned indifference, he endured the days of Shaming.

When Jua rose, two warriors would drag him from the *manyatta* set aside for him and prop him against its leather wall. Then the people would gather, from the oldest to the youngest—everyone who was not obligated to graze the *ngombe* or guard the borders of the clan's territory.

They reviled him with bitter words, and pelted him with dirt and offal. Most vicious of all were the youths who were almost of age for *olmaiyo*. There were few among them who did not secretly fear that they, themselves, might one day share Imaro's plight. And there were fewer still who did not silently resolve to die beneath the talons of Ngatun rather than face the Shaming.

Only once did Imaro allow the emotions roiling beneath the expressionless mask of his face to betray him. It happened on the first day, when one face stood out indelibly from the others: the face of Keteke, the Zamburu captive meant to be his mate after he returned from *olmaiyo*. Surely Keteke, who had told Imaro she loved him, would believe in him....

But when Keteke looked at him, her face was twisted in an expression of deep loathing. Behind her stood Kanoko, who had scathingly proclaimed to all the clan that both Keteke and Imaro's small herd of cattle now belonged to him. In response, Imaro had lowered his head until the sorrow receded. After that, there was nothing left inside him other than hatred.

The ropes were cutting so deeply into his muscles that he was beginning to lose feeling. But his hatred felt no pain. Still, he knew that if he lost much more of this strength, he would not be able to burst free before dawn. He had to force the grass serpent-coils away from him—*now*!

And his bonds finally surrendered, torn apart by the tremendous surge of Imaro's ultimate surge of power and will. Shaking the limp bond from him, he sat up, ignoring the tingling pain of the circulation that returned to his limbs. The pain was nothing, for he was now free—free to escape from his prison, for the Ilyassai had not deigned to post guards at the *manyatta* in which he was held.

There would be other sentries elsewhere, Imaro knew, for the *ngombe* had to be protected from two- and four-legged marauders. But Imaro was confident he could evade them.

For the first time since he had slain Ngatun, joy suffused Imaro's soul. *First, freedom,* he vowed. *Then—vengeance!*

It was then that he heard a slight, furtive noise at the entrance to the *manyatta.* And he saw a dim bulk pass through the circular opening. And moonlight glittered on a metal blade….

***

Imaro moved swiftly, soundlessly. One brawny arm hooked across the throat of the intruder to stifle any outcry. His free hand clamped onto the wrist of the hand that bore the blade that had flashed in Mwesu's light. A *simi* dropped from fingers suddenly rendered useless. With a soft thump, the weapon hit the floor of the *manyatta.* Imaro felt the tightening of throat muscles against his forearm, and he heard a strangled cry of agony.

Fiercely the intruder struggled, but Imaro inexorably forced his captive closer to the light at the *manyatta*'s entrance. The faint light illuminated features contorted in pain and fury. Astonished at what he saw, Imaro slackened his grasp, allowing the intruder to twist loose.

"You … you're free," Kanoko gasped in a choked whisper.

Cobra-swift, the warrior's hand darted toward his fallen weapon. Imaro's foot was faster. His heel crunched down on Kanoko's wrist just as the warrior's fingers touched the hilt of his *simi.* Although Kanoko's face writhed in a grimace of pain, he refused to cry out.

"Did you come here to kill me, Kanoko?" Imaro asked, his voice deceptively soft.

"I came to make you beg for death," Kanoko replied.

For a long, tense moment, the young warriors glared at each other, as they had on the day that Kanoko had given a flame-ant filled *kutendea* to Imaro's *ngombe.* Then another shadow obscured the light at the entrance to the *manyatta.*

As one, Imaro and Kanoko turned their heads toward the entrance. A slim figure stood there, bent as though about to enter. It was Keteke, eyes wide and mouth agape in astonishment.

Before either warrior could move, Keteke screamed. And with a desperate effort, Kanoko wrenched his hand from beneath Imaro's foot, nearly toppling him. While Imaro struggled to keep his balance, Kanoko again dove for his *simi.* But Imaro recovered quickly. By the time Kanoko reached for the *simi*'s hilt, Imaro's full weight crashed heavily onto the smaller man's back, driving the breath from his lungs and flattening him to the ground.

Even as Kanoko struggled beneath him, Imaro snatched the fallen *simi* and rose to his feet. Not only was he free; now, he had a weapon. He looked down at Kanoko. One slash of the *simi* would forever silence his tormentor's sharp tongue….

Then Imaro remembered Keteke and her cry—a cry that must have been heard by half the Ilyassai. He had time only for flight now. Vengeance must wait.

He whirled toward the entrance of the *manyatta*. Keteke was no long there. Betrayer, Imaro reflected bitterly as he moved toward the opening—and nearly fell when a hand clutched hard at his ankle.

It was Kanoko, driven beyond pain by a hatred that equaled Imaro's own. With a roaring curse, Imaro kicked free, his foot crashing against Kanoko's face. With a crack of breaking bone, Kanoko released his grip from Imaro's leg. Then Imaro bent and wriggled through the opening.

Already, the warriors of the night-guard were racing toward the source of the outcry that had aroused them. Others, alert even in sleep, poured from their *manyattas*. The weapons that never left their hands sprouted like iron thorns. When they spotted Imaro, the cry went out:

"The *ilmonek* is loose! Get him! Take him alive!"

Imaro knew he was trapped. He could outrun any Ilyassai, but he could not outrun an *arem*. They would aim at his legs....

His muscles bunched like those of a lion about to spring. He would not allow his mother's people to banish him under the custom of Shaming; he would slay them until they were forced to slay him. He cursed himself for failing to kill Kanoko when he had the chance....

It was when the warriors were almost upon him that an alternative occurred to him—an act that, more than any other, would express his ultimate repudiation of the Ilyassai. Snarling in defiance, he turned and fled from the *manyatta* that had housed him during the Shaming.

"The *ilmonek* flees!" the warriors shouted. "Get him!"

Keeping to the shadows, Imaro wove his way through the *manyattas*. Caught up in the frenzy of their chase, the warriors failed to notice that Imaro was running not toward the open plain, but toward the great thornbush *boma* in which the *ngombe* were penned for the night.

A short stretch of open ground separated the *boma* from the *manyattas*. Torches positioned at regular intervals cast a flickering glare across the gap. The ten youths designated to guard the *ngombe* shifted the *arems* in their hands. Alerted by the clamor rising from the *manyattas*, they were prepared to use their spears to defend the cattle in their charge.

Nothing, however, could have prepared them for Imaro's headlong rush into their midst. One moment, the herd-boys saw him leap from between two *manyattas*; then he was upon them, striking down the first youth he encountered with a blow of his fist.

Another young warrior challenged him with a thrust of his *arem*. Dodging the deadly point, Imaro lashed out with his stolen *simi*. The youth fell back, blood welling from a deep slash across his chest. The cut was not lethal; Imaro was reluctant to kill any of his mother's people, other than Kanoko and Muburi, now that the onslaught of hopeless rage had passed.

Shouting in consternation, the remaining herd-boys converged on Imaro. At any moment now, his other pursuers would be upon him. Already, the swiftest of them were racing toward the *boma*.

With his weaponless hand, Imaro tore the torch nearest him from the ground and thrust its lit end into the wall of thornbush. The resulting flames spread with frightening rapidity.

Another lesson from N'tu-mwaa, Imaro reflected ironically, remembering how he had used fire as a weapon against the Turkhana.

On the other side of the *boma*, the soft, musical lowing of the *ngombe* quickly changed to bellows of panic; among the few things that frightened Ilyassai cattle, fire was foremost.

As the blaze engulfed the thornbush, the warriors—men and youths alike—stopped short, shock graven on their faces. If Imaro had shoved the *simi* he was carrying into his own heart, they would have been scarcely less astounded. To set fire to the *boma* of the *ngombe* was an act so unthinkable that for an interminable moment, they could do nothing more than stand agape while their minds attempted to absorb the reality of Imaro's act of apostasy.

His opportunity won, Imaro bent and snatched up an *arem* dropped by one of the herd-boys. As he straightened, he heard a rending crash rise above the frantic bawling of the *ngombe*. Maddened by the sight and the heat of the flames, the long-horned cattle were smashing through the sections of the *boma* still untouched by the flames. The thorns that ripped painfully into their hides and pierced the flesh between their cloven hooves were as nothing in the face of their primordial urge to escape the bright, devouring flames.

In a vast tide of hooves and horns, the *ngombe* herd swept toward the savanna, stampeding away from the fire, the warriors, and the *manyattas*. Alone and free, Imaro fled in another direction, also headed for the open Tamburure. His desperate gamble had succeeded. He knew the clan would spend days, if necessary, to recapture their scattered *ngombe*, for cattle were the source of wealth, food, shelter, and life itself for the people of the plains. The clan members would not stop their search until the last *ngombe* was recovered.

And once that task was done, the Kitoko clan warriors would hunt Imaro as they would a beast that was a threat to the herds. Imaro had committed an act that was of far greater profanation against the rigid code of the Ilyassai than the one of which he had been falsely accused. The knowledge that some of the stampeding *ngombe* would fall to predators before they could be recaptured caused a twinge of remorse in Imaro's heart.

Then he remembered his own *ngombe*, unjustly claimed by the hated Kanoko. He remembered Kulu, slain by a wielder of *mchawi*—sorcery, foul magic of the same kind that had planted lies in the minds of the warriors who had accompanied him on his *olmaiyo*.

He scowled—a harsh, unyielding expression. Visions of vengeance swirled in red whirlpools in his mind as the night, and the Tamburure, swallowed him. He was naked, and his head shaven woman-bald. But he had a *simi* and an *arem*. He knew he would be hunted. But he also knew that he, too, would hunt....

***

Amid a flurry of purposeful activity, the *ol-arem* and the *oibonok* of Imaro's former clan sat in conclave. Around them, *manyattas* were being dismantled and loaded onto *ngombe*. Likewise, cooking pots, wooden bowls, and other women's utensils were bundled and strapped onto broad bovine backs. Warriors gathered their weapons and garments, and directed their children to take their positions in the long, snakelike concourse of people and *ngombe* preparing to migrate to other pastures.

Although the Ilyassai were a nomadic people, their wanderings followed a pattern that had been set in ancient times. When the season changed from dry to wet, they traveled to the extreme northern boundary of their realm to wait out the rains.

Shouts and admonitions filled the humid air while final preparations for the journey progressed. But Mubaku and Muburi paid scant heed to the turmoil that surrounded them.

"I still say it is bad to move onward while the *ilmonek* still lives," said Muburi, his face set in stubborn lines. "A person who is at once *ilmonek* and an abuser of *ngombe* should not be left alive."

Mubaku frowned in recollection of how long it had taken his warriors to recover the *ngombe* after Imaro had stampeded them—the better part of a week. Some of the cattle had fallen to Ngatun and Chui and Matisho, as well as packs of wild dogs. One group of blindly fleeing *ngombe* had blundered into a small cluster of rhinoceros. The ensuing carnage had left the Tamburure littered with the gored carcasses of cattle and Kifaru alike. It was a badly depleted herd that the Kitoko clan finally gathered into a new *boma*.

Each missing *ngombe* was a blood-debt that Imaro owed the clan. The bands of warriors that stalked him through the vast sea of grass were at once hunters and executioners.

Yet as the days passed, no trace of the fugitive had been found. And as the time for migration had drawn inexorably forward, the *ol-arem* could not delay his clan's departure much longer.

Ten clans comprised the Ilyassai tribe, and the north-to-south, south-to-north cycle of roving they followed had been planned long ago to allow each clan ample pasturage all year long for its herds. When one clan's area was sufficiently grazed, it moved on, and the area was left undisturbed until the grass had regrown tall enough to provide pasturage for the next clan in the cycle.

The success of the pattern depended on intricate timing. If one clan lingered overlong in its area, there would be diminished pasturage for the one that followed. In bygone rains, blood feuds had resulted from incidents of neglect, and when the Ilyassai fought among themselves, rival tribes gathered like packs of jackals around a conflict among lions.

As *ol-arem*, it was Mubaku's responsibility to ensure that the ancient cycle of migration continued. The most vehement arguments Muburi could muster for the clan to remain where it was until the hunt for Imaro was completed failed to forestall Mubaku's final decision to dismantle the *manyattas* and begin the long trek northward.

"The *ilmonek* is as good as dead," Mubaku said flatly.

No one among the Ilyassai referred to Imaro by his name anymore, or even as "son-of-no-father."

"If the beasts don't get him, the next clan to use this land, the Itayok, will," Mubaku continued. "I have sent runners to the *ol-arems* of all the clans, telling them that an *ilmonek* and harmer-of-cattle runs free—much to our clan's dishonor."

"Then our clan should kill him," Muburi persisted. "That way, we would regain our honor, and no young warrior would ever again think of doing what the son-of-no-father did."

He lowered his voice as he continued.

"And there are some who say one who is *ilmonek* could never have escaped from *all* the warriors of the Kitoko. . . ."

"But you've already explained that the *ilmonek*'s cowardice maddened him," Mubaku said. "The young men spit on the grass whenever he is mentioned. Why, then, should we risk war with the Itayok?"

"I have seen the messages in the clouds, and studied the omens in the entrails of hyenas," the *oibonok* replied darkly. "Ajunge may turn his back on us if we do not slay the *ilmonek*."

Mubaku considered those words before he spoke with finality.

"Our clan must move," he said. "But I will allow some of our warriors to stay in the area to hunt for the *ilmonek*. The *ol-arem* of the Itayok will understand."

Realizing that Mubaku would bend no further, Muburi nodded to signal his acquiescence. Without further conversation, both men rose from their squatting positions, and Muburi walked away.

The preparations for departure continued. The heat of Jua pressed like a hot, heavy hand on the backs of the toiling Kitoko clan. Like countless generations before them, they welcomed the sun's searing touch, and they soon completed their tasks. Then they began their northward march, stretched in a long line across the Tamburure.

Huge herds of grass-eaters made way for the Ilyassai and their cattle. Predators resisted the smell of meat and remained hidden in the grass until the last of the clan went by. Then they resumed their pursuit of easier prey.

There was one who followed the clan, however. This predator stalked on two legs. Stolen weapons were in his hands. And hatred was in his heart….

***

The Tamburure was less open in the northern part of the Ilyassai range. Trees grew thicker there, and small lakes lay scattered like the teardrops of a giant across the edges of the yellow plain. Pasture was good and game plentiful. Distracted by the work involved in settling into their new area, the Kitoko clan spoke less and less about the curious circumstances of Imaro's *olmaiyo*. The erecting of the *manyattas* and the parceling of grazing land became matters of far more importance than the fate of one who was both *ilmonek* and outlaw.

But there were others who did not forget.

Far from the *manyattas*, five young warriors, only two of whom had earned their *shingonas*, sat in a circle around a waning fire. They had hunted well this day, as the well-gnawed remnants of the buffalo they had speared attested. When the drums of war were silent, it was in hunts such as this that Ilyassai warriors slaked their thirst for conflict and maintained their weapons skills.

The youths had put up a small *boma* to keep scavengers away from their kill. They did not fear the packs of jackals, hyenas, and long-billed marabou storks that the smell of decaying meat would lure; the barrier simply saved them of chasing off the more adventurous of the carrion-eaters. The hoots and barks of the scavengers furnished a background against which the boasts and jests of the hunters sounded even louder.

Suddenly, the cries of the carrion-eaters changed, and a rustling of the grass signaled their sudden departure. Immediately, the warriors sprang to their feet, *arems* poised to strike swiftly. Over the jagged edge of the thornbush, they spotted a lone, armed figure passing close by.

Then the tension broke as they recognized the solitary warrior as one of their own clan.

"Easy, brothers; it's only old "Bent-nose" Kanoko out hunting for the *ilmonek* again," said one of the wearers of the *shingona*. The others joined him in laughter.

"Kanoko!" another gibed. "Why don't you go look in the Place of Stones for the *ilmonek*? Maybe you'll find him hiding under one of the rocks!"

The laughter increased. Kanoko glared at the hunters, spat in the grass, and moved on. Unconsciously, he raised his hand to touch his flattened nose, which had not healed properly after Imaro's foot had broken it during the night of his escape from the Shaming. Kanoko scowled at the memory that night….

Mubaku and the other elders had questioned him relentlessly about his presence in the *manyatta* from which Imaro had escaped. Kanoko told them the truth: his purpose had been to torment Imaro one last time; to offer him a clean death as an alternative to the final degradation of the Shaming. He had hoped to bring Imaro to the point of begging for the bite of Kanoko's *simi*, before withdrawing the offer in a final gesture of contempt and disdain.

But by the time he arrived at the *manyatta*, Imaro had already broken his bonds, and what followed was known by everyone in the clan.

The elders had been far harsher in their judgment of him than of Keteke, whose scream had alerted the night guards. She said she had awakened to relieve herself, and had spied Kanoko on his way to the *manyatta* in which Imaro was held, and had followed him there for no reason other than curiosity. The elders had accepted her explanation without question, or even much consideration.

After inspecting Imaro's bonds, which had been torn rather than cut, Mubaku and the elders decided Kanoko had not helped Imaro to free himself. But because he had failed to prevent Imaro's escape, and thus had an indirect role in the stampeding of the *ngombe*, Kanoko had been stripped of all but one of the cattle in his sizable herd. And his resolve to seek vengeance against Imaro had hardened.

Kanoko still possessed Imaro's woman, Keteke. But now he found, to his dismay, that he had himself become an object of derision among the younger warriors, almost as much as Imaro had been.

He did not respond to the taunts. But long after the other warriors had lost their fervor for the fruitless search for Imaro despite the urging of the *oibonok*, Kanoko persisted. He could not explain how he knew, but he was certain that Imaro still lived, hidden in the trackless reaches of the Tamburure.

And as long as Imaro lived, Kanoko would hunt him. And he would not rest until Imaro was dead.

Beyond the *boma* of the hunters, Kanoko scanned the grass, searching for even a slight sign of human passage. Finding nothing, he moved on, shutting his ears to the laughter that followed him from the *boma*.

***

Cautiously, Muburi threaded his way through a thin clump of trees. Although he bore his *arem* and shield and *simi*, the *oibonok* still moved furtively, as if to hide his movements even from the blind eye of Mwesu the moon.

Fully secluded by the trees now, Muburi laid down his shield and arem, then gathered a pile of fallen branches for kindling. He drew a fire-bow from his garment and twirled it rapidly. Soon, the tinder was ablaze. From a pouch belted at his waist, the *oibonok* extracted a handful of powder that glinted in the firelight. He tossed the powder into the dancing flames.

The moment the crystalline grains touched the fire, the orange blaze was transformed into an inferno of emerald incandescence. Muburi sat cross-legged in front of the green flare, eyes unblinking. As he sat unmoving, he attempted to control a rising sense of dread as a shape began to form in the center of the conflagration.

Rapidly, the shape assumed the outlines of a face that was human, yet eerily inhuman; a face of Ilyassai configuration, dominated by eyes that burned with an amber sheen that surpassed even the green glare that surrounded it.

Suddenly, the spectral visage swelled outward from the flames and hovered over the upturned face of Muburi. Sweat that was not caused by the heat of the fire beaded on the *oibonok*'s brow. Yet Muburi neither moved nor blinked. He waited for the glowing apparition to speak.

"You are a flawed tool, Muburi," it said at last, its voice deep yet alien: unpleasant to the ear. "Yet I, too, am flawed, and a tool. Tell me, tool of a tool, what you have accomplished for me since I last spoke with you."

Muburi, knowing that the face in the fire was already aware that he had accomplished nothing, spoke nonetheless. It was as though something was physically dragging the words from his unwilling tongue.

"The *ilmonek* has not been found," Muburi said. "I do not know whether he is alive, or dead. I cannot find him with the *mchawi* you taught me, and the warriors have wearied of hunting him—all except Kanoko. There is no more to say."

The flames expanded outward like emerald wings, stopping only inches short of Muburi's face. For the first time, the *oibonok* shut his eyes against the fierce glare. Perspiration trickled into the corners of his mouth.

"Why did it fail: my plan, my vengeance?" the face howled. "The deception during the *olmaiyo*; the Shaming—you had no trouble carrying out *that* much of what needed to be done. After he was driven in disgrace from the *manyattas*, it would have been so simple for you to cast the spell that would send him to me for my vengeance. So simple—*yet he escaped! Escaped, and remains alive!*"

The voice gave way to a wordless shriek. In a land that had never felt the breath of frost, Muburi shivered. The fiendish rage that twisted the features of the face hovering before him engendered a fear that even his warrior's pride—for he, too, had won a *shingona* when he was younger, before he had become the *oibonok*—could not quell. Still, he summoned the courage to ask a question of his own after the echoes of the outcry faded.

"But how can you know the *ilmonek* lives? The warriors have spent weeks searching for him, and have found nothing. How could one man evade the warriors of the Ilyassai for so long?"

"*Fool!*" the apparition shouted. "He is more than any Ilyassai could ever be! He's—*by all the Mashataan! He's here!*"

The face in the flame shifted its eyes to look past Muburi, focusing on the brush behind the *oibonok*. Muburi half turned to follow the apparition's gaze—then he hurled himself backward to avoid the point of an *arem* that flashed toward him from the foliage.

But the cast had not been meant for the *oibonok*. Unerringly, the iron point flew directly into the face that writhed in the green flames. The moment metal touched fire, the entire spear shaft burst into blinding combustion. The weapon did not pass through the fire; it *hung* in midair, transfixing the face as though its point had pierced flesh rather than flame. Screams of inhuman agony poured from the mouth of the apparition. Then, with a final flare of brilliance, the green fire vanished, leaving behind only the charred, smoking remnant of the weapon that had struck it.

Nearly blinded by the final discharge of the flames, Muburi barely made out the huge, dark shape that hurtled toward him. Rising to his feet, the *oibonok* dragged his *simi* from its leather scabbard. His assailant's reaction was swifter—far swifter. One sweep of a polished iron blade, and Muburi's weapon flew from his hand. Then Muburi stood very still, as the point of Imaro's *simi* dented the flesh at the base of the *oibonok*'s throat.

For the second time that night, Muburi knew fear as he stared at the figure looming before him. Imaro's pate, shaven woman-smooth weeks ago, was now covered with a short mat of wooly, unbraided hair. He was no longer naked; a makeshift garment covered his loins. Broad bands of muscle rippled catlike beneath his bare, umber skin. The red ocher that had once decorated his body was gone. There was nothing left of the Ilyassai in his appearance.

In their own way, Imaro's eyes were as merciless as those of the face in the flames. Those eyes now burned unwaveringly, unnervingly, into Muburi's. And Imaro's free hand clamped onto Muburi's arm in a crushing grasp.

This was not the Imaro Muburi had known, stalwart though the young warrior had been since the days of his boyhood. This was an Imaro unrestrained even by the blood-code of the Ilyassai; an Imaro as feral as the predators that stalked the Tamburure at night. Again, Muburi shuddered. The slight movement pushed the *simi*'s point deeper into his skin....

Hidden near the clan's *manyattas*, Imaro had observed Muburi's departure and stealthy progress toward the copse of trees. He had planned to slay Muburi as soon as the *oibonok* passed beyond the earshot of the people in the *manyattas*. It was Muburi's sorcerous deception that had caused the other warriors to brand him *ilmonek*; therefore, Muburi would be the first to die.

But curiosity had stayed Imaro's hand. Muburi's furtive and odd preparations once he had reached the trees had at first puzzled Imaro, and then aroused his interest. And so he waited to see what would happen. Crouching undetected in the brush, he had watched the malevolent face form in the midst of the green flame. He had listened with increasing interest to the colloquy between Muburi and the disembodied entity that appeared to be the *oibonok*'s master.

The words the face had spoken beat against his ears like hammers of truth—the truth about his *olmaiyo*, and the deceit and treachery that had followed his slaying of Ngatun….

Then, somehow, the apparition had *seen* him, despite the darkness and the concealing foliage. And the amber eyes had launched a spear of eldritch energy that seemed to burn directly into his brain, as though it were attacking his very thoughts. In a purely reflexive action, Imaro had hurled his own spear at his spectral tormenter instead of succumbing to the attack. When the face in the flame disappeared, so did the pain inside Imaro's skull.

Now, Imaro held Muburi at bay. And he wanted more than the *oibonok*'s death. He wanted answers. He pressed his *simi* deeper against Muburi's skin, drawing blood.

"Who was that face in the fire?" he demanded, his voice hoarse, as though he had not used it for a long period of time.

Muburi remained silent.

"Why did you and that … *thing* … betray my *olmaiyo*?" Imaro asked. *"Speak!"*

In response, Muburi … *changed*. Instead of Muburi, Imaro was suddenly holding a gigantic, writhing serpent, long and thick as a python, covered with unpatterned scales the color of human skin. Cold, ophidian eyes met Imaro's startled gaze, and a black, forked tongue flicked from an open, lipless mouth.

Before Imaro could react, the serpent plunged its fangs into the warrior's sword-hand. Imaro's hand opened involuntarily, and the blade dropped. The fangs sank deeper, but Imaro managed to tear his hand out of the serpent's jaws. Blood welled in the puncture marks on his skin.

Imaro reached for his fallen *simi*. Before he could get to it, coil after coil of sinuous serpent-muscle whipped around his body, then constricted in a deadly embrace. Somehow, Imaro was still able to seize the serpent's throat in a grip of iron. Then the contest for survival began.

Whether Muburi had actually transformed himself into a thigh-thick reptile, or had only cast an illusion like the one that had convinced the Ilyassai that Imaro had shown cowardice during his *olmaiyo*, the serpent was a deadly, all-too-real foe; a foe that was inexorably forcing the breath from Imaro's lungs and beginning to bend his ribs as if they were twigs….

Glaring his hatred into the serpent's lidless eyes, Imaro swayed precariously.

But he did not fall, despite the weight of the scaled loops that enveloped him. His breathing grew labored, and pain splintered through his upper body. The pain was a prelude to a death that would leave him limp and broken in the clutch of those terrible coils if the constriction continued much longer.

Yet the rage that fueled Imaro's strength was limitless. He redoubled his efforts to crush the serpent's neck, and he began to feel its scaly flesh yielding beneath his hands.

Abruptly, the coils relaxed their grasp. Then the serpent began to twist and jerk in spasmodic convulsions, and Imaro felt the terrible pressure on his rib cage slacken. The cold glare in the serpent's eyes dimmed, and a faint hiss that bore a disquieting resemblance to a strangled human scream wheezed from slack, gaping jaws. When Imaro finally released his hold, the serpent's thick coils fell away from him like a discarded rope.

Closing his eyes and exhaling heavily, the warrior sank slowly to his knees. When he inhaled, he welcomed the infusion of humid night air into his aching chest and depleted lungs. Slowly, the snarling set of his features relaxed, and the pain in his rib cage subsided.

Then Imaro opened his eyes—and his skin crawled as he stared wide-eyed at the sprawled corpse of Muburi, lit eerily by Mwesu's glow. The *oibonok*'s limbs seemed almost boneless, and his neck was bent at an unnatural angle, attesting to the force of Imaro's final surge of power.

Shifting his gaze to his wounded hand, Imaro saw that the blood-rimmed teeth-marks on his skin were human. There had been no serpent; Muburi's sorcery had deceived him as thoroughly and effectively as it had the warriors on his *olmaiyo*. Illusion or not, though, Imaro could still feel the crushing of the serpent's coils.

Rising to his feet, the young warrior looked down at the corpse of the *oibonok*. He uttered a bitter curse, for he had just killed the man who could have answered the questions that had plagued him since the day of his *olmaiyo*.

Yet he could not discount the enigmatic face in the green flames....

Imaro now realized that the apparition was his true nemesis, much more than the warriors of the Kitoko clan, and others, who still hunted him. With dreadful clarity, the demonic visage of Muburi's master was graven in his mind.

He knew—and cared to know—little about the workings of *mchawi*. But still, he realized that the sorcery of Muburi was as nothing next to that of a being that could project its face and voice into a fire. And he remembered the spearlike bolt of power the apparition had driven into his brain.

Yet Imaro had bested the thing in the fire's *mchawi* with a single cast of his *arem*, though despite the shriek of agony the apparition had uttered when the iron point pierced its face, Imaro sensed that he had not slain it.

Imaro looked to the north. He knew that beyond the horizon, beyond the borders of the Ilyassai range, lay an ancient ruin known as the Place of Stones. Even when the First Ancestors of the Ilyassai came to the Tamburure hundreds of rains ago, the Place of Stones had long been deserted.

In the tales handed down from generation to generation of elders, the First Ancestors had sensed an aura of archaic, slumbering evil about the moldering pile. The beasts of the Tamburure avoided it as they would a stretch of quicksand or a poisoned water hole. The First Ancestors had acknowledged the wisdom of the beasts, and forbade their people to approach the tumbled stones. This long-held taboo was the closest the Ilyassai had ever come to an acknowledgment of fear.

Imaro decided that he would break yet another tribal taboo, and go to the Place of Stones. He was certain that his enemy, the apparition in the flames, was hidden in the one place the Ilyassai shunned.

But there was one more debt of blood to be collected; one more draught to be swallowed from the cup of vengeance.

He stared northward a while longer. Then he bent to relieve Muburi's cadaver of clothing and weapons. He pitied the lion whose body the *oibonok*'s soul would inhabit. Then he turned his gaze southward again, to the land the Kitoko clan now occupied. As he thought about what he would do there, his hands clenched tightly around the shaft of Muburi's *arem*.

***

Keteke stood waist-deep in a warm Tamburure pool. Jua's light burnished her sleek mahogany skin and flashed diamond-bright in the droplets of water that clung to her slender body. Her fine-boned face held an enigmatic expression as a stream of water rilled from her cupped hands onto her high, pointed breasts.

Earlier in the day, she had come to the pool, which was located in a small patch of woodland not far from the pastures in which the *ngombe* grazed. She knew Kanoko would follow her there, and that she would see him before long. The pool, with its natural screen of trees and brush, was a favored spot for couples seeking privacy for their lovemaking. That the others in the *manyattas* would have noticed her departure, she was sure; and they would notice Kanoko's soon after. Even now, they would be enjoying crude jests about the pairing of the former mate of the *ilmonek* Imaro with his greatest rival.

Her lips curved in a mirthless smile at that thought.

A rustle from the bushes brought her hairless head up quickly. She knew that few dangerous beasts dared to come close to the *manyattas* of the Ilyassai. But sometimes, Chui the leopard was bolder even than Ngatun the lion. Still, she had neither seen nor heard signs of Chui, and Kanoko had to be near, though it was taking him longer to reach the pool than she had expected. The rustling seemed too hesitant to herald Kanoko's presence—yet it was, indeed, he who stepped from the concealment of the brush.

Weapons in hand, Kanoko stared wordlessly at the woman in the pool, absorbing every facet of her unclad body, from her smooth-shaven head to the slim, boyish hips half hidden beneath the surface of the water.

She is beautiful, even though she is Zamburu, Kanoko thought. *And she was Imaro's....*

"It took you so long to get here," Keteke said. "Why?"

"Before I left, Mubaku stopped me and asked me if I had seen the *oibonok,*" Kanoko replied. "Muburi has not been seen for two days now. Mubaku thought I might have come across some sign of him while I was hunting for the *ilmonek.*"

He touched his broken nose. Then he laid his oval shield aside, and began to strip off his garment.

"Why don't you stop searching, Kanoko?" Keteke asked. "Imaro has to be dead by now, or gone far from the land of the Ilyassai."

"Don't say his name!" Kanoko snapped, raising his hand as though to strike her.

Keteke shrank away from him, and he caught himself before he could act on his impulse. Masadu had always taught that a warrior was the master of his own anger, but too often, Kanoko's anger was mastering him.

"I *know* he's still out there," he continued, lowering his hand. I can *smell* him in the grass. I will find him, kill him, and bring his head to Mubaku!"

Then another voice spoke.

"Want to try it now?"

Kanoko whirled toward the brush behind him. And Keteke's hands shot to her mouth to stifle a cry of terror.

Imaro had slipped through the brush soundlessly after trailing Kanoko to the tree-girt pool. Easily, so easily, he could have cut Kanoko down from behind. But that was not the way he wanted to end their feud. He wanted vengeance, not slaughter.

In a single, swift motion, Kanoko took up his *arem* and hurled it straight at Imaro. Imaro raised the shield he had taken from Muburi and deflected the hurtling weapon, sending it spinning into the brush.

Then Imaro flung his own *arem* at Kanoko's feet.

"Try again, Bent-nose," he said contemptuously.

Goaded by Imaro's use of that despised sobriquet and his own obsessive animosity, Kanoko erupted into frenzied action. Snatching the proffered *arem,* he charged toward Imaro. He lunged forward and thrust its point toward Imaro's abdomen. Again, Imaro deflected the thrust. As Kanoko pulled back his arm to strike again, Imaro drew his *simi.*

Three more times, Kanoko attempted to slide his spear point past the rim of Imaro's shield. The first two times, Imaro blocked the thrusts by shifting the position of his shield. The third time, Kanoko's point penetrated the thick hide covering, but not enough to pierce all the way through it.

Imaro jerked his shield-arm back. Still holding on to his *arem*, Kanoko was dragged within range of a vicious sweep of Imaro's *simi*—the first blow Imaro had struck in the fight.

Only cat-quick reflexes saved Kanoko then. Releasing his grip on the spear shaft, he hurled himself backward, evading Imaro's blade by a mere hair's breadth. Thrown off balance, Kanoko fell heavily onto his back and lay momentarily vulnerable to a fatal thrust by Imaro.

But Imaro used that moment to discard his shield. With Kanoko's *arem* lodged in its covering, the shield would only be an encumbrance now.

Scrambling quickly to his feet, Kanoko drew his *simi* from its scabbard. His own shield lay nearby. Taking a desperate chance, he leaped toward it and shoved his arm through its inside loops. Then he turned to face Imaro, who had simply stood and watched him.

It was then that Imaro decided it was time to stop toying with his lifelong foe. With the speed that time and again belied his massive bulk, he sprang to the attack. A whirlwind of iron drove Kanoko back. Large chunks of leather flew from his shield. Occasionally, the smaller man's blade rang against Imaro's. But his fighting was strictly defensive, even though he had a shield and Imaro did not. He knew he had to do something to turn the tide of battle, or he would die....

With a quick snap of his arm, Kanoko flung the ragged remnant of his shield into Imaro's face. Stunned by the unexpected blow, Imaro stumbled, nearly dropping his *simi*. Kanoko's point darted toward Imaro's heart—only to be parried by Imaro's own blade.

Now they circled each other with silent caution, shifting and feinting with their *simis*, each hoping to draw the other into making an impulsive mistake. Only the shuffle of their bare feet across the ground broke the deadly quiet of the duel, which was the culmination of their endless antagonism.

Then, tiring of the cat-dance, Imaro renewed his assault. Kanoko countered well, using skills that were superlative even among the Ilyassai. But quick though Kanoko was, Imaro was quicker. And even with a weapon in his hand, he could not offset Imaro's superior strength. It was as though Imaro were wielding a hammer instead of a sword, crashing blows in a steady, unstoppable rain against Kanoko's notched iron blade.

Blood seeped from a dozen small wounds on Kanoko's body. He was wearying—and not once had his blade penetrated Imaro's guard.

Kanoko had always known he could not match Imaro's sheer strength. But with a weapon in his hand, he had been certain he was equal, if not superior, to his rival. Now, he realized that he was not.

Suddenly, Kanoko faltered, as though he had momentarily lost his footing.

As he flailed his arms to recover his balance, Kanoko's *simi* dipped low, leaving a broad expanse of flesh exposed for the killing stroke. It was an obvious trap, but Imaro trusted that his speed would overcome it.

Imaro lunged forward, aiming at Kanoko's heart. Then he twisted his entire body sideways, nearly wrenching his spine in a desperate effort to elude Kanoko's sudden counterthrust, for Kanoko had moved faster than Imaro would have believed he could. Had Imaro moved an instant more slowly, his hand would have been severed at the wrist. As it was, Kanoko's *simi* clanged loudly against Imaro's, and sent it flying from his hand. Suddenly weaponless, Imaro was doomed—unless he moved faster than he ever had before.

They were still at close quarters. Before Kanoko could draw his *simi* back for the final stroke, Imaro fastened his hand on the wrist of his foe's sword-arm. Then he squeezed, exerting the same strength that had burst his bonds in the *manyatta* from which he had escaped weeks ago. Bone cracked, and Kanoko bit back a cry of agony as his *simi* fell.

Yet true to what he had learned in *mafundishu-ya-muran*, Kanoko did not falter. He smashed his free fist against the side of Imaro's head. Any other man would have been stunned by the impact, but Imaro only curled his lip in disdain and struck a bludgeoning blow of his own full into Kanoko's mouth. Jaw broken and teeth sheared off at the roots, Kanoko sank to his knees.

Thoroughly beaten, Kanoko was still an Ilyassai. He groped for the hilt of his *simi* on the blood-specked ground, found it, and lurched painfully to his feet. Imaro awaited him, armed with his own *simi*, which he had retrieved at the same time.

Kanoko stumbled toward Imaro. With both hands, he raised his *simi*, then drove it forward. His target was Imaro's face.

Imaro easily parried the feeble stroke. Then he buried his blade deep into Kanoko's body, transfixing him just below the breastbone. As Imaro tore his blade free, Kanoko fell backward with a gurgling groan. A crimson sheet of blood cascaded down his abdomen.

Incredibly, Kanoko clung to life. Glaring up at Imaro, he choked out words barely intelligible in the red froth that bubbled from his mouth.

"Why … did … you run … from Ngatun … at the *olmaiyo*? *Why?*"

The last word was almost a scream.

"I did not run," Imaro replied quietly. "I have been telling the truth all along—Muburi used his *mchawi* to let you see what he wanted you to see—what you wanted and hoped to see."

Kanoko did not respond. Imaro leaned closer to him.

"Do you believe me now, Kanoko?" he demanded. "*Do you?*"

Those were the last words that passed between the bitter foes. Imaro never knew how Kanoko would have answered his question. When Imaro finished speaking, Kanoko's eyes were already glazed in death. And Imaro knew that the lion that encased Kanoko's emerging soul would prove a formidable challenge for any young warrior seeking to earn his *shingona*.

Then a rippling splash from the pool caught Imaro's attention. He raised his eyes from the corpse of Kanoko and looked at Keteke. She had sunk deeper into the water, so that only her head and bare shoulders were showing. Imaro's eyes frightened her. They were a killer's eyes, hard and merciless as those of Ngatun.

"Why are you still here?" Imaro asked. "Why didn't you run back to the *manyattas* while I was fighting Kanoko—your new man?"

"Are you going to kill me, too?' she asked in return.

"You betrayed me," Imaro said in a flat voice. "You were no better than the others who cursed me during the Shaming. You went with Kanoko as willingly as my *ngombe* did."

"And what else would you expect me to do?" Keteke flared. Her face suddenly contorted with a resentment that was as deep as Imaro's.

"*You* carried me away from my tribe as a prize of battle," she accused. "*You* brought me to the *manyattas* of the Ilyassai, the Feared Ones, the ravagers of the Tamburure. Oh, I hated you then, Imaro. But then, with time, I realized that you were a warrior unlike any other I had ever seen. I could not understand why your people treated you as they did.

"But you treated me well—better than any of the other Ilyassai would have done. You were going to mate with me honorably, not just use me as a captive. I never cared what the others called you. You were a better man than any of them.

"Then they brought you back from the lion-hunt as if you were the prey. I could not believe what Muburi and Kanoko said. *I* know you are not *ilmonek*. But the Ilyassai believed it, and I had to pretend to believe it too, if I wanted to live. And *I wanted to live*, even if it meant hating myself for turning against you. What else could I do, Imaro? I wanted to live.

"I went to the *manyatta* that night to give you what comfort I could before they sent you away—I told Mubaku a different story later. I couldn't believe it when I saw you free, and Kanoko there, too. I screamed—just as I screamed when you carried me away from my Zamburu people."

She looked at Imaro, who stared back at her, saying nothing. But his *simi* was still in his hand.

"Yes, Imaro, Kanoko took me for his own, just as you did," she continued. "And yes, I allowed him to. I was alone, a captive among the people whose name Zamburu parents use to frighten children into obeying them. Now, Kanoko is dead, and you stand there like a demon, come to take my soul. I have nothing left. If you mean to kill me, Imaro, then do it quickly!"

Keteke gazed up at Imaro through eyes blurred with tears. Her water-beaded shoulders trembled in anger and fear.

The murderous fires in Imaro's eyes were banked now. For the first time since he had stepped from the brush to battle Kanoko, he seemed human again.

"I will not kill you, Keteke," he said.

"Then take me back to my people, the Zamburu," Keteke said quickly. "There is nothing left for you among the Ilyassai, or for me, either. I think you are the reason Muburi has not been seen lately.... If you've slain him, as well as Kanoko, then you have already had your vengeance."

Imaro seemed to be considering her words. She went on, her words tumbling over each other in her haste to speak them.

"But if those deaths are not enough, and you still hate the Ilyassai, then join the Zamburu! My people will forgive you your part in the last raid against them if you lead their warriors into battle against the Ilyassai. You know all the Ilyassai secrets of warfare. You could teach the Zamburu to fight as the Ilyassai fight. With you at their head, the Zamburu could drive the Ilyassai out of the Tamburure!"

Slowly, Imaro shook his head.

"Why not?" Keteke demanded.

Then he told Keteke of the face Muburi had conjured in the green flames, and of his intention to go to the Place of Stones to confront his unknown enemy.

"Fool!" Keteke cried when he was done. "You are a fool, Imaro—and I am already dead!"

She kicked herself backward into the deepest part of the pool. Water closed over her head. She did not resurface.

Cursing in anger, Imaro cast down his *simi* and plunged into the pool. Diving deep, he spotted her floating limply near the bottom of the pool. Imaro's huge hands closed roughly on her limbs. Gathering her in his arms, he planted his feet on the silty bottom, then propelled himself and his burden to the surface.

The moment Keteke's face broke water, she sputtered and hissed cries of protest. The water churned wildly as she struggled in Imaro's iron embrace. When she finally spat out the water she had swallowed, she began to sob bitterly. Acrid tears trickled trails of accusation down Imaro's broad chest while he held her.

Then he astonished Keteke by gently covering her mouth with his own. His arms pressed hard against her wet, naked back, and moments later, her own arms circled his shoulders.

After a time, the water of the pool once again began to churn....

***

Imaro awoke with a start, still caught in the grip of the nightmares that had haunted his sleep. The details of the dreams were fading rapidly; he could recall little other than huge, amorphous shapes with blood-rimmed holes for eyes, and the sinister echo of inhuman laughter. He stirred sluggishly at the memory of that laughter—then snapped into full, wakeful alertness.

Quickly, he gained his feet and scanned the small encampment he had put up for the night, far from the pool where Kanoko's corpse lay hidden beneath a pile of rocks and grass.

Mwesu hung like a round, cataracted eye in the black shroud of the night sky. The fire Imaro had built to discourage predators was now only a pile of dimming embers. And the shelter of sticks and grass he had made for Keteke was … empty.

A quick, thorough search revealed the unsettling truth: while Imaro slept, the Zamburu woman had left the encampment. Angrily, Imaro berated himself for falling asleep. He could not remember dozing; one moment, he was gazing at the shadowy forms of the beasts slinking beyond the circle of light his night-fire cast; then he was groping his way back from uneasy slumber.

He remembered what had happened earlier, before Jua went down. After the ardor of their lovemaking in the pool had passed, Imaro had told Keteke what he intended to do. He would return her to the Zamburu, as she had asked. And then he would go to the Place of Stones. And when the confrontation with his enemy was over, he would join her in the land of the Zamburu.

But Keteke was convinced that Imaro would die at the Place of Stones, which was as taboo a place for her people as it was for the Ilyassai. When she was unable to dissuade him from his purpose, she slipped into a state of resigned apathy. Under her breath, she began to chant a Zamburu death-song, until, finally losing patience, he shouted her into silence.

Apprehensive over what Keteke might do in her current state of mind, Imaro had decided to forgo sleep so that he could make certain she would not attempt, once again, to take her own life. During his own past, thoughts of ending his seemingly unendurable existence among the Kitoko clan had sometimes crept into his mind. They were snake-thoughts; with the iron edge of his determination, he had slain them. Yet, snakelike; those thoughts had continued to writhe long after they had been slain.

Impatiently, Imaro shook himself out of his abstracted mood and peered intently at the grass. The pale light of Mwesu illuminated a story told by the patterns of bent blades and broken stems of grass.

The beasts that should have sought to attack him once the fire had died had approached the encampment, but their spoor ended only a few paces from where Imaro had lain. Once they had halted, the predators had wheeled and fled, as though impelled by sheer terror.

Then Imaro found Keteke's trail. The track led northward—toward the Place of Stones.

Even in Mwesu's pallid light, Imaro could see the strangeness of Keteke's spoor. Normally, a person's strides varied in length. Such variations were slight, but were easily detectable to a hunter's eye. But Keteke's tracks were spaced evenly, indicating a stiff, unnatural gait—the gait of one whose will had been usurped by *mchawi*, by sorcery that guided her footsteps.

His face set in resolute lines, Imaro swiftly donned his single garment and gathered his weapons: the *simi* of Muburi and the *arem* of Kanoko. His great thews tensed in anticipation of what he sensed would be a final battle against the enigmatic face in the emerald flame. It was as though he were about to face Ngatun again … but this foe would be far more dangerous than any lion.

Imaro snarled soundlessly. There was no need for his enemy to have utilized Keteke as bait to lure him to the Place of Stones. That was where he had intended to go since the night he saw the face in Muburi's flames. If Keteke had been harmed on his account …

Without further deliberation, Imaro began to follow the tenuous path to the Place of Stones. The force impelling him was as insistent as that which had ensnared Keteke. But Imaro's was by far the more dangerous compulsion, for its origin lay not in *mchawi*, but in the hatred that sustained his soul….

***

Night still cloaked the sky when Imaro came into sight of the Place of Stones. The land surrounding the ruin was marked by a change in the vegetation: the few trees there were stunted and warped, and the grass grew scraggly and sere, unlike the thick growth that carpeted the rest of the Tamburure.

In the distance, the warrior could see a pale, green glimmer emanating from what, at first glance, appeared to be a small hill. Hills of any size were a rarity on the flat Tamburure plain.

Green, Imaro thought. *The color of the fire when the face first appeared …*

There was an unpleasant, even offensive quality to that glow, a suggestion of a presence that had no place in the Tamburure. But when Imaro, suddenly repelled by the alien sensation the glow imparted, attempted to shift his eyes from the luminescence, he found that he could not do so. The glow was beginning to *pull* him. It beckoned him as a flame attracts a helpless moth.

Imaro did not succumb easily. Even as his feet involuntarily carried him toward the glowing excrescence on the Tamburure, he fought against the force that slithered insidiously into his mind. All the way to the edge of the looming mass of rock, he pitted his will against the *mchawi* that ensnared him. Yet still, it drew him to the Place of Stones.

Ages ago, the misshapen pile of crumbling masonry was a building, an edifice of colossal proportions. The gigantic stone blocks from which it had been constructed once fit together with immaculate precision. But that time was thousands of rains ago, as humans measure time. Now, the structure was only a mound of aging stone, futilely defying the passage of the rains even as the name of its long-dead builders had long since been forgotten. It hulked in the midst of the Tamburure like a monument to a time so distant that even the land surrounding it had changed.

Yet the ruin was not entirely dead. Keteke was there—her trail led directly into the ruin. And someone else was there, too—whoever it was that had created the ensorcelling green glare that controlled Imaro's movements as though invisible strings were attached to his limbs.

The owner of the face in the fire awaited him....

Sweat bathed Imaro's brow as he battled against the power that had invaded his mind. His struggles were to no avail. He began to clamber up an incline of jagged stone that had once been a stairway. At the top of the incline, an opening gaped like the mouth of a titanic lion, flanked by the stumps of pillars that had outlasted the long-vanished gates they had been built to support.

Imaro stopped—*was* stopped—at the summit of the ancient stairway. And he stared out onto the roofless, time-ravaged interior of the Place of Stones. Then unwilling legs carried him into a scene that had no counterpart in his previous experience. Never before had he encountered such decrepitude. And never before had he been enclosed by walls of stone.

The interior stretched like a counterpart to the Tamburure, with broken stones taking the place of grass. Shapeless heaps of rock from the fallen roof lay in clusters larger than an Ilyassai *manyatta*. The entire, eerie vista was lit by a lurid green glow that had no discernible source.

A shudder shook Imaro's massive frame. Unfamiliar though he was with structures other than *manyattas* and *bomas*, he could still sense an *alienness* about this ruin, an intuition that it belonged elsewhere. In the glare of the sourceless illumination, he could see faint outlines of grotesque images graven on the scattered stones. And he remembered what the elders said on nights when the stars were hidden behind curtains of cloud: whispers that the hands that built the Place of Stones had not been human....

Again, Imaro felt the tug of an unseen tether. The presence that had wormed its way into his mind had gained full control of his movements now. Against his will, Imaro paced toward a mass of stone larger than any of the others, and less affected by the passage of time. Though there remained only a hint of its original contours, its outline suggested it was a vast chamber that had somehow escaped the full effects of the collapse of the building's roof, ages ago.

When Imaro drew nearer to the half-fallen chamber, he saw a singular shape become visible among the shadows cast by broken walls. It was manlike, of prodigious height, towering over even Imaro. A voluminous, cowled cloak swathed the figure so completely that not a single feature was left unconcealed. But Imaro was certain that the face hidden in the folds of the cowl was the same visage that had appeared in Muburi's fire.

It was the face of his enemy: the enemy whose volition had usurped his own, and was forcing his legs to carry him closer … closer….

It was only when he advanced to within three strides of the cloaked figure that Imaro came to an abrupt halt. The same *mchawi* that had dragged him through the broken portal how held him fast, entrapped in sorcerous shackles that sapped his strength and will.

A new enemy rose against him now. It was an enemy he thought he had long since conquered, during the course of *mafundishu-ya-muran*. The enemy's name was fear.

Then the figure stepped out of the shadows. Its cloak shimmered iridescently in the green glare. Abruptly, the figure jerked its head backward, and the cowl fell away, revealing a face. As Imaro anticipated, it was the same face his *arem* had pierced while it hovered in Muburi's flames.

No longer distorted by the flickering of a fire, it was clearly the face of an Ilyassai man. Only its lambent green eyes were incongruous—no human on the Tamburure had ever possessed eyes that were not dark.

The head, though of normal dimensions, seemed much too small for the outsized body that bulked beneath it. Uneasily, Imaro wondered what kind of body was hidden beneath the folds of the glittering cloak.

Then the face opened its mouth and spoke, breaking the silence that reigned in the Place of Stones.

"Do you not know me, son of Katisa?" it grated. "Do you not know … Chitendu?"

***

Chitendu!

The name seared like a white-hot iron through Imaro's mind and memory. Had his tongue not been rendered as helpless as his limbs, he would have roared like Ngatun challenging an intruder.

Chitendu!

One of the few facets of her past that Imaro's mother had shared with him had been about Chitendu, the former *oibonok* of the clan. Imaro knew Katisa had fled southward to avoid a forced marriage to Chitendu. Then she had returned to the Ilyassai to expose the ultimate evil of Chitendu's *mchawi*. The spears of the warriors had driven Chitendu from the *manyattas*. When he was spoken of at all, Chitendu was considered a dead man, and the lion whose body his soul inhabited was thought to be defiled, and was pitied.

"The Ilyassai were fools to think I would not survive," Chitendu said, as if he had read Imaro's thoughts.

Again, the former *oibonok*'s head tilted back. His laughter was like the bark of Matisho.

"Oh, I am hard, hard to kill," Chitendu continued. "Even the Masters cannot kill me, though they confine me to this pile of fallen stone as punishment—punishment for my all-too-human desire for Katisa…."

Then Chitendu's face contorted into a mask of malevolence. His amber eyes blazed brighter, and a renewed mystic force assailed Imaro's mind. Pain unlike any he had experienced in *mafundishu-ya-muran* lashed at him like a whip made of thorns. Yet he neither moved nor cried out, for the paralytic bonds of Chitendu's *mchawi* continued to hold him in a relentless grip.

Still, the hot core of hatred within Imaro had not been diminished by the experience of helplessness. The core burned more fiercely than ever, for he was facing the man responsible for the events that caused the wretchedness of his life among the Ilyassai.

He still lived. And he still had his weapons….

Abruptly, Chitendu ceased his assault. Imaro gasped; breathing was the only function he could still control. His muscles felt as if they had been wrenched from their moorings. But he continued to glare defiantly at his enemy, ignoring the irony of his *arem* and *simi* clutched uselessly in his hands.

Chitendu laughed again.

"So much like Katisa you are," he said.

His eyes flared, as if to launch another assault. Then the glow subsided.

"I will tell you a tale, son-of-no-father," Chitendu continued. "Once I was nothing more than a caster of spells and a feeder of blood to a god who offers nothing in return. I began to do different magic—*mchawi*. Then, I was *called* … summoned by an emissary of the High Sorcerers of Naama, who are the Chosen of the Mashataan, the Demon Gods. Somehow, they had detected my secret wanderings into *mchawi*.

"The man from Naama offered me power—a place in the High Sorcerers' plan to conquer and dominate all. For even in faraway Naama, the ferocity of the Ilyassai was well known. Long had the Naamans desired to use the Ilyassai as a weapon to spread destruction in the lands of the east.

"Time and again, the Naamans tried, and failed, to gain contact of any kind with the Ilyassai—until I began my delvings into *mchawi*. I desired the power the Naamans offered me. But I desired Katisa more….

"Katisa rejected me, despised me, called me 'devil-man.' She loved a young warrior who was about to go on *olmaiyo*. I caused him to be slain by Ngatun, and the elders, and her father, had no choice other than to give her to me in marriage.

"But she escaped me, and not all the power the Mashataan had granted me could return her to me. So I carried out the Naamans' plan, and wove a web of *mchawi* around the Kitoko clan, causing them to think they were serving Ajunge when they were truly following the purposes of the Demon Gods. My control over them was nearly complete and the other clans would soon follow—*and then Katisa returned!*

"She bore *you* with her ... and something else—an amulet forged by the Kwenda Mawingu, the Cloud Striders, themselves. The amulet broke my power; it caused the Kitoko to see me as I truly was—and am. They attacked me, drove me from the *manyattas*, though they could not slay me. Not even the Naamans themselves could slay me....

"But they could punish me. For had I not caused Katisa to flee from me, she would never have come into possession of the amulet that destroyed the designs of the Naamans and the Mashataan.

"The Naamans imprisoned me here with mystic bonds. I need neither food nor drink. I live by the *mchawi* that has made me what I am. And I have lived for a purpose—one that you would understand well.

"Katisa was far beyond my reach. But *you* were not.

"Muburi was the one I needed. My *mchawi* can reach beyond the Place of Stones, even though my body is confined here. And a greater *oibonok* can always bend the will of a lesser one.

"Through Muburi, I caused you to be declared *ilmonek*, and to endure the Shaming. Then you escaped, and slew Muburi, thinking you had triumphed. Yet here you are, and in your own desire for vengeance, you have gained a more complete retribution for *me*!"

Chitendu's voice had risen to a keening shriek. Throughout the long diatribe, Imaro had striven vainly against the power that held him maddeningly immobile. He found Chitendu's rantings insane, yet tantalizing as well. They answered some of the questions that had plagued Imaro throughout his life, but there were still others that remained mysteries. And there was one other, the answer to which he was beginning to dread: *Was Keteke still alive?*

Again, Chitendu seemed to be aware of the warrior's thoughts.

"Your Zamburu woman is here, son of Katisa," he mocked. "She has been a guest of my friends. For I am not alone here. The original builders of this place are here, too. Through my *mchawi*, I restored them to life, although they are not as they once were.

"The Zamburu woman has entertained my friends well. They will return her to you now...."

Raising a shrouded arm, Chitendu uttered syllables in a language that jarred unpleasantly against Imaro's ears. From the shadows of the ruined chamber behind Chitendu, a horde of repellent shapes came forward, moving with a shambling gait. Yet for all their awkwardness, they moved swiftly, filling the space between the warrior and the wizard.

The builders of the Place of Stones were short, squat, manlike in shape ... and thoroughly nightmarish. Narrow, elongated eyes glittered balefully in the green light suffusing the ruin. Bestial fangs filled their gaping mouths. Colorless hair sprouted in thin patches across scabrous, unclothed skin. Catlike claws curved from the fingers of hands otherwise human in form.

These were the people of the Place of Stones, whose very name had long since been forgotten. Dead for unimaginable ages, the remnants of their life-essence had been locked by arcane necromancy into the eroded stone of their fallen edifice. Now they walked again, summoned into a macabre semblance of life by the *mchawi* of Chitendu. Of their former high degree of culture and intellect, not a trace remained. Now, they were only creatures of Chitendu....

But it was not the sight of the inhabitants of the Place of Stones that smote Imaro with sick horror. It was the thing the largest of them held upraised in its paws—a skeleton, human, with blood still dripping from glistening white bones. The flesh that had clothed the bones had only recently been stripped away.

The head, however, remained intact above the bare vertebrae of the skeleton's neck. The face—hideously distorted by an expression of inconceivable terror—was Keteke's.

A hoarse cry of despair tore from Imaro's throat. He remembered Kulu, his *ngombe*, the only being, human or otherwise, besides Keteke that he had allowed himself to care for. He remembered Kulu, dead, her heart ripped from her body by N'tu-mwaa. And now Keteke was dead, too, torn apart by demons in the thrall of another sorcerer, one who was far more powerful than the Turkhana had been. And both deaths were *his fault*, despite all his strength and prowess ...

Now a scarlet haze burned in front of Imaro's eyes, blotting out the emerald emanations of Chitendu's *mchawi*. The warrior's hatred surged within him as though it had suddenly acquired an independent life. The unseen bonds that held him helpless melted in the face of Imaro's incandescent rage. Then, abruptly, he was free, his body once again his own to command.

His action was instantaneous.

With one hand, he hurled his *arem* at Chitendu. With the other, he swung his *simi* in a sweeping, deadly semicircle.

The *arem* struck squarely in the center of Chitendu's cloak. And the *simi* slashed through the neck of the creature that held Keteke's remains. The beastlike head flew from the creature's shoulders and bounced toward the feet of Chitendu. No blood flowed from its wound.

As the resurrected inhabitant of the Place of Stones collapsed to the ground, dead for the second time, its hands loosed their burden. The blood-smeared bones of Keteke clattered loudly against broken rock. Her face stared skyward, mouth open in a soundless scream.

Chitendu, betraying no sign of pain despite the iron spear point lodged in his body, issued orders to his minions in a series of croaks and chitters that were never meant for a human tongue to utter. As one, the horde shuffled forward, momentarily driving Imaro back by sheer weight of numbers. They bore no weapons, but their fangs and talons were as deadly as those of any beast. Like a pack of Mbwa, the wild dog, attacking a buffalo, they leaped and tore at their towering foe.

Halting his retreat, Imaro lashed left and right with all the weapons he had at his disposal: his *simi*, his balled left fist, and his bare, callused feet. Like a scythe through grain, he sheared his way through the demonic horde. Although his foes' bodies were animated by Chitendu's *mchawi*, and could not be slain by mortal means, their ancient flesh was so brittle that even a glancing blow could inflict incapacitating damage.

Imaro bled from wounds the creatures' teeth and claws tore in his flesh when they first swarmed over him. But now, he waded through their ranks as though he were fording a stream, leaving a trail of shattered heads, severed limbs, and broken bodies behind him.

Battle madness claimed him fully now. The blood-blaze that had frightened Keteke lit his eyes, and curses spilled from his lips as he fought his way closer to Chitendu. His eyes locked with those of the former *oibonok*. It was then that Chitendu realized that he would never again gain control of the mind of the young warrior and keep him immobile. But there were other ways to complete his vengeance against the son of Katisa....

Again, Chitendu spoke to the inhabitants of the dead city. Those that had not been smashed asunder by Imaro's assault halted in midmotion, then stepped aside, leaving Imaro a clear path to their master. Teeth bared in a brutal snarl, the warrior charged forward, raising his *simi* for a slash that would have separated Chitendu's head from his shoulders—had it landed.

It did not land. For when Chitendu suddenly shrugged the cloak from his shoulders, Imaro halted his headlong rush as though he had run into an unseen, adamantine barrier. He stared in gaping disbelief, his *simi* nearly dropping from fingers rendered numb by the sight of what lay beneath the cloak....

***

Chitendu was even more inhuman than his resurrected minions. His elephantine legs rose from the ground like wrinkled tree trunks. Long, bony arms hung like sticks from a pair of narrow, knobby shoulders. The hands at their ends were incongruously delicate and graceful. Other than his head, those hands were the only human features Chitendu had left.

His torso was worst of all: a mass of tendrils that seemed imbued with a life independent from that of the rest of his hideous form. Like a swarm of maggots infesting a rotted carcass, the tendrils writhed, expanding and contracting in their anchors of grotesque, alien tissue. They glowed green, like fungus. Some of them curled around the shaft of Imaro's *arem*.

"Now you see the price I paid for my power," Chitendu intoned, looking at Imaro intently.

"No wielder of the *mchawi* of the Mashataan may long retain human form. Only the very *shape* of the Demon Gods may contain the true source of their magic. The Chosen of Naama know—and I quickly learned—that with each succeeding invocation of the power of the Mashataan, the wielder becomes less human and more Mashataan. I paid the price—gladly.

"But not for this! *Not for this!*"

The tentacles thrashed in wild agitation, as though animated by Chitendu's burst of bitterness and self-pity.

Then Imaro struck.

Of the horrendous consequences of the use of Mashataan magic, Imaro cared nothing. He knew only that beyond the wrong Chitendu had done to him and his mother, there was a deeper, more insidious evil that clung to the former *oibonok* like the cloak he had just discarded. That evil had to be obliterated.

The red tide of rage bursting through Imaro's mind washed away the moment of apprehension Chitendu's true appearance had engendered. Roaring out a battle cry, the warrior sprang across the few yards separating him from his enemy. With both hands, he plunged his *simi* deep into Chitendu's bulbous torso. Then, with a savage burst of strength, he ripped the blade upward, seeking to disembowel his monstrous foe.

Laughter was Chitendu's only response—laughter as inhuman as the form he wore; laughter that continued even as the serpentine coils of his intestines spilled to the ground.

Then an elongated arm lashed out, catching Imaro across the face. Despite its emaciation, there was disproportionate strength in that arm; Imaro fell as though he had been struck by a Turkhana club. Before he could regain his feet, a blinding beam of emerald light shot from a cluster of tentacles that had stiffened like pointing fingers.

Enveloping the iron blade of the *simi*, the green ray lanced down to its hilt and into Imaro's hand. Biting back a cry of agony, Imaro dropped the weapon. Its blade was a melted, smoking ruin before it hit the ground. Imaro's hand felt as though he had just pulled it from a fire.

The warrior stared in disbelief as the shaft of the *arem* embedded in Chitendu's body burst into green flame, then crumbled into ash. Again, the tentacles brightened, aimed, and launched a coruscating bolt of destruction—this time, directly at Imaro.

But there was no target for the blast. Reacting with pantherish speed, the warrior had hurled himself behind a block of fallen stone. It was unfeeling rock that bore the brunt of Chitendu's green fire.

No longer did Chitendu laugh. His demon-fire spoke for him. Bolt after bolt of emerald destruction seared into the stone that shielded Imaro. The rock began to glow with heat; heat that forced Imaro to abandon a shelter that had proven to be far too temporary.

Keeping his body low to the ground, the warrior raced across the broken stone, casting his gaze left and right in search of anything he could use as a weapon. His face betrayed no fear, only frustration at the thwarting of his vengeance.

Triumph imminent, Chitendu laughed again. He turned ponderously on his thick legs, stepped forward … and crashed heavily to the ground, feet entangled in his own spilled intestines.

A bolt of demon-fire, trapped between the ground and Chitendu's bulky body, consumed the alien flesh as ordinary flames or weapons never could. An unearthly shriek escaped the former *oibonok*'s lips.

Even as Chitendu strove clumsily to rise, Imaro sprang into action. Bending quickly, he caught a heavy slab of stone in an iron grasp. Muscles cracking and straining beneath his umber skin, he raised the slab high over his head. Then, teeth clenched in exertion, he staggered toward Chitendu.

Head half-turned in Imaro's direction, Chitendu thrashed and struggled in a frenzied effort to rise. But his ungainly Mashataan body hindered his efforts. Imaro towered above him, the weight of the slab of stone cording his arms.

Chitendu shuddered: his long-delayed doom was upon him at last. *Unless ….*

"Wait!" Chitendu screamed to Imaro. "I can tell you who your father is!"

Imaro hesitated. And in that brief moment of respite, Chitendu heaved his body onto its back. The waving tendrils stiffened, brightened …

And Imaro hurled the heavy slab downward. It smashed Chitendu's skull like an eggshell. Imaro had reasoned that the human parts of Chitendu's hybrid form were the most vulnerable, and his surmise had proven correct.

A grayish paste oozed from beneath the broken slab. The green-glowing tendrils writhed a moment longer. Then they faded and hung limply, whatever life they possessed having fled with Chitendu's. The green glare of Chitendu's *mchawi* faded, to be replaced by the clean light of Mwesu the moon.

But Imaro's fight was not yet over….

***

Strength ebbed abruptly from the warrior's limbs. It was not so much the battles with the creatures and Chitendu that had drained him of energy; it was the debilitating struggle to free his mind from the shackles of Chitendu's *mchawi*. Any sense of personal triumph he felt at having slain Chitendu was canceled by the sight of Keteke's face fixed in an eternal spasm of horror, echoing an endless, soundless scream.

Leaning against the remnant of a pillar, Imaro looked down at the piteous remains of Keteke. She had prophesied her own death, and Imaro felt responsible for it.

Then a slight noise brought his attention back to the Place of Stones. And he saw that not all of Chitendu's *mchawi* had died with him. The last denizens of the Place of Stones were advancing toward him. Imaro counted more than a score of them. In the blankness that had once been their minds, only Chitendu's final command remained: *Kill.*

Weakened and weaponless, Imaro knew he could not prevail against the undead horde. He would fight them, and kill some of them, but sooner or later, their teeth and talons would overcome him, and he would join Chitendu and Keteke in death.

He gathered the last of his strength, pulled himself upright, and knotted his hands into maul-like fists. If he must die now, his end would not be an easy one.

The creatures drew closer. Imaro crouched, ready to spring recklessly into their midst. Before he could move, the creatures were raked by a volley of Ilyassai *arems* launched from the darkness.

Blinking in disbelief, Imaro saw a score of warriors emerge from the shadows of the Place of Stones. They fell upon the undead things like lions, hacking them to pieces with their *simis*. Confused, bereft of the guidance of Chitendu's will, the creatures' resistance collapsed quickly. Before long, they lay scattered across the barren stone, once again as one with their fallen city.

The slaughter done, the warriors of the Kitoko clan approached Imaro. He glared at them like a cornered beast.

The warriors had broken the long tradition forbidding them to enter the Place of Stones. To Imaro, their only possible purpose in doing so was to kill him for having stampeded the *ngombe*. They had slain the creatures menacing him only so that they could save the satisfaction of slaying him for themselves.

In the light of Mwesu, Imaro recognized some of the warriors. Mubaku, the *ol-arem*, was there. So was Masadu. Many of the warriors in this band had accompanied Imaro on his ill-fated *olmaiyo*. Mubaku and Masadu continued to advance toward Imaro after the others halted several paces from him. Imaro's muscles tensed, as though he were about to hurl himself at them. Sensing the young warrior's mood, the *ol-arem* broke the silence.

"Kanoko and Keteke were missing," he said. "We found Kanoko's body at the pool, for everyone in the *manyattas* knew that was where he and Keteke would go. Your trail was not difficult to follow from there."

"So you came here to kill me?" Imaro snarled. "Do it quickly, then, for I have done what I had to do."

"You have slain fellow Ilyassai of your clan," Mubaku said sternly. "You loosed the *ngombe* from the *boma*, causing the deaths of some before we could recover all of them. Those are great wrongs."

"And have the Ilyassai not wronged *me*?" Imaro shouted.

For a fleeting moment then, the Kitoko clan warriors saw what lay beneath Imaro's impregnable exterior: a hurt child.

"Yes," Mubaku replied. "We have."

Astounded by those words, Imaro leaned back against the pillar, which suddenly was all that was keeping him on his feet.

"How long do you think we have been here, Imaro?" the *ol-arem* asked. "We followed your spoor quickly. Chitendu's *mchawi* was not as strong as he thought, or perhaps he was so intent on you that he failed to realize that we were coming. We heard everything: all his boasts and claims of the evils he had done to us—and to you and your mother. My daughter …

"Chitendu's *mchawi* did not capture us; we would have slain him, if you hadn't done so.

"But it was your fight — your second *olmaiyo*—and you won it. And afterward, we were not going to allow those demon-things to slay you. Nor would we slay you ourselves."

Masadu, the master of *mafundishu-ya-muran*, stepped forward then, and laid his own *arem*, *simi*, and shield at Imaro's feet.

"When Chitendu died, so did his lies," the scarred warrior said. "In our minds and memories, we finally saw the truth of what happened on your *olmaiyo*, not the lie Muburi made us think we saw."

He looked deeply into Imaro's eyes.

"Never before has a man of the Ilyassai slain Ngatun as you did," Masadu said. "And never before has an Ilyassai done what you have this night. Warrior—my weapons are yours."

Imaro remained impassive.

"Take them, Imaro," Mubaku urged.

Imaro still neither moved nor spoke. Mubaku's next words came haltingly, as if at great cost.

"The wrongs we Ilyassai have done to you are greater than any you have done to us," the *ol-arem* said. "If killing Muburi and Kanoko, and stampeding the *ngombe*, were part of what you had to do to destroy the evil that was Chitendu—an evil we did not even know was still among us—we can live with that.

"You are a man and a warrior, Imaro. You have done deeds greater than any Ilyassai of any clan since the time of the First Ancestors—of Ajunge himself. Return to the *manyattas* with us. We will do you honor—and we will honor the memory of Katisa, who brought you among us. No longer will you be called 'son-of-no-father.' I will make you my own son, for your mother's blood is mine, as is yours."

Imaro looked at him then. Mubaku, father of Katisa. Mubaku, his grandfather. He recalled a day, long past, when he had unwittingly called Mubaku "*mkale-ya-mzazi*"—father of my mother. On that day, Mubaku had beaten him senseless.

He bent, and took up Masadu's *arem* and *simi*. As he held the warrior-trainer's weapons in his hands, new strength flowed into his weary limbs. It was the strength of vindication. His lifelong goal—acceptance as a warrior among his mother's people—was his at last. For one painfully short moment, his heart sang in triumph.

Then the memories returned, crowding his mind like ants teeming from an overturned hill. Bitter memories, hateful memories, each one a brick in a soaring wall of acrimony that would forever stand between him and the people who had now, belatedly, acknowledged him. The Ilyassai were a proud people, a harsh people, a fierce people, a just people … but they were not his people.

And he could not forget.

His hands opened. Masadu's weapons fell with a clatter and a clang to the rock-strewn ground. His heart hardened. And the hurt child spoke.

"You did not accept me before," he said tonelessly. "I will not accept you now."

Then he turned and strode past the silent warriors. He descended the broken stairway he had climbed under Chitendu's ensorcellment. He left it to the others to see to Keteke's remains, though the image of her terror-stricken face would accuse him for the rest of his life.

Dawn spread wings of pink through the sky as Imaro left the Place of Stones. He headed northward, deliberately taking the opposite direction from the one his mother had taken long rains ago. Chitendu had lied—Imaro knew that only Katisa could tell him who his father was. But she had refused to tell him during the five rains he had been with her. And now—he had no desire to know, nor to seek her out for any other reason. He desired only solitude.

Then he heard the singing. It came from behind him, from the Place of Stones. He recognized the words of the song, punctuated by the rhythmic clash of spear butts against stone. It was the song sung by warriors when they returned triumphant from *olmaiyo*.

The deep-voiced words wrenched at his emotions. Almost … almost, he turned, almost he yielded to Mubaku's promise of honor and fellowship among the only people he had ever known.

But the wall of rancor was too strong. Without looking back, he strode onward, the echoes of the Ilyassai song fading as he resolutely shut his ears against it.

The weapon was out of the crucible. Now, the forging would begin....

PART II
THE HARAMIA

THE AFUA

In the country of the fierce,
An Ilyassai is king.
— Tamburure proverb

Imaro stood at the juncture between forest and savanna—two entirely different worlds. He hesitated, uncertain where his next footsteps should take him.

As he had wandered farther north in the Tamburure, far beyond the territory the Ilyassai claimed, he noted that the occasional copses of trees with which he was familiar were becoming larger and more frequent. And he was also beginning to see trees of types he had never before encountered. Gradually, the woodlands had thickened, until they became the towering palisade of bark, limbs, and leaves before which the warrior now stood.

He looked back in the direction from which he had come. In the distance, beyond the scatterings of trees, he could see the last of the golden grassland of the Tamburure. Mwesu the moon had waxed and waned six times since he had departed from the Place of Stones and left the Kitoko clan behind. During that time, he had avoided all contact with other people. And he had wandered through places into which no Ilyassai had ever before set foot.

During his travels, he had seen ample signs of human habitation: herds of cattle, *bomas*, and dwellings different from those of the Ilyassai. And he had caught glimpses of people who did not resemble the Ilyassai and their neighboring tribes. But because they did not look like him, either, he avoided them.

Having rejected the weapons Mubaku had offered him, Imaro had spent the first weeks of his exile living in a manner similar to that of his distant ancestors. Stones and sharpened sticks were his weapons, and with such crude equipment, his hunts were seldom successful. On some days, he went hungry; on others, he ate things the Ilyassai would have disdained. But he was no longer an Ilyassai, so it did not matter what he ate or did not eat.

One day, Imaro came across the corpse of a man. Or, at least, the parts of the carcass that the scavengers had left behind. From the skin that had not been torn away by the teeth of Fisi and Mbweha, Imaro could see that the man had been extremely dark in hue. He could also see that the man had been a warrior; his spear still lay in the grass, as did a bladed weapon that was smaller than a *simi*, but larger than the dagger N'tu-mwaa had carried.

The dead man's clothing had been torn asunder, but enough of it remained intact to allow Imaro to create a makeshift garment to wrap around his loins, for he no longer wanted to wear the clothing that had belonged to Mubiri. He took the man's weapons, as well. The spear was nothing like an *arem*. Its blade was not nearly as long, and its point was far narrower. It would, however, suit Imaro's purpose, which was to hunt with greater efficiency.

For a moment, he wondered why this warrior had been wandering alone, like him. He wondered how the man had died. And he wondered how he would have responded if he had met this man in life. Then he left his speculations, along with the man's remains, behind.

With better weapons at his disposal, Imaro's eating improved. His body, which had grown leaner, now regained the massive musculature that was reaching its maturity. His hair had grown into an unruly, wooly bush—never again would he wear it in the ocher-caked braids of the Ilyassai. And never again would he allow his head to be shaved like that of a Tamburure woman.

Although his eyes remained alert to the constant dangers of the wilderness, Imaro's face bore an expression of melancholy. The isolation he had welcomed after he left the Place of Stones was beginning to wear on him, though he would never have admitted it. At first, he had reveled in his freedom from the opprobrium he had endured during his life among his mother's people. Now, he longed for human contact—contact that was not hostile.

But he was not yet willing to incur the risks involved in initiating such contact. So he continued to embrace solitude as though it were a friend.

For a moment longer, Imaro stood at the threshold of the forest. Once again, he looked back toward the Tamburure. Even at a distance, its familiarity drew him. But that familiarity included unwanted memories—most of all, that of Keteke's face, mouth gaping in a silent scream in the moonlight....

He shook himself violently, as though his skin were covered with foul water. Then he turned to the woodland.

Never before had he seen so many trees clustered so closely together. The forest stretched as far as he could see, in all directions other than the one that lay behind him—the one he did not want to take. He could travel along the forest's edge, in the hope that he would eventually find a way around it. Or he could venture into the foliage to see what might await him there.

The question of whether he should enter the forest was far more straightforward than the ones that had plagued him since his confrontation with

Chitendu. The sorcerer's words repeated themselves endlessly, sometimes maddeningly, in his mind. And all too often, the Place of Stones intruded in his dreams, as did the faces of the creatures that dwelled there. So did the face of Chitendu—and, always, Keteke.

Imaro did not welcome those dreams. But he could not prevent them. And the questions continued....

Where was Naama? Who were the High Sorcerers? Who—or what—were the Mashataan?

None of those names had ever been mentioned in the tales of the past that Ilyassai clan elders told by firelight. Even so, Imaro was certain that Chitendu had been the least of his enemies. There were others who were far more powerful and dangerous than the disgraced former *oibonok* of the Ilyassai. Imaro needed to find them, before they found him.

But how?

Imaro pushed that question to the back as he always did when he could not find an answer to it. He listened to the sounds of the forest, which were unlike those of the savanna. To his ears, the chorus of birdsong was a cacophony. The screeches of the monkeys, which to Imaro looked like smaller, long-tailed cousins of the baboons that roamed the Tamburure, grated annoyingly. Even the voice of the wind was different, rustling noisily through leaves rather than sighing softly in the grass.

For a moment longer, Imaro stood, shifting his spear from one hand to the other as he looked from the forest to the plain.

Then he decided. The forest was a place of trees, not a Place of Stones. It was a living place, not a dead place. He did not think he would find Naama or the Mashataan in its depths. But he might well find something that would fill the emptiness that gaped like an abyss inside him.

Gripping his spear firmly in one hand, Imaro entered the forest. And the forest embraced him.

***

Imaro's first reaction to the forest was a sense of *enclosement*. The trees, most of which were far taller and thicker than those that dotted the Tamburure, crowded against him, even though there were spaces between them through which he could walk. Under his feet, the carpet of fallen leaves gave him an uncomfortable sensation, different from the familiar touch of trampled grass. Overhead, the foliage concealed the sky like the roof of a *manyatta*.

The shapes of birds and monkeys flitted across his line of vision, and hordes of insects flew around him and crawled along the ground. He saw shapes moving between the trees; the shapes of larger animals that were either evading him—or stalking him. He noticed the tracks of Chui, the leopard, but none of Ngatun or Matisho. And there was spoor of other beasts he could not identify.

His *kufahuma* sense, which had been honed in the wide spaces of the Tamburure, could not help him in this place. To survive, he would have to learn its signs of danger—and learn them quickly.

When Imaro first stepped into the forest, all sound ceased, as though the entire woodland was aware of the presence of an intruder. Then, after a short silence, the calls and cries resumed.

The forest was a much noisier place than the Tamburure, and Imaro could hardly hear the sound of his own footsteps. But he did hear the distant trumpeting of Tembo, the elephant, and he wondered how a creature that large could squeeze its bulk through the spaces between the trees.

And above the cacophony of forest sounds, Imaro heard another noise—one that was strange, yet tantalizingly familiar. It sounded like rain. Yet shafts of sunlight penetrated the spaces in the canopy of leaves high above his head.

Curiosity piqued, Imaro decided that he would seek the source of this new sound. Gripping his spear more tightly, the warrior pushed his way between the trees, and through patches of undergrowth splashed with flowers. He looked back once—and saw only trees. For the first time in his life, he could not see the Tamburure.

Then he heard a rustle in the trees, directly overhead. He looked up quickly, spear poised to hurl. High above, he saw an unfamiliar creature that resembled a monkey, but was far larger and lacked a tail. In face and shape, the beast was more manlike than those of monkeys or baboons. Thick, black hair covered its body. Even in the distance from its perch in the high branches, Imaro could see that the creature was observing him, examining him.

The beast made soft hooting noises as it gazed at Imaro. Then it screeched loudly, shook the branch on which it was standing, and sped off, using its long arms to swing from tree to tree.

Imaro paused for a moment longer, wondering if the manlike creature would return with others of its kind. For several heartbeats, he strove to extend his *kufahuma* sense through the loud noises of the forest. When he was satisfied that the beast of the trees was not returning, he continued toward the rainlike sound that had attracted his attention.

As he drew closer, Imaro could hear other sounds; sounds with which he was very familiar—human voices. He halted. People were the last thing he expected to find in the forest, for all the tribes of the Tamburure knew that the savanna was the only place where cattle could be grazed, and *manyattas* built. Yet the sounds he heard could only have been made by humans—men, not women, judging by the timbre of their voices.

Imaro wasn't certain he wanted to resume contact with his own kind. But the closest alternative he had seen was the hairy creature of the trees. Without further contemplation, Imaro pressed forward, moving more cautiously now. The watery sound grew louder, as did the voices, which conversed in a language Imaro did not understand.

Soon, only a thin screen of foliage separated Imaro from the sounds that had intrigued him. He pulled a bit of the brush away—and stared wide-eyed, transfixed by his first sight of a river.

The Tamburure was a land of lakes and ponds, not rivers. The sight of a wide ribbon of flowing water, tinged brown with silt, caused Imaro to blink several times in disbelief.

On the other side of the river, he saw another forest, like the one that now enclosed him. Then he turned his attention to the voices. And he saw two men on the bank of the river closest to him. The men were darker of skin than he, ebony to Imaro's own umber shade. They were shorter than the people of the Tamburure, but stockier in build. Loin-coverings of brightly colored cloth—which looked to Imaro like the hides of bizarre beasts—were their only garments, other than strings of beads that circled their wrists and ankles.

A large, hollowed-out log lay beside the two men, who were wrestling a large net filled with fish into the hollow. Imaro had seen fish in the lakes of the Tamburure, but the Ilyassai never ate them, and did not make nets. He wondered why these men were going to the trouble of hauling the fish into the log—then the river exploded in a shower of water, and a huge shape hurtled onto the bank and seized one of the men in its jaws.

The sudden cries of both men tore at Imaro's ears … and he immediately sprang into action.

***

Bursting through the foliage and raising his spear in both hands, Imaro raced down the riverbank. Neither the men nor the river-beast were aware of him—not until he plunged the point of his spear into the creature's scaly hide. Imaro's thrust was so powerful that the spear point drove completely through the creature's body, pinning it to the riverbank.

Imaro leaped out of the way of the river-beast's lashing tail. Its long, teeth-laden jaws opened in agony, releasing their hold on their intended prey. But Imaro paid no heed to the man. For instead of weakening, the river-beast's struggles grew stronger, and it was actually beginning to pull the spear point out of the soft soil of the riverbank, even as blood poured from the wound.

Quickly, Imaro pulled his other weapon—the dead warrior's dagger—from its sheath. Moving out of range of the snapping jaws of the roaring river-beast, he focused on the creature's eyes—small, reptilian, malevolent. The beast was almost free from the soil, and was turning toward Imaro. …

Striking with the swiftness of a cobra, the warrior thrust the point of his dagger through the river-beast's eye, and into its tiny brain. After a convulsive shudder that sent mud and blood flying in all directions, the huge creature finally lay still.

Imaro's gaze took in the length of the beast: its long jaws; short, splayed legs; and scaly hide that looked as hard as an Ilyassai shield. He could see how this creature of the water could be as formidable as Ngatun. It was Imaro's first encounter with a crocodile, and the creature was as alien to him as the monstrosities that inhabited the Place of Stones.

Then he turned to the men whose lives he had just saved. Already, he had pulled his dagger out of the crocodile's eye, and the weapon remained in his hand, blood dripping from its blade.

The fishermen stared at Imaro as though he was as dangerous as the crocodile. The man who had been caught in the beast's jaws lay on the riverbank. He was attempting to use his hands to stanch the flow of blood from the wounds the crocodile's teeth had torn in his leg. The other man crouched protectively beside his wounded companion. In one hand, he held a bladed weapon that was as long as a *simi*, but sharpened on only one side. It looked more suitable for slashing than for stabbing.

At close quarters, the differences between these men and any others Imaro had seen before were more pronounced. Their hair was braided into rows that ridged their scalps. Raised dots of skin formed swirling patterns on their faces and the upper part of their bodies. Their eyes were round and white in the darkness of their faces, and Imaro knew he was as strange to them as they were to him. But then, all his life, he had been the strange one.

He lowered his weapon. With his other hand, he pointed toward the wounded fisherman.

"He will die if you don't stop his bleeding," he said.

The two men looked at each other. The one the crocodile's jaws had spared lowered his own weapon, and spoke to Imaro. Imaro found the speech unintelligible, though he thought he could hear hints of the tongues of the Tamburure tribes. He spread his hands and shook his head, indicating that he did not understand what the man was saying. The other man pressed his lips together in frustration. Then Imaro wiped the bloody blade of his dagger against his garment, returned the weapon to its sheath, and made tying motions with his hands.

After a moment, the fisherman sheathed his own weapon and went into the nearby foliage, in search of vines. The wounded man continued to stare at Imaro. With what he hoped was a reassuring smile, the warrior turned his attention to the carcass of the crocodile.

He almost expected the river-beast to rise again as he approached it. But the crocodile remained still as he placed one placed one foot on its hide, grasped the shaft of his spear in both hands, and wrenched the weapon free in a shower of blood.

Then, grunting with the strain of the effort, he reached down and heaved the dead crocodile off the riverbank and back into the water. For a moment, the carcass floated lazily and began to drift downstream. It only moved a short distance before the jaws of other crocodiles broke the surface and dragged the beast Imaro had killed back underwater.

When Imaro turned back to the fishermen, he saw that they were once again staring at him, mouths agape. The second man had returned, arms laden with lianas and leaves. The two of them, together, would have had difficulty pushing the carcass of the crocodile into the river, and indeed, might not have been able to accomplish the feat. But Imaro had done it easily.

The wounded man groaned, and his companion shifted his attention from Imaro to more urgent matters. Imaro gestured to indicate an offer of assistance, and the fisherman, after a brief hesitation, accepted his aid. Soon, a lattice of leaves and vines covered the wounded man's leg. The man did not cry out during the ungentle ministrations. An Ilyassai would not have done so, either, Imaro observed. His opinion of the other men rose.

When the wrapping was done, all three men leaned against the side of the hollowed-out log, which still contained the net filled with fish. The fisherman who had escaped the crocodile's jaws gave Imaro a long, searching gaze. Imaro did not look away.

Finally, as though satisfied by what he had seen in Imaro's eyes, he pointed to himself and said:

"Msuli."

The wounded fisherman made a similar gesture.

"Busa," he said.

After a moment, the Ilyassai pointed to himself.

"Imaro," he said.

And for the first time in his life, Imaro had friends.

***

During the time that passed while Busa recovered from the wounds the teeth of the crocodile had inflicted, Imaro discovered a great deal about the forest and the river—lessons that might have cost him his life if he had not had help in learning them.

The name of the river, Busa and Msuli told him, was the Damba Bolong. The woodland was known as the Kajua. The two men's people were the Mtumwe, one of dozens of tribes that dwelled along the river's edge, farther downstream. Of the vast, flat plain that lay beyond the border of trees, they knew nothing.

The area of the Kajua in which Imaro had found Busa and Msuli was considered remote and dangerous by the river people. But the fishing was good there, and the two men had decided that the reward would be well worth the risk. Had Imaro not slain the crocodile and saved their lives, the Mtumwe would have mourned the passing of Msuli and Busa after it became evident they would not be returning—and they would have cursed the young men's foolishness.

Like all the river people, however, Imaro's friends were far from foolish in the ways of the woodland. They taught Imaro which of the abundant fruits of the forest were edible, and pointed out the ones that were so dangerous that a single bite of them was fatal. They showed him a leaf that, if crushed and rubbed onto the skin, kept the annoying hordes of insects away. He learned that poisonous snakes were, perhaps, the deadliest predators of all, including the leopard.

He learned the ways of Mjino the crocodile, and Kiboko the hippopotamus, which to Imaro looked like an overweight rhinoceros that had shed its horns. Gradually, he came to realize that the wildlife in the forest and river was as abundant as it had been on the Tamburure. But it was different in ways he never could have imagined.

He saw antelope of various shapes and sizes, none of which resembled the ones that roamed in huge herds across the savanna. Tembo did, indeed, dwell here, but the elephants of the forest were not as large as those of the Tamburure. There was also a smaller version of the fierce buffalo.

Imaro's companions were well acquainted with the large, tailless, monkeylike creature he had seen when he first entered the forest. They called it Mponga, the chimpanzee. Once, Imaro saw a beast that resembled Mponga, but was so large it made even him look puny by comparison. Ngagi was the name the Mtumwe gave to this manlike giant—the gorilla. They spoke its name in fearful tones.

In the meantime, Imaro absorbed as much of the Mtumwe language as he could, for he had no reason to believe he would ever again utter a word in Ilyassai. Before long, he was able to make himself understood in the new tongue, which was more melodious than the harsh sounds of his native language. And the fishermen no longer had to speak slowly to ensure that Imaro understood them.

The day came when Busa's wounds were healed to the point where he could walk with only a slight limp. A set of jagged, tooth-shaped scars now decorated his leg, accompanying the patterns of skin-marks that festooned the rest of his body. Busa and Msuli had once remarked on the smoothness of Imaro's skin, and asked him if all his people were scar-free. Imaro said they were. The others did not ask him many other questions about the Ilyassai, for they soon learned that Imaro was reluctant to speak of his origins.

A fresh catch of fish lay at the bottom of the boat, but it was not as large as the original haul, which the three men had long since consumed. Imaro had stared in amazement when the fishermen first demonstrated how their dugout floated, and could be propelled by poles and paddles along the river. Soon enough, he learned how to keep himself upright in the boat, and to paddle without splashing loud enough to frighten the fish.

Now, Msuli and Busa were gathering their nets and *pangas*—their name for the single-edged blades they carried—and were making room for Imaro in the dugout. But Imaro did not enter the boat. The Mtumwe fishermen gave him a puzzled look as he remained on the riverbank.

"Are you not coming with us, Imaro?" Msuli asked.

"I am not sure," Imaro replied.

"But Imaro," Busa said, "we have spoken of this before. You saved me from the jaws of Mjino. I owe you my life, as does Msuli, for Mjino might have killed him, too. What is mine, I must share with you. My family is your family; my people are your people. A place of honor awaits you among the Mtumwe."

Busa's face bore a stricken expression as he spoke, for he could not fathom Imaro's reluctance to join them. Still, Imaro hesitated. Friendship was still new to him; he did not know if he could adjust to the embrace of an entire people. And there was also the matter of Chitendu, and the sorcerers of Naama. Would he be bringing danger to the Mtumwe if he lived among them?

"Imaro," Msuli said softly. "No man should be alone."

Imaro was not certain he agreed with Mtumwe's sentiment. Nevertheless, he decided to join the fishermen in their boat.

***

Watercraft of all sizes crowded the Damba Bolong as Msuli and Busa brought Imaro to the Mtumwe *kijiji*, which was what the people of the river called the towns and villages that dotted its banks. The splashing of paddles and poles were accompanied by the rhythmic beat of unseen drums. Both sounds were overshadowed by the joyous songs that marked the return of the two fishermen, who were long since thought to be lost to the jaws of Mjino or Kiboko.

When the dugout was first sighted as it passed outlying *kijijis*, word of its appearance—and of the outlander who accompanied the fishermen—passed downriver quickly, as though borne by the wind. No boats emerged from the *kijijis* they passed, however. Although the people of the river tribes had traded, fought, and mated among each other for thousands of rains, and the news of the missing Mtumwe fishermen had traveled the length of the Damba Bolong, it was the privilege of their home *kijiji* to celebrate their return.

Now, the Mtumwe sang in their boats and from the shore. Imaro marveled at the people's ability to dance in their boats without falling into the river. Men, women, and children alike crowded into the watercraft, shouting and singing their greetings to Busa and Msuli. Yet even in their joy at the sight of two men returning as though resurrected, they stared in wonder at the stranger, Imaro. And he, in turn, gazed in open curiosity at them.

The Mtumwe men were garbed and scarified in a manner similar to that of Busa and Msuli, though some also wore more elaborate ornaments, as well as feathered headgear. Mtumwe children wore almost nothing, and their skin was unmarked. It was not the men or children, though, but the women of the river people who caught and held Imaro's attention, as nothing else had done since his departure from the Ilyassai.

They were clad in tight-fitting skirts that covered them from waist to ankle. The bark cloth from which the garments had been made was dyed in shades of scarlet, orange, yellow, and other colors that looked as though they had captured the brightness of Jua the sun. Above the waist, the women wore nothing other than strands of multicolored beads that looked like tiny, hardened nubs of flowers.

Like the men, the Mtumwe women bore scar patterns on their skin. More than anything else about them, though, Imaro was fascinated by their hair, and the way they wore it. Among the Tamburure tribes, the heads of girls were shaved as part of their initiation into womanhood, and remained that way thereafter—a custom so ancient its origins had long been forgotten. The only adult woman Imaro had ever seen with hair on her head was his mother, Katisa—and he always thrust his memories of Katisa aside whenever they arose.

None of the Mtumwe women shaved their heads. And the hair on no two of their heads was alike. Some wore their hair in rows of braids, like the men. Some wore long, thin, twisted braids that resembled vines tangled in trees. Others grew their hair in spikes and spirals.

Imaro could only shake his head in disbelief at what he saw, even as the Mtumwe whispered comments to each other about the huge-statured stranger with strangely unmarked skin.

Before long, the welcoming flotilla reached a wide stretch of riverbank. Dozens of dugouts were already beached at the spot, but there was room for many more. Imaro's friends were the first to beach their boats, and he climbed out to help the others push the fish-laden vessel ashore. Soon, all the boats were beached, and Imaro stood at the center of a swirl of people, the tallest of whom were a head shorter than him. Amid the cacophony of singing and drumming, Imaro detected a nuance he had never heard before—a tone of welcome.

Beyond the crowd and the shoreline, Imaro saw the dwellings of the Mtumwe. Instead of leather, the Mtumwe used reeds, poles, and thatch to construct their dwellings, which blended with the forest that surrounded them. The conical roofs of the dwellings reminded Imaro of anthills he had seen in the Tamburure.

No *boma* or barrier of any other kind protected the *kijiji*. On the borders of the dwellings, Imaro saw gardens filled with a variety of unfamiliar plants. One thing he did not see was cattle. He missed the sight—and the smell—of the *ngombe* of his clan.

On the whole, the village gave an impression of permanence that was foreign to the nomadic mentality of the Ilyassai. But Imaro had no time to reflect on that feeling, for a small knot of people were pushing to the forefront of the crowd: two pairs of older Mtumwe men and women, a group of others who were about the same age as Msuli and Busa, and several small children. They were the parents and family of the men Imaro had rescued. They engulfed the two fishermen, embracing them and praising all the ancestors that Busa and Msuli had returned safely to the *kijiji* after such a long, and ominous, absence.

In snatches of conversation between embraces, the fishermen told their families the tale of how Imaro had killed the crocodile that was about to drag Busa into the river. And the curiosity in the glances they gave to the Ilyassai quickly turned into a mixture of awe and gratitude.

One of the older men bent down and closely inspected the marks of the wounds on Busa's leg. When the man straightened and turned to Imaro, a hush gradually descended upon the crowd, and the drumming abated.

The man looked long and searchingly at Imaro, as though he was looking for a message in the warrior's eyes. Then he spoke.

"I am Najimu, father of Busa, and the *mku*—the chieftain—of the Mtumwe *kijiji*," he said. "You, Imaro, have given me the life of my son. You, Imaro, are welcome to remain among us as long as you wish, and what is ours is yours."

And he bowed his head to Imaro, as did all the others in the families of Busa and Msuli.

Imaro did not understand all of Najimu's words, but he caught most of their meaning. Again, he wondered at the differences between the river people and those of the Tamburure. Hostility, not hospitality, was the basis of relations among the tribes of the savanna, and sometimes even among the clans and families of the same tribe. Death would have greeted Imaro if he were to venture into the territory of the Turkhana or the Zamburu, and he would never have even considered saving the life of a member of a rival tribe.

Yet here, in this unfamiliar land enclosed by a *boma* of trees, strangers were offering him a welcome he had not received from his own people until it was too late to matter.

To Najimu, Imaro said two words that had never once issued from his mouth while he lived among the Kitoko clan:

"Thank you."

***

Night fell, and the drumming in the Mtumwe *kijiji* continued. Imaro wondered if it would ever cease. He had never seen so many different types of drum. Among the Ilyassai, each clan had only a single drum that was brought out only for ritual occasions, such as the return from *olmaiyo*. But the Mtumwe drums were as varied as the people themselves: some large, some small; some with a beat as deep as a lion's roar; others that sounded like the chattering of monkeys.

The Mtumwe were holding an impromptu festival to celebrate the safe return of Busa and Msuli, as well as the arrival of the stranger who had saved their lives. The people of the *kijiji* feasted heartily, and quaffed banana beer by the gourdful. Imaro had nearly choked the first time he tasted the concoction, which was called *ndizi-pombe*, but he soon learned to enjoy its taste, if not its effects.

Now the drummers' beat was changing, and the people began to dance. In concert, the drums of the Mtumwe produced rhythms and beats that worked their way into the blood of the listener and embedded the urge to get up and join the dancing.

But Imaro did not know dancing such as this. Men and women danced together, a thing that never happened among the Ilyassai. And the children danced among the adults, never missing a beat of the complicated cadence of the drummers' sound. The light of the moon and the *kijiji*'s night-fires glistened on the dancers' sweat-slicked bodies as they shuffled their feet and swayed their hips.

Imaro took another swallow of *ndizi-pombe*. He was sitting on the woven-grass mat of Busa's family, in a place of honor at the side of the *mku*, Najimu. The mat of Msuli's family was nearby.

During the few occasions on which the drumming receded, Imaro told his hosts tales of the broad, flat savanna that stretched beyond the perimeter of the Kajua. The Mtumwe listened in wide-eyed wonderment, for they could no more imagine a treeless land without rivers than Imaro could have visualized a land of nothing but trees before his departure from the Tamburure.

"Do your people dance, Imaro?" Najimu asked.

"Sometimes," the warrior replied.

"Can you show us one of your dances?"

Neither the tone of the *mku*'s words, nor the words themselves, bespoke anything other than a simple question. Even so, Imaro sensed he was being put to a subtle test in the eyes of his hosts—a test that would determine whether he would be a true guest of the Mtumwe, or only an interloper.

Then, perhaps born of the many gourds of *ndizi-pombe* he had swallowed, an idea came into his mind. He would show the Mtumwe the dance that had been denied him because of the *mchawi* of Muburi and Chitendu—the dance he had now twice earned the right to perform, having slain Ngatun, and now Mjino the crocodile, a beast that was more than a match for any lion.

Imaro rose to his feet. If the *ndizi-pombe* he had consumed had affected him, it didn't show as he walked toward the open area that was the *kijiji*'s dance space. The crowd of dancers gave ground as he approached, making way for their guest from afar. And the drumming subsided to a low background mutter as Imaro stood alone in the firelit dance space.

For a long moment, the warrior remained motionless, as though gathering energy into himself. Then, without warning, he sprang so high into the air it seemed he had disappeared. Even the drumming halted as the astonished Mtumwe waited for Imaro to return to the ground. And they wondered how he would manage to land without injuring himself.

When Imaro descended, however, his feet touched the earth as lightly as those of one of the small forest cats that lived in the shadow of Chui the leopard. Now he crouched in a fighting stance: one arm extended as though he were wielding an *arem*; the closer to his body, in the position of a shield.

Then his feet began to move, carrying him forward like a predator stalking prey. Tentatively at first, then with greater confidence, the Mtumwe drummers picked up the rhythm of his movements, and their beats kept up with the warrior as he suddenly began to leap and whirl and thrust with his imaginary spear.

As Imaro's motions became swifter and more fierce, the drummers quickened their beat. And Imaro wielded his unseen weapons not only against Ngatun and Mjino, but also against all the other foes he had faced during his short lifetime: N'tu-mwaa, Kanoko, Muburi, Chitendu, the misshapen creatures of the Place of Stones.... He slew them all, again and again, as he danced.

He ended his dance with a final, prodigious leap that again carried him almost out of the sight of the watchers. When he landed, he raised his face to the night sky and uttered the cry of victory and vindication the Ilyassai had denied him until it was too late to matter.

The drums fell silent as the echoes of Imaro's wordless shout died away. The Mtumwe were silent as well. They gazed at Imaro as though he truly had fallen from the sky ... a being of wonder, but of danger as well.

Amid the crowd, one person caught Imaro's eye. It was a woman, of an age with Busa's father, Najimu. Imaro had noticed her before. From the deference with which she was treated by everyone—including Najimu, for all that he was chieftain—the woman was obviously a person of great importance in the *kijiji*.

Amulets carved from wood and bone were looped in myriad strings around her lean body, which was otherwise unclothed. During the entire festival, she had not spoken. And she had not taken her eyes off Imaro.

Earlier, Imaro had asked Busa who the amulet-clad woman was. Busa told him her name was Ariathu, and that she was the *nganga*—the shaman and diviner—of the Mtumwe.

On the surface, Imaro remained impassive upon learning that the Mtumwe harbored a person whose role was similar to that of the *oibonok* among the Ilyassai. Still, he found that knowledge disquieting, as was Ariathu's constant attention, and the evaluative glint in her eyes.

His dance done, Imaro made his way back to his place beside Najimu and Busa. As he sat down, the drumming began again, and the Mtumwe resumed their dancing. However, their movements were more subdued than they had been before. And many of the dancers stole glances at Imaro—glances that were a combination of curiosity … and fear.

Leaning over to Imaro, Najimu said, "You have shown us more than just a dance."

Imaro did not respond. His eyes searched for Ariathu. And her eyes were still on him.…

***

Imaro woke to sounds that were at once familiar and unfamiliar: the chatter of the Mtumwe as they went about their morning tasks, the yapping of dogs, the clucking of the guinea fowl the Mtumwe kept in place of cattle, the rhythmic clatter of poles on pestles as the women of the *kijiji* pounded vegetables into the paste that was the staple of the river people's diet.

When he opened his eyes, the sunlight that filtered through the thatch of the dwelling that had been set aside for him filled his vision. When he rose to his feet, the top of his head nearly touched the roof of the building.

Memories of the night before dominated his mind.

Thus, Imaro was not surprised to see Ariathu waiting for him when he emerged from the dwelling. With her were Najimu, Busa, and Msuli. All four Mtumwe bore solemn expressions on their faces.

In her hands, Ariathu carried an object Imaro had not seen the night before. It was a staff made from the wood of the ebony tree. Its surface was covered with carvings of spirits, as well as beasts that could exist only in the imagination. White feathers decorated its tip. The *nganga* used it as a walking stick—but it could easily be employed as a weapon as well.

The sounds of the *kijiji* had abated upon Imaro's emergence from the thatched dwelling. The people of the tribe gazed quietly at the huge, smooth-skinned form of the stranger from beyond the Kajua.

Imaro waited for one of the others to speak. It was Ariathu who broke the short silence.

"Man-from-afar, there is another among us who must greet you," she said in a low, almost masculine voice.

She turned and walked away then, not bothering to look back to see whether Imaro was following her. Her amulets rattled in rhythm with her stride as she walked. After a moment's hesitation, Imaro did, indeed, follow, with the other two men falling into step beside him.

No one spoke as the *nganga* led the way through the *kijiji*. The Mtumwe gazed at Imaro as he passed, but he could read nothing in their eyes. Imaro and the others followed Ariathu through a tangle of pathways between dwellings. The warrior noticed that the *kijiji* was far more extensive than it had appeared to be from the vantage of the riverbank. Finally, they stopped in front of a structure that was different from any other in the village.

It was smaller than the typical Mtumwe dwelling, and was open-sided, with its poles bent to form a thatch-covered arch at the top. But the structure was not what caught Imaro's attention. As the *nganga* drew him and the others closer, he blinked in the glare of sunlight reflected from the object the structure sheltered.

The occupant of the structure was an effigy, human in shape, but with inhuman proportions. Its torso was long and tubular; its limbs stubby; its head large, with grotesquely exaggerated features. Imaro could not discern the substance from which the effigy was made, for its entire surface was covered with bright spikes of gold that resembled the spiny hairs of a hedgehog. This was Imaro's first sight of the precious metal that incited avarice in the lands beyond both the Tamburure and the Kajua. To him, it looked like iron of a strange color.

Although the effigy was slightly more than half Imaro's height, it stood on a wooden pedestal that raised its head to a level with that of the warrior. A frieze of unfamiliar designs was incised deep in the pedestal's surface. Imaro looked directly into the face of the sculpture. The only part of it not pierced by the golden spikes was its eyes—blank, empty sockets that nonetheless seemed to stare back at Imaro.

As he continued to gaze into the large, round holes that were the effigy's eyes, Imaro began to experience a sensation similar to the one he had felt when he had been drawn against his will to the Place of Stones.

Is this mchawi? he thought in sudden unease. Just as he tore his gaze away from the darkness that beckoned in the effigy's eyes, Ariathu spoke.

"Man-from-afar, this is the Afua," she said. "It was here when the Mtumwe first came to this place, and it will be here after we are gone. Since we have been here, the Afua has brought us good fortune. Our fishnets are always filled. Our crops never fail. No enemy has ever attacked us."

She looked at Imaro again, in the same intense manner that had marked her observation of him during the festival of the night before.

"And it brought you, man-from-afar, to save Busa and Msuli from the jaws of Mjino. "The Afua welcomes you. The Mtumwe welcome you. I welcome you."

Imaro forced himself to look away from the Afua, and turn to the *nganga*.

No longer did she look at him appraisingly. He could still see a glint of curiosity in her eyes. But the skepticism was gone.

Imaro nodded once in acknowledgment of Ariathu's words. He was relieved when she led him and the others away from the Afua, and he resisted the temptation to look back at the gold-spiked effigy, even though he could sense the continued stare of its empty eye sockets. And he wondered what would have happened if the Afua had not "welcomed" him....

***

Imaro crouched behind a screen of foliage, spear shaft gripped tightly in one hand. His friends, Msuli and Busa, were there as well, although they were positioned out of his line of sight. Three other Mtumwe men hid nearby. All were involved in a hunt for the *bongo*, an elusive forest antelope valued for its hide, which was cinnamon-colored with delicate white stripes. Najimu had ordered the hunt because such a hide was needed for a complicated bargain with an upriver tribe.

A *bongo* hunt required much patience. But that was a quality Imaro was beginning to lose.

For two cycles of the moon, he had lived among the Mtumwe. During that time, he had learned a great deal about his hosts, and about the river and the woodland as well. No longer did he feel imprisoned by the gigantic trees that surrounded him. And the sounds of the forest were no longer alien to his ears. His *kufahuma*, the sense that attuned him to his surroundings, had been honed in the Tamburure. Now, it was beginning to adapt to his new environment. But his woodcraft remained rudimentary compared to that of the Mtumwe.

And about the Mtumwe, he had much still to learn. His adjustment to the *kijiji* and its people was proving to be more problematic than learning the ways of the woodland. His proficiency in the language of the river people had improved, but conforming to their culture was much more difficult, for their customs were those of farmers and fishermen, not the herders and warriors among whom Imaro had lived for most of his life.

It had not taken Imaro long to realize that the Ilyassai would have felt only contempt for the Mtumwe and the other tribes of the Damba Bolong—people without cattle, and therefore, without wealth; people who did not make war on their neighbors, and therefore were without courage. They would have wondered how such a people could have survived.

But had the Ilyassai not also disdained Imaro? And had Imaro not rejected them in the end?

Imaro shifted his position in the brush and, to his satisfaction, made no noise in doing so. He scanned the lush foliage for even the slightest sign of a *bongo*. But he saw nothing. And in truth, the hunt was not foremost on his mind. Even if it proved unsuccessful, Imaro was glad that Busa had suggested it, for it provided him a reason not to be in the *kijiji*.

His thoughts drifted to the women of the Mtumwe, with the decorative scarifications on their skin, and the endless variety of spikes and braids into which they sculpted their hair—hair that would have been absent from their heads, had they been living on the Tamburure.

More than a few of the Mtumwe women had cast gazes of admiration—and longing—in Imaro's direction, even though, or perhaps because, he was unlike any man they had seen before. And a familiar stir awakened within him as he looked at them in turn, for all that they would have seemed as out of place among the Ilyassai as a fish from the Damba Bolong on land.

But those stirrings were always circumscribed by an image that interposed itself like a barrier—the image of Keteke, and the Place of Stones.

A slight sound broke Imaro's reverie. He could not even be certain he had heard anything. But his *kufahuma* had stirred, and it told him the noise had not been made by a *bongo*, nor by any of his fellow hunters.

Imaro's muscles tensed, and his grip on his spear tightened as he listened for a repetition of the sound. Had any of the others heard it? He could not see them. If he called out to them, the Kajua would explode with the cries of birds, monkeys, and ground-dwellers, and if a *bongo* was indeed nearby, it would quickly disappear, and that would be the end of the hunt.

Now, though, his *kufahuma* was growing in urgency, and he could not discount the warning it was giving. The meat and hide of the *bongo* were no longer important; his sense of danger had not flared this intensely since his encounters with the *mchawi* of Chitendu and Muburi.

Rising from his hiding place, Imaro was about to cry out a warning when he heard a sharp exhalation of breath. Then he felt a sting at the side of his neck. Immediately, his blood turned into fire and his thews slackened. A moment later, he toppled and his spear fell away from nerveless fingers. Before his consciousness fled, Imaro saw several bushes detach themselves from the rest of the Kajua's foliage and move, as though they were walking.

And walking, indeed, they were. For the foliage was actually camouflage, maintained by sorcery, that served to conceal the presence of men who were, like Imaro, intruders in the Kajua. Now, more and more of them were appearing, as though conjured into existence by the same sorcery that had kept them hidden.

Some of the intruders stooped to examine Imaro and his fellow hunters, all of whom had fallen when the tiny darts the strangers had shot from blowpipes pierced their skin. The victims of the poison that had been smeared on the tips of the darts lay as though dead: eyes closed and limbs so slack they seemed boneless. But the slow rise and fall of their chests indicated that life, if not awareness, remained within them, if only tenuously.

The camouflaged intruders lingered over Imaro longer than they did any of the Mtumwe.

"Ever seen anyone like this one before?" one of them asked, his bare, brown arms visible as he gestured toward Imaro.

"No," another replied. "Bet he'd fetch a good price at the markets, though."

"Never mind that," a third intruder snapped in an authoritative tone.

The other two backed away deferentially.

"That's not what we're here for, and you know it," the man with the commanding voice continued. "Now, let's get moving."

The others pulled their arms back into their leafy concealment. Only hints of their bodies and weapons could be seen beneath the elaborate lattices of leaves and vines that covered them. Scores of ambulatory bushes began to move away from the place where the hunters had been brought down. It was as though part of the Kajua itself was on the march.

Soon, the last of them was gone, and Imaro and the other hunters were left behind, immobile and insensate.

***

Like a wave of foliage, the invaders made their way through the forest, toward the Mtumwe *kijiji*. They encountered no other villagers along the way, for Imaro and the others were the only ones who had ventured into the Kajua that day. They moved confidently, fearlessly, as though they believed nothing could harm them.

Despite their elaborate camouflage, the progress of so many intruders should have generated enough noise that they would have been heard long before they were seen. Yet their movements were almost soundless. And the wildlife of the Kajua fell silent as well at the outlanders' approach, as though even the insects had been ensorcelled by the magic that suffused their disguises.

When they reached the outskirts of the *kijiji*, the intruders waited until they had all gathered beneath the shadows of the huge trees that formed the village's boundary. The Mtumwe saw nothing, suspected nothing. Then, to their disbelief, the forest that was their home attacked them.

Like images from a nightmare, moving mounds of foliage descended upon the Mtumwe. Before any of them could fight or flee, they fell, even though no visible weapon had been directed against any of them. The invaders attacked relentlessly, coursing through the Mtumwe like lions in a herd of antelope.

The Mtumwe who had not crumpled to the ground, struck down by the unseen force the invaders wielded, swiftly succumbed to a panic that stole their wits. Men, women, and children alike howled in sheer terror as they fled in all directions—some into the forest, others to the riverbank and into dugouts that they paddled frantically downriver. The courage of even the bravest of the Mtumwe evaporated in the face of this sudden, unfathomable assault. It was *ujuju*—deadly, evil magic against which they had no defense.

The intruders allowed the villagers who had not fallen to escape, for their purpose was neither conquest nor the capture of slaves for the markets of the great cities of the coastal lands. Instead, they ranged impatiently among the dwellings in the *kijiji*, seemingly certain of what it was they hoped to find.

Their search ended when they came to the shrine of the Afua. There, they saw not only the gold-spiked statue, but also the only Mtumwe who was willing to remain behind to defy them: Ariathu, the *nganga*.

As she faced the intruders, Ariathu held her ebony staff in front of her, its tip pointed straight ahead in a warding stance. The staff did not waver in her grasp. If fear of the *ujuju* she faced lurked within her, she hid it well.

Ariathu glared at the intruders a moment longer. Then she thrust her staff forward, as though it were a spear. As the amulets at the tip of the staff rattled, the *nganga* spoke a single word in a strong voice:

"Begone!"

A sharp bark of laughter was the invaders' only response to Ariathu's command. Then, with a loud crack, her staff split in two, and the top section fell to the ground. Ariathu's eyes widened in shock, and her fear finally betrayed her. She opened her mouth to utter a cry of hopelessness. But before any sound could emerge, she felt a slight sting at the base of her throat, and she collapsed, as had all the other Mtumwe who bore the brunt of the invaders' assault.

Ignoring Ariathu's crumpled body, two of the camouflaged intruders approached the Afua. Slowly and carefully, they worked the statue free from its pedestal, a task complicated by the sharpness of the protruding golden spikes. Finally, they removed the Afua and laid it on a litter some of the others had constructed, commandeering their materials from the shrine.

Having seized the object of their search, the intruders began to make their way out of the *kijiji*. An eerie silence marked their departure, for even the dogs and the guinea fowl had fled when the outlanders came. As the intruders departed, one of them spoke to the person who was in charge of the others.

"I still say we should take that big one, too."

"But Rumanzila told us to bring back only *this*," the leader said, his arm emerging from his camouflage to gesture toward the Afua.

"Rumanzila did not know we would find anyone like that man here," the other said. "Have you ever seen anyone like him before? He would fetch more gold in the market than all these scarred-up people put together!"

The leader did not say anything.

"What do you think Rumanzila would do if he were here?" the other persisted.

That argument proved to be the decisive one.

"All right," the leader said. "We'll take him. But if Rumanzila doesn't like it—it was your idea."

"Fair enough," the first speaker conceded.

Thus, as the intruders departed from the territory of the Mtumwe, they paused at the place where Imaro still lay unconscious. There, they constructed another, larger litter, loaded Imaro onto it, and tied him to it securely with bonds made from woven liana vines.

Then they were gone, carrying both Imaro and the Afua with them.

***

A day and a night passed before the Mtumwe who had fled from the invaders' attack recovered sufficient courage to return to the *kijiji*. There, they found that the ones who had fallen to the unseen forces the intruders commanded were only beginning to awaken from what was, to them, a deep slumber plagued by dreams they hoped one day to forget.

Soon enough, the Mtumwe discovered that the Afua was gone. They found Ariathu sitting with her back against the pedestal that had supported the effigy. She stared vacantly at the broken halves of her staff. Only when the hands of many of her people reached down and helped her to her feet did she begin to regain her awareness, and her authority.

Some of the younger men remembered that a group of their comrades—including the newcomer, Imaro—had ventured into the forest on the day the forest itself attacked the *kijiji*. Spears in hand, a small group of men began to search for the missing hunters. The trail to the place where they had concealed themselves was not difficult to follow, and the searchers soon reached the fallen hunters, who were slowly recovering their senses.

Busa was the first of the still-dazed hunters to speak to the men who had come from the *kijiji*.

"Have you seen Imaro?" he asked.

"No," one of the others replied. "Was he not with you?"

"Yes. But he is not with us now."

Still moving gingerly, the hunters led the others to the place where Imaro had hidden in wait for the *bongo* that never came. Flattened foliage was the only indication the outlander had been there.

Then the men scoured the brush for any clue that would show where the warrior had gone. The ones who had come from the *kijiji* told the hunters about the mysterious and devastating attack they had endured the day before. At first, the hunters were incredulous, for they had not seen their own assailants. Bushes that moved as though they were walking? Invisible weapons that struck people down where they stood? And the Afua—*gone*?

Yet the hunters could not dismiss their own experiences. One moment, they had been lying quietly in wait for the *bongo*.... Then they felt a slight sting, like the bite of an insect.... And after that, they awakened a day later, feeling as though they had drunk too much *ndizi-pombe*. They knew the story the others told was not a tale inspired by drunkenness, or some story to frighten children. It was the truth—a truth that was more than sufficient to terrify adults.

Of Imaro, they found no sign. After they finally accepted that the search would be fruitless however long it lasted, the hunters and the others returned to the *kijiji*. There, they found that a *kijiji* council had already begun.

Ariathu had now recovered enough of her senses to fully assert her authority. And she was the only one among the Mtumwe to retain so much as a shred of respect, for other than the ones who had fallen at the initial assault, she, alone, had not fled the *kijiji*. Even the *mku*, Najimu, whose status was higher than that of the *nganga*, deferred to her now.

"We must recover the Afua," she was saying as the Mtumwe who had returned from the forest joined the others who were now gathered around the statue's empty pedestal.

Ariathu's words incited a chorus of consternation. Najimu was the one who voiced the questions that were on the minds of all.

"How are we to do that?" he demanded. "How are we to overcome *ujuju* that causes bushes to walk, and people to fall as though their bones have turned into water?"

"Find the man-from-afar, and you will find the Afua," the *nganga* said.

"Do you think Imaro has something to do with this?" Busa asked incredulously. "Do you think Imaro stole the Afua?"

Others echoed Busa's skepticism, none louder than Msuli. Ariathu remained calm amid the storm of protest. She did not speak again until it eased.

"The man-from-afar is gone," she said. "So is the Afua. Is that chance?"

"But the same *ujuju* that took away the Afua might also have taken Imaro," said Busa.

"Why?" Ariathu asked. "Why take both?"

Busa had no reply to that question. But he refused to acknowledge any possibility that the stranger who had saved his life could in any way be involved in the theft of the Afua. However, if Imaro had been captured by the wielders of such overwhelming power, then he was in danger comparable to what Busa and Msuli had faced when the crocodile attacked them.

"Ariathu," Najimu said, speaking for the first time since the council began. The *nganga* turned to acknowledge him.

"Even if our warriors find the ones who have taken the Afua—and Imaro—what could they do? What can anyone do against people—or spirits—who can do *that*?"

He pointed to the *nganga*'s shattered staff.

Ariathu remained imperturbable in the face of such stark evidence of her own inability to forestall the attackers' *ujuju.*

"I was not ready when they came," she said. "None of us were. Now, I will have the time to prepare a protection against any *ujuju* our warriors may encounter."

Then she turned to the crowd of people gathered at the shrine.

"We must regain the Afua," she said, her voice low and intense. "If we do not get it back soon, we will have to leave this place, for without the presence of the Afua, our crops will wither and our nets will be empty. Now, who will go to bring it back to our *kijiji*?"

"I will," Busa said without hesitation. He exchanged only the slightest of glances with his father, the chieftain.

"So will I," said Msuli.

Other voices joined those of the two who had first encountered Imaro. In all, a dozen of the *kijiji*'s bravest young men agreed to undertake the task of recovering the Afua.

It took the *nganga* another day to prepare the protections, which she fashioned in the form of amulets to be worn around the neck. In the meantime, she fitted the halves of her staff together again. The pieces slowly rejoined, like broken bones reknitting.

Then the day came when the Mtumwe sang farewell to the twelve warriors as they entered the Kajua, spears and *pangas* in hand, amulets bumping against their chests. And even as they sang, the people of the *kijiji* wondered if they would ever see these young men—or the Afua—again.

***

Far beyond the reach of any pursuit from the Mtumwe, the invaders emerged from the Kajua at a point that was on the opposite side from the place where Imaro had entered the forest. An unimaginably vast distance now lay between the warrior and the Tamburure. But Imaro did not yet know that. He remained securely trussed to the litter on which his captors carried him. And he also remained unconscious; whenever he stirred, one of the intruders would jab a dart into his neck, and his movements would subside.

The landscape through which the invaders now traveled contrasted sharply with both the Kajua and the Tamburure. It was a harsh-looking country: a land of thinly forested crags of rock interspersed with stretches of flatland covered by grass that was green, rather than the yellow of the Tamburure. A variety of beasts roamed the area, from giraffe to gnu. The animals gave a wide berth to the camouflaged men who had come from the forest.

When they had put a large amount of distance between themselves and the Kajua, the invaders halted and laid down the litters that held the Afua and Imaro. Then they discarded their disguises. Within moments, all that remained of the camouflage was piles of shrubbery on the ground.

The men beneath the disguises came from many nations and tribes in the lands east of the Kajua. Their skin tones ranged from amber to ebony, and their clothing was as varied as their complexions. They were outlaws: criminals, exiles, and escaped slaves who had banded together to prey on the wealthy kingdoms of the East Coast of Nyumbani. Although they, and others like them, were known by many names, the most common one was *haramia*—bandits. The leader of their band was Rumanzila, who was known far and wide as "the Ravager."

Never before had any *haramia* band ventured so far from the territory through which they normally ranged, moving from hideout to hideout, constantly pursued by the authorities of the lands they pillaged. But never before had the promise of riches been so immense. The golden-spiked idol Rumanzila's men now carried would be worth more to them than any other treasure they, or any other *haramia*, had ever stolen—of that, they were certain.

"I'm so glad to be out of this getup, and out of that damned jungle, too," one of the *haramia* said as he stretched his arms over his head.

The speaker was a brown-skinned man of medium height and stocky build, with a shaven head and a thick black beard that hid the bottom half of his face. His name was Mwenze, and he was the one who had suggested that the *haramia* bring Imaro out of the Kajua, along with the Afua.

"Me too," said another, a slightly built man named Chimba, whose skin had a yellowish cast. "I hope I never have to smell monkey turds again."

The others laughed raucously—with the exception of the one Rumanzila had chosen to lead the group that had gone into the Kajua. His name was Kongolo, and he was a squat boulder of a man whose skin was the same color as that of the river dwellers. But the scars his skin bore were not decorations; they were the marks of battle.

"I'm still not so sure about this one," he said, gesturing toward Imaro. "Something tells me we should have left him back there with the scar-faces."

"I've got a feeling Rumanzila will be glad we brought him," Mwenze insisted.

"You and your 'feelings,'" Kongolo muttered.

"We should get moving now," another voice said. "The longer it takes us to return, the more impatient Rumanzila will be. And I don't think any of us wants him to become impatient."

The attention of all the other bandits turned to the new speaker. His name was Angulu, and he was a *wa-nyanume*—a sorcerer of the highest rank—who had fled from the kingdom of Azania after his delving into forbidden arts was uncovered by rival magic users. Embittered by what he considered betrayal,

Angulu sought refuge among the *haramia*. Now, he was helping Rumanzila's band to gain ascendance over all the others.

Angulu had created the poison on the tips of the blow-darts the haramia had used to render Imaro and the people of the *kijiji* senseless. He had also cast a spell to enhance the effectiveness of the bandits' camouflage. And for him, it had been a simple matter to overcome the feeble sorcery that was all Ariathu could muster.

Kongolo was the nominal leader of the foray. But he, like all the others, deferred to the *wa-nyanume*.

Suddenly, the captive uttered a low groan and began to strain against his bonds. His eyes rolled beneath their lids, and the litter to which he was bound shifted as he rocked from side to side. Quickly, Angulu reached into his garment and pulled out a small, feathered dart. Its point pricked the skin at Imaro's throat, drawing a tiny bead of blood. Immediately, the warrior's struggles ceased.

"He's a strong one; I'll give him that," Kongolo muttered.

He could feel Angulu's gaze on him, even though he was not looking at the sorcerer.

"Let's move," he said curtly, still avoiding Angulu's eyes.

The *haramia* assigned to carry the litters hoisted their burdens, and the bandits resumed their trek through the rugged lands beyond the Kajua, heading toward the north and east.

***

Sometimes, Imaro knew he was dreaming. And when those times came, he tried to will the dreams to stop. But they never did. Then his awareness would fade, and he would slide back into an unquestioning acceptance of unreality....

He was at olmaiyo, *facing Ngatun the lion.... But this lion was many times larger than the one he had slain ... and Imaro himself was only a small child, as he had been when his mother, Katisa, left him with the Ilyassai, left him to fend for himself.... He was only a boy, and his hands were too small to fit around the shaft of the* arem, *and the shield was too heavy for him to lift.... Roaring like thunder, Ngatun sprang....*

He was battling N'tu-mwaa hand to hand, his forearm jammed against the sorcerer's throat to prevent the transformed, lionlike jaws from closing on his face ... but N'tu-mwaa was changing ... the pale spots on his skin were disappearing ... fur was sprouting on his body, and claws were growing in place of his fingernails....

Imaro was chasing his cow, Kulu, across a Tamburure empty of anything other than grass ... but this grass was different, unnatural.... Its edges were as sharp as the blade of a simi.... *They cut cruelly into his legs as he ran, but he could not stop.... Kulu could not stop running, either.... The* ngombe *drew farther and farther away from him, bawling in pain in a voice that seemed almost human....*

He was fighting Kanoko.... Death blazed in his rival's eyes, and sparks flew from the warriors' simis *as the blades clashed again and again.... Imaro beat down Kanoko's guard, and drove the point of his weapon deep into his tormentor's chest ... but Kanoko did not cry out, and his expression did not change, and when Imaro pulled his blade free, no blood flowed from the gaping wound....*

He was in the Place of Stones, held fast by the mchawi *of Chitendu.... The creatures that dwelt in the ruined edifice surrounded him.... Then the nameless creatures began to change ...and they became the Ilyassai.... Hatred contorted their features as they shouted abuse and epithets, as they had during the Shaming.... Suddenly, Chitendu himself appeared before him.... With a mocking laugh, the* oibonok *opened his cloak.... The tendrils that writhed along his torso glowed brighter ... and still, Imaro could not move....*

Sometimes, there were no images at all ... only blackness deeper than that of a starless, moonless night. Those were the times when Imaro came closest to regaining consciousness. It was then that he became dimly aware that he was bound, as he had been by the Turkhana, and as he had been by his own people when they believed he had displayed cowardice during his olmaiyo. *It was then that he struggled against bonds he could feel but could not see, only to be plunged once again into visions that were beyond nightmares.*

Then came a day when the blackness faded ... when his limbs felt as though flame ants were crawling through them ... when his senses registered the sensation of ropes tied tightly across his skin ...when he could, at last, open his eyes....

***

When Imaro's vision swam into focus, his first thought was that his dreaming had not yet come to an end. The last thing he remembered from waking life was crouching in the foliage near the *kijiji* of the Mtumwe, and then a sudden flaring of his *kufahuma*, followed by dream-haunted oblivion.

Now ...

He was no longer in the Kajua. He was in a place even more unlike the Tamburure than was the land of trees. This was a land of rocks: crags of red, yellow, and black stone that bit at the sky like the teeth of a giant. Scraps of foliage clung to the sides of the peaks; otherwise, this land was the most barren he had yet seen.

Despite the harshness of its landscape, however, this new place was inhabited. There were people on either side of Imaro, holding him upright. His bonds chafed against his skin, but that was the least of his discomforts. Hunger gnawed at his stomach, and his mouth was dry from thirst. The weakness of inactivity had depleted the strength in his limbs, and his head throbbed from the aftereffects of the poison that had kept him unconscious and immobile for so many days.

None of those ailments mattered to him now. His entire attention was claimed by the people who were gathered before him—people the like of whom he had never seen even in the most bizarre of the dreams that beset him while he was in the grasp of the poison.

The people stared at him and made comments to each other, speaking words Imaro did not understand. It was easy enough, however, for him to discern that his welcome among them would not be as friendly as the one he had received from the Mtumwe.

In appearance, these new people were diverse, with none resembling the inhabitants of either the Tamburure or the Kajua. Some were tall; others, as short as half-grown Ilyassai children. The complexion of most was a deep, umber brown, not unlike the color of Imaro's own skin. But some were as dark as midnight, and others had skin the color of cinnamon and amber. Some bore ritual scarification, though not as extensive as that of the Mtumwe.

The garments in which these people were clad were bewildering in their variety. Some wore trousers, called *suruali*, of white or black cotton; others wore loin-wraps. Some went naked above the waist; others wore vests of cloth, or leather harnesses studded with silver and gold. Turbans covered the heads of some; others wore their hair bushy or in rows of braids. Imaro was astonished to see that some of the men shaved their scalps as bare as those of the women of the Tamburure tribes.

There were women among these people, as well. Most wore only long, colorful skirts, with their upper bodies bare except for ornaments of beads and metal. A few, though, were clad in the garb of warriors.

All of the people who surrounded Imaro were armed. They carried swords, which to Imaro resembled oversized *simis*, as well as spears, daggers, cudgels, and bows—a weapon Imaro was seeing for the first time.

For all their diversity, the people among whom Imaro now found himself had one element in common. The eyes of each of them were cold and pitiless—like those of the Ilyassai and the other warrior-tribes of the Tamburure.

Beyond the crowd of people, Imaro could see what looked like a *boma* made from wood. In it were animals that resembled large zebras without stripes. He blinked to make certain the creatures were real rather than illusionary. Then he returned his attention to the people.

As the focus of Imaro's vision became clearer, certain individuals among the *haramia* made an impression upon him beyond the others, who became part of the background.

Directly in front of him stood a squat, extremely dark-skinned, heavyset man who was a head shorter than Imaro, but whose shoulders were nearly as wide as the Ilyassai's. Even though he was looking up, Kongolo's gaze locked onto Imaro's as though he were attempting to determine his measure as a man.

Angulu stood to one side of Kongolo. At the sight of the tall *wa-nyanume*, Imaro stiffened, for he could sense that this man was a user of sorcery. Although the evil of *mchawi* did not exude from Angulu as it had from Chitendu, Imaro was immediately wary of the *wa-nyanume*, in no small part because the Afua lay in a litter at Angulu's feet.

Imaro's gaze was then drawn to the tallest man he had ever seen—a man who overtopped him by as many inches as Imaro stood above Kongolo. The man's height was emphasized by his lean, almost cadaverous physique and the way he wore his hair—swept upward into a wooly peak like the crown of a king. His skin was as dark as charcoal, and the features on his long face were sharply chiseled, like those of the Ilyassai and the other tribes of the Tamburure. His long, red-and-white garment left one bony shoulder bare, again reminiscent of the Ilyassai.

Sympathy glimmered momentarily in the man's eyes as he looked at Imaro. His name was Ngodire, and he was an exile from the Ndashikuya, a people whose very existence was half legend and half reality.

As Imaro's gaze shifted, the peacock-like attire of another haramia caught his attention. The man stood only slightly above medium height, but carried himself as though he were much taller. Patterns woven in brilliant colors festooned his *suruali*, as well as his embroidered vest. A long, scarlet feather was set in a jewel at the front of his turban. His skin was sienna-colored, and his handsome features were highlighted by a thick, black moustache—a sight that disconcerted Imaro, for among the Ilyassai, facial hair was as frowned upon among men as head hair on women.

This was Bomunu, a minor nobleman from the coastal city of Zanj, whose underhanded plans to climb higher in the aristocracy had gone so badly awry that the *haramia* had been his only possible refuge. Among them, he had risen, standing second only to Rumanzila himself.

Then Imaro saw another man who was more than his match in girth, rather than height, although he was the Ilyassai's equal in that regard. A leather loincloth was the man's only garment; otherwise, his elephantine bulk was fully exposed. Rolls of cocoa-colored flesh spilled across his torso and limbs, but Imaro surmised that hard muscle lay buried beneath the flab.

The huge man's head seemed to grow directly out of his shoulders. The dark moon of his face was devoid of expression, and his small eyes stared vacantly. In his right hand, he held a whip as thick as a python. He carried no other weapon—he needed none.

His name was Mbuto. His wits were as small as his body was large, but he was as loyal as a dog to Rumanzila, whose side he seldom left. Mbuto could not speak, but he could hear and understand simple commands, such as "beat" and "kill."

Rumanzila was also a large man, standing nearly as tall as Imaro and Mbuto. But he was leaner in physique, like the people of the Tamburure. He was clad in the garments of a wealthy city-dweller, with *suruali* made from ivory-colored silk and an overshirt, or *shati*, and turban of the same fabric. A multitude of jeweled ornaments sewn into the cloth winked in the sunlight.

Rumanzila's skin was the color of umber, like Imaro's. A full beard covered the bottom of his face, and his hawkish features bespoke the blood of the foreigners who came from across the sea to trade in the coastal cities. But Rumanzila never discussed his origins, and none of the *haramia* dared to ask him about his parentage.

The bandit chief eyed Imaro appraisingly, as though assessing a livestock specimen or a piece of merchandise. Kongolo was not yet certain that Rumanzila would approve of his deviation from the orders he had been given. He had explained to Rumanzila why he thought the huge outlander would be valuable—there were many in the coastal cities who would pay huge sums of gold for a slave of such obvious strength and vitality.

Rumanzila remained noncommittal. At least, Kongolo thought, his leader had not, as yet, yet commanded Mbuto to kill him for failure to follow orders....

Then Rumanzila spoke. Imaro did not understand what the bandit leader was saying, but Kongolo translated, speaking in a garbled version of the river people's language that Imaro could barely understand.

"Who are you?" Kongolo translated. "Where do you come from?"

"I am Imaro," the warrior replied. "I come from ... the Tamburure."

The word "Tamburure" caused a ripple of whispers to run through the *haramia*. Some of the bandits had quizzical looks on their faces; others were incredulous, disbelieving.

Imaro spoke again, looking directly at Rumanzila rather than Kongolo.

"Who are *you*?" he demanded. "Why have you brought me here? Why did you steal the Afua from the Mtumwe?"

In reply, Kongolo drove his balled fist into Imaro's abdomen.

"*We* ask the questions here, not you," the *haramia* said. "Got it?"

Imaro said nothing, and betrayed no reaction to the blow he had received. Kongolo's first impulse was to hit him again. But he thought better of it, for his hand felt as though it had struck stone instead of flesh.

Rumanzila spoke again, at greater length this time.

"You are among the *haramia* of Rumanzila," Kongolo translated. "This is our country. Everything that is here belongs to us, including you—and *that*."

Kongolo's eyes strayed toward the Afua as he spoke.

"Do you understand?" the *haramia* asked.

Imaro did not reply. He was still disoriented. One moment, he was with the Mtumwe, among whom he had found the first friends he had ever known; the next, he had awakened among strangers—strangers who behaved like enemies, not friends. Strangers who behaved like the Ilyassai.

Mistaking Imaro's silence for insolence, Kongolo struck him again, this time with an open hand across the face.

"I said, *do you understand*?" Kongolo shouted, trying not to show the extent to which his hand stung from the impact of blow.

Imaro did not reply, and the expression on his face did not change. In the meantime, Bomunu had sidled over to Rumanzila, and now he was whispering urgently into the *haramia* leader's ear. Rumanzila frowned, as though he was about to dismiss what his underling was saying. Finally, and grudgingly, Rumanzila nodded.

Then the bandit chieftain spoke at length, forcing Kongolo to struggle to keep pace with his translation.

"I, Rumanzila, offer you a choice, outlander: join my *haramia*, or be sold as a slave. To join us, you must prove yourself worthy. And to prove yourself, you must endure twenty lashes on your back from the whip of Mbuto—with no outcry."

Kongolo then pointed in Mbuto's direction, to emphasize the stark nature of the choice Rumanzila offered.

Imaro frowned.

"This word, 'slave,'" he said haltingly. "What does it mean?"

For a moment, Kongolo was taken aback. When he translated Imaro's response to Rumanzila, a chorus of bitter laughter rose from the *haramia*—but not from Rumanzila.

"Explain it to him," Rumanzila said.

As Kongolo tried to define the concept of slavery with the few words of the river people's speech he knew, Imaro's eyes widened in incredulity. He could never have conceived or dreamed of the notion of one man belonging to another, like a weapon or piece of clothing. In the Tamburure, such a practice was unknown. But since his departure from the savanna, Imaro had encountered much that was unknown, and even unthinkable, to the people he had left behind.

He glanced at Mbuto, and at the thick whip in the *haramia*'s hand. Then the warrior looked directly at Rumanzila.

"I will join your *haramia*," the Ilyassai said.

A murmur rose from the crowd after Kongolo translated Imaro's words. This was not the first time the challenge had been accepted—but no one who had done so had lasted longer than ten lashes before shrieking in agony and begging Mbuto to stop.

"You mean, you will *try* to join us," Rumanzila said, amusement edging into his tone.

Kongolo repeated those words. Imaro's expression did not change.

***

As the assembled *haramia* looked on, the two who had been holding Imaro untied the ropes that bound him, while a third stood in front of him, with a sword pointed directly at the warrior's abdomen. Then the other two secured him to a slab of basalt in the encampment. His arms were spread wide and manacled to iron rings sunk deeply into the sides of the stone. He faced the black stone, and his broad back was exposed to offer the best target for the swings of Mbuto's whip.

Mbuto stood behind Imaro, stolid and inert as the stone of the whipping block. His eyes were no longer vacant; they gleamed avidly as he gazed at Imaro's back. Then Rumanzila's voice cut through the chatter of the crowd.

"Begin," he said.

Mbuto's massive arm rose high above his head. The thick whip wriggled as though it were alive in the harsh glare of the sun. Then, with deceptive speed, Mbuto's arm levered forward. His whip cracked loudly against Imaro's back and rebounded as though it had struck the trunk of an ironwood tree. Imaro neither moved nor cried out. But this was only the first lash.

Again and again, Mbuto's whip fell. By the tenth lash, the *haramia* began to murmur in disbelief, for no one else had lasted this long without crying out. Yet Imaro remained silent and motionless. The rigid thews of the warrior's back seemed to deflect the lashes, rather than absorb them.

Imaro's skin remained unbroken, for Mbuto's whip was not designed to inflict cutting blows. But thick welts were beginning to form on Imaro's back, and the smash of the whip against those swellings had to be agonizing. Yet Imaro remained silent. The only sound the crowd heard was the repeated smack of leather against flesh.

When the fifteenth lash landed, a recognizable expression appeared on Mbuto's face—a frown. By now, this stranger should have been a writhing, shrieking travesty of a man—or dead. But he was neither. It was as though the punisher were whipping the stone slab, rather than the man who was bound there.

Sweat dripped copiously from Mbuto's massive frame as he applied the whip with renewed fervor, grunting with the effort he exerted with each blow. When the twentieth lash landed with no outcry from Imaro, a spontaneous cheer erupted from the *haramia*. For they feared Mbuto no less than they did Rumanzila himself. The mute giant was a weapon their leader could turn against them at any time he desired.

"Stop," Rumanzila said sharply. He was speaking not only to Mbuto, but to the rest of the *haramia* as well, to quiet their cheers.

Mbuto's arm dropped, and the end of his whip dangled in the dust. His mouth hung open in disbelief, and his eyes seemed to bulge from his round face. The *haramia* fell silent.

"Free him," Rumanzila commanded.

The two *haramia* who had been guarding Imaro unlocked the manacles that bound the warrior to the stone. As they turned him to face the others, his knees sagged momentarily. Then he shook off the outlaws' grasp and stood erect. The price he had paid for his silence under Mbuto's lashes showed plainly on his face, for blood dripped from his lips, which he had bitten brutally to stifle any outcry—a tactic he had learned during *mafundishu-ya-muran*.

He looked first at Mbuto, then at Rumanzila. He spoke in a clear, strong voice. Then his legs would no longer support him, and the *haramia* beside him caught him before he fell.

"What did he say?" Rumanzila asked Kongolo.

The squat bandit shook his head in disbelief before replying.

"He said: 'Was that supposed to hurt?'"

Murmurs of astonishment and admiration rose from the crowd, and they continued even after Rumanzila glared angrily at his followers. Then he turned and vented his ire on the closest target: Bomunu.

"You *had* to insist that he be offered the Choice," Rumanzila said harshly. "Now, he is one of us, and we've lost the profit we would have made by dealing him to the slave markets!"

"If we had not offered him the Choice, the others would have noticed, and wondered why we didn't," Bomunu said calmly. "How was I to know this man would prove to be stronger than Mbuto's whip?"

Rumanzila eyed the Zanjian for a long moment.

"This Imaro is your responsibility now," the bandit chieftain said. "Teach him how to speak our language, and show him what he needs to know to be a *haramia*. And do it fast."

"As you wish," Bomunu said.

But as Bomunu approached the semiconscious Ilyassai, he allowed himself a brief, secretive smile. For events had turned out almost exactly as he, not Rumanzila, had desired.

***

Imaro's hand tightened on the hilt of his sword. His horse snorted and shook its head. Imaro leaned forward and spoke soothingly to his mount, much as he would have spoken to a restive *ngombe*. Immediately, the horse calmed. Then Imaro sat erect in his saddle, and scanned the horizon of the rocky landscape before him. In the distance, he could discern a tiny puff of dust.

"They come," he said.

The *haramia* who were with him looked in the same direction, using their hands to shade the sun from their eyes.

"Where are they?" demanded Chimba, who had been among the *haramia* who had brought Imaro out of the Kajua. The yellowish man had taken an active dislike to the outlander, and he did not bother to conceal it.

Imaro didn't answer him.

"I see nothing," Chimba grumbled, his face set in a scowl.

"If Imaro says it's there, it's there," said Kongolo.

Chimba responded with a wordless snort.

Kongolo looked at Imaro and shrugged, a gesture Imaro did not return. Unlike Chimba, Kongolo had come to admire the Ilyassai, as did most of the rest of the outlaw band. Imaro had first earned their respect by enduring Mbuto's blows without any outcry, and later by his quickness at mastering the speech of the eastern people, as well as the ways of the *haramia* and new skills, such as riding a horse. And the outlander's ferocity in battle had won their awe. The loot they had gathered since Imaro had joined their ranks more than compensated for the loss of the price he would have brought from the slavers.

Other than Chimba, the only *haramia* who genuinely disliked Imaro were the sorcerer, Angulu, who was in turn disliked by Imaro; Mbuto, whose normally blank expression turned into a scowl whenever Imaro went near him; and Rumanzila, who hated Imaro because he knew the warrior was the only one among the *haramia* who did not fear him. And that lack of fear made Imaro dangerous.

"I see them, too, said Ngodire, the Ndashikuya, whose vision was nearly as keen as Imaro's.

Moments later, all of the *haramia* saw the growing cloud of dust that approached the valley in which they were concealed. Kongolo, who was in charge of the bandits' latest raid, gave them a signal with his hand. Steel sang as the *haramia* drew their weapons from sheaths and scabbards.

Imaro eyed the blade of his sword. The metal from which it was made was much sharper than the iron smelted by the people of the Tamburure. So much was different.... Had anyone among the Ilyassai or the Mtumwe seen him as he was now, they would have had difficulty recognizing him. Indeed, Imaro would have had trouble recognizing himself.

Bright crimson *suruali* encased his legs. Above the waist, he wore nothing other than a leather strap that held the sheath of his sword. His hair was cropped close to his head. His eyes smoldered with dark intensity, as they had when he began his *olmaiyo*.

Imaro never thought he would one day ride the back of a beast like a tick-bird perching on a rhinoceros. Nor did he imagine he would live among outlaws, plundering the wealth and property of others in the same way that the Ilyassai stole the cattle of neighboring tribes. Cattle were the only objects of value he had ever known. Now, he was discovering there was more that people treasured—much more.

What satisfied him most about his life among the bandits was that when he rode on raids, or battles against rival *haramia* bands, he could forget the words Chitendu had spoken in the Place of Stones; and he could forget the presence of malign, unseen foes; and forget that he did not know where, or how, to seek out those enemies and deal death to them.

Imaro concentrated on the dust cloud, which was drawing closer. Shapes could now be seen in its swirls—the shapes of riders.

The *haramia* were at the top of a defile that cut into a valley of stone. Multicolored strata brightened the sides of the valley, as though the stone had been painted by the brush of a god. At Kongolo's command, the bandits began to descend the defile. When they reached the bottom, they remained hidden by outcrops of rock. There, they awaited their prey.

Before long, the riders arrived—armed men, clad in leather armor decorated with beads and cowrie shells. Plumes sprouted from the helmets that protected their heads.

Peacocks, Imaro thought. *Like Bomunu.*

The Zanjian was courteous enough to Imaro on the surface, and had taught the warrior a great deal during the days that followed Imaro's acceptance into the ranks of the *haramia*. But he detected a different undercurrent in Bomunu's attitude toward him: a touch of disdain and condescension.

Bomunu had been away from the *haramia* for a time. He was in the faraway kingdom of Kundwa, negotiating payment for the Afua with the rogue sorcerer who had hired Rumanzila's bandits to steal it for him. Rumanzila had raised the price, knowing that the sorcerer's lust for the effigy would overcome his outrage over the prospect of giving up more gold in return.

Among the riders, Imaro noticed one who was different from the rest—covered from head to foot in a dusty, white garment, called a *kuva*, that left only a slit for the rider's eyes. The hands of this closely guarded rider were tied securely to the front of the saddle. Armed men flanked the mysterious figure.

The shrouded rider was the target of the *haramia*. Rumanzila's spies had told him that a nobleman of Bomunu's home kingdom, Zanj, had bought a woman from the Shikaza, a remote people renowned for the beauty of its female members and the timidity of its males, for his seraglio. But another noble from the neighboring kingdom of Azania had offered a huge bounty for anyone who could obtain the Shikaza woman for him—and that was a bounty Rumanzila was determined to win.

Kongolo counted the Zanjian soldiers as they clattered past. Some of them looked toward the opening of the defile, but between the shadows cast by the rocky outcrops and the dust the soldiers' mounts raised, the bandits were all but invisible.

After the last soldier went by, Kongolo turned to Imaro.

"Not very many of them, are there?"

Imaro nodded agreement. In truth, however, the soldiers escorting the Shikaza woman outnumbered the *haramia* by nearly two to one. But the *haramia*'s advantage of surprise would outweigh those odds—or so they hoped.

Quietly, the bandits emerged from concealment and rode behind the Zanjians. The hoofbeats of the *haramia*'s horses blended with those of the soldiers' mounts. The *haramia* quickly closed the gap between them and the Zanjians, and only the sudden sound of bodies falling to the ground after swords pierced through flesh alerted the Zanjians that they were under attack.

Then the chaotic sounds of combat overwhelmed the clatter of hoofbeats. Steel clanged against steel; *haramia* and soldiers alike cursed and cried out as blades struck their targets; horses neighed in fright and fury; and more bodies crumpled to the ground to be trampled by flying hooves.

The Zanjians' numerical superiority over the bandits vanished with startling swiftness. Before the soldiers could defend themselves effectively, nearly half of them were cut down. To the greater disadvantage of the Zanjians, a number of them were needed to guard the Shikaza woman, and to prevent her horse from bolting with her bound helplessly to the saddle. The woman's horse danced nervously as the fighting raged around her.

Imaro accounted for more Zanjians than anyone else in the raiding party. The Ilyassai's sword streaked like a steel lightning bolt, shattering the weapons of his adversaries and slashing through the leather of their armor as though it were mere cloth. The other *haramia* followed his lead more than they did Kongolo's, but Kongolo took no offense, for he knew no slight was intended. Like all the *haramia*, he was well aware that the best place to be in a battle was at Imaro's side—and the worst place to be was in front of him.

Before long, only the Zanjians who were guarding the shrouded woman remained alive. And it was time then for Kongolo to assume his position of leadership for the raid. Riding slowly toward the Zanjians, he spoke to the one who appeared to be in charge of the remnants of the escorts.

"Throw down your weapons, and we will allow you to live," he said in passable Zanjian. "It is the woman we want, not you."

The Zanjian leader, a lean man whose mustache bristled like the quills of a hedgehog, let out a short bark of mirthless laughter.

"You know full well, bandit, that if we return to Zanj without the Shikaza woman, we will pay for that failure with our lives," he said.

"Then don't go back," said Kongolo. "Join us, and live in freedom."

The officer spat on the ground, as did the rest of the surviving soldiers.

"Better to die with honor than to live as a thief," he said.

And with a cry that could have been a prayer or a curse, the Zanjian spurred his horse forward and swung his bloodied blade at Kongolo's skull. The *haramia* barely had time to lift his own weapon in time to parry a stroke that would have separated his head from his shoulders. Following their commander's lead, the other soldiers charged into the bandits, slashing in a blind frenzy as though madness had claimed them.

The ensuing combat was short but savage, with the *haramia* prevailing in the end. But another *haramia* fell before the last of the Zanjians died. That brought the bandits' death toll to four, and Kongolo knew he would have to answer to Rumanzila for that loss. He also knew, however, that even more *haramia* would have been killed had Imaro not been among them.

In the meantime, some of the bandits had surrounded the Shikaza woman. The hand of one was clamped firmly on the bridle of her horse. With her hands bound, the woman could not have escaped, but the *haramia* had wanted to make certain that her horse did not bolt after the Zanjians abandoned her. Through the eye-slit of her *kuva*, the woman's gaze was unreadable.

Kongolo addressed her in a harsh, peremptory tone.

"You are going to a different destination," he said. "If you do not give us any trouble, there will be no trouble for you. Understood?"

"Understood," said the woman, her voice muffled by the cloth that covered her mouth.

She spoke to Kongolo—but she was looking at Imaro. If the warrior noticed the direction of her gaze, he gave no sign. In truth, he was thinking not of the captive, but of a word the Zanjian officer had spoken, a word he had not heard before: "honor." He wondered if its meaning of it was the same as the Way of the Warrior, the stiff-necked integrity of the Ilyassai.

At a word from Kongolo, the *haramia* rode back up the defile, with the Shikaza woman in tow. They left their dead companions behind, along with the corpses of the proud Zanjians.

***

Jua hung low in the sky as the bandits returned to Rumanzila's latest hideout. It was, as always, located in an area that would be difficult for rival *haramia* bands, or the authorities of the kingdoms on which they preyed, to locate. The current encampment was in a wooded area, in territory that was part of the disputed borderland between Zanj and Azania. However, the remote area was so unsuitable for farming or herding that neither kingdom made much of an effort to enforce its claim. Few people dwelled in the region, and those who did gave the bandits a wide berth.

Even though darkness had not yet fallen, some of the *haramia* were already erecting their sleeping shelters, which consisted of lengths of cloth draped over a framework of poles lashed together with twine.

As Kongolo and his riders clattered into the encampment, a cheer rose from the *haramia* who had remained behind, for the sight of the shrouded Shikaza woman signaled that the raid had been successful. At the sight of the four riderless horses led by the bandits at the rear of the column, however, the celebration wavered. Four comrades had been lost—rivals and competitors in the sharing of the loot, but comrades nonetheless.

As their fellow bandits gathered around them, the raiders dismounted. Kongolo untied the hands of the Shikaza, and helped her down from her horse. Then, while the raiders boasted of their prowess in overcoming a far larger number of Zanjian soldiers than they had actually confronted, Rumanzila approached them. And all conversation ceased.

Mbuto was at Rumanzila's side, a place from which he seldom strayed. The big man's face remained impassive, and the ever-present whip hung motionless in his hand. When Mbuto looked at Imaro, however, the whip moved in a slight twitch that only those who were sharp of vision could detect.

Imaro saw it. And he touched the hilt of his sword lightly in response. If Rumanzila was aware of the subtle exchange between Imaro and Mbuto, he gave no indication.

"You have the woman," Rumanzila said to Kongolo. "That's good."

Then he turned his attention to the four riderless horses, and a frown creased his brow.

"But you lost four men. That's not good."

"One of them was Mwenze," Kongolo said.

A glimmer of sympathy appeared for a moment in Rumanzila's eyes. Mwenze, who had been with Kongolo during the journey to steal the Afua, had been Kongolo's best friend, and among the *haramia*, such friendships were difficult to find. Then Rumanzila's eyes hardened again.

"Mwenze and the others were your responsibility, Kongolo," he said. "When the Azanian pays our price for this woman, your share will be … nothing."

Kongolo nodded acceptance. His punishment could have been far worse. Rumanzila could have decided that Mbuto's whip was necessary to remind Kongolo, and the others, of the consequences of failure.

Rumanzila turned his attention to the Shikaza woman, who stood before him like a dust-shrouded apparition from the Bush of Ghosts—the afterlife.

"What's your name?" he demanded.

"Tanisha," the muffled voice replied.

"Well, Tanisha, you are a very valuable woman," Rumanzila said. "So valuable, in fact, that a certain nobleman of Azania is willing to pay more for you than the Zanjian who bought you in the first place. The Azanian hired us to … secure the transaction."

A sound that might have been either a gasp or a snort of laughter came from beneath the *kuva*. Rumanzila frowned, then continued.

"Zanjians can be clever, though," he said. And he shot a glance at Bomunu, who smiled in return.

"How am I to know that you are truly the Shikaza woman who is so much desired by both the Zanjian and the Azanian?" Rumanzila continued. "You could be a decoy, and the actual woman of the Shikaza could be safely in Zanj by now."

Now a sardonic grin replaced his previous scowl.

"I am, of course, well aware that according to the customs of your people, no one is permitted to look upon you before you are delivered to the one who has bought you. But surely you can understand why that custom must be broken now, so that we can be certain you really are a woman of the Shikaza."

Tanisha said nothing in response. Rumanzila's scowl returned.

"Remove your *kuva*," he said, a dangerous edge creeping into his tone. "Or we will remove it for you."

"As you wish," Tanisha said.

Bending forward, she took the hem of her garment in both hands. Then, in a single, deft motion, she stood upright, pulled the *kuva* over her head, and let it fall to the ground behind her.

Sharp intakes of breath greeted the sight of what the all-enveloping garment had concealed.

Tanisha was tall for a woman. Her obsidian-black skin gleamed in the sunlight. Two long, narrow rectangles of pale-yellow silk hung from a chain of gold looped low around her waist: one in front of her, the other behind. The translucent rectangles were her only garment, other than the strands of gold that circled her neck, arms, and ankles. Golden hoops hung from her ears, and studs of the same metal pierced her navel and the tips of her large, round breasts.

Her waist was so narrow that Imaro could have circled it with both his hands. So could Mbuto. Her hips, however, were far from narrow, arcing from both sides of her scanty garment.

A cloud of wooly, black hair framed Tanisha's face. Full lips parted beneath her nose, showing a flash of white teeth. Her midnight eyes gazed with amusement at the dozens of wide *haramia* eyes that goggled back at her.

After seeing her, the *haramia* knew that the tales of the beauty of Shikaza women were true. Only the snorts of the horses and the shuffle of feet and hooves against the ground broke the silence that had descended after Tanisha removed her *kuva*.

It was Tanisha who ended the moment.

"Have you seen enough?" she asked Rumanzila.

"Yes," the bandit chieftain replied. "Put your *kuva* back on."

Tanisha smiled again—a dazzle of teeth that captured the sunlight. Then she shook the dust from her *kuva* and shrugged it back over her head, again in a single motion.

"Chimba," Rumanzila said, turning to the small, yellowish man. "Go and tell the Azanian we have what he wants. And because we lost four men in obtaining the Shikaza for him, the price has now doubled."

Nodding his acknowledgment of the command, Chimba mounted his horse and rode out of the encampment.

Rumanzila then rattled off a series of other orders. Tanisha was to be given her own shelter, and would be guarded at all times. No *haramia*, man or woman, was to touch her until she was delivered to the Azanian—unless it was to prevent her from escaping from the hideout. No harm was to come to her while she was among the *haramia*.

"Anyone who disobeys will answer to Mbuto," Rumanzila concluded.

The mountainous man beside him twitched his whip. All the rest of the bandits—except Imaro—trembled inwardly at the thought of Mbuto's lashes thudding into their flesh. Quickly, they dispersed, two of them leading Tanisha away.

Rumanzila had noticed something when the Shikaza woman had turned away. He had seen her looking at one person among the *haramia*, and it hadn't been him. Through the eye-slit of her *kuva*, she had been gazing at Imaro.

Rumanzila's scowl deepened.

***

Night had fallen. In the encampment, everyone was asleep, except the sentries—and Rumanzila and the *wa-nyanume*, Angulu. They sat beside a small fire in front of Rumanzila's shelter. Angulu's face bore an expression of concern. Rumanzila's did not. Both men sipped from cups of palm wine.

"I do not like this waiting," the sorcerer said. "We're going to be in one place for far too long a time."

"The risk is high," Rumanzila agreed. "But the reward will be worth it."

"More loot to share with rogues?" Angulu asked.

Rumanzila stared at him a long moment before replying. Angulu hid his sudden discomfort. Of all the *haramia*, he was the only one who could speak to Rumanzila without deference. Because Rumanzila respected his skill at sorcery, Angulu could, with impunity, give the chieftain blunt advice and, sometimes, even contradict him. But perhaps he had now crossed a dangerous boundary.

"There's more to it than that," Rumanzila finally said. "And I thought you, of all people, would see it. Neither you nor I wish to spend the rest of our lives robbing caravans and sacking villages. With the gold we will receive for the

Shikaza and the idol, we can begin the work of carving out our own kingdom in this wasteland—a kingdom that will one day cause Zanj and Azania and Kundwa to tremble at the sound of its name. It will be a kingdom worthy of my heritage, for it is the blood of the *rajas* from the Lands across the Sea that flows in my veins—not the blood of bandits and beggars!"

Firelight glinted in the bandit leader's eyes—firelight, and the flame of ambition. For all his knowledge of the darkest sorcerous arts, Angulu feared Rumanzila at times such as this—moments when the man's true face showed, rather than the impassive mask he wore most of the time.

Angulu knew Rumanzila's father was no *raja*. He was a sailor on one of the ships that came from the Lands beyond the Sea to trade in the ports of the East Coast. After seducing a merchant's daughter and leaving her with child, he had sailed away with his ship. The merchant had cast his daughter away, and as a child, Rumanzila had, indeed, been a beggar in the streets of Mugishu after his mother had died. He had suffered many indignities before he became strong enough to repay them in kind. When the ships came from across the sea, he had haunted the docks, searching for the man who had sired him. But he had never found him, and he was never certain what he would have done if he had.

When Rumanzila grew to manhood, he had joined the Azanian army. But he deserted after killing an officer who had disparaged Rumanzila's half-caste ancestry. He became a *haramia*—a *raja* of outlaws.

Rumanzila had told none of this to the *wa-nyanume*, or any other *haramia*. But Angulu knew.

"Bomunu is taking a long time to return," the sorcerer said, hoping to steer Rumanzila's thoughts elsewhere. "Do you suppose he—"

"Has betrayed us?" Rumanzila finished, letting out a short laugh.

"Would you put it past him?" Angulu asked.

"No," Rumanzila said. "That one will betray me, one day. But not yet. He will wait until I have done all the work of building before claiming it for his own. I know his kind all too well, whether they're from Azania or Zanj."

Rumanzila spat into the fire. Then he took a long swallow of palm wine.

"Bomunu may think he is the greatest threat to you," Angulu said. "But he is wrong, as you know all too well."

"Who is it, then, that I 'know' to be so dangerous?" Rumanzila asked, his voice deceptively soft.

"Imaro," Angulu said.

Rumanzila's eyes narrowed.

"That one?" he said scornfully. "He has no ambition to lead. All he wants to do is fight and kill—which he does better than most, I'll grant you. But it takes more than that to make a leader."

"Still," Angulu said, "the men—and women—respect him. And there is also this to consider: among all the *haramia* who ride with us, only Imaro has no fear of Mbuto. And he is the only one who has no fear of you."

"That's still not enough to make him a leader," Rumanzila said stubbornly.

"No. But it could make him an effective weapon in the hands of one who *is* a leader—or would like to be."

"What do you mean?" Rumanzila asked.

"It was, perhaps, a mistake for you to put Bomunu in charge of the newcomer," said Angulu. "Bomunu would like Imaro to become to him what Mbuto is to you. Of course, Bomunu is no match for you. But Imaro is more than a match for Mbuto, and I think you know that."

Rumanzila did not say anything. Again fearing he had gone too far, the *wa-nyanume* spoke on.

"During my studies, I learned of far-off places," he said. "And I saw maps that were old before the time of our grandfathers' grandfathers. I remember seeing this 'Tamburure' Imaro says he comes from on one of those maps. It is almost as far away over land as the traders' country is over the sea. And I read of a fierce, savage people called the Ilyassai—Imaro's people. According to the stories, an Ilyassai youth must slay a lion single-handed before he can be counted as a man. Imaro certainly looks as though he could have done that."

Rumanzila snorted in derision.

"I have one more test for this lion-slayer," he said.

"What would that be?" Angulu asked.

Instead of responding directly, Rumanzila asked a question of his own.

"Why are you so anxious to get rid of the river people's idol?" he demanded. "Are you afraid of it?"

"Yes," the sorcerer replied without hesitation.

The two men said little more before Angulu rose and went to his shelter. Rumanzila sat alone for a long time afterward, staring into the fire.

***

"Imaro."

The warrior recognized the voice that called to him as he sat in front of his shelter. He was using a stone to whet the blade of his sword. With its greater length and steel blade, this weapon suited him far better than the Ilyassai *simi*.

Imaro looked up, tilting his head back farther than usual. Standing in front of him was Ngodire, the Ndashikuya. With the hand that held the whetstone, Imaro motioned Ngodire to sit near him. As Ngodire lowered himself to the ground, with his long legs folded, he resembled a gigantic mantis. Awkward as the Ndashikuya's position appeared, however, Imaro knew Ngodire was capable of springing to his feet, weapon in hand, with a quickness that rivaled the Ilyassai's own.

Even in a seated position, Ngodire still looked down on Imaro. He was the only one among the *haramia* who could do that. Patiently, Imaro waited for the other man to speak further.

The silence between the two men was companionable. Theirs was a friendship born of similar circumstances, for among the *haramia*, they were the outsiders. At the beginning of his time among the bandits, Imaro found that Ngodire was the only one who treated him in a way that did not bring back memories of his time among the Ilyassai.

But there was a sharper edge to Ngodire as well, as Imaro had discovered when he asked the Ndashikuya how he had managed to withstand the Choice.

Ngodire had laughed derisively.

"The Choice is only for captives, like you," he said. "I was no captive. I am here because this is where I belong. I stole treasure from my country's king, and I barely escaped with my life. I came to the *haramia* because a thief should be with other thieves."

Then he had given Imaro a long, penetrating gaze.

"You belong among warriors, not thieves," he said. "One day, you will understand that."

Now, in a low tone that barely carried above the noises of the encampment, Ngodire said a single word.

"Beware."

Imaro made a sound that was not quite a laugh.

"That is what I've been doing all my life," he said.

"This is different," said Ngodire.

"How?"

The Ndashikuya shifted his eyes away from those of Imaro. Following the direction of Ngodire's gaze, Imaro saw the shrouded form of Tanisha. The Shikaza captive was guarded lightly, but guarded nonetheless, usually by at least two *haramia* women. Tanisha and her warders stood a fair distance from Imaro and Ngodire. But from the position of the eye-slit in her *kuva*, Imaro realized that she was looking in his direction.

Imaro turned his attention back to Ngodire and gave him a look that asked an unspoken question.

"That one has been watching you ever since we captured her," Ngodire said.

"And that's what I should beware?" Imaro asked.

"Rumanzila has been watching you, too."

Imaro's only response to that observation was a tightening of his grip on the whetstone.

"What do his eyes have to do with hers?" he demanded.

"I do not know," Ngodire admitted. "I see only what I see. It is up to you to see more—if you want to."

"If I do see more, I will have you to thank," Imaro said.

Ngodire nodded. Then he rose to his feet in a single motion and left Imaro to his sword and whetstone.

Imaro thought about what the Ndashikuya had said. From the time he had withstood Mbuto's lash without crying out, Imaro had known he needed to be wary of Rumanzila. The bandit chieftain reminded him of Chui the leopard, lying in wait, hidden in the tall grass.

But the woman …

He stole a glance in Tanisha's direction. She had not moved, and neither had the *haramia* who guarded her. She was still looking at him.

***

Several days passed with no sign of either Bomunu or Chimba. Like their leader, the *haramia* were becoming even more restless. The iron discipline Rumanzila maintained was beginning to show cracks, though no one was yet so blatant as to require a session with Mbuto.

One night, as he lay on the grass sleeping mat in his shelter, Imaro once again compared the *haramia* to the Ilyassai. He was beginning to believe the two were not as similar as he had first thought. Although Ilyassai warriors respected leaders like the Kitoko clan's *ol-arem*, Mubaku, they did not fear them, as the bandits did Rumanzila. And although Masadu dispensed painful punishments during warrior training, he was not a mindless tool, like Mbuto.

Imaro had long since been aware that Rumanzila considered his lack of fear as a lack of respect. And he knew Rumanzila believed that others would eventually emulate Imaro's disrespect, and that that would lead to the bandit leader's downfall. And who did Rumanzila think would take his place? The newcomer, the warrior, the man who had withstood Mbuto's lash …

What Rumanzila did not know was that Imaro had no desire to usurp the leadership of the *haramia*. Indeed, the warrior was considering leaving the band of outlaws.

His dreams of the Place of Stones were becoming more frequent. The names Chitendu had spoken echoed through his mind, even when he was awake. Although he did not sense any presence of the type of *mchawi* Chitendu had wielded, he was beginning to believe the enemies of which the *oibonok* had spoken were somewhere, somehow, hunting him. He should be the one hunting them, he thought. But how was he to find them?

He remembered what Ngodire had told him: *You belong among warriors….*

A slight sound interrupted Imaro's musings. It came from outside his shelter. As he looked toward the narrow entrance of the makeshift structure, he saw a moon-shadow on the ground.

With the stealth and speed of a panther, Imaro rose from his sleeping mat, reached outside, and pulled the intruder into the darkness of the shelter. Imaro expected a struggle; he expected teeth to tear into the hand he had clamped over the intruder's mouth. But that did not happen. The intruder did not move.

Although he could not be entirely certain of the identity of the person he held in his arms, Imaro believed he knew who it was. At the very least, he knew it was a woman.

"You are the one called Tanisha," he said in a low voice. "The one we captured from the Zanjians."

The woman nodded her head.

"I'm going to take my hand away from your mouth," Imaro said. "Then I'll decide what I am going to do with you. Do not cry out. Understand?"

Tanisha nodded again. Imaro removed his hand. Tanisha's mouth opened, but only to take a gasping breath, not to scream. Then, with a subtle twist for which Imaro was not prepared, she turned her body to face the warrior—and her mouth found his. Her hands caressed the hard muscles of his shoulders, and she pressed her gold-bedecked skin against his.

Imaro's arms tightened around Tanisha as their tongues danced. For a single, frightful moment, the image of Keteke as he had last seen her flashed through his mind. Then it was gone, banished by the taste of Tanisha's mouth and the scent of her skin.

But another vision entered unbidden into his mind—the face of Rumanzila, laughing....

Abruptly, Imaro pulled his mouth away from Tanisha's.

"Who sent you to me?" he demanded. "Guards are at your side day and night. You could not have gotten away from them on your own."

Tanisha let out a laugh that was almost inaudible. Then, even though Imaro was holding her in a tight grasp, she wriggled free before he could react. But she made no attempt to escape. She remained in front of Imaro, kneeling in the darkness, her shape a silhouette among shadows.

"The guards are fools," she said. "They see my *kuva*, and think they see me."

She laid her hand against the warrior's chest.

"No one sent me, Imaro," she said. "I am here because I want to be."

"Why?" Imaro demanded.

Tanisha did not reply immediately. As the silence stretched, Imaro's suspicions grew ... as did his desire. Then Tanisha spoke.

"Among my people, women are trained from birth to serve men, to please men … to know men," she said. "We of the Shikaza are a small tribe, a weak tribe. But we are also a free tribe, because we trade our women in exchange for safety. To the outsiders, a Shikaza woman is worth more than her weight in gold or jewels."

Her hand slid across his skin as she spoke.

"The Shikaza women are taught something else as well," she continued. "We are taught that no matter how many men buy us, and use us, there will be, for each of us, one man to whom we will truly belong, whether or not he buys us. For me, that man is you. And I knew that from the moment I saw you, even though you came to steal me from the men of Zanj."

Imaro could barely think, let alone say anything in response. In all his life, no one had spoken of him in this way—for the most part, what he heard was the opposite. Yet now, a woman over whom bandits and solders were willing to fight and die, and for whom treasures were traded as though they were trinkets, was prepared to risk all her value to give herself to him.

And he desired her more than he ever had wanted Keteke. Tanisha's presence had already helped him to begin to overcome the guilt that had eaten at him since Keteke's death.

But still …

"You do not know me," he said. "You do not know who I am, or what I must face."

"Tell me," said Tanisha.

And, to his surprise, he did exactly that. He spoke of his past in a way he never had before. He told her about his life among the Ilyassai; about *olmaiyo*; about his encounter with Chitendu at the Place of Stones; about the unseen, unknown menace of the sorcerers of Naama and the Place of Stones.…

After he finished, Tanisha murmured: "Naama … Mashataan … I have heard those names before."

Imaro's hand tightened around her wrist. If the pressure of his grasp was painful, Tanisha did not acknowledge it.

"What do you know about those names?" he demanded.

"Only this," Tanisha replied. "Those names are so evil that they must be spoken only in whispers … so that they do not echo in the ears of those who should not hear them."

Imaro relaxed his grasp.

"Now you know I have enemies who are worse than Rumanzila," he said.

"Yes. But Rumanzila is the enemy you can see and touch," Tanisha said. "And with him, you have but one choice: kill him before he kills you, or leave the *haramia*. If you stay, I will stay with you. If you go, I will go with you. Either way, you must decide soon."

Once again, Tanisha covered his mouth with hers. And her hands pulled his garments aside. As their bodies joined, the image of Keteke receded in

Imaro's mind until it was gone, if not forgotten. At the end, when both he and Tanisha were sated, she left him with a single word:

"*Soon.*"

***

In the time that followed, Tanisha visited Imaro's shelter as often as she could—not every night, but enough times to build a bond between herself and the enigmatic warrior who had come from afar.

She told him of her life among the Shikaza: how the most beautiful girl-children of the tribe were taken from their parents at a young age to be instructed in the many arts involved in pleasing a man. They learned dances that were unmatched in all of Nyumbani, and their lovemaking skills were legendary. It was through the sale of those skills that the Shikaza survived the wars and conquests of neighboring tribes and kingdoms.

The training Tanisha had undergone reminded Imaro, in its own way, of *mafundishu-ya-muran*. The Shikaza women protected their people; and so did the men of the Ilyassai. The more time he spent with her, the more he learned of what it meant to be one with a woman; to allow himself to love. And he realized that what he had felt for Keteke had not been love at all; not even a shadow of what love truly was. It had previously been an emotion as foreign to him as fear. Despite what he felt for Tanisha, however, he would forever regret that Keteke had died because he had stolen her from her people.

But had he not also stolen Tanisha? That question did not enter his mind when she was with him. She would appear suddenly, as though she had an ability to conceal her appearance until she wanted to be seen. Yet Imaro could not detect any taint of *mchawi* about her. If she was indeed practicing sorcery, it was of an entirely different kind, and Imaro surrendered to it.

Not only did Imaro and Tanisha speak of their past lives, they also considered the future. What would happen when Chimba returned from his negotiations with the Azanian noble? Tanisha was certain the Azanian would meet Rumanzila's demand for a higher price. And Imaro would not allow her to go to the Azanian for any price.

Days passed slowly as the *haramia* awaited the return of both Chimba and Bomunu, for Rumanzila had commanded that no further raids would occur until the transactions for the Afua and Tanisha were completed, and the proceeds duly divided. Only foragers were allowed to leave the encampment, to replenish dwindling food supplies.

The forced inactivity irritated the bandits. They chafed against each other like grains of sand against the skin, and quarrels broke out constantly. Only the *haramia*'s dread of Mbuto's whip prevented the arguments from becoming physical fights that would eventually lead to fatalities. If Bomunu and

Chimba did not return soon, even the fear of Mbuto, and of Rumanzila himself, would not be sufficient to contain the rising tension.

***

Tanisha stirred in Imaro's arms. They were lying together in the darkness of Imaro's shelter, their bodies silhouettes in the minimal light that filtered through its cloth walls. Skin to skin, they held each other. There were no longer any secrets between them—only a choice; one that needed to be made soon.

"Imaro," Tanisha whispered, her lips moving against his shoulder.

The warrior made a wordless sound. He had nearly fallen asleep. On more than one occasion, he had slid into slumber while still holding Tanisha close to him. And each time he had awakened, she had been gone, slipping out of his grasp without awakening him.

Tanisha sat up and looked down at him.

"You must decide now," she said. "There are only two alternatives."

Imaro was well aware of the truth of her words. They had discussed—and discarded—all options other than the ones Imaro now identified aloud.

"To escape with you. Or to challenge Rumanzila for the leadership of the *haramia*."

"Which do you choose?" Tanisha asked.

Imaro had given long consideration to both alternatives. Escaping from the encampment would be a difficult feat, but it was possible, given that the *haramia* were distracted by their impatience and restlessness. But if he and Tanisha fled, Rumanzila would pursue them, and they would be only two against dozens of relentless foes. Imaro's friends among the *haramia* would be compelled to join the hunt for him and Tanisha—join it, or face Mbuto's whip.

And even though he had rejected the Ilyassai, the ways of the warrior tribe were still rooted deep within him. Those ways demanded that an Ilyassai warrior must never run from a foe.

Yet overthrowing Rumanzila would not be a simple task. Even outlaws lived by rules and traditions. If Imaro challenged Rumanzila over Tanisha, his justification would have to be a disagreement with the price that would be paid for her. However, that price had not yet been determined, and would not be until Chimba returned.

The result of such a challenge would be the death of either Imaro or Rumanzila. And even if Imaro prevailed, his leadership would not immediately be accepted by all the *haramia*. Some, like Chimba, openly disliked him. Others would have doubts about being led by an outlander. And there were still others, like Bomunu, whose own ambitions were obvious.

The dangers of challenging Rumanzila were clear. But so, too, was the incentive—Tanisha. As leader, Imaro would have the choice to cancel her sale to the Azanian. The bandits would object to the loss of so much gold—but that was a consequence Imaro was willing to accept.

"I will not run," he said.

Tanisha squeezed his shoulder.

"I knew you would not," Tanisha said.

Then she leaned down and darted her tongue into his mouth. But when he reached up to draw her down to him, she pulled away.

"I will not come to you again until the challenge is won," she said. "We cannot take any more chances, now that the decision is made."

Imaro opened his mouth to speak, but before he could utter a word, Tanisha was gone. Only a quickly vanished shadow and a slight stirring of the cloth walls of the shelter marked her passage.

The warrior remained awake for a long time after Tanisha departed. But she remained in his thoughts. So did Rumanzila. And so, as always, did the Naamans and the Mashataan. Much of the night passed before Imaro fell into a fitful slumber filled with dire dreams.

***

Imaro awakened suddenly. If his *kufahuma* had possessed a voice, it would have shouted a warning. But it was a different voice he heard.

His eyes snapped open, and his hand reached for the closest weapon—his sword. He looked toward the entrance through which Tanisha had gone the night before. Now, that opening was filled with daylight—and spear points.

"Come out," the voice said. It was the voice of Rumanzila.

Imaro moved his arm across the ground, making a noise loud enough for those outside to hear. The spear points immediately moved away from the opening, making a way for him.

"Come out, Imaro," Rumanzila said again. "Now."

The warrior considered his chances for survival if he took his sword and tried to cut his way through the *haramia* who were gathered at the entrance of his shelter. It did not take him long to realize that the chances were nonexistent. Thus, he reached for his *suruali* rather than his sword, and pulled the garment over his legs.

The scent of Tanisha lingered as Imaro pushed his way past the spear points and crawled out of the shelter. Was it the smell of betrayal?

Outside the shelter, he saw what he expected: Rumanzila. Strangely, however, the hulking Mbuto was not at his usual place at the bandit chieftain's side. Other *haramia* were there, though, weapons in hand. Even Imaro's friends, Ngodire and Kongolo, had the points of their swords and spears aimed at him. The expressions on their faces were neutral.

Silently, Rumanzila raised one hand, which was clenched into a fist. Then he opened it, palm upward, in front of Imaro. Resting in the center of Rumanzila's hand was a hoop of gold. The last time Imaro had seen it, it was hanging from the ear of Tanisha.

"We found this outside your shelter," Rumanzila said.

Imaro said nothing.

"There are laws among the lawless, Imaro," Rumanzila continued. "The Shikaza woman is for the Azanian, not you. We *haramia* steal from all—but not from each other."

"And what now?" Imaro asked.

"Punishment. For you and her."

Rumanzila gestured with his other hand. The gathered *haramia* moved aside to give Imaro a clear view of Tanisha. The Shikaza woman was chained to the large rock that served as the whipping post of this encampment. Manacles secured her arms to the sides of the rock in a position that was a cruel parody of an embrace. Her body was naked; the haramia had stripped away her *kuva* and other garments, leaving only the golden ornaments that circled her neck and arms. Even from a distance, Imaro could see that she was trembling.

Mbuto stood near Tanisha, whip in hand. He gazed impassively at the woman in front of him. The end of his whip moved back and forth incessantly, like the flick of a lion's tail.

"Here is your choice, Imaro," Rumanzila said. "Ten lashes from Mbuto for the Shikaza woman—or ten times ten for you. Which will it be?"

Rumanzila and Imaro both knew what the answer would be. Ten lashes from Mbuto would kill Tanisha. And one hundred could kill Imaro. But well did Imaro know that even if he chose not to accept the lashes, Mbuto's whip would never touch Tanisha's skin. Her value was too great; Rumanzila would not allow her to be damaged before the sale to the Azanian was complete.

Regardless of Imaro's answer, Rumanzila would benefit. If the warrior accepted the punishment and died, the bandit leader would be rid of a potential rival. If he lived, he would not be the same man he was before. And if he chose to allow Tanisha to take the punishment in his place, the other *haramia*'s contempt for his cowardice would force him out of the bandits' ranks.

Like a wily and patient hunter, Rumanzila had ensnared Imaro—thoroughly and easily. And Imaro knew it.

"Let the punishment be mine," he said.

Triumph kindled in Rumanzila's eyes.

"Unchain her," he said to the *haramia*. "And chain this one in her place."

The bandits quickly carried out Rumanzila's command. The tips of their weapons touched Imaro's skin as they prodded him to the rock to which Tanisha was chained. Then two of the *haramia* led her away. Tanisha kept her head down, avoiding Imaro's eyes. Other *haramia* chained Imaro to the rock, manacling his arms in the same position in which the Shikaza woman had been confined—his bare back an offering to Mbuto.

The encampment was quiet, save for Mbuto as he flicked his whip near Imaro, waiting for Rumanzila to give the order to begin, waiting to savor his vengeance against the man who had humiliated him.

But before Rumanzila could issue the command, a sudden disturbance diverted the attention of everyone in the encampment—everyone except Imaro and Mbuto. The bandits reached for their weapons.... Then they relaxed and called out greetings. For the cause of the disturbance was Bomunu, who had finally returned from his negotiations with the rogue sorcerer over the Afua.

***

Two *haramia* sentries accompanied Bomunu on horseback into the hideout. As all three dismounted, Bomunu's dusty, disheveled state was in striking contrast to his usual fastidiousness. And as Bomunu approached Rumanzila, no one failed to notice the absence of the smile that usually curved the Zanjian's lips, even though it seldom reached his eyes.

With the arrival of Bomunu, the *haramia's* attention shifted away from Imaro. The warrior could not see Bomunu, but he had heard the hoofbeats that marked his coming, and he heard the *haramia* greet the Zanjian by name. Although he wanted to see what was happening, Imaro did not move or struggle against the chains. Positioned as he was, he knew there was no chance he could break free. He could only await the first stroke of the whip.

Suddenly, Imaro felt a light touch against his back. It was the end of Mbuto's whip. Then he heard a low, rasping laugh. It was the most articulate sound he had ever heard the punisher make. And Imaro realized then that Mbuto was not as simpleminded as he appeared to be....

In the meantime, Bomunu stood in front of Rumanzila. His smile flickered in a brief crescent of white teeth before he spoke.

"I'm back," he said.

"That's obvious," Rumanzila said impatiently. "What about the sorcerer? Will he meet our price?"

"He will ... and he won't."

Rumanzila clamped his hand onto Bomunu's vest and twisted the embroidered cloth so hard it almost ripped.

"I'm not in the mood for games, Bomunu," he said. "*What happened?*"

If Bomunu was intimidated by Rumanzila's wrath, he showed no sign.

"The sorcerer still wants the statue," the Zanjian said. "And he will pay what we ask. But he doesn't want the *whole* statue. He only wants its spikes. He says the spikes are the true source of the statue's magical power."

Rumanzila released his grip on Bomunu's vest. Then he laughed cynically.

"I'm beginning to think this man isn't a *wa-nyanume* at all," he said. "I'll bet he's just another bandit, like us. I can even see what he has in mind. He'll sell the spikes one by one, claiming that each of them holds great magical power. And he will end up making back far more than what he paid for them."

The bandit leader laughed mirthlessly.

"If he can play that game, so can I," he said. "I could sell the spikes myself. But I'm no sorcerer. Who would believe me if I tried to sell these spikes as objects of power?"

He turned his attention to Angulu.

"People would believe you, though," he said.

"They would," Angulu agreed. "But I think it would be better for us if we find another buyer. This statue needs to be away from us … far away."

Rumanzila stared hard at the *wa-nyanume.*

"What are you afraid of, Angulu?" he asked. "Is there something about the statue you've been keeping from me?"

"No," the *wa-nyanume* replied after a short pause. "Do what you will."

"As always, Angulu," Rumanzila said. "As always."

"And you will convince all your fellow sorcerers that these spikes are objects of such great power that they will pay any price to own them."

"Yes."

Rumanzila did not take his eyes off the *wa-nyanume.*

"If it makes you feel better, Angulu, I'll pull the spikes out of the statue now, and we can use the rest of it for firewood," he said.

Angulu's only reaction to that statement was a slight, almost imperceptible, flicker in his eyes. He did not speak further. For all his skill in sorcery, Angulu feared Rumanzila, for the bandit leader was as dangerous as any of the demons that dwelled in the netherworld.

Rumanzila strode toward the Afua, along with Angulu and Mbuto, who had returned to his place at the leader's side. When he reached the statue, Rumanzila contemplated it for a moment. Then the bandit leader reached out and grasped one of the golden spikes.

"This shouldn't be too difficult," he said. "The wood looks soft."

Then Rumanzila pulled the spike out of the Afua. As he did so, Angulu's body stiffened, then shook, as though he had been struck by one of his own poison-tipped darts.

"Put it back!" he cried, his voice shrill with terror. "*Put it back*!"

But it was too late.

***

The moment Rumanzila removed the spike from the Afua, Imaro's *kufahuma* flared, and he strained instinctively against the manacles that bound him to the rock. Although he could not see what was happening behind him, he had heard what Bomunu said to Rumanzila, and what Rumanzila had, in turn, said to Angulu. Now, he heard loud outcries and running footsteps … and, overwhelming all other noises, a creaking groan, like the sound of a large tree bent by the strong winds of the rainy season.

Then Imaro heard a series of reverberating thumps, like the footfalls of a giant. He struggled harder against the chains, but his arms had been spread too wide to allow him any leverage. Behind him, some of the shouts turned into cries of agony, accompanied by crunching sounds.

Suddenly, from the corner of his eye, Imaro caught a glimpse of black. Then he heard a click, and felt a slight tug on one of his manacles. Skin brushed briefly against his back, and the click and tugging motion were repeated on the other manacle.

A familiar scent filled his nostrils—Tanisha. And her voice whispered urgently in his ear:

"Imaro! Put the spike back into the statue. It's the only chance we have! Rumanzila has it…."

Then she was gone.

Imaro pulled his arms away from the rock, and the chains and manacles clattered to the ground. He turned and looked for Tanisha. He caught only a fleeting glimpse of her golden ornaments flashing against her bare skin before the fleeing, fear-crazed mob of *haramia* blocked his vision.

The encampment resembled an overturned anthill. *Haramia* were running in all directions, some chasing panicked horses that were fleeing as well. But it was not the terrorized bandits that caused Imaro to suddenly stand immobile, mouth falling open, eyes wide, muscles as stiff as those of a beast at bay, staring at a sight nearly as grotesque as what lay beneath the robes of Chitendu.

It was the Afua. The statue had … *grown*. It had become as tall as a tree, and its golden spikes were now as lengthy as spears. Blood dripped from some of the spike points—the ones closest to the ground. A hole the size of a man's fist marked the place from which Rumanzila had pulled one of the spikes.

Haramia corpses lay strewn on the ground, crushed horribly. For the Afua was not immobile. The effigy's steps were lurching and ungainly, like those of a child just learning to walk. With each movement, the wood from which the Afua was made groaned, as though the motion caused it great pain. Its head turned slowly, and its hollowed-out eyes appeared to be *searching*, even though the statue had to be sightless. The Afua's footsteps shook the ground, and anyone luckless enough to fall before it was crushed beneath the stumps of its feet.

With Tanisha's words echoing in his ears, Imaro's moment of inaction ended. His eyes scanned the crowd of fleeing *haramia*, none of whom paid him any heed even though he was free from his chains. He was looking for

Rumanzila—and finally, he spotted the bandit leader.

Rumanzila was moving toward, rather than away from, the Afua. Imaro could see the gleam of the golden spike in Rumanzila's hand. The bandit leader was attempting to find a way to put the spike back into its proper place. But each time he came close to the Afua, the sight of the effigy's legs, which had grown to the size of tree trunks, moving his way unnerved him, and caused him to retreat.

Imaro saw no sign of Mbuto, Angulu, or Bomunu. He did see Ngodire, towering over everyone else, and Kongolo. Both men were attempting, with limited success, to quell the panic.

Although he was still unarmed, Imaro had no time to find a weapon now. He pushed his way through the fleeing *haramia*, heading in the direction of the Afua and Rumanzila. He had almost reached Rumanzila's side when the bandit chieftain turned and saw him.

The fear that etched Rumanzila's features turned into rage the moment he recognized Imaro.

"You!" he shouted, his voice rising above the din of the *haramia* and the slow thump of the Afua's footsteps.

Even though the Afua was coming closer, Rumanzila reached for his sword and pulled it from its sheath.

"Don't be a fool!" Imaro shouted. "Give me the spike. I'll put it back if you can't!"

Rumanzila opened his mouth to utter a curse.... Then his eyes suddenly widened, giving Imaro a warning that came a fraction of a second too late.

Before he could turn to see what was behind him, Imaro suddenly found himself enfolded in a grasp of steel, with flesh that was both soft and hard pressing against his back. Mbuto, Imaro realized even as the hulking punisher began to lift him off his feet. And he saw Rumanzila rushing toward him, his sword pulled back to deliver a killing thrust.

Imaro knew he would be dead if Mbuto succeeded in lifting him all the way off the ground, for the warrior would then have no way to defend himself. He had only one chance to survive. With all his strength, he pulled himself forward. Then, with his feet planted firmly, Imaro bent at the waist, forcing Mbuto's feet, rather than his own, to leave the ground.

Briefly, Imaro tottered beneath the punisher's enormous bulk. Then he turned, so that his back, and Mbuto's, faced Rumanzila. Even as he heard Rumanzila shout in anger and consternation, a jolt from behind nearly sent him tumbling. A loud cry of agony from Mbuto preceded a light touch against Imaro's back.

Then Imaro straightened his body. The motion forced Mbuto's bulk, which had suddenly gone slack, to fall away from him. He heard a shrill curse from Rumanzila, which was abruptly cut off by a crashing thud and the crackle of breaking bones, then silence.

Struggling to maintain his balance, Imaro turned and saw Rumanzila's body, almost completely hidden by that of Mbuto. Mbuto was dead; his eyes stared sightlessly, and the point of Rumanzila's sword protruded from his huge abdomen—the same point that had barely touched the skin of Imaro's back.

Rumanzila was not yet dead. But his life rapidly ebbing; Mbuto's mountainous bulk had crushed him so thoroughly that he could neither move nor speak. He could only glare in hatred of Imaro during his final moments alive.

Imaro paid Rumanzila no further heed once he realized the spike from the Afua was trapped beneath Mbuto. Mindful that the effigy was nearly upon him, Imaro seized the corpse of the punisher, and with a single heave, he rolled it away from Rumanzila. He saw that the bandit chieftain's hand still clutched the spike. Imaro pried Rumanzila's hand open and took the spike from his fingers.

Then the shadow of the Afua blanketed him. He whirled away from the bodies of Rumanzila and Mbuto … but not before the edge of the Afua's foot caught him with a blow to the side of his skull—a glancing blow that still had enough force to send him senseless to the ground.

***

When Tanisha saw Imaro fall, she cried out in fear—for him, rather than for herself. The crowd of fleeing *haramia* had pushed her far from where Imaro and the Afua were, but she had made her way closer again. Now, as she was about to rush toward the fallen warrior, a thin, spidery hand reached and seized her by the arm.

With a wordless exclamation, Tanisha turned, her other hand raised to lash out—but her intended blow stopped in midmotion as she looked far up at the face of Ngodire, the Ndashikuya.

"You can't help Imaro now … even though you helped him before," Ngodire said.

"How do you know what I did?" she demanded.

"I saw you unchain him," said Ngodire. "It was clever of you to steal the key to the manacles from the one who unchained you – and you were lucky Mbuto was distracted by that … statue. But there's nothing you can do for Imaro now."

"I have to try!" Tanisha said fiercely, struggling against the Ndashikuya's surprisingly strong grasp.

Her lips were drawn back from her teeth in a primal snarl, and if she had been carrying a weapon, Ngodire would have been a dead man. Seeing the look on her face, Ngodire released his grip on her arm.

"I agree," another voice said.

"As do I," said yet another.

Turning in the direction from which the voices had come, Tanisha and Ngodire saw Angulu and Kongolo. The *wa-nyanume*'s eyes held a haunted look. Kongolo appeared to be fighting fear, but he had remained behind when almost all the other *haramia* had fled in panic, much as the Mtumwe had bolted when the bandits raided the *kijiji* and stole the Afua.

"Can you not use your sorcery to help?" Tanisha asked Angulu.

The *wa-nyanume* shook his head.

"The only way to end this is to replace the spike," he said, raising his voice so the others could hear him over the sounds from the Afua's movements.

"I have no magic that can accomplish such a thing," Angulu continued. "The only hope is Imaro. Otherwise ..."

"Look!" Kongolo shouted suddenly. "He's getting up!"

They saw Imaro rising unsteadily to his feet. But the Afua remained near him, and he was still in danger of being crushed beneath its feet. Without further hesitation, the four who had remained behind rushed toward Imaro and the towering effigy.

***

Imaro had briefly lost consciousness when the Afua struck him. Yet even in that moment of oblivion, he had managed to stay out of the way of the effigy's footsteps. When his mind snapped out of its daze and back into focus, he saw golden spikes coming toward him again. Scrambling shakily to his feet, he was able to evade the sharp, gleaming points.

He looked toward the spike he had taken from Rumanzila—*but it was gone*!

It had dropped from his grasp after he had fallen. Head throbbing from the pain of the blow he had received, Imaro frantically searched the ground, seeking the gleam of the spike while at the same time avoiding the footfalls of the Afua, each of which reverberated like a thunderclap.

Imaro could have simply given up and fled then, and allowed the Afua to continue its rampage. But now that he was close enough to the statue to touch it, an unpleasant cognizance suffused his senses ... an awareness akin to *kufahuma*, but not exactly the same ... an awareness spawned from his encounter with Chitendu in the Place of Stones ... an awareness of the *mchawi* that was linked to the masters the *oibonok* had served: the High Sorcerers of Naama.

When Rumanzila removed the spike, the *mchawi* had been unleashed, and Imaro's senses had flared like the sunrise. In his deepest core, Imaro knew he had to put an end to this *mchawi*, as he had that of Chitendu.

But where was the spike?

Desperately scanning the ground, Imaro barely avoided impalement on the spikes of the Afua's leg as it swung toward him. He did not know whether the effigy was consciously attacking him, or was simply moving without volition, like a river or the wind. He did not know whether the Afua was truly alive, or merely animated by the power of the *mchawi* within it. He knew only that he had to find the spike, and return the Afua to what it had been when he first saw it in the Mtumwe shrine.

Then his eyes caught a gleam of gold on the rocky ground. He reached for it—but the Afua's leg came between him and the spike.

"Ajunge!" he shouted in frustration, invoking the name of the Spear God of the Ilyassai, a god that had long since forsaken him.

When the path was clear again, Imaro saw that the spike had vanished.

"Ajunge!" he cried again.

But the voice that answered him was not that of the god. It was Tanisha's.

"Imaro! Here!"

Imaro turned toward Tanisha, again narrowly avoiding the Afua's footfall. She was standing close by. She was clad only in a scrap of cloth torn from her *kuva* and knotted around her waist. Between her thumb and forefinger, she held the golden spike. Her eyes were wide with fear, but she did not retreat. Ngodire was at her side, as was Kongolo. Angulu was standing apart from the others.

Imaro rushed to Tanisha's side. As he plucked the spike from her fingers, their eyes met, and what he saw in her gaze was not an enigma. Then the warrior turned to face the Afua.

The effigy loomed before him like a mountain clad in a forest of golden foliage. Never, not even when he was a child left behind by his mother, had he felt so small, so powerless.

But he was not entirely powerless. The spike glistened in his hand. Far above, he could see the hole from which the spike had come—a hole large enough to swallow his hand and arm.

The reflection of the sunlight from the enlarged spikes on the statue nearly blinded Imaro. To climb them would be like trying to ascend a wall studded with *arems*. But that was the only way the *mchawi*, which was emanating in waves from the Afua, could be curtailed.

Imaro lifted the spike to his mouth, and clamped his teeth hard onto the metal. This time, when the Afua's leg swung toward him, he did not dodge it. Instead, he seized one of the spikes and hauled himself upward, securing holds for hands and feet.

He tried to avoid the points of the Afua's spikes, but some of them pierced his skin, and blood began to trickle down his body as he clambered upward. Although the spikes were embedded firmly in the wood, they were as flexible as the branches of trees—and far more slippery, as Imaro discovered to his dismay when he lost his footing and nearly fell.

As he dangled from a spike by one hand, Imaro swayed back and forth while the Afua continued to walk. Imaro ignored the cries of consternation he heard from below. He did not look down. And he did not open his mouth.

Seizing a spike with his other hand, Imaro regained his footing and continued his climb. The loud creaks that accompanied the Afua's movements were deafening, but he kept his focus on his destination, which was still high above him.

Unmindful of the pricking of the spikes against his skin, Imaro finally reached the hole where the spike clenched between his teeth had been. When he was eye-level with the hole, Imaro again almost toppled. *Mchawi* poured from the opening like the wind during the wet season. The magical force was neither focused nor purposeful, as it had been when wielded by Chitendu and Muburi. Instead, it was unharnessed, and almost irresistible.

Using one hand to cling to the spike closest to the hole, Imaro used his other hand to pluck the spike from his teeth. He closed his eyes against the force of the unleashed *mchawi*, and pushed the sliver of gold deep into the hole. Then he pulled his hand back quickly, before the opening could close over it.

The Afua's movements halted with a lurch that nearly flung Imaro from his foothold. He held on with both hands even as his feet slipped from the spikes. Then a new sound replaced the groan of walking wood—a sharp crack, like the sound of lightning hitting a tree trunk. Imaro felt the spikes rapidly shrinking in his grasp....

And suddenly, he was falling.

Imaro looked down then, and it appeared that the ground was rushing up to meet him. The cracking sounds grew louder. The spikes he was holding, now small, slipped out of his hands. Pieces of wood fell like rain around him as he plummeted to the unyielding earth.

Imaro braced himself as best as he could for the inevitable crash. When it came, its impact was harder than any he had ever experienced, including the repeated blows of Mbuto's whip. Then pain and oblivion claimed him.

***

Consciousness slowly returned to Imaro—but he wished it hadn't. He felt as though every bone in his body had been shattered—yet he found that he was able to move his limbs, painful though that process proved to be. When he opened his eyes, his vision blurred for a moment, then came into clear focus.

He saw a circle of concerned faces surrounding him. Foremost among them was Tanisha's. She leaned close to him, her hands touching his face. The emotions on her face, in her eyes, were clearly delineated: relief and love.

Kongolo and Ngodire were there, too, as was Angulu. So were many others. For after their first outburst of blind panic had subsided, most of the *haramia* returned to the encampment to aid those who had not fled. They had witnessed Imaro's feat, and now they regarded him with undisguised awe, as though he were more than human.

Bomunu was the only *haramia* whose expression conveyed anything other than respect. Anger smoldered in the Zanjian's eyes. Anger … and envy.

At the moment, Imaro did not care what was on the mind of Bomunu, nor anyone else other than Tanisha. Even though the smallest of movements sent lances of pain through his body, he struggled to his feet, brushing aside the hands that tried to hold him down.

"The Afua," Imaro said, his voice thick with the struggle to speak. "Where is it?

As the warrior swayed, determined to remain on his feet, Tanisha slipped an arm around his waist to steady him. He gave her a look of gratitude.

"There it is, Imaro," she said, gesturing with her free hand.

The *haramia* stood aside. When Imaro looked at the ground a few paces away, he saw shards of wood scattered over a wide area, none of them larger than a finger. Interspersed among the fragments of the Afua were the golden spikes that had once adorned it. Now, tarnish blackened the metal like the decay of death.

Imaro raised his eyes—and looked upon a scene of devastation. The body of Rumanzila still lay beneath that of Mbuto. The crushed remnants of the luckless bandits who had fallen beneath the Afua's feet were strewn across the ground. In the distance, more *haramia* were straggling into the hideout. Some of them led horses that pranced nervously, wary of the fading residue of *mchawi* from the Afua.

The Ilyassai's *kufahuma* had calmed, however. The *mchawi* Rumanzila had released when he removed the spike was dissipating like morning mist. No longer was the unleashed sorcerous energy a menace—but it was still a concern.

Then Bomunu's voice broke through the undercurrent of murmurs that had accompanied Imaro's return to consciousness.

"It's time to stop standing around," he said. "This place is cursed. We've got to get out of here. Gather up your gear; we need to find another place to camp before the sun goes down."

The murmurs rose in volume, and Kongolo spoke for most of the other *haramia*.

"Who are you to give us orders?" he demanded.

The Zanjian brushed a few specks of dust from his clothing before deigning to reply.

"I was second-in-command to Rumanzila," he said. "Rumanzila is dead.

So now, I am your leader. Is that so difficult to understand?"

Kongolo's response was a sneer.

"That may be the way things are done in the palaces of Zanj," he said. "But it's not the way the *haramia* do things. I would've thought you'd have learned that by now, Bomunu."

Bomunu's eyes shifted for a moment, but his bravado remained intact.

"How, then, did Rumanzila become leader?" he asked.

"He earned it," Kongolo snapped. "He didn't inherit it."

"And what have you done lately to earn it, Bomunu?" Angulu asked. The *wa-nyanume*'s tone dripped with contempt.

"I can't think of anything," Ngodire said, speaking, literally, above others who were making similar remarks. "Can anyone else?"

"Where were you when that accursed statue was trampling us like bugs?" Kongolo demanded, his eyes narrowed in anger as they focused on the Zanjian.

"Who was it that finally saved us all, Bomunu?" asked Ngodire. "It certainly wasn't you."

Other bandits shouted in agreement. Bomunu knew the direction in which the *haramia* were leaning, and he knew it wasn't toward him. He glanced in Imaro's direction. The Ilyassai's face revealed nothing of what he was thinking. Tanisha, however, was smiling.

"We cannot be led by an outlander," Bomunu argued, desperation creeping into his voice.

"Why not?" Angulu asked. "Are we not all outlanders? Or, at least, outcasts?"

"You know what I mean!" Bomunu shouted. "We need a leader who has experience."

He gestured toward Imaro.

"*He* doesn't have the experience. I do."

"Did your 'experience' help us this time, Bomunu?" Angulu asked. "Did mine? Did anybody's?"

To those questions, Bomunu had no reply.

Kongolo spoke then, loudly enough for all the *haramia* to hear.

"Which one do we want to lead us? Bomunu? Or Imaro?"

The *haramia*'s answer was immediate and overwhelming, shouted from dozens of throats:

"Imaro! Imaro! Imaro!"

Their shouts echoed throughout the encampment. Imaro listened in amazement as the *haramia* repeated his name and waved their weapons over their heads. Imaro turned to Tanisha, who tightened her grasp around his waist and smiled up at him. Her smile, and the adulation of the *haramia*, eased the ache of his injuries—and of the old wounds he carried inside.

He leaned closer to Tanisha.

"Will you stay with me, even though death is on my trail?" he asked.

"I would rather die with you than live without you," she said.

As the *haramia* continued to call out for Imaro, Bomunu's shoulders slumped in defeat. Jealousy smoldered in his eyes as he glared at Imaro and Tanisha. And the humiliation of having the position he considered rightfully his usurped by a barbarian from some faraway tribe was already eating into his soul.

Eventually, the clamor subsided. Kongolo looked at Bomunu with an expression that mingled pity and contempt.

"There's your answer," he said.

Then he turned to the Ilyassai.

"You have heard the will of the *haramia*, Imaro," Kongolo said. "We want you to lead us. Will you?"

Imaro looked at him, and the others. His aches continued, and his dark skin had acquired darker bruises. Blood from the wounds the tips of the Afua's spikes had made trickled down his chest and abdomen, and soaked into his *suruali*. He wanted nothing more than to lie down in his shelter until the pain abated.

"I will lead you," he said.

Again, the *haramia* erupted into shouts, this time in celebration. Some cried out Imaro's name; others simply yelled out in exuberation, as well as relief that the danger the Afua had posed was gone. Only Bomunu remained silent.

Amid the tumult, few noticed a commotion at the fringes of the crowd. The distraction grew as two *haramia* pushed their way forward, firmly gripping the arms of a person they half dragged and half carried between them.

When they reached the front of the crowd, near the place where Imaro and Tanisha were standing, the bandits shoved their captive ahead of them. It was a man—a man who was emaciated, weaponless, bedraggled, and nearly naked. Patterns of scars covered his skin. The man looked up at the Ilyassai, and uttered the same word the *haramia* had been shouting:

"Imaro."

And for all the visible privations the intruder had obviously undergone, as well as the dirt that splotched his skin and the recent wounds that cut across his scarifications, Imaro knew this man, even though he had never thought he would see him again.

"Busa," he said.

***

"This one has been saying your name ever since we caught him sneaking around here," one of Busa's captors said.

"It's like that's the only word he knows how to say," the other added.

Those among the *haramia*, including Kongolo, who had gone to the Kajua to steal the Afua recognized Busa as one of the river people.

"You know him?" Kongolo asked Imaro.

"Yes," the warrior replied.

Busa's gaze shifted between Imaro and the area where the fragments of the Afua were scattered. Despair darkened his eyes. And bitterness tinged his tone when he spoke to Imaro.

"So, these are the ones who took away the Afua. And you were part of it all along, weren't you?"

Imaro slipped out of Tanisha's grasp and took a step toward the Mtumwe, who did not flinch or change his expression.

"I had nothing to do with it, Busa," he said, speaking slowly, for he had half forgotten the river people's tongue. "These people took me, as well as the Afua."

"Then why are they treating you as one of their own?" Busa demanded, his voice rising even though he was a captive.

Some of the *haramia* put their hands on the hilts of their weapons. They did not understand Busa's language, but the angry tone of his voice was unmistakable. Kongolo, who had a rudimentary grasp of the river people's speech, was also apprehensive, for all that the scarred man was an unarmed, helpless captive. Had Imaro not been just as helpless when he first came among them?

Imaro remained calm.

"Did you see what happened to the Afua?" he asked.

The haunted, anguished look that reappeared in Busa's eyes answered the question even before he spoke.

"I ... saw."

"There was evil in the Afua, Busa," Imaro said. "Evil magic that would have destroyed the Mtumwe, sooner or later. You thought the Afua would bring good luck to the *kijiji*. Now you have seen it for what it really is."

Busa looked at the ground. His shoulders trembled, and his hands clenched into fists. He shook his head in sadness. When he looked up again at Imaro, his face was as bleak as the face of death.

"Ariathu sent us to bring it back," he said.

"'Us'? Imaro asked. "Where are the others?"

"Dead. All dead, except me."

Imaro fell silent then, thinking of the long distance Busa and the others had traveled in search of the Afua, and of the dangers they must have faced in a country that was at once hostile and unfamiliar.

"Was Msuli with you?" he finally asked.

"Yes."

Imaro's only sign of emotion was a long, slow exhale. He deeply mourned the death of Msuli, and he wondered whether he had done either Msuli or

Busa a favor by saving them from the crocodile.

"I cannot go back to the *kijiji* without the Afua," Busa said.

And I cannot go back to the Ilyassai, Imaro thought—for once, without bitterness.

"I understand," he said to Busa.

"I have nowhere else to go," Busa said, his voice devoid of inflection.

"That is not true, Busa," said Imaro.

The Mtumwe gave him a puzzled look. Imaro's arm swept outward in an expansive gesture that included all the *haramia*, who were listening intently to the exchange even though it was in a language few of them could understand.

"These were not my people before," Imaro said. "They stole me, just as they stole the Afua. But they are my people now. You once offered me a place among your people. Now, I offer you a place among mine."

Busa considered Imaro's words. His choice was stark: become part of the band of outlaws that had terrorized his people and stolen their most sacred object—or live a life of lone exile, a life likely to be short in this harsh land where the trees were sparse and rivers tumbled down hills instead of flowing between banks in the forest.

"I accept," he said.

Imaro turned to the *haramia*.

"We have a new member," he said.

The bandits murmured among themselves, having learned of Busa's origins through Kongolo and the others who had gone on the raid in the forest. In their eyes, the scar-skinned newcomer had no reason to be loyal either to Imaro or the *haramia*. They did not know that Busa owed his life to Imaro.

Kongolo spoke for the others.

"You are our leader, Imaro," he said. "We must accept what you decide. But this one has a reason to turn against you one day. You may have pointed a dagger against yourself."

"I will take that chance," said Imaro.

Tanisha touched his arm.

"Imaro," she said. "What about this?"

She gestured toward the remnants of the Afua that were strewn like unplanted seeds across the ground.

"We will bury the Afua," Imaro said. "Along with Rumanzila, Mbuto, and all the others who died here. And we will never camp here again."

As the outlaws moved to carry out the bidding of their new leader, another straggler arrived at the encampment. It was Chimba, returning from his mission to negotiate the new price the Azanian noble would be paying for Tanisha. When his fellow *haramia* recounted all that had occurred while Chimba was gone, his eyes widened incredulously.

Still, he had to believe what he saw: his fellow *haramia* tossing pieces of wood and tarnished spikes of gold into a large, freshly dug pit; the corpses of Rumanzila and Mbuto, as well as others, lying at the side of the burial hole; the outlander, Imaro, receiving the adulation of the bandits with the Shikaza woman at his side.

Chimba shook his head in disgust. He had been one of Rumanzila's favorites, and his dislike of the outlander was hardly a secret. Regardless of who the leader was, though, he still had a duty to perform, and information to provide. After elbowing his way through the throng, he stopped in front of Imaro and Tanisha.

"So, you're the leader now," he said, looking up at Imaro.

"I am—whether you like it or not," said Imaro.

"Well, here's a decision for you to make," Chimba said, a sneer only half hidden in his tone. "Our friend in Azania is willing to pay twice as much as he first offered for this one."

He gestured toward Tanisha, who looked at him with undisguised disdain, which he ignored.

"What do you say?" Chimba asked.

Bomunu, who was standing not far from Imaro and Tanisha, smiled when he heard Chimba's words about the increase in price. Before he had been forced to flee Zanj, he had been acquainted with the nobleman of his country who had originally purchased Tanisha. The acquaintanceship had been unpleasant, and Bomunu had long suspected that the man had played a role in the events that had forced him to flee for his life. Bomunu was the one who had suggested the theft of the Shikaza woman, to keep her out of the hands of the countryman who coveted her.

This outlander may have stolen my place as leader, Bomunu reflected, *but I'll still have my share of the price this woman commands....*

"I say the Azanian can keep his gold," Imaro declared.

He turned to Tanisha, and despite the continuing pain from his fall and the wounds the Afua's spikes had made, he pulled Tanisha into an embrace, and his mouth found hers. And even though the *haramia* would now profit from neither the Afua nor the Shikaza woman, they shouted praises for Imaro, for they believed that he would lead them to even greater spoils.

Anger and envy smoldering in his eyes, Bomunu did not join the praise-chants. Neither did Chimba. And neither did Busa, who, instead, watched while the bandits threw dirt into the grave that held what was left of the Afua.

The forging of the weapon continued....

***

The Mtumwe awaited the return of the Afua, and of the young men who had set out to recover the statue. As time passed, some of the people of the *kijiji* lost hope that they would ever see either the Afua or the searchers again.

In the meantime, the good fortune the Afua had bestowed upon the *kijiji* quickly vanished. Fish avoided the Mtumwe's nets, and a mysterious blight ruined their crops. People from other *kijijis*, having heard tales of the magical invaders and the theft of the Afua, avoided all contact with the Mtumwe. No longer did the dugouts of the tribe ply the Damba Bolong in search of fish or trade. Along the length of the Damba, the river people agreed that the Mtumwe were cursed, and their fate was to be shunned by all, to prevent the effects of the curse from spreading.

Only the iron will of Ariathu prevented the Mtumwe from abandoning their *kijiji*. The *nganga* insisted that the Afua belonged to them, and that it would find its way back to the shrine the people had rebuilt at her suggestion, regardless of how long it might take for the return to occur.

Then Ariathu died. Soon thereafter, the *mku*, Najimu, also passed away.

Isolated and starving because their crops still would not grow, the surviving Mtumwe gathered for a council after the deaths of the *mku* and the *nganga*. The elders decided there was no longer any reason to continue their wait for the return of the Afua and the seekers. If the warriors who had gone had not found it after three rains, it was unlikely they ever would. And if there was no longer any reason to wait, there was also no longer any reason to remain in the *kijiji*.

The rest of the people agreed. And the next day, they abandoned the place that had been their home for many generations. Well aware that they were not welcome anywhere along the river, the Mtumwe retreated into the Kajua, leaving behind their dwellings, their dugouts, and the empty shrine that still awaited the Afua.

Soon after the Mtumwes' departure, the *kijiji* fell into ruin, and the forest swallowed it whole. No other tribe attempted to claim the site as its own, for its reputation as an accursed place had grown. When dugouts passed the area, the paddlers averted their eyes and propelled their watercraft as swiftly as possible until the former land of the Mtumwe was out of sight.

The Mtumwe people were never heard from again. Their retreat carried them deep into the forest, far from the sight, or even the sound, of the Damba, or any other river. The Kajua yielded enough food to forestall starvation, but not much more than that. Generation after generation, the Mtumwe lived in isolation, and their numbers dwindled, and they developed new customs that would have disquieted their ancestors who had lived in the *kijiji*.

With each change from the wet season to the dry, the Mtumwe enacted a ceremony of loss, in which they remembered the beautiful and bountiful land from which they had departed. They remembered the Afua, which had brought them good fortune for so long, and they praised its name.

And they cursed the name of the demon that had come among them, and taken their good fortune away—a demon whose name was Imaro.

HORROR IN THE BLACK HILLS

Mightier than all,
Mightier than all
Is Imaro! Imaro!
—haramia chant

In the pale light of Mwesu the moon, the Black Hills loomed like a horde of gigantic, crouching beasts, waiting to spring. On another night, only the calls of birds and the irascible chatter of baboons would have broken the somber silence of the thickly wooded slopes. Now, though, the hills reverberated to the chanting of hundreds of human voices and the thunder of scores of drums.

The chant was part praise, part challenge; flung with pride and defiance from the throats of nearly a thousand men and women. To the animals that dwelt in the hills, the chant meant nothing beyond the indication that mankind had invaded their shadowy realm. Where there were men, there were spears; where there were spears, there was death. The birds roosted motionlessly in the uppermost branches of the trees, and the baboons moved on to safer surroundings.

But in the depths of a still, stagnant pond sunk into the summit of the highest of the Black Hills, there slumbered a thing that was neither bird, nor baboon, nor human. A thing now awakened by the disturbance caused by the shouts of faraway voices; a thing that comprehended the words of the chants of praise and prowess as no beast ever could.

Projecting its awareness beyond the slimy surface of the pond, this thing that should never have been aroused pursued the drifting vibrations of the chants to their source. There, it listened … and probed … and learned.…

***

The *haramia*'s raucous celebration overflowed the confines of their newly erected encampment. They had ample reason to celebrate. Not only had they pillaged Tangwe, an important Azanian border town; they had also decimated the detachment of troops the Sha'a—the monarch of the kingdom of Azania—had sent to protect Tangwe from just such an attack.

After drawing the soldiers of the Sha'a into a carefully laid ambush, the bandits had cut the Azanians to pieces, then had easily overrun the defenseless town. Laden with their plunder of ivory, precious metals, and captives, the *haramia* had left Tangwe a flaming ruin, streets strewn with Azanian dead.

And now, the *haramia* reveled. By the time word of the sacking of Tangwe reached the ears of the Sha'a in his distant capital of Mulundu, the bandits would have long since departed from their current encampment. Thus far, no soldiers from any of the East Coast kingdoms had dared to pursue the *haramia* into the hinterland between the East Coast kingdoms and the Kajua, for in that trackless terrain, the bandits held all the advantages.

Imaro's *haramia* danced. The glare of the night-fires flickered in crimson flashes from sweat-slicked bodies cavorting to the rhythmic pulse of the drums. The dancers swayed in a huge circle around the drummers and the crackling fires. While they chanted and danced, they clapped hands still encrusted with the blood of the luckless people of Tangwe.

The ranks of the *haramia* band that was once Rumanzila's had swollen since Imaro had become its leader. *Haramia* from rival bands were quick to desert their own groups and join that of N'tu-nje—the Outsider—as Imaro was now known in the borderlands of the East Coast. The success of his bold tactics and his ferocity in battle attracted others as well: criminals, dissidents, escaped slaves, and adventurers who would remain loyal as long as the loot lasted.

Even though the band's numbers had increased since Imaro's ascension to their leadership, some of those who had acclaimed him were no longer in the ranks. Some had been killed during raids and battles against other *haramia* bands.

And one had simply ... vanished.

Angulu had not been the same since the *haramia*'s encounter with the Afua. The *wa-nyanume* had grown distant from the others as the days and weeks passed, and the *haramia*'s successes under Imaro's leadership mounted. Often, Angulu brooded alone. Although he was obviously troubled, he shared his thoughts with no one other than himself.

No one believed Angulu begrudged Imaro's status as the successor of Rumanzila. But sometimes, the sorcerer would stare intently at the Ilyassai, as though he was searching for something no one else could see.

Clearly, the experience with the Afua had wrought changes within *the wa-nyanume*—changes even he could not understand.

Imaro was concerned about Angulu's troubled demeanor. But he never questioned the sorcerer about his worries. For Angulu had remained behind when most of the *haramia* had fled after the Afua came to life, and Imaro respected the courage he had shown.

Then, not long before the taking of Tangwe, Angulu disappeared. Neither track nor trace of him could be found.

Kongolo had advised Imaro to mount a search for the *wa-nyanume*.

"That one knows everything about us," Kongolo said. "He could end up becoming our worst enemy."

"No," Imaro disagreed. "He will be of greater danger to himself than to us."

Kongolo had accepted Imaro's decision. He could only hope that the warrior would not be proven wrong.

Now, leaping and whirling in gyrations made capricious by the *ndizi-pombe* they had swilled, the *haramia* continued their celebration. Among the dancers were women, who undulated their lithe bodies in nuances of motion that fed the flames of the men's passions. Some had joined the men willingly, accepting a life of lawless peril. Others had been seized in raids like the one just perpetrated against Tangwe, and some had become willing members of the outlaw horde. They danced just beyond the reach of the men, who for now were engaged in the praise of their own prowess—and that of their leader.

And as they danced, they sang a praise chant:

"Greatest of all, greatest of all is Imaro, Imaro!"

"Mightier than all, mightier than all is Imaro, Imaro!"

"Conqueror of all, conqueror of all is Imaro, Imaro!"

One woman danced apart from the others as they sang: Tanisha, her midnight-dark body clad only in a length of crimson Eastern silk knotted at her waist and golden ornaments that flashed in the firelight. Her dance was different— a series of sensual movements unique to her Shikaza people. For only one man did Tanisha dance: Imaro, whose iron will had welded the expanded *haramia* horde into a formidable fighting force that was more than a match for the armies the East Coast kings had sent against them.

Watching the dance like a sated lion, Imaro reclined against a glittering pile of gold ingots, elephant tusks, and bolts of cloth that came from the Lands across the Sea. Even in repose, the Ilyassai's thews rolled in magnificent symmetry beneath an iron-studded harness stretched across his massive torso. Scarlet *suruali* swathed his legs. Unlike his predecessor, Rumanzila, Imaro eschewed ostentation. His weapons—sword and dagger—were his only ornamentation.

In contrast to the gaiety that surrounded him, Imaro's mood was pensive and introspective. His mind was consumed with thoughts that had been absent for a time: thoughts of Naama and the Mashataan, thoughts that threatened to tarnish his moment of triumph.

Imaro's lieutenants sat near him on the pile of loot. Kongolo was to his right. Imaro trusted the squat, bull-necked bandit more than he did anyone else among the *haramia*, other than Tanisha, even though he had also stood high in the esteem of Rumanzila. Kongolo's judgment was sound, and the *haramia* respected him, for he had been among them a long time. And Kongolo showed no sign of harboring ambitions to take Imaro's place.

Ngodire sat to the left of Imaro. Some of the *haramia* were not comfortable with having the towering Ndashikuya in a position of leadership in their ranks. But Ngodire was no more or less an outsider among them than Imaro, and he had remained at the Ilyassai's side when the Afua had rampaged through the *haramias'* previous hideout. His was the advice Imaro heeded most when he needed to make a decision.

Bomunu stood apart from the others. The Zanjian was resplendent in the silken *suruali*, overshirt, and befeathered turban he had donned in place of his bloodstained battle garb. After the death of Rumanzila and the *haramia*'s rejection of him in favor of Imaro, Bomunu had shifted his loyalty to Imaro and convinced the Ilyassai that at least three lieutenants were needed to maintain efficient command over the large number of adventurers who had joined the outlaw army.

Even as he appeared to accept his subordinate position, Bomunu remained ambitious. He realized his chances of wresting the leadership from Imaro were, at this time, negligible. So he accepted his continued role of underling—and he waited, for there was something else Imaro had that he wanted as well....

Busa stood near Imaro and the other leaders, but he spoke to no one, and he did not participate in the chanting or dancing. The scarred Mtumwe had proven to be a good fighter, but he made no friendships among the *haramia*, and he followed Imaro as though he were the Ilyassai's shadow.

Sipping *ndizi-pombe* from a gourd, Imaro paid scant heed to either his lieutenants or to Busa. Even Tanisha could not divert him from his reverie. Lowering his nearly empty gourd, Imaro stared thoughtfully at the liquid pooled at the bottom. His reflection was dim, wavering—as inconstant as his own perception of his new status, as opposed to who, and what, he had been only a single rain ago, in a way of life that was now only a memory.

No longer was he an outcast, a son-of-no-father, whose acceptance among the Ilyassai had come too late to matter. No longer was he a lone wanderer. Only a few of the *haramia* he led cared about his uncertain heritage. The bandits respected his strength and battle prowess, and asked no questions concerning his ancestry, for all his lack of resemblance to the races of Nyumbani's East Coast.

Never before had Imaro enjoyed true companionship, or recognition for his deeds. The pulsing drums and the voices chanting his praises—those were his well-earned due. Yet for reasons he could not explain, the adulation he received now left him as uncomfortable as had the overdue tribute the Ilyassai had rendered when he left the Place of Stones.

That he was an outlaw, hunted by the armies of two kingdoms, had little to do with Imaro's current state of disquiet. He knew only the law of the Ilyassai: the law of courage, of conquering fear. And even that primal code had, until it was too late, been denied him.

Here, among the *haramia*, his word was the law. He liked that. Yet he could never fully acknowledge the esteem in which his comrades held him. The part of him that would never allow him to forget the pain of his early life was a sword that cut with a double edge, for it would also never allow him to believe he truly deserved the admiration of others.

"What's in that gourd that looks better to you than I do?" a familiar voice demanded, interrupting Imaro's introspection.

He looked up to see Tanisha standing before him, smiling as her hand smoothed her silken garment across the curve of her hips. Firelight reflected from the strings of gold looped around her body, and from the gold studs at the tips of her bare breasts.

"Nothing," Imaro replied, a slight smile curving his lips.

Setting the gourd aside, he reached up and pulled a laughing Tanisha down to him. She pressed her body against his as they embraced, and only a small outcry betrayed the pain she suddenly felt as the studs projecting from Imaro's war harness poked into her flesh.

Responding to that almost inaudible cry, Imaro ripped the harness from his chest and tossed it aside, disdaining buckles and thongs. The *haramia* had stripped the armor from many dead Azanians; he could always find another harness to don.

But there was only one Tanisha. No longer did the Shikaza woman share Imaro with the ghost of Keteke; her place in his heart belonged to her alone, and no other. Her arms encircled Imaro's neck while she covered his mouth with her own. Imaro and Tanisha were oblivious to the gradual diminution of the drumming and chanting, and they did not hear the commotion the *haramia* caused as they emulated their leader. Nor did they hear the laughter of the bandits as they swept dancing women into their arms and carried them off to shelters, bushes, and other trysting places. Only the women who had been captured in the raid on Tangwe showed signs of fear as the *haramia* descended upon them.

Imaro's lieutenants rose from their places, leaving their chieftain to his own amatory pursuits. Ngodire walked away silently, towering like a stork among quail. Kongolo and Bomunu lingered.

All evening, Kongolo had been keeping his eye on a lissome Tangwe captive who had darted him shy glances that were a combination of invitation and apprehension. She stood waiting for him in the firelight along with several other captives; no other bandit had approached her once Kongolo had passed the word that he wanted her.

As he started toward her, Kongolo noticed that Bomunu was now walking rapidly away from the dwindling group of captive women.

"Aren't you going to try your luck?" Kongolo asked jovially.

Muttering an inaudible reply over his silk-clad shoulder, Bomunu kept walking.

"Suit yourself, then," Kongolo said to Bomunu's back.

Then he took the arm of the captive, who was not many rains past girlhood, and led her toward the privacy of his makeshift shelter.

Bomunu cast a single backward glance at Imaro and Tanisha. The words he had not dared to utter aloud rattled like loose stones in his mind.

He, Bomunu, should have been the one enjoying the caresses of the Shikaza woman, and he, Bomunu, should have been the one who was leading the *haramia* to their greatest victories. Imaro had thwarted the Zanjian's ambitions. But they had not been extinguished.

Someday, Bomunu vowed silently. *Someday* ...

***

The thing in the pool completed its probings. Tendrils of thought had touched the minds of all the inhabitants of the *haramia*'s encampment. Most were dismissed with a flick of psychic disdain, for they were less consequential than insects. In the minds of others, the intangible tendrils scanned with momentary curiosity before withdrawing. And in one, they lingered, gripped by a sudden agitation of emotions that had until now been as stagnant as the liquid immersing the body of the prober.

Abruptly, the undetected perusal ended. It was time to act.

***

The sound struck without warning, like a leopard pouncing from a tree. It was a sound like the shrieking of a thousand tortured souls united as one. It was a doom-laden orison cried out by the worshippers of a dying god; it was the wail of a woman who had given birth to a stillborn child.

In the *haramia*'s encampment, lovers tore free from entwining embraces and thrashed spasmodically on the ground, their hands clutched at the sides of their heads. Other stood frozen in place, their hands clawing at their ears in a vain attempt to shut out the excruciating pain the awful sound produced. Even Imaro lay prostrate, rendered helpless by an assault that inexorably threatened to destroy his hearing.

As suddenly as it had begun, the sound ceased. Numbly, as if recovering from shock, the *haramia* pawed gingerly at their ears to ease the ache the mysterious noise had left behind. Nothing in their experience could explain what they had just undergone. Yet somehow, perhaps through a long-dormant trace of atavistic memory, many of the bandits were aware that what they had heard was a *song*—a song sung by something that was neither human, nor bird, nor beast.

Although his Tamburure-honed senses had suffered more than most from the effects of the sound, Imaro was the first to recover.

"What in Motoni was *that*?" he muttered, borrowing an East Coast curse he had learned.

He looked down at Tanisha to see how she had fared. She shook her head slowly, wiping tears of pain from her eyes. Although Imaro had not been expecting a reply to his question, Tanisha provided one.

"You should ask Ochinga," she said, referring to one of the newer members of the *haramia*.

"Why him?" Imaro asked.

"Bomunu told me Ochinga's tribe herded goats in these hills long ago."

A frown creased Imaro's brow. Bomunu was spending too much time with Tanisha, he reflected darkly. He would speak to the Zanjian about that.... But the confrontation would have to wait. For now, he needed information so that he could take action.

"Bring Ochinga to me," Imaro said.

The mood of the bandits had altered in the space of only a few moments. Their riotous gaiety was gone now. A pall of fear had settled over them like morning mist on swampland. Low voices mumbled supplications to obscure gods and half-forgotten ancestors. Trembling fingers fondled amulets previously valued only as trinkets or ornamentation. The tree-clad slopes that girded the valley in which the encampment was located seemed suddenly menacing, like the jaws of some gigantic beast about to snap shut.

Finally, Ochinga came forward. He was a lean, short, bandy-legged member of the Ndurubu tribe, which roamed the wooded areas. He bore a strong resemblance to Chimbu, but he had nothing of the latter's sour disposition. Ochinga was given to taciturnity in speech and reckless courage in battle.

Now, he sweated, but the perspiration bespoke anxiety rather than heat. The Ndurubu refused to meet Imaro's eyes as he stood before him.

"I have heard that your people once lived in these hills, Ochinga," Imaro said. "Can you tell us anything about that ... *sound*?"

"The Ndurubu call this place Weusi Milima—the Black Hills," Ochinga replied, still not meeting Imaro's gaze.

"We herded goats near here many rains ago," the Ndurubu continued. "But the elders say our ancestors fled this place because of a ... *thing* ... that dwells in the woods."

"Dog!" cried Bomunu, who had slipped quietly to Imaro's side.

Before Ochinga could turn to face him, Bomunu dealt him a treacherous blow to the side of his head, sending the Ndurubu sprawling to the ground.

"If you knew these hills were cursed, why in Motoni did you not tell us before now?" Bomunu raged, aiming a kick at Ochinga's midsection.

Curling into a defensive ball, the Ndurubu awaited a second kick from Bomunu's booted foot. It never came.

A heavy hand clamped onto Bomunu's shoulder. Then the Zanjian was hurled to the ground even more violently than Ochinga had been. Bomunu landed on his face, and he stifled a groan as he hit the ground.

"Have you forgotten who leads the *haramia*, Bomunu?" Imaro said quietly.

Bomunu did not reply. Rolling onto his back, the Zanjian used his elbows to lever himself into a sitting position. Blood seeped from his nostrils into his thin black mustache. He glared sullenly at Imaro, who had helped Ochinga to his feet. And he did not fail to notice that Kongolo and Ngodire had appeared at the Ilyassai's side, as well as Tanisha.

"This 'thing' you mention," Imaro asked. "What is it?"

Ochinga was shaking like a sick man. It was not Imaro he feared; like all the other *haramia*, Ochinga knew the Ilyassai's disposition was harsh, but fair. It was the tales from his childhood that frightened him now—tales the Ndurubu elders told; stories that were rampant with menace.

His throat was constricted, making it difficult for him to speak. Yet he did speak, each word costing him considerable effort.

"The dweller in the forest is called Isikukumadevu," he said. "The elders said it is a thing of evil, imprisoned in these hills long rains ago. Isikukumadevu never dies. And Isikukumadevu sings the doom of those who come too close—so the elders say."

"Why didn't you tell us before about this ... creature?" demanded Bomunu, who had regained his feet, along with a measure of composure.

Ochinga looked at Imaro rather than the Zanjian, even though Bomunu had been the one who asked the question. Bomunu seethed with resentment at the slight, but he didn't show it.

"Tell us now," Imaro said.

After a visible struggle to bring his trembling under control, the Ndurubu continued his story.

"Many rains have passed since Isikukumadevu last sang," he said. "That is why I said nothing when we came into the Black Hills. People like Bomunu would have laughed at me, and called me ignorant and superstitious. Even I had come to believe that Isikukumadevu was only a tale told by drunken old men. But we all heard that terrible *sound....*"

"Was it a call of some kind?" Imaro asked.

"No. That was Isikukumadevu's song of ... greeting. She calls the one she wants by name."

"*She?*" Tanisha asked incredulously.

"Yes, *she*," Ochinga said sharply, reacting to the disbelief that was clear in Tanisha's tone. "The elders always said Isikukumadevu was—*is*—a female creature."

"Whatever it is, we're going to break camp and get out of here now," Imaro said. "There are other places we can go that are beyond the reach of the soldiers."

"Is our leader frightened of this she-demon?" Bomunu asked, a sneer plain in his tone, if not his expression.

Imaro gazed at him levelly and dispassionately.

"After what happened with the Afua, you, of all people, should know better than that," the Ilyassai said.

Bomunu could only look away from Imaro's pitiless gaze, and from the truth in the warrior's words. Then Imaro turned to the rest of the *haramia*, who were, indeed, frightened of the she-demon.

"We'll need torches if we expect to walk out of these hills at night," he began to say.

At that moment, a new sound susurrated through the encampment. It was a hiss, yet there was nothing of the ophidian in its aspect. Unlike the previous spear of sound that had brought the *haramia* to their knees, there was no direct attack on the senses this time. Instead, it was a message—spoken softly, caressingly, rustling again and again like a sinister wind sighing in the ears of the outlaws:

imaroimaroimaroimaroimaroimaroimaroimaroimaroimaroimaroimaroimaroimaroimaro...

Abruptly, the whispering call was gone. As before, the echo it left behind died quickly.

Ochinga fell to the ground and tore at his hair.

"We are lost! Lost!" he wailed. "The elders spoke truly. Isikukumadevu has not died, and now she claims Imaro for her own! Imaro is lost, and so are we!"

"Be quiet!" snarled Kongolo, who had torn himself away from his Tangwe captive when Isikukumadevu first struck.

"Do you believe Imaro is one to be overcome by a *whisper*?" Kongolo demanded.

"Can you not see that Isikukumadevu is more than a whisper?" the Ndurubu, who had calmed somewhat, retorted.

A low, agitated murmur rose from the ranks of the *haramia*. Fear quavered in their voices as it never had before under the leadership of Imaro. They would have followed him headlong into battle against all the armies of the East Coast kingdoms, for they knew the Ilyassai would hurl himself so ferociously into the forefront of their enemies that it sometimes seemed that he won their battles by himself.

But an unseen foe that crippled with sound and called its victims to their doom … This, the *haramia* feared greatly, even with Imaro leading them.

Imaro knew that one more manifestation from Isikukumadevu would send the bandits fleeing senselessly through the wooded hills. And once they emerged from the shelter of the trees, they would be easy prey for the soldiers who hunted them.

He knew something else as well.… Isikukumadevu bore the taint of the *mchawi* that had been wielded by Muburi and Chitendu, and that had been unleashed when Rumanzila removed the spike from the Afua. Isikukumadevu was, therefore, a foe that had to be destroyed.

The time to act was now. Imaro exchanged a glance with Ngodire, whose counsel he valued. The Ndashikuya gave him a barely perceptible nod, as though he knew what the warrior was about to say.

"Ochinga!" Imaro said sharply, cutting through the Ndurubu's fear. "Where will I find this Isikukumadevu?"

Tanisha dug her fingers into the warrior's arm. But she did not protest; she knew it would be futile to do so. She did not want Imaro to die, but she also knew that a direct confrontation between him and this creature, whatever it might be, was the only chance she and the others had to survive—even if, in the end, Imaro didn't.

Imaro looked down at Tanisha. Then he looked again at the Ndurubu.

"The elders say Isikukumadevu guides her chosen in her own way," Ochinga said.

Before Imaro could ask Ochinga what he meant, a streak of pale light appeared on the ground at the feet of the Ilyassai. The light twisted in a luminescent trail across the ravine, leading into a thick tangle of dark hill-forest.

Isikukumadevu had answered Imaro's challenge.

For many of the *haramia*, the sudden manifestation of the eerie pathway of light proved the final strain for minds already burdened with apprehension. One voice—strident, unidentifiable—cried out.

"Run, before the demon claims *us*, too!"

That outcry triggered the incipient panic of the bandits, and some of them flung down their *ndizi-pombe* gourds and began to flee in the direction opposite to the one taken by Isikukumadevu's silver trail.

"Stop!" Imaro roared. "Anyone who runs, dies!"

Startled by Imaro's harsh words, the would-be deserters halted abruptly, as though they had collided with an unseen wall. Never before had Imaro threatened the *haramia*. He always led by example. Shamefaced, they hung their heads. But their braver comrades were too preoccupied with their own fear to chide them for their moment of weakness.

"Now, listen well," Imaro said. "Isikukumadevu called only me. I will answer the call—alone. If I am not back here by sunrise, you will have a new chieftain: Kongolo. Follow him, and continue to loot and slay, or fall apart and allow your pursuers to slay you. If I fall to Isikukumadevu, it will not matter to me."

The *haramia* gazed uneasily at the towering figure of their leader. Firelight daubed his lion-thewed frame in crimson and orange. Often, they forgot that Imaro had seen the passing of fewer rains than most of the others. He looked more than a match for any demon ever spawned.... Yet the *haramia* had seen him writhing on the ground like the rest of them, felled by Isikukumadevu's deadly song. In the very lair of this demon, how could even Imaro withstand another such attack?

Imaro turned to Tanisha.

"You understand that I have to go alone?" he asked, his hands gripping her bare shoulders.

"Yes," she replied.

Without further words, Imaro turned and followed Isikukumadevu's beckoning pathway. Apprehensively, the *haramia* watched as their leader disappeared into the woodland.

Tanisha longed to rush after him and envelop him in a farewell embrace. But she knew him—knew him well enough to realize that the bleak, unfeeling part of him she had never been able to reach, despite their love for each other, was at the forefront now. When he was like that, it was as though he had never known a tender moment in his life. Sadly, she at the entrance of the shelter she and Imaro would have shared that night. Her vigil had begun.

Of Bomunu, who had listened with growing incredulity while the man he hated more than any other had suddenly given to someone else the position he desired more than any other, besides the status he had once held in his homeland of Zanj, there was no sign.

***

Isikukumadevu's path led Imaro on a twisted, random course through the Black Hills. In the pale beams of Mwesu the moon, dark trees loomed like sentinels of nightmare. Creepers and lianas clung leechlike to his skin as he forged along the tortuous track of the shimmering streak of light. The normal night sounds of the forest were muted.

Dark, bitter broodings crowded Imaro's mind even as his *kufahuma*—attuned now to the forest after his time in the Kajua—told him no beasts of prey lurked behind the screens of foliage flanking his path. He did detect something else: faint sounds, far behind him. But they were of scant consequence. Whatever true danger there was, he would find it at the end of the winding trail Isikukumadevu had lain. And he would do his best to destroy it.

Mashataan. The name of the Demon Gods Chitendu had served reverberated in his mind now. Well did he remember the *mchawi* that had nearly destroyed him at the Place of Stones. He remembered the helplessness he had felt when Chitendu had held him motionless by sheer force of will. He had experienced a similar inability to act when Isikukumadevu's song brought him down at the *haramia* encampment. Feelings such as those came closer than anything else to unravelling the resolute fabric of Imaro's courage.

Yet whatever the unease that was awakened by this new intrusion of the Mashataan and the Naamans into Imaro's life, after he had been able to push them, and his futile search for a way to confront them, to the back of his consciousness for a time, it remained no more than a guttering candle next to the inferno of his rage. For he hated the Mashataan and their minions more than anything else in existence. It was their interference, through the machinations of Chitendu, that had caused his early life to be such an endless misery.

Memories of that life dominated Imaro's thoughts now. Hate lit wrathful fires in his dark eyes and transformed his features into something very similar to the face of a stalking lion. He was unaware of the passage of time as he forged deeper into the woodland.

Suddenly, he halted. At a point near a particularly thick growth of foliage, the path of light separated into four branches, each of them trailing away in a different direction.

Eyes narrowed in thought, Imaro considered Isikukumadevu's latest ploy. Was one of the paths genuine, and the others illusions? Would all four eventually lead to the demon, each in its own capricious and devious way? Or was Isikukumadevu now ... behind him?

A faint rustle in the brush had suddenly reached Imaro's ears. He whirled, sword at the ready. Mwesu's light flashed along the sharp steel blade. Muscles tensed rock-hard beneath the Ilyassai's dark skin as he stood in a half crouch, poised to strike. But he saw nothing—no eldritch shape shambling out of the darkness, no treacherous spear point about to be thrust from behind.

Yet he had heard *something*.

He was certain of it.

Imaro turned again to face the fourfold fork in the path—and nearly dropped his sword in astonishment at what he saw.

Each branch of the path now had an occupant. None of the four, Imaro knew, could be Isikukumadevu. For he recognized each of them, and he knew each was dead, slain by his own hand. But if they were dead, why were they moving toward him now, weapons raised and grim purpose glittering in their eyes?

Rumanzila was there. The moon's light picked out every detail of the garish ornamentation on the clothing of the former bandit chieftain as moved toward Imaro, sword sliding soundlessly out of its scabbard....

Mbuto was there. The punisher's mountainous bulk absorbed the moonlight rather than reflecting it. As he lashed his thick whip through the air, Mbuto's dull eyes focused on Imaro....

Chitendu was there. Towering higher than both Rumanzila and Mbuto, the *oibonok*'s body was swathed in a voluminous, iridescent cloak. Chitendu's head seemed disproportionately small; his body, oddly asymmetrical. The *oibonok*, who had been exiled from the Ilyassai, began to open his cloak....

N'tu-mwaa, *n'tu-mchawi* of the Turkhana, was there. He was naked. The pale splotches on his mahogany-colored skin glowed like phosphorescent fungus in Mwesu's light. His head was an unholy amalgam of the face of Ngatun the lion and the horns of an Ilyassai ngombe. Two blood-dripping beast hearts hung from an intestine looped around the Turkhana's neck. In his upraised hand, N'tu-mwaa held a curved blade; a blade splotched with blood....

In silent, deadly unison, the specters from Imaro's past attacked.

Rumanzila's sword clove the night air in a deadly crescent, aimed at the head of Imaro.

Mbuto's whip snaked toward Imaro's face, its tip snapping in a way that would blind or maim what it struck.

Chitendu's cloak gaped wide, exposing a brightly glowing mass of wriggling, maggotlike tendrils. The tendrils flared, and a bolt of emerald demon-fire lanced toward Imaro's body.

N'tu-mwaa hurled his dagger of sacrifice straight at Imaro's heart.

The deadly, simultaneous attack hit—nothing. Only a moment before, Imaro had stood in stunned disbelief, shaken by the sheer impossibility of what he was seeing. Yet the moment his former foes launched their onslaught, he had flung himself to the ground, rolled, and sprang to his feet behind the shelter of an ironwood tree.

Chitendu's burst of demon-fire had torn loose a huge chunk of the bole of the tree. The concussion of its impact rang in his ears. Imaro could see N'tu-mwaa's dagger buried deep in the scorched, smoking wood.

Crouching warily behind the tree, Imaro saw that his attackers remained in their places at the branches of the path. Chitendu's tentacles continued to glow. Mbuto's whip lashed back and forth like the tail of a great cat. Rumanzila's sword rested lightly in his hand. And N'tu-mwaa had somehow acquired another dagger, exactly like the one he had hurled at Imaro.

The irony of Isikukumadevu's choice of weapons to use against him was not lost on the Ilyassai. But he had killed each of these nemeses once before. Now, he would lure them deeper into the woods and kill them as many times as he had to, until they rose no more.

Then a memory came to him—vivid, but only in his mind, not before his eyes. He was back in the *manyattas* of the Ilyassai, on the day of his ill-fated *olmaiyo*. He was listening in disbelief to the lies that spewed from the mouths of Masadu, Kanoko, and the other warriors who were branding him *ilmonek*. To the warriors, the lies had been truth. Muburi, the *oibonok*, the tool of Chitendu, had used *mchawi* to cause the warriors to see what he wanted them to see—what they themselves secretly wanted to see. But what they thought they had seen was not real; it was not true.

"Not real," Imaro whispered between clenched teeth. "*Not real* ..."

Suddenly, the outlines of his four foes blurred, then broke apart like a reflection on the surface of water into which a stone has been cast. Then they snapped back into clear focus, each appearing as he had at the moment of death.

Rumanzila collapsed under the bulk of Mbuto, whose body had been impaled by the bandit chieftain's sword. Both men sprawled on the ground. Their eyes stared directly into Imaro's: vengeful, hating.

Chitendu, writhing like a dying serpent, his skull crushed, his alien intestines spilled and seared by his own demon-fire, raised his head in a final, supreme effort. His eyes daggered into Imaro's: vengeful, hating.

N'tu-mwaa, his beast-face twisted in agony, his sacrificial blade buried in his heart, lay unmoving on the ground. Yellow lion-eyes burned into Imaro's: vengeful, hating.

Then the figures began to blur. Stepping from behind the tree, Imaro watched them slowly disappear. His eyes were vengeful, hating.

When the apparitions were finally gone, the path changed. Once again, it was a single strip of shining brilliance leading directly into a thick tangle of foliage. The path seemed to beckon and mock Imaro at the same time.

Imaro looked at the ironwood tree. N'tu-mwaa's dagger no longer jutted from its wood. But there was still a gaping, smoking wound in the tree's trunk. Gingerly, Imaro touched the part of the tree that had been seared by the demon-fire. Heat flared on his fingertips. He quickly drew his hand back and glared at it angrily, as though it had betrayed him somehow. If the phantoms from his past had not been real, what, then, had so severely damaged the tree?

The implications of that conundrum caused Imaro's skin to crawl—but only for a moment—before he again followed Isikukumadevu's path of light. As he slashed and shoved his way through bushes and vines, he did not waste any thoughts speculating on what he would find at the end of the silver trail, or on who might be lurking treacherously behind him.

Whatever awaited him there, he vowed, would die.

***

After a seeming eternity of chopping through undergrowth that may or may not have been real, Imaro finally broke through to a small, circular glade that looked as though it had been scooped like a cup into the summit of the highest hill in the range. At the center of the glade lay a pool of a viscid liquid that was not water. Gnarled, stunted trees that grew in unnatural, eye-wrenching loops and whorls lined the margins of the pool. The area closest to Imaro, however, was barren of foliage. A narrow stretch of foul-smelling muck rimmed the shore.

The shining trail laid by Isikukumadevu led directly into the pool. Imaro tightened his grip on his sword-hilt and planted his feet in a fighting stance. For he had decided that he would not follow the silver path any longer.

He would not be so foolish as to meet Isikukumadevu in her own element. If the fetid pool was, indeed, the demon's lair, she would have to emerge from it to meet the Ilyassai. He steeled himself against a renewed onslaught of Isikukumadevu's song, even as he remembered the first time he had heard it. When it came, his only chance would be leap once and slash, and even that chance would only come if the demon-creature revealed herself, even if only for a moment....

A sound did, indeed, burst upon Imaro's ears. But Imaro did not go down with his hands clapped against his ears, as he had in the encampment. For the sound was not Isikukumadevu's song. Instead, it was one Imaro knew well. He had shouted it himself countless times in the past, in battles against the other tribes of the Tamburure—it was the war cry of the Ilyassai.

The cry did not come from the direction of the pool. Alerted by a rustle of limbs from the distorted trees that grew nearby, Imaro turned—and he saw a huge, lithe figure appear as if by magic from the foliage. In graceful, catlike bounds, the shape, still partially obscured by darkness, approached Imaro. Then it sprang fully into the glare of Mwesu's light.

Imaro prepared himself for an imminent attack. Then he uttered a half-strangled gasp of disbelief.

For the newest foe from the warrior's past that Isikukumadevu had sent him was—*himself*!

A single, incredulous glance told Imaro this was no mirror image he faced, nor was it a trick of his senses. It was the Imaro who had embarked so hopefully on his *olmaiyo*. His plaited hair was plastered with red ocher; his body was daubed with crimson clay; his *simi* gleamed in his massive hand.

It was the Imaro who had just slain Ngatun the lion, and was about to cut off the great cat's head and display it to the warriors of his clan. Seeing himself as he had been then, Imaro became one with the warrior who had just won the right to full manhood among a people who despised him. The hot scent of Ngatun's blood filled his nostrils; both Imaros cried out in joy and vindication....

Yet even in the Imaros' moment of triumph, the other Ilyassai were encircling them, their faces grim-set, their eyes hard. The Imaros knew then that betrayal was at hand. Roaring like the lion they had just slain, the Imaros swung their *simi* in a vicious arc....

A primal urge to survive jolted the warrior from his double-consciousness. Imaro raised the blade of his sword just in time to parry the death-slash from his earlier self. Sword and *simi* clanged together with an impact that numbed Imaro's arm and nearly caused him to drop his weapon.

The Imaro from the past struck again. Imaro leaped backward. Only by a hairsbreadth did he avoid evisceration. The other Imaro pressed his attack, the blade of his *simi* flickering like an iron wand.

Bewildered, Imaro fell back, fighting defensively. The metallic ring of Ilyassai iron clashing with *haramia* steel echoed in his ears. The other Imaro moved quickly—so quickly that Imaro could hardly follow the pattern of the *simi*'s blade as it repeatedly darted toward him, eager to taste his blood. His own movements seemed sluggish in comparison.

"Not real," Imaro muttered. "Not real ..."

But how could he believe that, when his former self was gradually backing him into the muck that bordered Isikukumadevu's pool? The other Imaro's red-daubed face snarled, and battle-lust blazed in his dark, narrowed eyes. His movements were graceful, like a lethal dance.

In contrast, Imaro's efforts were lethargic, almost desultory. It was as though he had become spellbound by the sight of his own mighty arm rising and falling, beating out a cadence of death against his own faltering blade. Only a nearly unconscious evocation of his fighting skills had prevented him from going down at the beginning of the other Imaro's attack. Even so, he felt the sting of half a dozen wounds, while the other Imaro remained unscathed.

Suddenly, Imaro's feet came into contact with the fluid of the pool. The viscid liquid sucked at his heels like quicksand. For a moment, Imaro's attention wavered, and his sword did not move. In that moment, the other Imaro's *simi* flashed and twisted, and slammed just above Imaro's hilt. The impact tore Imaro's blade from his hand, and it whirled into the muck. And the iron of the *simi* shattered against the steel of the sword, leaving the Imaro of the past holding only a hilt spiked with slivers of jagged metal.

The other Imaro swung the hilt in a sweeping blow aimed at the head of Imaro. Imaro ducked under the lunging swing, and the hilt flew by without touching him. Contemptuously, as he had done on many occasions, Imaro tossed the useless hilt aside—then, in almost the same motion, he smashed a heavy fist against Imaro's jaw. Caught unaware, as he had caught so many others, Imaro's head was snapped sideways, and he pitched backward into the pool.

Imaro struggled to raise his head above the foul, choking liquid. But before he could reach the surface, an iron-hard hand clamped onto the top of his head and shoved him deeper into the pool. Another hand closed crushingly around his wrist and began to force his arm behind his back. Feet slipping in the ooze at the bottom of the pool, Imaro strained his gigantic thews to their utmost. But the other Imaro seemed immovable as a mountain, and Imaro could not budge his adversary. Imaro's head remained beneath the surface of the pool, and his arm felt as though it was about to be wrenched out of its socket.

Not since his childhood had Imaro been rendered so helpless by any foe. Slowly, inexorably, he was drowning, dying in a futile struggle against his own strength, the strength that set him apart from all others—except himself.

Why? Imaro cried out in his mind as air emptied from his lungs. Why could he do nothing to fend off another self who was younger, less experienced and ever so slightly less strong than he?

The answer came to him with all the intensity of the pains stitching through his oxygen-starved lungs: *hate!*

It was a core of hatred that fueled his strength, expanding it to levels beyond the limits of other men. Hate had sustained him through the bleak years *of mafundishu-ya-muran*, when the hands of all the other Ilyassai of the Kitoko clan were raised against the son-of-no-father. And now … now, he had to redirect his hatred, to aim it against his earlier self, the fool who had actually believed he could be one with his mother's people, and earn the approval of those who hated him in turn—those whose approval finally came too late to matter.

Could he channel his hatred against himself? *Yes*. For he had done it before.

As his strained lungs seemed about to explode, Imaro gathered his legs beneath him, found purchase on the slippery bottom of the pool, and shoved upward. All the strength remaining in Imaro's thews powered that single, mighty surge. He burst through the pool's surface in a shower of viscid spray, and even as he blinked the loathsome liquid from his eyes, he reached out to grapple with his foe—himself.

He felt nothing—the other Imaro's crushing grasp was gone. And when his vision cleared, he saw nothing.

Shaking off the liquid of the pool and gratefully gulping air back into his lungs, Imaro awaited the reappearance of his other self. He heard a sound behind him, and he whirled, careful to maintain his footing. Ripples began to spread from a spot not far from where Imaro stood.

Then Isikukumadevu rose from the pool, making almost no sound despite the large amount of liquid the demon displaced.

As Ochinga had said, Isikukumadevu was a female creature. But she was far from human—as far from it as the *oibonok* Chitendu had become at the time of his demise.

Isikukumadevu was an enormous, squatting lump with a swollen, melon-like head that bore jaws similar to those of a hippopotamus. Pale, fishlike eyes glared chillingly beneath a tangled mane of mossy filaments that only slightly resembled hair. Mottled, grayish skin covered her naked, bloated body. Multiple breasts that were huge sacs of flesh spilled slackly over an abdomen that was grossly distended. Huge arms tapered into incongruously delicate hands that clenched in anticipation as Isikukumadevu scrutinized her latest prey.

Then Isikukumadevu spoke.

The syllables that slid from her mouth pricked at Imaro's mind like a handful of nettles pulled across naked skin. Isikukumadevu spoke in the same repellent, yet at the same time seductive, whisper that had drawn Imaro away from the encampment of the *haramia*.

"Imaro," Isikukumadevu said, her voice caressing the warrior's name. "The chants that praised your name, and disturbed my slumber, spoke the truth. Not since the conflict between the Cloud Striders and the Mashataan have I encountered a human being such as you. The Cloud Striders made your kind, even as the Mashataan made mine. Are you not aware of that, warrior?"

Imaro did not reply to the demon, even though he had questions of his own.

Who are the Cloud Striders?

What do you mean, they 'made' me?

But the creature's answers, he suspected, would be of no more use to him than Chitendu's.

"For the sake of your kind, Imaro, the Cloud Striders imprisoned me in this pool, where humans rarely venture," Isikukumadevu continued. "But when your kind comes close enough, I sing to the one who most deserves my … love. I will love you, Imaro, better than any woman of your kind could. In my love, you will die as all your kind should have done, so long ago."

Imaro still betrayed no reaction. Isikukumadevu grinned then, her mouth stretching wide, showing rows of peglike, grinding teeth.

"Love me, Imaro," the demon crooned. *"Now!"*

With preternatural speed, Isikukumadevu hurled her bloated mass toward Imaro. Her maw, fully open, hung above the head of the Ilyassai. A single snap of her jaws would have crushed Imaro into a crimson pulp—if he had been standing still as they closed.

The demon had read Imaro's thoughts well—but not well enough. She had plucked images from his mind, given them a semblance of life, and directed them against the warrior. She had studied him closely.… But she did not know him.

Isikukumadevu was the focus of Imaro's hate now, because her manipulations of his mind had undone all the forgetting he had forced upon himself since he had left the Ilyassai. With pantherish speed, Imaro evaded Isikukumadevu's jaws a moment before they snapped shut. Then he jammed his forearm beneath the creature's lower jaw. Bracing his left hand beneath his forearm, Imaro began to lever Isikukumadevu's head upward.

The demon croaked in pain—the first such sound she had uttered in many hundreds of rains. Wrapping her massive arms around Imaro's back, Isikukumadevu pressed him against the pendulous folds of her body. It was as though she intended to *absorb* him into the substance of her gray flesh.

His face a mask of fury, Imaro shoved his forearm harder against the point where Isikukumadevu's underjaw met her throat. Like a bar of black iron, Imaro's arm sank deep into the demon's flabby flesh. Isikukumadevu's head tilted farther upward. Strength undiminished by his struggle against the illusion of his former self, the Ilyassai redoubled his efforts to break the neck of his foe.

For a seemingly endless span of moments, man and monster strained against each other in a grotesque parody of a lovers' embrace. Then Imaro's foot slipped on the silty bottom of the pool, and he lost his balance. Instantly, Isikukumadevu seized her advantage and lifted Imaro off his feet, robbing him of his leverage. Then she sank deeper into the pool. Like the simulacrum she had created of Imaro's former self, the demon now intended to drown the warrior.

Back and shoulder muscles knotting beneath the pressure of Isikukumadevu's arms, Imaro forced the she-demon's head so far upward that her eyes stared directly into the face of Mwesu the moon. But he still continued to sink downward until the liquid of the pool closed over his head.

Now, only the upward-bent head of Isikukumadevu remained above the surface. Alarmed at the pain lancing through her creaking neck, Isikukumadevu unleashed the song that had disabled the *haramia*. The surface of the pool roiled in sudden agitation. Then Isikukumadevu sank from sight.

And the surface of the slimy pool became still and smooth again.

***

Bomunu rose slowly from his hiding place in the foliage through which Imaro had hacked. The Zanjian rubbed cautiously at his ears, as if that action could erase the remnants of the pain that still throbbed through his skull and left a ringing sound behind. He thanked his gods and ancestors that Isikukumadevu's song had finally ceased—for the second time that night.

The Zanjian had followed Imaro from the encampment, keeping to the shadows, hiding behind bushes and trees each time the Ilyassai turned his head in Bomunu's direction, moving as silently as he could. He had followed Imaro all the way to the pool at the summit of the hill. And then he had seen the warrior go mad—or so, at first, he had thought.

Eyes wide in disbelief, Bomunu watched as Imaro swung his sword wildly, ducking and dodging as though he were engaged in deadly combat. Yet Bomunu saw no foe in front of Imaro. Then Bomunu's mouth dropped open in astonishment when Imaro threw away his sword and plunged backward into the pool, as though he had been struck by some unseen force.

For a few moments, Bomunu thought Imaro had drowned himself. Then he saw the warrior resurface—and he saw Isikukumadevu.

A paralysis of terror had rooted the Zanjian to the spot where he crouched as he watched the ensuing struggle between Imaro and the she-demon. And after Isikukumadevu succeeded in dragging the warrior beneath the surface, Bomunu's heart leaped in unholy joy. But when Isikukumadevu's wordless song attacked his ears, Bomunu crumpled to the ground, writhing and whimpering like a punished child.

The surface of the pool lay placid and serene when Bomunu finally recovered his poise. Dark gratification suffused his soul as he realized the full significance of what he had witnessed.

Imaro was dead! And now he, Bomunu, could lay claim to the leadership of the *haramia*, even though Imaro had named Kongolo as his successor. But Bomunu had no doubt he could take the leadership—and Tanisha.

Without another glance at the pool, Bomunu turned and raced back down the jagged trail Imaro had cleared. To his horror, the Zanjian saw that Isikukumadevu's pathway of light was beginning to fade. Stumbling and cursing as his silken garments tore on protruding twigs and thorns, Bomunu ran frantically down the wooded hillside. To the ancestors who had long since disowned him, Bomunu prayed that he reached the encampment before Isikukumadevu's pathway disappeared completely and he became lost.

The final glimmer of the path died when Bomunu finally burst into the encampment. The *haramia*, who had maintained a sleepless vigil since Imaro had gone, rushed toward Bomunu, peppering him with questions about where he had gone, and whether he had seen Imaro. Bomunu paused before answering them, savoring his moment of triumph.

"Imaro is dead!" the Zanjian shouted. "He's dead! Isikukumadevu has taken him. I saw it with my own eyes!"

Tanisha broke loose from the *haramia* who surrounded her and confronted Bomunu. Her eyes blazed, and her breaths came hard with anger.

"You lie," she said. "Imaro cannot be dead. I would know it if he were."

Bomunu caught Tanisha's wrist in a grip that caused her to wince in pain.

"I tell you I saw him die," he insisted. "And with him gone … you belong to me now."

"No!" Tanisha shouted, struggling fiercely to free herself.

"Let her go," a new voice said.

It was Kongolo, who had swiftly grasped the import of Bomunu's actions, as well as his words.

"Let her go," Kongolo repeated. "We have only your word that Imaro is dead. How do we know you are telling the truth?"

"Who are you to be giving me orders?" Bomunu said, with a sneer reminiscent of his days as a courtier in Zanj, speaking to a servant. "And why do you doubt the truth of my words?"

Even as he spoke, though, he released his grip on Tanisha. She gave Bomunu a glare of contempt, then moved to the side of Kongolo.

"Have you forgotten what Imaro told us before he left?" Kongolo rejoined. "He said if he did not return here by dawn, I would become leader. That's who I am."

The others around Kongolo, including Ngodire, Busa, and Ochinga, murmured words of support and encouragement.

"As for how truthful you are," Kongolo continued, "if Imaro is dead, why are you still alive? Why did you not help him if he was being attacked by Isikukumadevu? Who are *you*, Bomunu?"

An angry rumble rose from the ranks of the *haramia*. Many of them preferred to believe that they would have aided Imaro against Isikukumadevu, however fearsome the demon may have been. Others remembered that Bomunu, like so many others among the bandits, had fled when the Afua came to life.

Bomunu was becoming uneasy. This was not going at all the way he had anticipated.

"Did you not hear the demon's song?" he demanded. "I was helpless, paralyzed. The demon killed Imaro and vanished with him before I could do anything."

"We heard no song, Bomunu," said Ngodire. "At least, not a second time. We only heard it once, while all of us were here."

"No ... song?" Bomunu repeated numbly.

Could it be that Isikukumadevu had concentrated her song so that it could only be heard at the summit of her hill, and nowhere else? Had his ancestors truly cursed him with such ill fortune, to thwart him at every turn?

Thinking quickly, Bomunu decided that only a desperate gamble would save his ambitions—and possibly his life—now.

"You ask me who I am," he said. "But, in turn, I ask you this: who is—or *was*—Imaro?"

The *haramia* stared at him as though he had lost his senses. Bomunu pressed on before any of them could reply.

"Imaro has brought us great riches," he continued. "But at what price? Do you not remember the gold-spiked statue that came to life and almost killed us all? Is it not strange that Imaro and the statue came to us at the same time? Is it not strange that he led us to where this Isikukumadevu lurks?"

Doubt appeared on the faces of some of the *haramia*.

"Imaro is dead," Bomunu repeated. "If you want to obey the wishes of a dead man, then follow *him*."

The Zanjian gestured toward Kongolo, who was scowling at him.

"If you want to be led to more riches, and not to demons and statues that walk, then follow me."

"If you want to follow a coward and a liar, follow him!" Kongolo shouted. "If you want to go and see what truly happened to Imaro, follow me!"

Bomunu's sword sang from its sheath.

"You dare to speak to me that way?" he said, his tone dangerously soft.

Kongolo drew his own sword.

"I dare to speak the truth," he said.

As the bandit lieutenants faced each other, the *haramia* split into two groups. One, with Chimba the most prominent among them, stood behind Bomunu. The other, led by Ngodire, Busa, and Tanisha, stood behind Kongolo. When the sorting of the factions ended, Bomunu quickly realized that he and his followers were outnumbered by a factor of five to one.

A wicked grin creased Kongolo's wide, ebony face.

"Do you still want to fight, Bomunu?" he asked. "As you can see, the odds are against you."

"No!" Bomunu cried, enraged at the ignominious unraveling of what had appeared to be his greatest opportunity.

"What if Isikukumadevu challenges more of us?" the Zanjian demanded. "What would you do then? I've *seen* Isikukumadevu. Only I can protect you from this demon. Are you all fools, to gamble your lives on loyalty to a dead man? How many times must I tell you that Imaro is—"

"Here."

All heads turned toward the sound of that deep, quiet voice. And a chorus of choked gasps, muffled screams, and muttered curses greeted Imaro's return to the *haramia*.

The slimy liquid of Isikukumadevu's pool dripped from Imaro's massive frame as he stood in the moonlight. His eyes burned with a light the *haramia* had never seen before, not even in the heat of combat. His features were set in a rictus that denoted supreme effort as he staggered toward the bandits, who quickly backed away to give him room.

In one hand, Imaro held his sword, its blade coated from point to hilt with a greasy, gray ichor that bore only a slight resemblance to blood.

In his other hand, Imaro carried something that caused even the most hardened of the *haramia* to turn away, hot gorge surging to their throats. The Ilyassai's fingers were twined tightly in the filamentous mane that covered the head of Isikukumadevu. There was no body beneath the head. The she-demon's wide-open, silvery eyes glowed lambently in the moonlight as her head swung from Imaro's hand like a huge, grotesque pendulum.

Slowly, Imaro walked toward Bomunu. Slack-jawed and wide-eyed in terror, the Zanjian retreated, his sword hanging forgotten in his hand. He attempted to speak, but only strangled sounds escaped his throat.

"Do you think I did not know you followed me, Bomunu?" Imaro grated between clenched teeth. "Here. Take this gift!"

With an effort that nearly pulled the muscles of his arm from the bone, Imaro swung Isikukumadevu's head in a circle, releasing his grip on the filaments at the end of the arc. Then the head shot straight at Bomunu, who uttered a single, piercing cry before the macabre missile crashed into his body.

The Zanjian fell, and lay motionless, the gaping jaws of Isikukumadevu cradling his head. But Bomunu was not dead. He had lost consciousness from the shock of seeing Imaro alive—and vengeful.

Whatever respect Bomunu had accrued among the bandits was gone now, vanished like an impala at the scent of a lion. The *haramia* who had sided with Imaro now fell to their knees, begging Imaro to forgive their disloyalty.

"Please spare us, Imaro," one of them implored. "We thought you were dead...."

Ochinga the Ndurubu stared in morbid fascination at the head of the demon his people had feared for more rains than he could count. Then he prostrated himself at Imaro's feet and began to chant:

"Mightier than all, mightier than all is Imaro, Imaro ..."

"Get up," Imaro snapped, his voice suddenly a whip. "All of you—get up and be quiet. And don't ever kneel to me again."

Uncertainly, the defectors—and Ochinga—rose, the Ndurubu doing so with great reluctance. Without another word, Imaro turned his back on them all and went to Tanisha.

"I knew you could not be dead," she said.

Imaro did not speak. But she could read his eyes. His eyes told her that Imaro needed her. And she knew he would never say that aloud. Tanisha took Imaro's hand and led him toward the shelter they shared. The *haramia* watched silently as he followed her with stiff, weary steps, as though he had reached the limit of his endurance.

For the rest of the night, the *haramia* talked about what had happened. Their reactions were varied. There was, however, one impression that underlay all others. Before they had come to the Black Hills, the *haramia* had respected and admired their young chieftain. Some almost worshipped him, as though he were a war god destined to lead them to victory against all foes. Those who admired his prowess had done so without envy, unlike Bomunu.

But now ... they all feared him.

There were flaws in the forging....

BETRAYAL IN BLOOD

Your worst foe,
Can be your best friend.
—Nyumbani saying

Imaro's blade sang a song of death as he attacked his foes. Neither swords nor shields nor leather armor nor flesh and bone could disrupt his deadly rhythm. He slashed rather than thrust, for he could not afford to waste the time it would take to pull his sword out of an impaled enemy.

Imaro was armed with a shield as well, but he used it to batter his foes as much as he did to protect himself from their weapons. Whenever he battered a soldier with his shield, his sword would flash in front of him, turning aside swords and spears alike.

He was clad in leather armor, stripped from the corpse of a foe who had fallen in a previous battle. It was barely large enough to fit Imaro's huge frame, but it was sufficient to protect him from the slashes he didn't deflect.

A helmet—also scavenged—protected Imaro's head. Beneath its brim, his eyes blazed with a ferocity that appeared only when he was fighting. His nostrils widened, as though they were smelling the blood from the wounds he inflicted. His lips pulled back from his teeth in a grimace that was half smile, half snarl, and totally terrifying to his enemies.

As Imaro engulfed the soldiers who faced him in a storm of steel, a group of *haramia* stood behind him, weapons poised to foil anyone who attempted to circle around the Ilyassai and strike him from the rear. Only a few of the soldiers made the attempt, and they died swiftly.

Corpses littered the ground at Imaro's feet. As the reality of the damage the warrior could inflict became clear, the soldiers fell back. Imaro looked back to the bandits behind him, and gave them a brief nod. At that signal, the *haramia* shouted a close approximation of the Ilyassai war cry and surged forward toward the demoralized soldiers, who continued to retreat.

Stepping aside, Imaro raised his own voice in a cry that carried above the clash of weapons and the shrieks of the wounded and dying. He waited a moment. Then he heard an answering shout, partly muffled by the foliage of the forest in which the battle raged. Cutting down yet another foe, Imaro raced off in the direction of the cry he had heard—which had been a signal that he was needed elsewhere.

The *haramia* were facing two armies that would, on any other occasion, have been fighting each other. Zanj and Azania were neighboring kingdoms that had been rivals for preeminence on the East Coast longer than anyone could remember. Peace between them came only intermittently. Most of the time, they engaged in warfare, with neither kingdom holding an advantage over the other for more than a few rains.

However, the threat that Imaro's *haramia* horde posed to the borderlands of both kingdoms created the need for an alliance neither of them truly wanted. Negotiating through clandestine emissaries, the monarchs—the Sha'a of Azania and the Mwamu of Zanj—agreed to send a combined army to crush the bandits, and to bring back the head of their leader, who was known as N'tu-nje—the Outsider.

Under the joint command of each kingdom's highest-ranking military officer, the huge army marched into the hinterland, overweeningly confident in its capacity to crush a rabble of outlaws led by a barbarian outlander. Quickly, and painfully, they learned that the *haramia* were formidable fighters, and none more so than N'tu-nje himself.

The bandits refused to engage in direct combat. Instead, they harassed the army like a pack of wild dogs snapping at the flanks of a buffalo. When the commanders sent out smaller units to hunt down the attackers, the *haramia* ambushed them and cut them to pieces. And whenever the *haramia* suffered setbacks, N'tu-nje would rally them with a new strategy, or simply through the example of his own demonic ferocity in battle, even though the combined armies vastly outnumbered their bandit foes.

Well aware were the East Coast commanders of the fate that awaited them if they returned to their respective monarchs in defeat and disgrace. Thus, they continued their wilderness campaign, hoping to break the will of the *haramia* through sheer attrition.

Recently, fortune had appeared to favor the soldiers. They had herded the *haramia* into a woodland, which the armies soon surrounded. Then they advanced inward, like the closing jaws of a trap.

Soon enough, they realized their error. In the forest, their advantage in numbers was negated, and tangles of brush rendered their horses almost useless. The *haramia* remained elusive, and they attacked the soldiers in small clusters, vanishing before reinforcements could arrive.

And then there was N'tu-nje....

The commanders, and many lesser-ranking officers, had scoffed at the stories they had heard about the mysterious barbarian who came from no known kingdom or tribe, who had welded the *haramia* into a disciplined combat force, and who fought as though he were possessed by a djinn, or was, himself, a djinn in human guise. Now, they knew the truth of those tales. And some of them were beginning to believe that the Outsider was, indeed, a djinn....

***

Imaro responded to yet another call for aid. Azanian and Zanjian soldiers alike were learning to fear the sound of the warrior's answering cry, for they knew that before the echoes died away, he would be among them like a lion, rending and tearing at their ranks, heartening the bandits and eroding the soldiers' will to continue.

Even as his sword reaped a red harvest, Imaro observed the soldiers' demeanor. Despite the loud urging of their commanders, the troops of both kingdoms were falling back toward the edge of the woodland. With sufficient numbers, the *haramia* could have turned the soldiers' encircling tactic against them, and the battle would have become a slaughter. Instead, Imaro used calls and runners to instruct his forces to drive the soldiers out of the forest, then pursue them—but only until the enemy was out of sight.

One by one, the isolated units of soldiers broke and fled, dragging their wounded with them and leaving their dead behind. The bandits followed, cutting down stragglers and taking no prisoners. They knew that in comparison to what had happened to those from their own ranks who had fallen into enemy hands, the swift death the *haramia* provided was merciful.

Jua the sun was sinking when the battle ended. Scores of corpses—mostly soldiers, but some *haramia* as well—lay on the forest floor. Blood soaked into soil that would not otherwise have received moisture until the beginning of the wet season.

Birds, monkeys, and other animals that had fled the incomprehensible fighting among the two-legs slowly returned to their territory. Scavengers that flew, walked, and crawled soon began to feast on the dead. The setting sun painted the scene of the battle in a deep, crimson hue.

And the *haramia* savored another hard-won victory.

***

Two armies trudged away from a battlefield not of their own choosing, united in defeat. Clad in the colors and accouterments of Zanj and Azania, the kingdoms' soldiers marched in separate ranks. The leather of their armor was slashed and torn; the metal of their shields dented; the blades of their swords nicked, and in some cases broken. Blood seeped through the scraps of cloth that bound their wounds. Those whose wounds were more severe hobbled, or were carried on improvised litters.

Bitterness burned in the eyes of the battle's survivors, even as they mourned the fallen comrades they had left behind, buried in shallow woodland graves topped with mounds of stones they hoped would be too heavy for the hyenas to push aside before the spirits of the dead could join their ancestors.

Once again, the combined forces of the two most powerful kingdoms on the East Coast of Nyumbani had been defeated by a rabble of outcasts from both kingdoms, and beyond. Once again, the *haramia*'s enigmatic leader, N'tu-nje, had triumphed over the finest troops the gold of two monarchs could buy.

Only the iron-handed discipline imposed by their commanders prevented the two armies from turning on each other in frustration and refighting ancient wars. And only the threat the *haramia* posed to Zanj, Azania, and their lesser neighbors could have compelled them to continue marching under the same banner despite the string of defeats they had suffered.

The *haramia*'s ranks had swollen since the days when they were led by Rumanzila the Ravager. With N'tu-nje fighting at their forefront, the bandits believed they were invincible, and they were making ever-deeper inroads into the kingdoms' territories, pillaging towns and even small cities. And they always returned to the hinterland, where they held sway as effectively as the Sha'a and the Mwamu ruled their kingdoms.

As the defeated armies made their way back into the their huge *kambi*, or encampment, in the borderland between Zanj and Azania, the only sound that could be heard was the weary tramp of feet and hooves, and the low, muttered curses of the soldiers who had yet again failed to gain victory.

And in the largest of the multitude of tents that dotted the flat wilderness land like a crop sown by some capricious god, the commanders of the two forces exchanged blame.

***

"Why did you want to chase them into that cursed forest in the first place?" demanded Mkojo, the *mwenye*, or commander, of the Azanian forces.

"It is their element, as water is to the fish," Mkojo continued. "Why fight them on their own ground?"

"Would you prefer that they come to us, and cut us down where we stand?" countered Chuwumba, *mwenye* of the Zanjians.

"You probably wouldn't have minded that at all," Chuwumba added. "Not as long as it was my men who were dying, and not yours."

The two men glared at each other across a dark space lit only by low-burning candles. They were the only ones in the huge command tent, for they preferred that others did not hear their strategy sessions, which had of late consisted of little more than mutual recrimination.

"We would not have been forced to fight the *haramia* in the woods if your troops had cut them off before they got there," said Mkojo.

"We *couldn't* cut them off," Chuwumba retorted. "Your troops were too damned slow to get into position. And it shouldn't have mattered anyway, once we had them surrounded."

Mkojo's only reply was a curse. He was a large man, and only his activities as a soldier prevented him from becoming obese. A broad-featured, bearded face the color of umber scowled from beneath the elaborate plumes atop his helmet—his only concession to his rank. His armor was as worn and battle-stained as that of the lowest troops under his command.

In contrast, Chuwumba was, as always, accoutered as though he were leading his soldiers in a parade before his monarch, the Mwamu. Gold ornaments glittered in the muted light of the candles, and Chuwumba's lean, narrow-featured face maintained an expression of studied neutrality. His eyes provided the only hint of his true character. They glinted as pitilessly as those of a serpent.

In any other circumstance, these men would be leading their armies against each other, fighting on a battlefield or besieging a city. For all their similarities in language and ancestry, Zanj and Azania had been foes for rains beyond counting—the consequence of a feud between two clans of a tribe that had wandered the East Coast lands in the time before the great trading kingdoms were founded. From time to time, one kingdom would gain an advantage over the other, but those periods of ascendance tended to be temporary. The smaller kingdoms and city-states that dotted the East Coast maintained their independence by manipulating the antagonism between their powerful neighbors.

Now, the smaller kingdoms viewed the current alliance between Zanj and Azania with apprehension. If it continued after the bandit army was defeated, then their own independence would be threatened.

However, if their kings could have observed the thinly veiled animosity between the two commanders, their concerns would have abated. The coalition was on the verge of failure. One more setback at the hands of N'tu-nje would cause it to collapse, and the consequences of that outcome would be immense.

Chuwumba was the one who pulled back from the brink of speaking words that might have begun a battle that would have engulfed the sprawling *kambi* in fire and blood. It had been his idea that the *mwenyes* hold their latest strategy discussion alone, without the presence of underlings who would have bared their blades at the slightest hint of an insult. The decision had been a wise one. But now, the tensions caused by repeated losses on the battlefield were undermining the forced courtesy that had marked the commanders' relationship.

"We have both made mistakes, Mkojo," Chuwumba said.

The Azanian *mwenye* said nothing. He was not inclined to acknowledge shortcomings, especially not to a Zanjian.

"But we are not the problem," Chuwumba said. "*He* is."

The scowl on Mkojo's face deepened. But his ire was no longer directed toward his counterpart—just as Chuwumba had intended.

"You are right," Mkojo said, his voice like a leopard's growl as he thought of N'tu-nje. "On that, at least, you are right."

Chuwumba chose to ignore that slight, with was subtle by the Azanian's standards.

"We would have left the bandit rabble for the scavengers long ago if N'tu-nje were not leading them," Mkojo continued.

"It is because of him that they're *not* a rabble," Chuwumba said.

"Is he a man?" Mkojo wondered. "Or is he a djinn?"

At the sound of the name of the demons of East Coast legend, Chuwumba's hands rose in a warding gesture.

"A djinn does not need a sword," he said.

"No," Mkojo agreed. "But this one, be he man or djinn, has turned the *haramia* into something very much like a sword. And he wields it well."

Both commanders fell silent then. The defeats the bandit chieftain had inflicted caused wounds that were hard to heal. Never before had either commander encountered tactics like those N'tu-nje employed. Large groups of *haramia* would emerge from the back country in lightning raids, striking swiftly, then retreating before the soldiers could mount an effective counterattack. And in the lone direct engagement between the troops and the *haramia*, which had just concluded, the bandits had more than proven their mettle, fighting with a single-minded discipline that the Zanjians and Azanians, who were as much at odds with each other as they were against the common foe, were hard-pressed to match.

Yet the soldiers might still have prevailed, had it not been for the presence of N'tu-nje himself. The bandit chieftain did not direct his forces from afar, like the *mwenyes*. Instead, he fought at the forefront of the fray. Well did Chuwumba understand why Mkojo had likened the man to a *djinn*. N'tu-nje was a huge man, of a race unknown in the East Coast kingdoms or their hinterlands. In combat, he fought with the strength and ferocity of a lion; none could stand before him. And he was a shrewd strategist as well.

During the last battle, Chuwumba had seen N'tu-nje redirect his forces in response to the soldiers' shifts in tactics. Even if he was not a djinn, the Outsider was a man of uncommon courage and cunning.

If I had him in my army, I could conquer Azania, Chuwumba mused.

But he did not say that aloud.

"What does he want?" the Zanjian wondered, speaking as much to himself as to Mkojo.

"What do you mean?" Mkojo demanded.

"What does N'tu-nje really want? Is he content merely to loot and kill? Or does he want to carve out his own kingdom, like the one before him, Rumanzila?"

"Rumanzila," Mkojo said, stifling an urge to spit on the ground. "That one had ambition, for certain. But he was only a half-caste from Mugishu. Most of the other bandit leaders opposed him because of who he was. This N'tu-nje … he is far more of a threat than Rumanzila could ever have been. The *haramia* follow him because of what he does, not who he is."

Chuwumba blinked in surprise. For the normally taciturn Azanian, those words were a long speech—and an astute one.

"As for what he wants—who knows? And how can we find out?" Mkojo continued. "The spies we send to infiltrate the *haramia* have an unfortunate habit of failing to return."

"Well, we cannot continue to chase after N'tu-nje like blind men," said Chuwumba. "We must find a way to make him come to us."

Mkojo snorted.

"Great thinking, Chuwumba," he said derisively. "What's your plan?"

Chuwumba laid his hand on the hilt of his sword and opened his mouth to utter a sharp retort. The words remained unspoken, for a voice that belonged to neither of the *mwenyes* interjected.

"I believe I can help you."

Both commanders swore in surprise. They rose to their feet, swords rasping free from their sheaths. And they both stood in wide-eyed, open-mouthed astonishment at the sight that greeted them.

***

The celebration at the latest *kambi* of the *haramia* had long since ended, and in the light of Mwesu the moon, the unruly sprawl of tents and shelters resembled a city of the dead. Drunken bandits sprawled where they had fallen in the spaces between the shelters. Only those who remained sufficiently sober to manage sentry duty showed signs of life. And even some of those leaned sleepily against their spears.

If the armies of Azania and Zanj could have fallen upon the *kambi* at that moment, they would have wreaked an unimaginable slaughter upon the *haramia*. But the defeated soldiers were far away, licking their wounds and dreaming of vengeance.

The usual piles of loot were absent, for the latest *haramia* triumph had not been the result of a raid on a caravan or borderland town. It was a defeat of those who had come to destroy them, and the spoils consisted only of weapons and armor taken from dead soldiers—and the lives of the surviving bandits.

A long time had passed since the *haramia* had last plucked the prizes of their calling: gold, silver, jewels, ivory, cloth, and captives—who were held for ransom, but never sold into slavery. Now, their primary occupation was avoiding death at the hands of the soldiers who continued to pursue them despite being continually defeated. Of necessity, the ranks of Imaro's horde had swollen. Any small, independent band of outlaws that ran afoul of the soldiers was massacred mercilessly, for in the minds of the Zanjians and Azanians, all *haramia* were legitimate prey, regardless of who led them. Necessity was the reason the outlaws joined N'tu-nje. When lions were at war, it was best to belong to the strongest pride. And no lion was more fierce than the Outsider.

Yet even as the warrior-from-afar continued to lead them to triumph over the armies of two monarchs, some of the *haramia* were becoming restive. They had no desire to be soldiers; indeed, more than a few of them had begun the bandit life as deserters from the very forces they were now fighting. Circumstances had forced them to accept the discipline that allowed them to inflict deep wounds on the soldiers, and to become a power in their own right in the borderlands. But it seemed that the demands of those circumstances would never come to an end. A life of fighting, retreating, then fighting and retreating again held scant appeal to men—and women—who were, essentially, lawless.

Ngodire, the tall Ndashikuya who was the most trusted of Imaro's lieutenants, captured the dilemma of the *haramia* in a conversation with the warrior that was heard by only a few others.

"We are like a python that attempts to swallow a buffalo," he said. "If the python succeeds in that endeavor, he soon wishes he hadn't."

Imaro did not dispute Ngodire's counsel. But he did not give any indication of what he intended to do next.

As the night deepened, and the aches of the day's battle eased, the *haramia* who remained awake cast an occasional glance toward the largest tent in the *kambi*, where Imaro and Tanisha slumbered. They thought about how their chieftain had changed since the slaying of the demon Isikukumadevu; how distant and implacable he was becoming.

Where are you taking us, N'tu-nje? the more thoughtful among them wondered. *And will we survive the journey?*

***

Inside the tent, Tanisha awakened suddenly from a deep sleep. Immediately, she knew why she woke. As her eyes adjusted to the dim firelight that filtered through the cloth walls of the tent, she saw Imaro lying beside her, a massive silhouette in the semidarkness. She was facing his back. One of her arms encircled his waist. Her hand rested on the hard muscles of his abdomen. The sweat from their previous lovemaking had long since dried, but his skin remained hot against hers.

Imaro's breathing had become ragged, his body rigid. It was the change in his breathing that had awakened her. Tanisha had become attuned to Imaro's nightmares. She knew what was coming now. Quickly, she wrapped her arms and legs around him, and placed a hand over his mouth.

A moment later, Imaro erupted into motion. His arms lashed out; his legs churned; he mouth opened; an outcry beat against the palm of Tanisha's hand. She stifled most of the sound. Only someone whose ear was pressed directly against the cloth of the tent could have heard it. Tanisha knew no one would dare to come that close.

Tanisha was well aware that she could not hold Imaro for long. Yet she also knew that if she did not restrain him until he came fully awake, he might charge out of the tent and wreak havoc in the *kambi*. It was the touch of Tanisha's skin, the scent of her body, and the soft murmur of her voice that released the warrior from the grip of his nightmare.

Abruptly, his movements stopped, and his mouth closed under her hand. She removed her hand then, and she rolled on top of him and covered his mouth with hers. When their tongues touched, Tanisha knew that the demons that had haunted Imaro's sleep were gone.

"It is getting worse," she said in a low whisper after their lips parted.

Imaro was silent for so long that Tanisha thought he was not going to respond.

"Yes," he finally said.

"Were you in the Place of Stones?"

"Yes."

Tanisha tightened her arms around him. He had told her before about his encounter with the sorcerer Chitendu in the crumbling ruin at the edge of Ilyassai territory. Chitendu had slain Keteke, the woman who had been with Imaro at the time. And the sorcerer had come close to killing Imaro as well.

The warrior had learned much during his confrontation with Chitendu. He knew the names of his enemies: the High Sorcerers of Naama, and their Demon Gods, the Mashataan. But he did not know where, or when, they would strike at him again. And he did not know how he would fight them.

Chitendu was dead. But he continued to live in Imaro's dreams, which were becoming more frequent, and would have been terrifying for anyone other than him. And even for him, they were causing concern.

"There were more of the High Sorcerers with him this time," he said. "I could not see their faces—I never can."

Imaro spoke in a low, calm voice, but his muscles were like stone beneath Tanisha's hands.

He keeps so much inside, she thought. *And it is probably best that he does....*

"They said they will find me, and kill me ... and everyone around me," Imaro continued. "They ... *showed* me what they would do to you."

Tanisha tried, and failed, to suppress a shudder. Imaro's arms tightened protectively around her.

"I will not let that happen," he said.

"Do you think they can reach us?"

Imaro let out a snort that might have been laughter. Tanisha knew it wasn't.

"If they could, they would have done it long before now," he said. "They seek to weaken me with fear. But I do not fear—for myself."

Tanisha raised herself on one elbow and looked down at him. In the darkness, she could not see his eyes. Still, she knew he was looking at her. She wished she could look into his eyes then, to see what lay behind his words.

"What will we do?" she asked.

Tanisha had deliberately said "we," for her worst fear was that Imaro would one day decide to challenge the High Sorcerers on his own, leaving her behind and out of danger. She would never allow that, for she was a woman of the Shikaza, and when such a woman found the man to whom she would belong, she was his forever.

As though he were reading her thoughts, Imaro said, "I will not leave you."

She kissed him then, and for a moment, more lovemaking was imminent. But Imaro then said something Tanisha hadn't expected to hear.

"I will have to tell them."

Tanisha knew he meant the *haramia*.

"Tell them what?" she asked.

"I will have to tell them they face more than just the armies of the men who live in stone houses," Imaro said.

Tanisha sat up then, and hugged her knees against her breasts.

"And what do you think will happen then?" she asked.

"Some of them will go, and take their chances with the Zanjians and Azanians," he replied. "Some will stay. The ones who stay will be my people."

"Your people?"

Again, Imaro was silent for a time. When he spoke again, he chose his words carefully, as though he was expressing thoughts he had never before considered.

"The Ilyassai were my mother's people, not mine," he said. "The Mtumwe of the river could never be my people. Their ways could never be mine. But the *haramia*—they are outsiders, like me. The ones who will stand with me against the Naamans will be my people."

Now it was Tanisha's turn to be silent. She understood what Imaro had said, and she admired his ambition to create a tribe of his own to substitute for one he had left behind. Even so, she wondered how many of the bandits would be willing to remain at Imaro's side after he told them about his inevitable confrontation with the Naamans and the Mashataan. His tribe could turn out to be far smaller than he hoped.

"When will you tell them?" she asked.

"Not now. But soon."

The warrior put an arm around her and drew her down to the sleeping mat they shared. Tanisha yielded, as always. She anticipated that the time to enjoy such pleasures was becoming more limited by the day. The wet season was still far away, but she could sense that storms were coming.

***

Imaro was not the only *haramia* whose dreams were beyond the ordinary. The slumber of Chimba, the bandit who would be least likely ever to count himself as one of Imaro's people, was also restless, though he showed few outward signs of any disturbance.

No woman lay at Chimba's side. He slept in a tent filled with other *haramia* who had swilled enough *pombe* to render themselves insensate. The others drank because they had survived yet another battle, and had defeated armies from which they would have fled had they not been led by Imaro. Chimba, however, drank because of his dreams, and what they compelled him to do.

Chimba had been a favorite of Imaro's predecessor, Rumanzila, and also of Rumanzila's lieutenant, Bomunu. He had resented Imaro's arrival among the *haramia*, and when the Ilyassai rose to the leadership, Chimba had almost departed rather than follow an outlander. In the end, he stayed, and for a time the looting was better than it had ever been under Rumanzila. But his dislike of Imaro, which was rooted in envy, did not abate.

He had almost departed again after Bomunu's disgrace in the Black Hills. The Zanjian had slipped away from the *haramia* not long after that debacle, unwilling to bear the contempt in the eyes of his fellow bandits, or the scorn with which Tanisha regarded him, or the utter indifference of Imaro, who behaved as though Bomunu no longer existed.

Bomunu had departed in secret. Despite the misgivings of Ngodire and Kongolo, Imaro had simply said, "Good riddance."

Chimba would have gone as well, had it not been for the dreams, which began at that time. No nightmare images haunted his dreams. A single presence pervaded them: the voice of one who had departed from the *haramia* long before Bomunu had done so. Words dominated Chimba's dreams:

words that cajoled, words that promised, words that advised, words that threatened....

The voice told him not only to remain among the *haramia*, but also to ingratiate himself with Imaro; to gain the trust of the Ilyassai, if not of his lieutenants; to become one whose advice Imaro heeded. Success would bring great rewards, the voice assured him. Failure, or an attempt to escape, would result in consequences that would cause death to be welcome in comparison.

Chimba obeyed the voice's commands. Slowly, grudgingly, he had gained Imaro's ear, if not his camaraderie. For all his bitterness, Chimba was a sharp-witted man, and not even the skeptical Ngodire could find fault with the advice he offered.

Yet times came when Chimba simply could not stomach the role he played, or the mask he wore—especially when the *haramia* fought harrowing battles against trained troops instead of looting helpless caravans or villages. Chimba had not joined the *haramia* to become a warrior. With each battle he survived, his reluctance to remain in the *haramia*'s ranks increased.

It was when his thoughts turned to desertion that the dreams would come again, more intensely than before. Words were no longer sufficient: now, he was shown, in sickening detail, the punishments that awaited him if he failed or fled. Chimba had seen more death and destruction than most men, other than his fellow *haramia*. But the images that seared his sleeping consciousness were more than sufficient to dissuade him from reneging on the pledge he had made to the one who had sent them.

On this night, Chimba had come closer than ever before to succumbing to the urge to flee. He had barely survived the latest battle, even though the soldiers had been routed in the end. He would remain, though. Well did Chimba know the sender of the dreams. And well did he fear him.

***

Bomunu cursed bitterly as he pushed his way through the woodland that surrounded the *kambi* of the Zanjian-Azanian army. Even though Jua hung high in a bright azure sky, the brush was thick enough to conceal him from the eyes of sentries. But twigs and branches caught at his clothing like hands bent on impeding his progress—and announcing his presence to someone with keen hearing.

The Zanjian had acquired a modicum of woodcraft during his time among the *haramia*—more, at least, than the city-bred soldiers in the *kambi* would ever know. He prayed to the gods of Zanj that the sentries would attribute the small noises he was inadvertently making to the movements of animals. Most of the wildlife of the hinterland chose to avoid such a large gathering of two-legs. Yet the smaller, more furtive creatures remained.

Since his departure from the *haramia*, Bomunu had lived like such an animal—scavenging for food, hiding in terror whenever the predators of the wild stalked. With a scowl of disgust, he brushed at his tattered, threadbare garments. That he, the scion of the House of Kariunge in Zanj, was reduced to such squalid circumstances galled him as little else could have done. Little—save for the circumstances that caused him to crouch near the Azanian side of the *kambi* rather than that of his homeland. Well did he know that if he showed his face to his countrymen, he would be slain immediately.

His chances with the Azanians were only marginally better. Accordingly, he had bided his time carefully, waiting until a succession of setbacks had demoralized the combined armies. Now, while they were licking the wounds the *haramia* had inflicted, the Azanians might be more amenable to accepting the assistance he would offer.

And then, his vengeance against Imaro would begin.

Bomunu breathed deeply, made a final attempt to arrange his attire, smiled beneath his thick, black moustache, and stood up, no longer concerned about the rustling noise that accompanied the process. Then, keeping his hand well away from the hilt of his sword, he strode toward the first sentries he saw.

As soon as he emerged from the brush, two Azanian sentries confronted him. In the wake of the defeat they had recently endured, they looked scarcely less bedraggled than Bomunu. The leather armor both men wore was slashed and torn, and bandages circled a wound on one man's arm. The points of their spears showed signs of hard use. However, the weapons were still capable of skewering Bomunu where he stood. He waited for the guards to speak.

"Who are you, and what do you want here?" the taller of the two sentries demanded.

"I am a friend, with news for your commander," Bomunu announced, speaking as he would to a servant in his father's house.

"He look like a 'friend' to you?" the taller soldier asked his companion.

"No," the other replied. "Looks more like a bandit."

"Smells like one, too," the other added, not to be outdone.

Indeed, Bomunu's once-sumptuous attire had been reduced to little more than faded rags that hardly covered his body. Even the peacock feather that adorned his turban had been broken in half sometime during his wanderings. And he hadn't bathed in days.

But he still knew how to behave like a highborn.

"You could never even imagine what I went through to obtain the information I have for your commander," he said haughtily. "And I cannot imagine what you will go through if he does not receive it."

Bomunu assumed his tone would intimidate the soldiers. The assumption proved mistaken.

"You sound like a Zanjian," the shorter sentry said. "Why don't you take your 'assistance' to their side of the camp?"

"I decided that the most important side should be the one to have it," Bomunu retorted.

A few other soldiers were now gathered to see what had caused the minor commotion. Bomunu's words raised a few chuckles; the soldiers had little else to laugh about.

"Never thought I'd hear a Zanjian say something like that," the taller guard mused. "Be that as it may, we can't leave our posts unless we're ordered to, and we're sure as Motoni not taking orders from you."

He turned to the newcomers.

"Why don't you escort this one to *Mwenye* Mkojo's tent?" he suggested. "Let him decide if our 'friend' has anything worthwhile to offer."

His partner nodded agreement, happy to shift the responsibility for Bomunu to someone else.

"Why not?" said one of the others.

He motioned peremptorily to Bomunu.

"Come with us, Zanjian," he said.

Seething inwardly at such impertinence from commoners, regardless of their nationality, Bomunu obeyed. He caused something of a stir as the soldiers escorted him through the *kambi*. To Bomunu, the troops resembled a demoralized mob more than they did the army of a civilized kingdom. Some of the soldiers honed their weapons and patched their armor. Others drank deeply from gourds, and Bomunu suspected they were swallowing something stronger than water. And some simply stared vacantly, awaiting the next command to go into battle.

Bomunu shook his head as he approached the *mwenye*'s tent. Perhaps he had chosen the wrong side after all. But it was much too late for him to change his mind now.

Two soldiers, cleaner and looking less dejected than the others, stood guard at the entrance to the tent. When Bomunu and his escort came closer, the guards crossed their spears to bar the way.

"Who is this?" one of them asked, indicating Bomunu.

"Somebody who wants to talk to the *mwenye*," one of the escorts replied.

The guards were about to respond when a voice from inside the tent forestalled them.

"Let him in."

Resentment flickering momentarily on their dark faces, the guards uncrossed their spears. But they did not step aside. One of them held out an open hand.

"Your weapon," he said.

Bomunu unbuckled his sword-belt and handed his sheathed weapon to the guard. After taking it, the guard moved away from the entrance.

The Zanjian pushed aside the entrance flaps and walked into the tent. His eyes widened in reaction to the dimmer light inside—then they grew even wider in astonishment.

He had never before met Mkojo, but he had known of the commander by reputation even before his exile from Zanj, and he had a general idea of his appearance. It was the man standing beside the *mwenye* who caused the renegade to take an involuntary step backward.

"You!" was the single word he managed to choke out as the entrance flaps closed behind him.

***

The man at Mkojo's side was one Bomunu had never expected to see again. He had not known whether this person was alive or dead, nor did he particularly care. Much time had passed since the man had occupied Bomunu's thoughts.

"Angulu," Bomunu said, his voice reduced to a mere whisper.

For it was, indeed, the *wa-nyanume*, the rogue Azanian sorcerer who had served Rumanzila and then disappeared after the *haramia* were nearly destroyed by the Afua. In the time since Imaro's ascension to the leadership, Angulu's name was no longer mentioned among the bandits, although the memory of his magic lingered.

The sorcerer had changed since Bomunu had last seen him. His face had become leaner, almost skeletal. And his entire body was covered by a cloak made of cloth that was so dark it seemed to swallow the light. And Angulu's eyes threatened to swallow Bomunu.

"Indeed, it is I," the *wa-nyanume* said. "I saw you coming. We instructed the soldiers not to harm you. *Mwenye* Mkojo would like very much to hear what you have to say. So would I."

Struggling to maintain a measure of aplomb, Bomunu bowed low to both men. He addressed his first words to Mkojo.

"As Angulu must have told you, *mwenye*, I am a former member of the *haramia*," he said. "How it is that I joined them is of no consequence. Eventually, I became sickened by the excesses of the barbarian who leads them. I realized that he must be defeated, and his bandit army scattered. If that does not happen, the entire East Coast could collapse into chaos."

Neither the commander nor the sorcerer spoke. Fear was beginning to turn Bomunu's courage into water. But he pressed on, for his wits were the only weapon he had left to wield.

"I am well acquainted with N'tu-nje, the barbarian," he said, his words tumbling quickly, desperately. "I know his secrets. I know how he thinks. I could help you bring about his downfall—"

Mkojo laughed then, and Bomunu's fear congealed into a small, hard knot at the pit of his stomach.

"What could you tell me, Bomunu of Zanj, that I have not already heard from Angulu?" the *mwenye* asked. "He has told us of how N'tu-nje came to be among the *haramia*, and he has told us the outlander's true name—Imaro. And he has told us more than that. What knowledge can you add?"

Bomunu had no answer to give.

"I cannot think of any possible use I could make of you," Mkojo said. "However, I am certain that my fellow *mwenye*, Chuwumba of Zanj, would be grateful for a chance to speak with you."

It took all of Bomunu's will not to drop to his knees and beg for his life. He knew that such a display of cowardice would earn only the disgust of the commander and further reduce his rapidly diminishing chances of leaving the *kambi* alive.

"Your fame—or is it infamy—has reached even into Azania, Bomunu of Zanj," Mkojo said with a smile that caused Bomunu's knees to tremble. "The 'Highborn *Haramia*,' I believe you were called.... Yes, you and Chuwumba will have much to discuss...."

"Wait," said Angulu.

Mkojo paused, then nodded in acknowledgment of the *wa-nyanume*. That display of deference caused Bomunu to forget his overwhelming fear, if only for a moment.

"Bomunu could still be of some value to us," Angulu said.

"In what way?" Mkojo asked.

"He has been with Imaro longer than I was," Angulu replied. "He may be able to help us anticipate what the barbarian will do next."

Bomunu gave Angulu a glance of gratitude, which the sorcerer did not return. Mkojo's brows creased in thought. Then he nodded.

"That may well be," he said. "Sit, Bomunu of Zanj. Let us hear what more you have to say."

Bomunu almost sank onto the stool toward which Mkojo motioned. The three men talked well past sunset. And in the darkest hours of that night, Angulu's voice intruded into Chimba's dreams, imparting new instructions.

***

Towering cliffs dominated the site at which the *haramia* had located their latest *kambi*. It reminded Imaro of the place where he had first become involved with the *haramia*, even though that place was far away. The heights provided a vantage point from which the sentinels Imaro had posted could see the enemy coming from afar.

And they would come....

Regardless of how decisively the *haramia* defeated them, the soldiers of Zanj and Azania continued to pursue them. The losses the bandits inflicted on the ranks of the soldiers were heavy, yet reinforcements continued to arrive from both kingdoms.

In contrast, few newcomers augmented the ranks of the *haramia*. In earlier days, not long after Imaro succeeded Rumanzila as their leader, other outlaws had flooded to his side. The pickings were plentiful; the chances of death, minimal. After the *haramia* had sacked the small border city of Tangwe, however, the Sha'a and the Mwamu had intensified their efforts to eradicate the bandits. Now that the kingdoms' armies had joined forces, the hunt had become relentless, and the appeal of the Outsider's banner had dimmed considerably. Bomunu had been only the first of several *haramia* to make a clandestine departure from the ranks.

A spring flowed from a crack in the yellow-and-red rock that formed the face of one of the cliffs, leading to a stream far below, where the *haramia* washed and slaked their thirst, as well as that of their few horses and pack animals. Water was plentiful here; food was another matter. Between the supplies they took from the soldiers and the meat the *haramia* who could hunt provided, Imaro's forces were not starving. But a reliable food source was becoming a concern, especially since Imaro would not allow the *haramia* to slaughter any cattle they captured. The part of him that was still Ilyassai could not countenance such a defilement—he still felt guilt over the fate of the cattle he had freed when he escaped the Shaming.

In a secluded area not far from the waterfall, Imaro conferred with several other *haramia*. Despite the victory the bandit army had achieved over its foes, the gathering was more somber than celebratory. The *haramia*'s triumphs were proving more costly to them than to the Zanjians and Azanians, a reality of which Imaro and the others who were gathered near the waterfall were fully aware.

Tanisha was there. Imaro trusted no one more than her. The Shikaza woman had long ago eschewed the gold, jewels, and other finery that usually bedecked her. She was clad like the other bandits: in *suruali* trousers and a leather breastplate that had been looted from a dead soldier and modified to accommodate her proportions. A short sword was sheathed at her side; Imaro had taught her how to use it, and its blade had already tasted blood.

Ngodire was there. He was the first of Imaro's lieutenants, and no one among the *haramia* could match the sagacity of the towering Ndashikuya. The counsel he offered Imaro reflected that wisdom, though the Ilyassai did not always heed Ngodire's advice. The Ndashikuya posed no threat to Imaro's leadership. His sharp tongue had wounded more than a few *haramia*, and some of them would prefer to kill him rather than follow him.

Kongolo was there. The stolid, ebony boulder of a man stood equal to Ngodire among the *haramia*. Kongolo had transferred his loyalty from

Rumanzila to Imaro without question and, outwardly at least, harbored no ambition to take Imaro's place, even though Imaro had said Kongolo was to lead the bandits if Imaro fell.

Chimba was there. The dour bandit was not one of Imaro's lieutenants, and he was hardly a friend of the Ilyassai's. However, his shrewdness came close to matching that of Ngodire, and on the battlefield, he was a deadly combatant. Despite the objections Kongolo had raised, Imaro had invited Chimba to the gathering. Chimba's words were often worth heeding.

Busa was there. The Mtumwe did not rank highly among the *haramia*, and he rarely had advice to offer. But he seldom strayed far from Imaro's side. Behind his back, some of the other *haramia* called him "N'tu-nje's dog." With his intricately scarred skin and his aloofness from everyone except Imaro and Tanisha, Busa was the true outsider among the bandits. And in the endless battles against the soldiers of the Mwamu and the Sha'a, he fought as though he was daring death to claim him.

Ngodire spoke words that encapsulated the plight of the *haramia*.

"We are like a rope that is being pulled by elephants at each end," he said. "We are a strong rope—we couldn't be any stronger. But sooner or later, the elephants will pull the rope apart."

"What would you have us do, then?" Kongolo asked, a frown furrowing his dark face.

"There are only two things we can do," Ngodire replied. "Either we kill the elephants, or we find a way to make them drop the rope before it breaks."

Both lieutenants looked at Imaro then. The warrior appeared to be distracted. But when he spoke, it was clear that he had been listening to, and evaluating, Ngodire's words.

"We can kill one of the elephants," he said. "But there are not enough of us to kill both of them."

"Then how can we make them drop this 'rope' Ngodire's talking about?" Kongolo asked.

"We could become an elephant, instead of a rope," the Ndashikuya replied enigmatically.

Kongolo laughed humorlessly.

"By what sorcery do you expect to accomplish that?" he asked sardonically. "In case you haven't noticed, Angulu is no longer with us."

"We are better off without that one," said Tanisha.

Imaro looked at her, but she did not say anything else. In the meantime, Ngodire answered Kongolo's question.

"Rumanzila always wanted to be more than just a bandit chieftain," he said. "He wanted to build a kingdom of his own in the lands beyond the borders of Zanj, Azania, and all the other East Coast countries. That is how we could become an elephant. And ... Imaro would make a far better king than Rumanzila."

All the others looked at Imaro now. Only Tanisha could guess at what Imaro was thinking.

Ngodire's analogy of the elephants and the rope applied not only to the *haramia*, but to Imaro himself. In his case, the elephants were his desire to destroy the Naamans, and his obligation to the people he led. And ... he had never as much as imagined himself to be a king. Not while he lived among the Ilyassai, who had never accepted him as one of their own until it was too late to matter. Not among the Mtumwe, whose ways he could not fathom. Not even among the *haramia*, who were a band of marauders rather than a tribe or clan.

Even though they were outlaws and outcasts, the *haramia* were his people now. He was responsible for them. Their fate depended on his decisions. They were his people—and, if Ngodire was speaking for them all, they wanted him to be not just their chieftain, but their king.

Him—the "son-of-no-father."

Yet the *haramia* knew nothing of the dreams that came to him each night. They did not know the danger that he brought to them. Had the time come to let them know? Imaro was not certain.

Kongolo broke the silence.

"Where would we go to begin our own kingdom?" he asked. "The lands beyond the borders are useless, worthless. That's why no one lives there."

"We could make these lands useful and worthwhile to us," said Ngodire. "Others have done more, with less."

"If we go far enough away, it would not be worthwhile for the Sha'a and the Mwamu to continue to pursue us," said Tanisha.

"If we're that far away from everyone else, what would we do to live?" Kongolo asked. "Farm? Herd? We are not farmers or herders. We are thieves and robbers. If we settle down, we will no longer be *haramia*."

"I was once a herder," Imaro said, looking directly at Kongolo, who quickly looked away.

Ngodire spoke then, hoping to forestall the flicker of anger he saw in Imaro's eyes.

"Whatever we once were, we are not bandits anymore," he said. "We are an army—an army without a home."

"I do not want to live behind walls of stone," Imaro said then. "And I do not want to continue to fight against an enemy whose numbers are as endless as the ants in an overturned hill. We will go to another place."

"Where?" Kongolo asked.

Imaro was about to reveal his secret then: the conflict between him and the High Sorcerers of Naama, and his determination to destroy his enemies, and his need for their help to accomplish that aim. But Chimba spoke first.

"I know of a place," he said.

"Do you, now?" Ngodire asked, his skepticism evident.

"I know more than you think," Chimba retorted.

"Tell us," said Imaro.

"The other side of the Kakassa River," said Chimba.

The name meant nothing to Imaro or Busa. The others, however, reacted with varying degrees of disbelief when they heard it. Tanisha's eyes widened. Kongolo let out a harsh bark of laughter. Ngodire's long, ebony face showed a grimace of disgust, and he gave voice to what the others were thinking.

"Are you mad, Chimba?" the Ndashikuya demanded. "Are you a fool? Or are you both?"

"Have you ever been to the Kakassa?" Chimba retorted.

"No! Who, in their right mind, would ever go there?"

"I have been there," Chimba said in a deceptively soft tone. "And I was in my right mind at the time."

Although he was as a child next to Ngodire, who towered over even Imaro, Chimba's eyes betrayed no hint of fear as he glared up at the Ndashikuya. He seemed to relish the other man's enmity.

"What is the Kakassa?" Imaro asked.

"It is said to be a river like no other," said Ngodire. "It moves as swiftly as this waterfall, and it is filled with sharp, jagged stones that would rip out the bottom of any boat that attempted to travel on it. That is why the Kakassa is called the 'River of Blood.'"

He turned back to Chimba.

"Yet you found a way to cross it."

"It was before I joined Rumanzila," Chimba said, ignoring Ngodire's incredulity. "I was on my own then. A robbery in Zanj went wrong, and the city guard was chasing me as hard as these soldiers are chasing us. I finally gave them the slip near the Kakassa, or else they finally decided I wasn't worth any more of their time. I was trying to find a way to double back when I saw it: a way across the river that was free of the rocks. It was luck more than anything else that led me to it."

"Did you go across?" Imaro asked, his curiosity aroused.

"No. There was no reason to. All I wanted to do was get away from the city guard, and I'd already done that."

"Then you don't know what's on the other side," said Ngodire.

"Whatever's over there, it can't be any worse than the armies of two kingdoms seeking to wipe us off the face of Nyumbani."

"So, you would lead us from the leopard we know to the leopard we don't know," said Ngodire.

Chimba did not respond. He was looking at Imaro, as were all the others at the gathering.

Imaro's thoughts raced along trails they had never traveled before. He did not trust Chimba—few of the *haramia* did. Even so, the dour bandit's counsel had sometimes proved valuable as the *haramia* fought their running battle against the combined might of two kingdoms.

The veracity of Chimba's claims was at the forefront of Imaro's considerations. If Chimba was telling the truth, then Imaro saw a way to continue his association with the *haramia* a while longer, and a way to postpone telling them about the Naamans. If he could lead them to this unknown land across an impassable river, then he would have a better chance of convincing the *haramia* to join him in the destruction of the shadowy High Sorcerers.

And there was something else as well—something he had never before admitted to himself. For all his need to be apart from others, Imaro could not deny his desire to hold on to the tribe he had forged with his own hands—the only people he could call his own.

I will not let you take that away from me, he vowed silently to the phantoms that haunted his dreams. *I will not.*

Imaro stared hard at Chimba. He did not delude himself into thinking that Chimba harbored any greater liking for him than he had when Imaro had first arrived among the *haramia* as an unconscious, trussed prisoner. Yet Chimba would suffer the same fate as anyone else if the soldiers ever captured him.

The warrior turned his gaze to Tanisha. Her expression was neither encouraging nor discouraging; this decision was to be Imaro's alone. Without further delay, he chose.

"You can find the way to this crossing again?" he asked Chimba.

"Yes."

"Then we will go there."

***

The attack on the village of Umtala was totally unexpected. Located in the vicinity of the Kakassa River, Umtala had long remained apart from the sway of the coastal kingdoms, which did not consider the lands deep in the interior worthy of conquest or contention. The ancestors of the Umtala had fled such conflicts hundreds of rains ago, and when they reached the impassable river, they found a secluded area where they could plant their crops, graze their cattle, and live in tranquility. Subsequent events that reverberated throughout the eastern lands left the Umtala untouched, and there were some among them who believed the rest of Nyumbani would never breach the isolation they had chosen.

Their sanctuary was near the Kakassa, but not close enough that they could see the great river. Its constant roar had a menacing note.

Abruptly, their long seclusion came to an end. Marauders swept into the Umtala village like a swarm of locusts. The Umtala had no chance to defend themselves; the few who managed to pick up weapons were cut down before they ever had a chance to wield them.

Yet only a few people died during the assault. The raiders were more concerned about capturing than killing the Umtala. Only those who resisted died. The Umtala who surrendered were bound and hurled to the ground. Some of the villagers managed to escape; the raiders did not pursue them.

When the brief attack came to an end, the marauders forced the captives to their feet and lined them up in a clearing at the center of the village. Then they closely inspected the Umtala, as though they were appraising cattle. The attackers were of the East Coast race, as were the Umtala. But appearance was the only similarity between them, for the raiders were clad in the garments of several coastal kingdoms, none of which the Umtala recognized. Nor were they accustomed to the obvious contempt with which the invaders regarded them.

The Umtala had been isolated for so long that they could comprehend only a few of the words their captors spoke. Their actions, however, were easily understood. One by one, the young women and men—those who were on the verge of undergoing the rites of passage to adulthood—were pulled aside. The invaders kicked all the others back to the ground, leaving their bonds intact.

More than a score of the Umtala village's youths stood in a trembling knot amid the hard-faced intruders. As some of the raiders surrounded the captives and forced them to leave the village, others used still-burning cooking-fires to light brands, which they then tossed into the Umtala dwellings. The Umtala had long ago given up the practice of building in stone; their thatch-and-straw dwellings quickly turned into gigantic torches.

Frantically, the remaining Umtala struggled to free themselves while the raiders departed with their captives. Some of them managed to wriggle loose from their bonds before their burning houses collapsed, sending flaming debris flying in all directions. Others were neither quick nor fortunate, and they died screaming in the roaring flames.

The survivors could only watch helplessly as their village burned. And while they struggled to comprehend the calamity that had engulfed them, they remembered the one word they had heard more than any other from the intruders—a word they identified with those who had wronged them; a word they despised, but could not forget.

The word was *haramia*.

***

"Is it not like times of old?"

The voice from the darkness startled Bomunu out of his reverie. He had been standing alone, beyond the night-fires, wishing he were somewhere—*anywhere*—else.

Gone were the tatters that had clothed him when he first approached the *kambi* of the East Coast armies. The garments he now wore were not as elaborate as he would have liked, but they were clean and intact. Less intact were the ambition and bravado that had goaded him out of his comfortable life in Zanj, and into the precarious existence of the *haramia*.

The voice belonged to Angulu. In his all-enveloping cloak, the *wa-nyanume*'s substance had become shadow, as though he were a part of the night that had somehow taken on human form. Fear was never far from Bomunu whenever he encountered Angulu now. In the time before Angulu had departed from the *haramia*, relations between him and Bomunu had been cordial, if not particularly close. Since then, however, the *wa-nyanume* had … changed.

"You always wanted to lead the *haramia*," Angulu continued. "Now, you do."

The mocking tone of the sorcerer's voice stung Bomunu.

"Not like this," Bomunu said.

Bitterness laced the Zanjian's words. The men he had led on the raid against the Umtala village were not true *haramia*. They were soldiers, drawn from both the Zanjian and Azanian ranks, who wore the eclectic garb of the outlaws instead of their military accouterments. The disguised troops had followed Bomunu and Angulu into unknown territory, not far from a river that had previously been more legendary than real.

This was not the first time Bomunu had been among bandits who raided a remote village for captives. Slave markets were no more scrupulous about dealing in stolen property than any other.

But the purpose of this raid was different, in a way that sickened even the jaded, amoral Bomunu. Even though he had participated in the planning of this part of the strategy Angulu and the *mwenyes* had devised to destroy the *haramia*, he could not think about what he was doing without feeling revulsion—for himself and for Angulu, even though he owed his life to the *wa-nyanume*.

When Chuwumba, commander of the Zanjian forces, learned of Bomunu's presence on the Azanian side of the *kambi*, he had demanded that the outlaw be turned over to him without delay. *Mwenye* Mkojo's refusal to do so had come close to causing an irreparable rift between the two armies. Angulu's insistence that Bomunu had a vital part to play in the plan finally convinced Chuwumba to relent—but he did so only grudgingly.

Now, as he looked toward the dark, barely discernible forms of the Umtala captives, Bomunu knew their fate would be far worse than being sold into slavery in one of the East Coast cities. His regret for that outcome lasted only for a moment.

Better them than me, he thought.

"Soon, we will both get what we want," Angulu said.

Bomunu looked at him. The *mwenyes* had promised both men freedom from retribution for the misdeeds they had committed while they were with the *haramia*. Bomunu wanted more than that, and he was prepared to make full use of his opportunity to get it.

He did not know what Angulu wanted. He had no desire to know.

"Soon, indeed," was all Bomunu would say as he watched the shadows the wavering firelight cast.

***

In a long, ragged line, the true *haramia* marched warily through the unfamiliar country south of the Kakassa River. Some were mounted; most trudged on foot. The land here was incongruous; it was as though several types of terrain had been jumbled together by gods who were either mischievous or drunk. Rocky, broken outcrops jutted from flat plains; ragged copses of forest stood adjacent to swamps; natural barricades of thornbush lay athwart the path the *haramia* followed. Wildlife was abundant, but herds and solitary beasts alike gave way to the two-legs. Even the mighty elephant shunned the smell of so much steel.

The bandits' numbers had decreased since their last victory over the soldiers, for Imaro had given them the choice to follow him to the Kakassa, or fend for themselves. A small, but not insignificant, number chose to remain in the borderlands in the hope that they could continue their lawless ways after the alliance between Zanj and Azania ended.

And there was another reason the *haramia*'s ranks had thinned....

Shouts and curses emanating from the rear of the *haramia*'s line alerted Imaro, and he waited for news that had become far too familiar.

"Halt!" he commanded.

Then, he waited. Soon enough, a runner came from the rear. Breathing in ragged gasps, the runner, who was barely beyond boyhood, looked up at the Ilyassai.

"They got another one," the youth said.

Imaro did not have to ask who "they" were. Not long after the *haramia* had ventured into this unknown territory, unseen assailants had begun to pick off single bandits in stealthy attacks. Arrows and poisoned daggers were the attackers' weapons of choice, and they left no sign of their coming or going. The killings were random; they could occur at night, or in the middle of the day. Despite the *haramia*'s efforts at tracking, the assailants remained elusive. It was as though they were wraiths rather than humans.

Imaro turned to Chimba, who marched with him at the head of the *haramia* column, leading the way to the Kakassa and its crossing. Tanisha was also at Imaro's side, as was Busa. Ngodire and Kongolo were farther down the line, helping to keep the march in order.

"You said no one lives in this land," Imaro said to Chimba, not for the first time.

"No one did, last time I was here," Chimba retorted.

Tanisha spoke then.

"Well, you're wrong now," she said. "And if you were wrong about that, what else might you be wrong about?"

Before Chimba could respond, Busa spoke.

"This one is a snake," he said in the Mtumwe language. "You should have killed him long ago."

Imaro was the only one who understood all of Busa's words, for the river peoples' language was only distantly related to the Kiswa the coastal people spoke. Chimba, however, understood the gist of what Busa had said. The scrawny bandit laid his hand on his sword-hilt.

"Why don't you try it yourself, scar-skin?" he sneered.

Busa put his hand on the hilt of his *panga*, the chopping weapon he had retained since his departure from the Kafua forest.

"Enough," Imaro said, the impatience in his tone unmistakable.

Both men moved their hands away from their weapons. However, their mutual dislike remained clear on their faces.

Imaro was about to send some of the *haramia* to search for the attacker when a new disturbance claimed his attention—more shouts from the rear of the bandits' formation.

Another killing? Imaro thought. *They have become bolder.*

But this time, the *haramia*'s cries had a different tone. They weren't shouting in surprise or panic. Instead, Imaro heard taunts and jeers, and the sharp sound of blows struck by fists and spear butts. The sounds grew louder as more people joined in the beating.

A large group of *haramia* approached Imaro now. Eschewing even the limited discipline the bandits were willing to accept, others broke ranks and joined the crowd that was surging toward their leader. When they reached Imaro, the *haramia* at the forefront stepped aside.

Standing in their midst was Kongolo. Another *haramia* was with him. Between them, they held a captive who could barely stand unaided. Blood dripped from wounds caused by the many blows the captive had received while the *haramia* dragged him to Imaro. Now, he was barely clinging to consciousness.

"We finally got one of these sneaky dogs, thanks to Mtobo, here," Kongolo said, a wide grin splitting his ebony face.

The young *haramia* on the other side of the captive grinned as well.

"I was lucky," Mtobo admitted. "But it's better to be lucky than it is to be dead."

The other *haramia* roared with laughter, expressing their relief after so many days of facing death from the shadows.

With a single heave of his huge hand, Kongolo forced the captive's head upward, so that he was looking at Imaro. Outwardly, the man looked no different from the other people of the East Coast: brown-skinned, lean, taller than average, and long-faced, with protruding front teeth. Instead of *shati* and *suruali*, however, he was clad in a bark-cloth garment that covered him from waist to knees. His only other accouterment was a quiver, from which all the arrows had been removed. In his other hand, Kongolo carried the pieces of a broken bow.

"Who are you?" Imaro demanded. "Why are you attacking us?"

When the captive opened his bleeding mouth, broken teeth were revealed. Instead of replying, he spat on the ground at Imaro's feet.

Kongolo raised his fist to strike the captive for his effrontery. But Imaro raised his hand to forestall the blow. Then he motioned to Kongolo to give him the halves of the stranger's bow.

The weapon was fashioned from hard, resilient wood. Imaro squeezed his hand on the pieces, and the wood cracked loudly. When Imaro opened his hand, splintered pieces of the bow fell to the ground. Wide-eyed, the captive stared at Imaro. He did not spit a second time.

"Who are you?" the warrior asked again.

The captive spoke then. His words flowed in a torrent, only barely recognizable as Kiswa. Imaro and the others could not follow what he was saying, but the outrage in his tone was evident.

"Speak slowly," Imaro said.

The stranger obeyed, and now the *haramia* were able to make out enough of his words to understand him.

"I … Kulutu," he said. "My people … Umtala. Strangers come … to Umtala. Strangers kill … take many away. Strangers say they … *haramia*. You … come. Strangers … too. Look like … *haramia*. *Haramia* … kill Umtala. Umtala … kill *haramia*."

Several of the bandits raised their voices in anger and disbelief, and Imaro scowled in disgust. He did not allow the *haramia* under his command to steal people for the purpose of selling them to the slave markets. The tribes of the Tamburure sometimes took captives during their wars, but they were treated as prisoners, not slaves. Imaro himself would have been sold into slavery had he not withstood a brutal initiation into the *haramia*'s ranks—an experience he had never forgotten.

When he spoke to Kulutu, Imaro pronounced his words slowly and carefully, so that he could be certain he was not misunderstood.

"We are not the ones who attacked you, and took your people away," he said. "If you stop hunting and killing my people, we will help you to recover yours."

The *haramia*'s reaction to Imaro's pledge were varied. Tanisha looked at him in admiration. Chimba's lips curled in contempt; then he quickly neutralized his expression. Kongolo and Mtobo shook their heads in disbelief, a sentiment Kulutu shared.

"You do this … even after … we kill yours?" he asked.

"Yes," Imaro said.

"Are you sure this is wise?"

Ngodire was the one who asked that question. He had joined the others in the group surrounding the captive. Before Imaro could answer the question, Chimba spoke.

"Why should we delay crossing the Kakassa to help a dog like him?" he demanded. "Even now, the soldiers could be gaining on us. We have no time to lose."

"They may not be coming after us at all," said Ngodire. "Our back-scouts have not reported anyone on our trail. Maybe the Zanjians and Azanians believe their work is done—that they have driven us out of the borderlands, and there is no longer any reason for people who can't stand the sight of each other to continue to fight on the same side."

"You wish," said Chimba.

"We will help Kulutu's people," Imaro said. "Then Chimba will lead us to the Kakassa."

From the tone of Imaro's voice, the *haramia* knew he would not tolerate further discussion.

"Let him go," he said to Kongolo and Mtobo.

The two *haramia* released their grasp on the Umtala's arms. He almost fell forward, but he managed to maintain his balance and his dignity.

"Did your warriors try to follow the ones who stole your people?" Imaro asked.

"Yes. Some follow … none come back."

"Are there any more—hunters, like you?"

"Yes … some."

"Call them off," Imaro said. "Then show us the way the people-stealers went with your youths."

Imaro turned to Mtobo.

"You go with him."

The face of the young *haramia* no longer bore a smile. N'tu-nje was asking him to place himself in the hands of people who could still be enemies. Yet he also understood his presence would be a gesture of good faith that the Umtala could not fail to recognize.

Mtobo nodded. A moment later, he and Kulutu trotted past the bandits who, only moments before, had wanted to kill the stranger.

That night, dreams came to Chimba. But for the first time in many nights, none came to Imaro.

***

The river to which Bomunu and Angulu took their captives was not the Kakassa. It was a tributary that flowed less furiously, and dangerously, than the River of Blood. Only a few of the soldiers in *haramia* guise accompanied them. There was no need for more; the Umtala's fear of Angulu was stronger than the yokes and ropes that bound them.

Night had fallen. Although only half of Mwesu showed its face, the light was sufficient to show the captives the nameless river, which, until now, no Umtala had ever seen. Despite their youth, the faces of the captives showed signs of experiences that had aged them well beyond their rains. Their eyes stared vacantly, as though the captives' spirits had already fled their bodies.

"Untie them," Angulu commanded. "They will not move."

Inwardly, Bomunu bristled at the *wa-nyanume*'s imperious tone. Outwardly, he showed no sign of discontent, for his fear of the sorcerer was in no way less than the fear the captives harbored.

More than ever, he understood that this was not the same Angulu he had known before. If Angulu had been pursuing the same forbidden knowledge that had led to his exile from his native Azania, it had taken him to places no human was meant to go. Now the *wa-nyanume* seemed hardly human at all....

Bomunu and the other soldiers untied the yokes from the captives' necks and removed the rest of their bonds. As Angulu had promised, none of the Umtala attempted to escape.

"Strip them," said Angulu.

The captives had few garments to remove. The soldiers pulled them off and laid them in a pile beside the discarded ropes and yokes. Now the Umtala stood naked in the mud of the riverbank. In a land that had never known the touch of cold, they shivered.

"Step back now," Angulu told the soldiers. "Your work is done."

The soldiers obeyed as though the command had come from Mkojo or Chuwumba. Bomunu was not the only one among them to have become wary of the sorcerer.

As the Umtala stood unmoving, Angulu began to utter syllables in a language neither they nor their captors had heard before. The *wa-nyanume*'s voice changed into a serpentine hiss that caused Bomunu's skin to crawl in revulsion.

Angulu's voice rose to a sibilant crescendo, and Bomunu fought an urge to cover his ears. Then the air stirred. The moonlit surface of the river rippled. Then, abruptly, Angulu's incantation ended. But even though the alien syllables no longer issued from the sorcerer's throat, the surface continued to roil as though lashed by the winds of a storm.

Then the surface broke. And Bomunu and the soldiers flung their arms over their eyes to block the sight of what was emerging from the river. The captives cried out more loudly than the soldiers. But they could not cover their eyes. They were unable to move at all.

Long after the screaming stopped, and the furious splashing of the water ceased, and the soldiers and Bomunu uncovered their eyes to see the forlorn pile of clothing that was the only remnant of the Umtala captives, they would remember their single glimpse of what Angulu's chant had summoned from the river.

And when they returned to the *kambi* of the combined armies, bearing the news that they had accomplished their task, the memory remained, like a parasite that burrows beneath the skin.

For they knew they would see that awful sight again. Even as they awaited the order to begin to march, they knew it.

***

The pile of garments remained on the riverbank when Imaro and the *haramia* arrived several days later. Recognizing the sad relics of the people who had been stolen, Kulutu and the other Umtala guides dropped to their knees and sent an ululating chorus of mourning into the sky.

Respecting the Umtala's grief, the bandits stepped back from the riverbank. Before they did, however, they saw the footprints of the captives in the mud. They also saw peculiar gouges and furrows at the river's edge. And they saw red smears of blood, and other signs that hinted at the horror that had occurred in this desolate place.

Imaro stood apart from the others, with only Tanisha at his side. Although his face showed no expression, his eyes had become as hard as onyx. But it was not what his eyes showed him that caused the tension in his stance, which was reminiscent of a great cat poised to spring.

Since the time of his encounter with Chitendu at the Place of Stones, the warrior had developed a sense that was akin to *kufahuma*, the affinity with his surroundings that often warned the warrior when danger was imminent. All who were raised in the Tamburure possessed *kufahuma*. The other sense was Imaro's alone—an awareness of the presence of *mchawi*, the evil sorcery that Chitendu had practiced, and the power that had animated the Afua when Rumanzila had removed one of its golden spikes.

If *mchawi* were an odor, it would smell like carrion.... But the manner in which Imaro sensed it made it even more unpleasant. The taint was as powerful here as it had been at the Place of Stones, and the warrior's lips involuntarily pulled back from his teeth in a silent snarl.

Tanisha touched his arm. Her face bore an expression of concern as she looked up at him. He had seen him bare his teeth in this manner before:

in the shadow of the night, when the dreams held him in their grasp. The dreams that made his nights a battleground had not affected him recently. Were they now plaguing him while he was awake?

"Imaro?" she asked. "What is it? What is wrong?"

The snarl faded from the warrior's face. But his eyes remained hard as he answered her.

"*Mchawi,*" he said, in a tone that reflected his loathing of that term, and all it implied.

Tanisha nodded. The reach of Imaro's foes was long. But why did they strike here, at people who had no involvement in the conflict? Why not strike directly at Imaro?

The warrior turned and headed back to the group of Umtala, who had ceased their mourning and now stood quietly, staring at the slow-moving river as though its water could bring the captives back from its depths. Little more than half a dozen of them had accompanied the *haramia* on the search for the captives, and they remained wary of the bandits, despite Kulutu's assurances that the raid on their village had been the work of others.

Tanisha was at Imaro's side as he spoke to Kulutu. So was Busa. The other *haramia* remained in the background, muttering among themselves. Ngodire and Kongolo stood aside as well, for they knew that Kulutu, for reasons they could not understand, seemed more comfortable in the presence of the Ilyassai than anyone else among the bandits.

Kulutu eyed the three people who stood before him. Imaro, with his huge stature; Busa, with his marked skin; Tanisha, with her uncommon beauty—all of them so different from the Umtala, who had remained secluded for so long that they had almost forgotten the existence of other people. They wished they could remain apart from all others—but that was no longer possible.

"Do you know what happened here?" Imaro asked.

Kulutu shook his head.

"No," he said. "We never come to this river. It leads to the River of Blood … and we never go there, either."

The Umtala's speech had become easier to understand during their time with the *haramia*. Even as he listened, Imaro's eyes followed the flow of the river, which was not nearly as wide as the Damba Bolong, where Busa's village was located. If the sight of the river caused stirrings of nostalgia for the Mtumwe in Busa's heart, he kept them well hidden.

"These marks," Imaro said, indicating the gashes that were interspersed among the footprints. "Do you know what made them?"

Kulutu and the other Umtala looked at each other, unease apparent in their expressions and in the way they moved away from the riverbank. Finally, Kulutu spoke a single word, in a near-whisper:

"*Tuyabene.*"

"What does that mean?" Imaro asked.

Again, the Umtala hesitated. Imaro waited them out.

"Water demons," Kulutu finally said, as though the mere mention of their name could summon them.

"Very evil," said another of the Umtala.

"So are the ones who brought your people to them," said Tanisha.

Kulutu looked at her with an expression that combined sorrow with incredulity.

"We live far from the river to be away from the *tuyabene*," he said.

"Not far enough," said Busa.

Kulutu blinked in surprise. Busa spoke so seldom that the sound of his voice was startling.

In the meantime, Imaro looked as though he wanted to dive into the river and confront the *tuyabene* single-handed. He was looking at the spoor of others who had been at this place, along with the captives. The tracks of a small number of people could be seen in the mud, following the flow of the river. From the distance between the tracks, Imaro could see that these others had departed quickly, and had stumbled in their haste to get away.

The taint of *mchawi* was almost unbearable, but Imaro showed outward sign of its effects. He turned his attention back to Kulutu.

"We cannot bring back your people," he said. "But we will find the ones who gave them to the *tuyabene*. And we will kill them."

Seeing the fury that had gathered like storm clouds in Imaro's dark eyes, Kulutu knew the warrior would fulfill that vow.

"We, too, will kill them," the Umtala said.

Tanisha looked at Imaro with approval—and admiration—as he called the *haramia* to him. After the bandit army assembled, he spoke to them in tones that carried above the rush of the river.

"We have another enemy," he said. "It is neither the Zanjians nor the Azanians, and it is an enemy that uses our name against us. We must destroy this enemy."

"What about the Zanjians and Azanians?" asked Chimba. "Do you think they will just sit back and watch us chase after these false *haramia*?"

"Where are the Zanjians and Azanians?" Ngodire asked Chimba. "Have you seen them?"

Chimba did not reply.

"We will send scouts to keep watch on the soldiers," Imaro said, paying no heed to the bickering. No one else asked questions or raised objections.

"We go now," said Imaro.

"Wait," said Kulutu.

Imaro turned to him.

"We must bury what is left of our youths, and sing their spirits to the ancestors," Kulutu said.

Imaro nodded.

Later, as the voices of the Umtala provided the pathway along which the spirits of the *tuyabene*'s victims would travel, one of the *haramia* muttered, "Another fight, and nothing to show for it but our lives—if we are lucky."

He was not the only one to harbor that thought.

***

"Imaro. We must talk," said Ngodire.

The Ndashikuya was the only person, other than Tanisha, who could address the *haramia* chieftain in such an insistent tone. Imaro looked up at Ngodire's troubled face. Then he nodded.

The two men stepped away from the night-fires at the haramia's latest *kambi*, which sprawled across a rare open area of country that was mostly woodland. They had been following the trail of the false *haramia*, which paralleled the river, for days. So far, they had not come close to catching them.

Ngodire and Imaro had established a bond of trust and respect before Imaro became leader of the *haramia*, and the Ndashikuya's loyalty to the Ilyassai was unquestioned. Ngodire had no intention to become leader himself, for he knew he was even more of an outsider than Imaro, or even Busa. Few would be willing to follow him.

And now, some were not willing to follow Imaro, either.

Imaro looked toward the shelter he shared with Tanisha. The bandits no longer had the time to pitch semipermanent encampments, with tents and other amenities. They were spending all the time and energy they could muster in pursuit of the false *haramia*, who were proving to be maddeningly elusive prey.

The warrior preferred to be with Tanisha now. He could guess the reason Ngodire wanted to talk, and it was the last thing he wanted to discuss. But he knew it was necessary for him to do so.

Beyond the perimeter of the firelight, the two men presented contrasting silhouettes: Imaro's tall and broad, Ngodire's taller and reedlike. Some of the *haramia* who had not yet gone to their shelters for the night cast glances toward the two men and whispered to each other as they watched, although Ngodire had told no one what he intended to say to Imaro.

"Some of the men—and women—are wondering if you know what you're doing," Ngodire said.

Imaro took no offense to Ngodire's bluntness. Better bluntness and truth than flattery and lies: that was a lesson he had learned well during his life among the Ilyassai.

"I am not Rumanzila," he said after a short silence. "I do not force anyone to follow my lead."

"That's why most of the *haramia* do follow you … because you *don't* force them to," said Ngodire. "But that isn't—or wasn't—the only reason. These rogues and renegades have followed you because you are the strongest and fiercest warrior anyone has ever seen, and they could fill their sacks with more loot under your banner than that of anyone else."

He paused for a moment, choosing his next words carefully.

"Until now."

Imaro remained silent, waiting for Ngodire to continue.

"You have made us into warriors, Imaro," the Ndashikuya said. "And we are warriors beyond compare, more than a match for the mightiest armies of the East Coast kingdoms."

Imaro still said nothing.

"A bandit wants to loot and live, not fight and die," Ngodire said.

"A warrior wants to kill, and not to die," said Imaro. "But a warrior is not afraid to die, if he has to."

"That's the problem," said Ngodire. "There are many among us who don't understand why we have to die for the sake of the Umtala."

"I gave them my word that we would bring back their people," Imaro said. "Failing that, we must help them to get their vengeance."

Now it was Ngodire's turn to fall silent.

"What about Chimba's plan to cross the Kakassa?" he finally asked.

"We can still do that."

Ngodire was quiet again. The two men gazed at the firelight and did not look at each other. Ngodire was the first to speak.

"There is something you are not telling me—or the rest of us," he said. "If we are going to cross the Kakassa, then what does it matter that the false *haramia* did harm to the Umtala? They are nothing to us. Why risk being caught by the soldiers on the Umtala's account, even if you did give your word?"

He looked closely at Imaro. Even in the dim firelight, he could see the conflict that raged like a battle behind his eyes. Ngodire could not know how close Imaro came then to telling him about the High Sorcerers, the Mashataan, Chitendu, and the dreams that had recently returned to plague his sleep. In the end, though, he could not.

"There is something else," he finally said. "But it must wait until another time."

Then Imaro turned and walked away. Ngodire's gaze followed him as he headed toward his shelter.

"Another time may be too late," the Ndashikuya murmured.

He was right.

***

Imaro had still not broken his silence when the *tuyabene* attacked.

The *haramia* had remained closer to the river than they would have liked. But that was where the tracks of their quarry led them. Outwardly, the river was like any other. The *haramia* could see the shadows of large fish beneath the surface, and crocodiles and water antelope fled the approach of the bandit army. They saw no sign, however, of the river demons as sunlight glinted from the slow-moving water.

Imaro's *kufahuma* provided the only warning for the *haramia*. He stopped short, then stared closely at the river. The others who were with him at the head of the column also stopped, for they had learned to recognize that the cock of the warrior's head and the intent look in his eyes signaled an awareness of impending danger that their own senses could not match.

Imaro pulled his sword from its sheath.

"Beware!" he shouted, loudly enough to be heard throughout the ranks.

A moment later, the river's surface erupted, and the *tuyabene* leaped out of the water and charged toward the *haramia*. The river demons were man-shaped, but their resemblance to humankind was only superficial, for the knees of their long legs bent backward. Yet they moved with lethal speed and grace. Their slippery, naked skin was the color of the soil at the river's bottom. Elongated jaws gaped wide, exposing rows of needle-sharp teeth. The only sound they uttered was a low, gurgling growl.

The *tuyabene* did not carry weapons; they needed none. From the first fingers of their hand and the first toes of their feet grew long, hooklike claws that ended in joints that were as sharp as the tip of a dagger.

Those claws quickly ripped into the first ranks of the *haramia*, who were too stunned at the sudden appearance of the *tuyabene* to react in time to save their lives. The *tuyabene*'s numbers seemed endless; it was as though the river itself were spawning them.

Only Imaro's swift actions prevented a slaughter from occurring—but not before a *tuyabene*'s claw tore through the throat of Kulutu. The Umtala's eyes never lost their expression of horrified astonishment, not even as he sank to the ground in a welter of his own blood.

With one hand, Imaro thrust Tanisha behind him. With his sword, he cut off the hand of the *tuyabene* that had slain Kulutu. Although her eyes were wide with terror, Tanisha had already drawn her own weapon. Busa was at her side, clutching the hilt of his *panga* with both hands. But neither of them had any foes to engage, for the *tuyabene* in their immediate area had been driven back by the fury of Imaro's counterattack, which left a crop of fresh corpses in its wake.

The warrior's rage was nearly matched by that of the surviving Umtala. Their grief over the slaying of Kulutu overcame their dread of the *tuyabene*, and when they saw that the river demons could be slain, they rushed headlong at their foes, slashing at them with a ferocity their people had never before exhibited in their long seclusion from conflict.

When the *haramia* recovered from the initial shock of the *tuyabene*'s attack, they retaliated mercilessly. Unlike their strategic battles against the soldiers, however, this was a melee of humans and *tuyabene*, sliding in the mud of the riverbank as they tore at each other with steel and claws. The *tuyabene* were not capable of formulating tactics, and the bandits' only strategy was to survive.

For a short time, the momentum of the struggle shifted from one side to the other, then back again. The gurgling death cries of the *tuyabene* vied in volume with the shrieks and groans of the *haramia*. Then another cry rose above the din of combat: the war cry of the Ilyassai. When the *haramia* heard that call, they redoubled their efforts, and the *tuyabene* fell back, though they continued to fight tenaciously and exact their toll of dead.

Finally, their survival instinct superseded the compulsion that had brought the *tuyabene* out of the river. Hopping like gigantic amphibians, they returned to their subsurface lairs, their wounds staining the water crimson as the ripples marked their passage. For a short time, it was this nameless stream, not the Kakassa, that was truly the River of Blood.

Some of the *haramia* splashed into the river in pursuit of the *tuyabene* before Ngodire's voice stopped them.

"Are you fools, to think you can breathe underwater like those demons?" he shouted.

Stung by the Ndashikuya's tone but aware of the truth of his words, the bandits ceased their pursuit and returned to the riverbank. Before long, the current carried away the blood of the *tuyabene*.

The corpses of the river demons were interspersed with those of the *haramia*. Even as the weary survivors of the battle tended their wounds, a crocodile emerged and carried a *tuyabene* carcass back into the river.

Imaro lowered his sword blade. The *tuyabene*'s claws had gashed the leather of his armor, along with his arms. Tanisha was unmarked. The blade of her sword dripped *tuyabene* blood. So did Busa's *panga*.

The *tuyabene* dead far outnumbered the fallen and wounded *haramia*. Even so, the *haramia* had suffered far too many losses—more than they had in their last battle against the forces of the Sha'a and the Mwamu. Now the survivors looked at Imaro, who had saved most of their lives this day. But he had also led many of them to their deaths.

Before anyone could speak, more crocodiles came from the river to claim corpses. When one of the reptiles clamped its jaws on the leg of a dead *haramia*, Imaro shouted, "That is not for you!"

Charging forward, he slashed at the crocodile until it released its grip on the corpse and returned to the river.

"Give the demons to the crocodiles," Imaro commanded. "Don't let them take our dead!"

The *haramia* heeded the warrior's words. Some of them kicked and shoved the corpses of the *tuyabene* into the mouths of the crocodiles; others dragged the *haramia* dead away from the riverbank. Between the efforts of the crocodiles and the bandits, the riverbank was soon cleared of all corpses, and the crocodiles slipped beneath the water's surface.

By the time the bandits buried their dead and performed their various rituals to send their spirits to their ancestors, the sun was about to set. Again the *haramia* focused their attention on Imaro. In his eyes, they saw a weariness that had never been present before. His broad shoulders sagged, as though they bore a burden that had become too heavy even for him. The thought of becoming the ruler of an infant kingdom was far from his mind now.

Only two of the Umtala had survived the battle against the river demons. But they, as well as the ones who had died, had slain many *tuyabene*, and they had gained a measure of vengeance for those who had been stolen and sacrificed. Even so, they wondered if they would ever see their village again, and tell the people who remained there a tale they wouldn't believe.

Ngodire and Kongolo stood at Imaro's side. Tanisha was there, too. Her arm circled the warrior's waist, as though she was all that was keeping him on his feet. The rest of the *haramia* leaned heavily on their weapons. Other than their breathing, which was ragged with exhaustion, the *haramia* remained silent, waiting for their chieftain to speak.

Imaro gestured toward the row of earthen mounds piled with large stones, beneath which the *haramia* dead had been buried.

"The ones who brought these deaths to us owe us a debt," he said. "We will make them pay it."

He raised his sword skyward. Blood fell from its blade to the ground. The others, including the surviving Umtala, lifted their weapons as well, and they echoed the war cry Imaro uttered.

Even as he held his long, slender sword high above his head, Ngodire wondered, *What debt do you owe, Imaro? And how will you pay it?*

***

The *haramia* heard the Kakassa River long before they could see it—a rumbling reminiscent of the sound of distant thunder during the wet season. But the wet season had not yet come. The sky was free of clouds. The hearts of the *haramia* were not.

Even though no more attacks came from the *tuyabene*, Imaro had ordered his scouts to keep a constant watch on the river. The *tuyabene* would not take them by surprise again. Onward the *haramia* marched, following the tantalizing spoor of their quarry.

Like bait leading to a trap, more than a few of the bandits thought as they saw the marks of hurried footsteps. But Imaro would not relent.

The Ilyassai was well aware that the false *haramia* could be deceitful in more than one way. He took all the precautions he could. Scouts ranged far ahead of the main body of the bandit army; the *haramia* marched in a formation that was flexible enough to be effective in either attack or retreat; and he concentrated his own sense of danger, both natural and supernatural, to their utmost.

From a distance, Imaro saw riders approaching—three of them, their horses' hooves spattering mud. Scouts—or foes? Like the others at the front of the outlaws' column, Imaro kept his hand close to his sword-hilt as the riders came closer.

When they arrived, the *haramia* relaxed, for they recognized the face of Chimba, and those of the other two who had volunteered to join his scouting party. Because he was more familiar with this country than any of the others, including the Umtala, Chimba did most of the *haramia*'s reconnaissance. Imaro trusted him only as far as was necessary.

Chimba and the other scouts swung down from their saddles. All three wore glum expressions, a signal that their news would not be what their fellow bandits wanted to hear.

"The ones we seek are near the Kakassa," Chimba said to Imaro and his lieutenants.

"Did you see them?" Imaro asked.

"No," Chimba replied. "We could not even see the river. Mist covers everything. It's like a cloud that has fallen to the ground."

The other two scouts nodded in corroboration of Chimba's words. Imaro was not the only one who frowned in response to the report.

"Was it like that when you were here before?" Ngodire asked Chimba. "When you found the 'passage' across the river?"

"No."

"I don't like this," said Kongolo. "It smells of sorcery. Why else would there be a mist like that in the middle of the dry season?"

"Sorcery can be defeated," Imaro said.

Kongolo nodded slowly. He knew Imaro was right. He had seen the warrior prevail over the *mchawi* that animated the Afua, and he had seen him carry the severed head of the demon Isikukumadevu into the *haramia* encampment in the Black Hills. Yet he could not suppress his feelings of apprehension.

"Do we turn back, or do we go on?" Ngodire asked.

"What do you think?" Imaro asked Chimba.

"I say we should go on."

Before Imaro could go on, Busa spoke.

"Imaro," he said. "Do not follow the advice of a snake."

Rage twisting his features, Chimba took a step forward.

"Shut your mouth, you scar-faced son of a—"

"Enough," said Imaro.

Chimba did not take another step. He continued to glare at Busa, whose own eyes were brimming with hatred. Chimba's anger, however, did not prevent him from completing his report to Imaro.

"We have no other choice but to go on," he said.

"Why?" Imaro demanded.

"Because the mist is not just sitting at the Kakassa," Chimba said. "It is moving—moving in this direction."

"It is so thick, it blots out the sun," said another of the scouts. "And it just keeps coming, like it's swallowing the ground in front of it."

Now, all eyes were on Imaro. But he directed his own gaze to the one who stood beside him: Tanisha. As she gazed up at him, he could see a glimmer of fear in her eyes. But he also saw trust: trust, and confidence that he could overcome whatever it was that was hidden in the mist the scouts had seen. That trust almost overcame him.

Then Imaro turned back to the *haramia*.

"Our enemy comes to us, hiding behind the mist," he said. "I do not fear a foe that cannot show its face. Do you?"

"No!" came the reply from scores of throats.

"When the enemy comes, we will be ready."

Imaro believed his own words. But there were some among the *haramia* who did not. They did not give voice to their misgivings. Nor did they deny them. Now that they had come so far, however, they would stand or fall with N'tu-nje. And he would stand or fall with them.

***

Mist shrouded Angulu so thickly that it obscured even the midnight-black cloak that covered him. He could see nothing other than the swirling white clouds that shifted and coalesced around him. That did not matter to him, though, for his vision extended far beyond the vapor, as well as beyond all the limits that had confined him before he made common cause with the High Sorcerers of Naama.

Once before, during the time when he was still welcome in his native Azania, Angulu had come close to stepping on to the forbidden path of *mchawi*. At the last moment, panic had overcome him, and he had pulled back from that pathway. Even though he did not carry out the final ritual that would have bound him to the Mashataan, other sorcerers had discovered what he was doing, and he had barely escaped Azania with his life.

Among the outlaws of the borderlands, Angulu's sorcerous skills were coveted, and he had joined the strongest of the *haramia* leaders: Rumanzila. And as he cast simple spells for the benefit of the bandits, the *wa-nyanume* tried to forget the promise of power he had allowed to slip out of his grasp.

Then came the mission to steal the Afua ... and the capture of Imaro ... and the disaster that had occurred when Rumanzila rashly plucked one of the Afua's golden spikes ... and the subsequent death of Rumanzila ... and Imaro's ascension to the leadership of the *haramia*.

When Imaro replaced the spike in the Afua after the idol had come to life, he stemmed the flow of *mchawi* from the opening that had unleashed it. Some of the sorcerous energy, however, found a host that was not unwilling to accept it—Angulu. His exposure to the concentrated *mchawi* swept aside the trepidations that had inhibited him before. This time, he opened himself to the High Sorcerers—and they plucked him like a fruit from a tree.

He was under their influence when he departed from the *haramia*. In the deep wilderness, far from even the outlaws, Angulu absorbed the knowledge that had frightened him before. The High Sorcerers revealed their intentions, and the part he would play in their plans, to him. They showed him the rewards that would be his if he succeeded in the tasks they set for him, and the punishments that were the consequence of failure.

And they showed him the price he would have to pay if he became one of them. This time, he was willing to pay it.

Finally, the Naamans showed Angulu the main obstacle that could prevent the achievement of their goals: Imaro. The destruction of the Ilyassai would be Angulu's responsibility.

Angulu had disliked the outlander from the beginning. He had always wished the *haramia* had left the warrior in the Mtumwe village after the bandits stole the Afua. And when he saw how Imaro prevailed against the Afua after the idol was animated by *mchawi*, Angulu realized that the Ilyassai was an uncommonly dangerous man. Now, Angulu would be the instrument of Imaro's downfall.

He had easily insinuated himself into Chimba's dreams—but not into Imaro's. The High Sorcerers themselves were the ones who afflicted the warrior's sleep. It had been easy, also, to intimidate the likes of Bomunu, and even the *mwenyes*, Mkojo and Chuwumba. Mkojo had known of Angulu's past in Azania, but he was willing to overlook the *wa-nyanume*'s previous misdeeds in exchange for his help in defeating the bandit army.

Summoning and controlling the *tuyabene* was more difficult, but he had managed to do it, and their attack had weakened the *haramia*, though the river demons had failed to slay Imaro.

Now, as he gathered his *mchawi* in the thickening mist, Angulu experienced a moment of doubt akin to the uncertainty that had thwarted his first attempt to wield *mchawi*. For Imaro was, in his own way, as formidable as the High Sorcerers.

Still, Imaro was only a man. The High Sorcerers were more—much more. And so, now, was Angulu.

The sorcerer's hands wove intricate patterns in the air. He spoke words of power that resonated deep within him. The mist moved in cadence with his speech. The *mchawi* flowed through him.

The time had come....

***

Like a vast, moving wall of white, the mist approached the waiting *haramia*. The bandit army had moved inland, away from the river and the *tuyabene*, for there was no longer any reason to follow the trail of the false *haramia*. Now the enemy was coming to them.

The mist was as white as a cloud, as Chimba had said. But it had not whorls or ridges, or even a shape. As it drew nearer, the mist appeared to consume all that stood before it—even the sky. The wildlife in the area had long since fled its approach, and the bandits who had horses were experiencing difficulty keeping their mounts under control.

In the background the *haramia* could hear the muted roar of the Kakassa, into which this nameless but deadly stream flowed.

Imaro had deployed his forces in concentric circles. Spearmen and mounted bandits formed the outer circle; sword wielders stood a few paces behind. The two surviving Umtala stood in the inner circle: bows raised, arrows nocked. Tanisha and the other women among the *haramia* were also in the second circle. The weapons in their hands did not waver as the mist came closer.

In his customary place at the front of the *haramia* ranks, Imaro was already under attack. The taint of *mchawi* assailed his senses relentlessly. Yet he showed no sign of discomfort as the vapor crept forward.

When the featureless haze came to within a few paces of the *haramia*, it halted. Its substance was so opaque that it was impossible to see what it hid—or shielded. The only sound other than the Kakassa's rumble was the horses' nervous snorting and pawing of hooves.

Then, as though it were a curtain pulled aside by the hands of a giant, the mist parted, then quickly disappeared. And the sight of what the haze had concealed raised cries of consternation in the *haramia*'s ranks.

This was not the ragged group of false *haramia* Imaro's army thought it was chasing along the river. Instead, the *haramia* were facing the full, combined host of Zimbabwean and Azanian soldiers who had been, in turn, pursuing them. As if the overwhelming number of troops were not demoralizing enough for the *haramia*, the soldiers were accompanied by a teeming horde of *tuyabene*. Like the water from which they had emerged, the river demons flowed in front of the soldiers, standing between them and the *haramia*.

But it was not the *tuyabene* that claimed Imaro's attention. Instead, his eyes focused on four figures at the head of the soldiers' ranks. Two of them were the force's commanders, Mkojo of Azania and Chuwumba of Zanj. Imaro had seen them from a distance in previous battles, and if he hadn't, the deference with which they were treated by the other soldiers would have marked their rank.

With the commanders were two others whom Imaro knew well, though he had not seen either of them for a long time, and had doubted that he would ever encounter them again.

One was Bomunu—a grinning, confident Bomunu, not the chastened wretch whose humiliation had forced him to slink surreptitiously away from the *haramia* he had once aspired to lead. Imaro noticed that Bomunu was standing at the side of the Azanian *mwenye* rather than that of his countryman, Chuwumba. Bomunu raised his hand to Imaro in a mocking salute.

As for the other ... At first, Imaro almost didn't recognize Angulu, for the *wa-nyanume* had never swathed himself in black during his time among the *haramia*. And never before had Angulu reeked of *mchawi*—the sorcery Imaro's Naaman enemies employed.

Like Bomunu, Angulu lifted his hand. But the motion was not an ironic gesture. The sorcerer's lips moved as well. Imaro could not hear the words Angulu was speaking. But the *tuyabene* could.

The river demons surged forward; behind them, the troops advanced at a slower pace, content to allow their inhuman allies to begin the battle. As the *tuyabene* approached, the *haramia* could see the damage that the long period the creatures had spent outside the water had inflicted. Their eyes were dull and glazed, and scaly flakes of skin fell to the ground with each step the *tuyabene* took. But the *tuyabene*'s claws were still lethal, and the creatures' ferocity remained undiminished as they tore into the bandits.

As the fighting commenced, Imaro shouted a single command:

"Don't let them break the circle!"

The *haramia* obeyed, even as the *tuyabene*'s claws again ripped into them as lethally as any weapon made from steel. Following Imaro's example, the *haramia* used their shields to attack as well as defend, and *tuyabene* corpses collected at the bandits' feet. But the claws of the tuyabene exacted a toll as well, and more than a few *haramia* went down, blood pouring from jagged wounds.

Yet the bandits held their formation in the face of the *tuyabene*'s savage onslaught. They were familiar with these foes now; the shock and horror that had accompanied their first attack was gone. While the *haramia* were occupied with the *tuyabene*, however, the two armies moved into position, surrounding the *haramia*. For a time, they watched as the *tuyabene*, urged forward by the sorcery of Angulu, wreaked havoc in the bandits' ranks. Then

Chuwumba and Mkojo issued simultaneous commands, and the soldiers joined the attack.

***

Two sword blades slashed toward Imaro: one aimed at his face, the other at his abdomen. With a flexibility that seemed impossible in a person of his size, he twisted out of the path of the point that was about to impale his stomach and brought his own blade up to parry the slash aimed at his head. Then the warrior swung his sword twice, and both his assailants went down, one of them dead before he hit the ground, the other groaning from a wound that cut halfway through his body.

Taking advantage of the brief respite, Imaro scanned the battlefield. Not all of his fellow *haramia* were faring as well as he, but the outer circle held firm, even as both the soldiers and *tuyabene* attacked. Although the *haramia* were vastly outnumbered, their ferocity offset that disadvantage. They knew their only chance to survive would be to stand firm and break the will of their enemies.

Imaro looked for Tanisha, and he saw that she was still safe, in the midst of a group of men and women who were fighting in the second line. Kongolo and Ngodire were rallying the *haramia* in other parts of the circle. Busa remained close to Imaro. He wielded his *panga* crudely but effectively, chopping at his foes as though they were trees in the Kajua.

Then Imaro turned his attention to the enemy. He saw Angulu standing apart from the others, his cloak swirling around him like the wings of a gigantic bird. If the sorcerer could control the movements of the *tuyabene* and conjure the concealing mist, what other damage was he capable of inflicting on the *haramia* with the power of his *mchawi*?

Imaro made an instant decision. After dispatching yet another soldier, he bent down and shouted into Busa's ear, cutting through the clash of weapons and the cries of the wounded and dying.

"Cover my back!" he said.

Busa nodded, and his *panga* slashed in a whirlwind of steel, momentarily keeping soldiers and *tuyabene* alike at bay. Sheathing his sword, Imaro bent down and snatched a spear from the hand of a dead foe. He hefted the weapon, assessing its balance. The *arem* of the Ilyassai was designed for stabbing, not throwing. But the Ilyassai used throwing spears as well, and Imaro's motion was fluid and flawless as he hurled the weapon high over the heads of the combatants.

Angulu was so intent on monitoring the movements of the *tuyabene* that he did not heed the sudden, frantic warnings the soldiers closest to him shouted. He only became aware of danger when the point of the spear Imaro had thrown tore into his throat. For a moment, the *wa-nyanume* stood transfixed, as though the spear had pinned him to an unseen wall. The shaft of the spear bobbed, and gore spurted from Angulu's mouth as he tried to cry out. But he couldn't make a sound.

Then the sorcerer fell backward, and the spear shaft pointed upward like the stem of a plant rooted in bloodstained soil.

A great cry rose among the *haramia* when they saw Angulu fall. They redoubled their efforts against the soldiers and the *tuyabene*, and for the first time since the battle had begun, the *haramia* forced their foes to give ground. Another factor, however, was threatening to turn the battle into complete chaos.

Freed from the sorcerous compulsion Angulu had forced upon them through his sacrifice of the Umtala youths, the *tuyabene*'s sole desire now was to return to the water before further exposure to the alien element of air finally killed them. To that end, they attacked all who stood in their path, soldiers and *haramia* alike. The clear divisions among the antagonists suddenly disappeared, and an inchoate melee deadly to all involved began.

Now Imaro saw a chance to achieve victory. If he could rally the *haramia* to use the amok *tuyabene* to their advantage, they could rout their foes, despite the soldiers' advantage in numbers.

Imaro opened his mouth to shout new commands—then something crashed against his legs, nearly knocking him off balance. He looked down and saw Busa lying on the ground, clutching his stomach, blood seeping between his fingers. Standing behind Busa, sword blade dripping blood, was not a Zanjian or Azanian soldier, but Chimba. The *haramia*'s face was twisted into a mask of frustration, and Imaro immediately understood the reason.

The blow Chimba had struck was intended not for Busa, but for Imaro. Busa had jumped in front of Imaro, and had repaid the Ilyassai for saving him and Msuli from the crocodile in the Damba Bolong what seemed like a lifetime ago.

Enraged by Chimba's treachery, Imaro swung his sword. But Chimba was too quick. He leaped backward, and the blade barely missed him. With a wordless curse, Chimba spat on the ground at Imaro's feet. Then he turned and fled.

Imaro looked down again at Busa. He never had a chance to thank Busa for saving his life, for the Mtumwe was already dead. And he owed both his life, and his death, to Imaro.

Then, looking across the swirling mass of confusion the battlefield had become, Imaro saw something that caused him to forget Busa, and to cry out in anguish and disbelief.

***

Tanisha's faith in Imaro's prowess as a warrior had never wavered. However, her own confidence in her ability to survive what raged around her was an entirely different matter.

Imaro had taught her well; when her blade cut into flesh, the wound it left was as lethal as any a man could inflict. But she could not match a man's strength. Speed and guile were the other weapons that complemented her blade. Now that both the *haramia*'s circles were breaking, the soldiers were pressing closer, and she was losing the few advantages she had.

Grimly, she fought on, along with the others who were with her. Some of them were women bandits; others were captives who had become camp followers. *Haramia* men were battling on the women's behalf as well, and she was grateful for their presence. Imaro, however, was worth more than all of them combined on a battlefield, and she would have felt safer if he alone were at her side.

She understood why he could not be with her. His responsibilities included all the *haramia*, not just her. Yet she could not bear the thought of dying without him, or of him dying without her.

And, she thought when she had a moment's respite from concentrating on survival, she was certain she would be the first Shikaza woman to die on a battlefield, rather than in the palace of an East Coast noble or king to whom she had been sold.

Perhaps if more Shikaza had died this way, none of us would have to die the other way, she thought.

A soldier's blade came perilously close to cutting off her hand as well as her thoughts. Tanisha barely managed to parry the slash. Then she laid open a wound on the soldier's arm that caused him to cry out and drop his sword. One of the women at her side brought him down with a cut that severed his hamstrings.

Momentarily, the attackers fell back. Tanisha looked for Imaro. She saw him just as he hurled the spear that brought Angulu down. A cry of triumph rose in her throat—then it died when she saw Chimba's treacherous attempt to kill Imaro, and Busa's act of self-sacrifice.

Then the soldiers closed in again, and she was forced to take her eyes off Imaro and fight for her life. She lost sight of Chimba as well. Even as she slashed, parried, and dodged, Tanisha was determined now to go to Imaro. But before she could tell the others her intention, she was suddenly struck on the head. Pain overwhelmed her consciousness as rough hands seized her from behind. As her sword dropped from her hand and she was pulled backward, a familiar face swam into her blurred field of vision.

Then she knew no more.

***

Imaro saw Chimba strike Tanisha down. The *haramia*'s action stunned the others around her long enough to allow him to sling her unconscious body over one shoulder. Chimba's slight frame contained deceptive strength. In a moment, he was gone, carrying Tanisha as though she were weightless.

Before the other *haramia* could pursue the treacherous Chimba, they again had to battle the soldiers, who had renewed their attack, even as they were trying to fend off the *tuyabene* at the same time. A mass of struggling combatants separated Imaro from Tanisha and her abductor. Yet even as he defended himself against his foes, he could see where Chimba was going. He was headed toward the perimeter of the fighting. There, one man and two horses waited. Even from the distance across the battlefield, Imaro recognized the man. It was Bomunu.

Chimba wove through the fighting like a serpent through blades of grass. When he reached Bomunu, he handed Tanisha to him. The Zanjian slung her inert form over the front of his saddle, and he mounted the horse. Chimba mounted the other steed.

Across the horde of struggling combatants, Bomunu locked eyes with Imaro. With a smile on his face, and another salute, the Zanjian rode away, bearing Tanisha with him. Chimba rode at his side.

The sound that issued from Imaro's throat then was like nothing anyone had heard before, in or out of the wilderness. Those who were near him—friend and foe alike—drew back at the sight of the rage and torment on his face and the lethal glare in his eyes. The respite lasted only for a short time. Then the fighting resumed, with renewed ferocity.

During his time of distraction, Imaro lost his chance to salvage a victory. For the soldiers' commanders had seen the same opportunity he had observed, and they were quick to take advantage of it.

Instead of fighting the surviving *tuyabene*, the soldiers prodded and redirected them toward the *haramia*. The tactic succeeded. Between the *tuyabene* and their numerical advantage, the soldiers were beginning to prevail against the bandits.

Imaro continued to take his own deadly toll of attackers. But other *haramia* were falling. Kongolo went down, as did the last two Umtala. Even *haramia* who fought near Imaro were dying. Ngodire was still alive, and still fighting.

In the distance, Bomunu and Chimba's horses had become mere dots, headed toward the Kakassa River—toward the passage Chimba had promised to reveal to the *haramia*.

Never before had Imaro retreated from a battle against man, beast, or demon. Fleeing a fight was not the way of the Ilyassai, nor would it be the way of the *haramia* under Imaro's leadership. But he had led them to a defeat that was growing more imminent by the moment. And Bomunu had stolen Tanisha. . . .

"To me!" Imaro commanded. "To me!"

The *haramia* who were still standing fought their way to their leader. Some of them did not make it to his side. Those who did gazed at him with battle-weary eyes. Much of the Ilyassai's leather armor had been hacked away, and not all of the blood that spattered his limbs belonged to his foes.

The *haramia* feared him, and some of them were beginning to hate him. Yet their hopes of surviving what was becoming a massacre rested solely on him.

"Get in two lines and follow me," Imaro said.

The remaining *haramia*, who numbered only a few score, obeyed Imaro's command. Ngodire stood at the vanguard, at Imaro's side. A moment later, the warrior charged forward, his sword slashing a bloody path through the tangled ranks of soldiers and *tuyabene*. Like the spear it resembled, the *haramia*'s formation plunged through the enemy, and suddenly, there was open space in front of them.

"Keep moving!" Imaro shouted.

Again, the *haramia* obeyed. Some of them had fallen, but all of them would have died had Imaro not led them through their foes. They ran. The few of them who were mounted outdistanced the others. All the survivors headed in the same direction the traitor Chimba and the woman-stealer Bomunu had taken.

Under other circumstances, the soldiers would have pursued the fleeing, defeated enemy. However, with the *haramia* gone, the remaining *tuyabene* focused their fury solely on the Zanjians and Azanians, as Imaro had anticipated. By the time the soldiers managed to kill all the river demons, the *haramia* were gone from sight.

"Do we go after them now?" *Mwenye* Mkojo asked, as he and Chuwumba surveyed the corpse-strewn field of their costly triumph.

"No," Chuwumba said. "It's not worth the loss of one more man from either of our armies."

The Zanjian commander shook his head as he watched the clouds of flies that were already descending on the dead.

"The *haramia* are finished," he said. "N'tu-nje is finished. After what happened here today, his own followers will probably kill him."

"What about N'tu-nje's head?" Mkojo asked. "Both our monarchs demanded it."

Chuwumba gestured toward the *haramia* corpses.

"Any one of them will do," he said.

Mkojo nodded agreement. The two commanders parted then, realizing that their alliance of convenience had effectively ended, and that the next time they saw each other, it would be on a different battlefield, against each other. Separately, they supervised the burial of their armies' dead, leaving the *haramia* and the *tuyabene* for the scavengers, which would feast for days and leave an army of unmourned spirits behind.

When a pair of Azanian soldiers lifted Angulu's body to drop it into a common grave, the midnight-black cloak he wore caught on one of the men's weapons, and it ripped apart. At the sight of what the rip revealed, the soldiers turned their heads away in disgust and quickly threw the corpse in with the others.

The *wa-nyanume*'s body had . . . altered. Protruding pustules had formed on his skin, and the proportions of his limbs had changed in a way that repelled the soldiers, hardened though they were to the horrific sights of war.

Not recognizing what they saw, the soldiers assumed the protuberances were the marks of a disease. Saying nothing to anyone else, they piled other bodies on top of the Angulu's.

Had Imaro been there to see the deformities, he would have recognized them immediately. For he had seen similar protuberances, fully formed, on the misshapen body of Chitendu, in the Place of Stones.

***

As Jua set, the remnants of the bandit army rested. Some of the *haramia* leaned on their weapons. Others, too exhausted to stand, lay on the ground. Little more than two score of the *haramia* had survived the battle against the soldiers and the *tuyabene.* All the survivors bore wounds, some serious enough to be fatal if left untreated.

The country to which they had fled was rugged, with an abundance of thornbushes and huge rocks that seemed to grow out of the ground. As always, the wildlife remained wary of the two-legs and their steel.

Thus far, no one had detected any signs of pursuit. Some of the bandits thought the soldiers would be satisfied with the massive defeat they had inflicted. Others believed they would be hunted down until the last of them was dead. Still others preferred not to think at all about what might happen the next day, and the day after that. They were alive. That was enough for them.

It was not enough for Imaro.

"We will stay here for the night," he said. "In the morning, we will follow the trail of Bomunu and Chimba—and Tanisha."

"'We?'"

The speaker was Ngodire. Bitterness laced the Ndashikuya's tone as he looked at Imaro in a way no *haramia* had since the day the warrior had withstood the initiation—and in a way Ngodire had never looked at him before.

"There is no more 'we' among us, Imaro," Ngodire continued. "The 'we' is dead, as are all the others the hyenas are eating now."

"And they will eat us, too, if we continue to follow you," said Mtobo, the young bandit who had captured Kulutu, unknowingly sealing the doom of the Umtala and all the others who had accompanied him.

Imaro could only stare at the two men, not believing what he was hearing.

"You were going to lead us to a new kingdom," said Mtobo. "And so you did—to a kingdom of the dead."

The other *haramia* nodded in agreement. Even the ones who had been too fatigued to stand a moment ago were now on their feet, eying Imaro warily. Their hands touched the hilts of their swords.

"Do you not want vengeance against Chimba and Bomunu?" Imaro asked. "Do you not want to help me to get Tanisha back?"

"If you get your woman back, that is good for you," said Ngodire. "And if you kill Chimba and Bomunu, that is what those jackals deserve. But you will have to do those things by yourself."

Ngodire kept his hand on his sword-hilt, for the expression on the Ilyassai's face was frightening to behold. But he spoke on, regardless of what the words were costing him, for he had not lost his respect for the Ilyassai as a man and a warrior—only as a leader.

"We will not follow you anymore, Imaro," he said. "And you will not follow us. It's better that we all go our separate ways. When the soldiers realize they will have to hunt us one by one, maybe they'll leave us all alone."

Again, the others agreed. Now all of them had their weapons drawn. So did Imaro.

"We don't want to kill you, Imaro," said Ngodire. "We owe you our lives. But you owe too many deaths. Death follows you."

Imaro stared hard at the *haramia*. But he was not seeing them. He was seeing the Ilyassai. The rancor in the eyes of some of the *haramia* was reminiscent of the way his mother's people had looked at him during all the time he had been among them, until the death of Chitendu in the Place of Stones.

And Imaro's own emotions were traveling along a familiar path, as well. He shoved his sword back into its sheath.

"Go your way, then," he said, his tone as bleak as the landscape that surrounded him.

The bandits did not attempt to conceal their relief. With their advantage in numbers, they could have overcome Imaro sooner or later. But many of them would have died before he went down. It was better to end it this way, with no more deaths among them.

Without further words, the *haramia* turned and left Imaro behind—just as he had left the Ilyassai. He had not looked back at the Ilyassai; only one *haramia* looked back at him—Ngodire. Long after they had dwindled into the distance, Imaro stared in the direction they had gone.

My people, he thought.

***

Imaro was alone.

Without the Ilyassai …

Without the Mtumwe …

Without the haramia …

Without Tanisha …

The last time Imaro had been so isolated was immediately after he had left the Ilyassai, when he had wandered through unknown country before his encounter with the river people. His solitude then had been self-imposed. Now, he had been cast out by outcasts.

As the warrior had expected, the trail of those he sought led him close to the banks of the Kakassa River. Chimba was indeed leading Bomunu and the captive Tanisha to the promised passage. The roar of the river drummed in Imaro's ears. His first sight of it had caused him to gape in amazement.

Unlike the Damba Bolong, or the nameless stream from which the *tuyabene* had come, the Kakassa flowed swiftly, like a predator pursuing its quarry. Also unlike the other rivers, the Kakassa was studded with rocks—not round, smooth stones that could be used as a pathway across its breadth, but sharp, jagged rocks like the ridges along the back of a crocodile. It was the rocks, more than the current, that made the Kakassa impassable.

Imaro sensed *mchawi* as he came closer to the river. But the presence of the sorcery was old, like a trail washed to near-invisibility by the passage of many rains. It was as though some sinister force had exerted an unnatural change in the river a long time ago.

Scrub bush was the only vegetation on the Kakassa's banks. The tracks of the horses Bomunu and Chimba rode were clearly visible. Their mounts had given them a long lead over Imaro. He wished he could run as fast as the Kakassa flowed. He knew that he would eventually find the way across the river, wherever the hoof marks finally ended.

Toward the middle of the day, Imaro saw the horses. They were riderless, and as they drew closer, Imaro could see that their gear had been stripped away. The horses were running, eyes rolling with fear, for a pair of lionesses were pursuing them across the scrubland. Fast as the horses ran, the great, golden cats ran faster.

The lionesses brought one of the horses down, and its dying shriek echoed above the roar of the Kakassa. Having taken their prey, the lionesses allowed the other horse to escape.

As he watched the great cats devour the horse, Imaro knew he could not be far from the passage now. Bomunu and Chimba would not have abandoned their mounts very long ago. If they had, the beasts of the wilderness would have killed them before now.

The warrior picked up his pace, loping as he once had through the grass of the Tamburure. He focused on following the tracks and finding the passage. Resolutely, he banished all thoughts of the *haramia* from his mind. Consumed as he was by the need to rescue Tanisha and slay her abductors, that was not a difficult task.

By the middle of the afternoon, he found the place where the hoof marks ended. He saw the horses' saddles and bridles, which had been carelessly cast aside. And he saw—and heard—a huge cataract that led straight downward.

Gingerly, Imaro peered over the precipice. The roaring waterfall ended far below, sending up thick clouds of mist that were unlike the unnatural vapor Angulu had conjured. Beyond the mist, he could see that the Kakassa, and its rocks, extended to the distant horizon.

He also saw the passage: a narrow ledge near the top of the precipice, which led behind the waterfall.

Imaro wondered how Bomunu and Chimba could have carried an unconscious Tanisha along such a narrow pathway.

And if she was conscious …

He looked down again. Imaro was no climber; he was a man of the flat savanna. He would have preferred wrestling with Isikukumadevu to clambering down to the ledge, then following it under the waterfall. Still, if city-bred men like Chimba and Bomunu could do it, so could he.

Breathing deeply, Imaro levered his way over the edge of the cliff, and clung to whatever hand- and footholds he could find. He did not dare to look down again, not even when his feet touched the ledge.

Then he inched carefully along the ledge until he reached the waterfall. Its roar deafened him; his *kufahuma* sense was useless. The relentless cascade nearly knocked him from the ledge before he managed to pull himself to safety behind its flow.

The ledge widened behind the falls. But the rock was slippery, and the path far from smooth. As he made his way across, Imaro's existence was reduced to water, rocks, and the loudest noise he had ever endured. At the point when he thought the passage would never end, it sloped upward. A few moments later, he was free from the falls.

He felt as though he had just stepped out of the jaws of a gigantic, growling beast. Not since his childhood had he felt so small and insignificant.

Drenched as though he had been standing in a rainstorm, Imaro climbed to the other side of the Kakassa. The terrain there differed little from what he had left behind—except for a smudge of green on the horizon. A forest …

Vultures were circling and landing nearby. With a sense of foreboding, Imaro approached the carrion birds. They scattered resentfully, loath to leave their feast. Not much remained of the corpse on which the vultures were feeding. But it was enough to allow Imaro to identify Chimba, and to see that the treacherous bandit's throat had been cut.

"You trusted the wrong man," Imaro muttered.

He read the signs of what had happened after Chimba's death. Two sets of tracks led to the forest in the distance. One of the trails showed furrows in the dirt, as though the person who made it was being dragged unwillingly. At one point, it was clear that the person had fallen, only to be made to walk again.

Imaro looked down at Chimba's carcass one last time as the vultures circled impatiently. Then he looked at the Kakassa, and at the chasm that now separated him from his past.

Everything he thought he had gained since he departed from the Place of Stones was gone now. As he began to follow the spoor of Bomunu and Tanisha, three purposes pushed his footsteps forward: to save Tanisha, to kill Bomunu—and to destroy the Naamans.

The weapon was unsheathed....

GLOSSARY

The Tamburure

Ajunge: The Spear God; the highest deity in the Ilyassai pantheon.

arem: The spear used by the Ilyassai for war and ritual lion hunts. Length—six to seven feet, half of which is edged iron.

boma: A thornbush enclosure the Tamburure tribes erect to pen cattle and protect temporary encampments.

Chui: The leopard.

Fisi: The carrion-eating hyena.

ilmonek: An Ilyassai youth who exhibits cowardice on his ritual lion hunt. Literally, "un-man." An Ilmonek is banished from his clan in a ritual called the Shaming.

Ilyassai: A tribe of nomadic warriors and cattle-herders, dominant among many other such tribes that roam the Tamburure savanna.

Itayok: A clan of the Ilyassai.

Kifaru: The rhinoceros.

Kitoko: The Ilyassai clan to which Imaro and his mother, Katisa, belong.

kufahuma: The sensory attunement or rapport between the Ilyassai warrior and the environment of the Tamburure that sometime warns them of imminent danger.

Kupigana: The god of the Turkhana tribe.

kutendea: A gift of succulent grass given by an Ilyassai herder to the cattle of a friend.

mafundishu-ya-muran: A period of warrior-training lasting from the fifth year of life to the late adolescence of an Ilyassai male. During this period, the youths are isolated from the rest of their clan.

manyatta: The basic Ilyassai dwelling, constructed from hides stretched across poles. To facilitate transport, the *manyatta* is collapsible.

Matisho: The hunting-hyena of the Tamburure, a species distinct from the more common, carrion-eating Fisi.

Mboa: The buffalo.

Mbwa: The wild dog of the Tamburure.

Mbweha: The jackal.

mchawi: Malign magic, evil sorcery, witchcraft.

Ngatun: The lion.

ngombe: The cattle of the Ilyassai; a long-horned, powerfully built stock bred over many generations by the tribes of the Tamburure.

n'tu-mchawi: A practitioner of sorcery among the Tamburure tribes.

oibonok: The Ilyassai shaman, who interprets the will of the god Ajunge. Magic—of the benign variety, not *mchawi*—is an important adjunct to the role.

ol-arem: A clan chieftain of the Ilyassai. Literally: "first spear."

olmaiyo: The ritual lion hunt that marks the final test of manhood for Ilyassai youth. Ngatun must be slain single-handed.

Place of Stones: A prehuman ruin in a remote part of the Tamburure that is shunned by the people of the savanna.

shingona: An Ilyassai ceremonial headgear made from the mane of the lion a youth slays on *olmaiyo*.

simi: a short sword favored by the Ilyassai and certain other tribes of the Tamburure.

Tamburure: A vast plain of yellow grass in the east-central part of the continent of Nyumbani, analogous to the Serengeti of Africa.

Tembo: The elephant.

Turkhana: A Tamburure tribe that is the greatest rival to the Ilyassai.

Zamburu: A Tamburure tribe the Ilyassai raid regularly for cattle and women.

The Kajua

Afua: A wooden statue festooned with spikes of gold, sacred to the Mtumwe tribe.

bongo: An antelope of the Kajua forest.

Kajua: A large rain forest located far to the north and east of the Tamburure.

Its main feature is the Damba Bolong River, alongside which many tribes dwell.

Kiboko: The hippopotamus.

kijiji: A town or village of the river people.

Mjino: The crocodile.

mku: A chieftain of the river people.

Mponga: The chimpanzee.

Mtumwe: One of many of the tribes that dwell on the banks of the Damba Bolong.

ndizi-pombe: Banana beer.

Ngagi: The gorilla.

nganga: A shaman and diviner among the river people.

panga: A sharp, single-edged knife favored by the river people.

ujuju: Magic practiced by the river people.

East Coast Kingdoms and Borderlands

amir: A noble of Azania.

Azania: The most powerful kingdom on the East Coast.

haramia: Bandits who roam the borderlands of the East Coast kingdoms.

kuva: An enveloping, shroudlike garment worn by women of the Shikaza tribe.

Mulundu: The capital of Azania.

Ndurubu: A nomadic tribe of the East Coast hinterland.

Ndashikuya: A kingdom of very tall people located far to the west of the coastal lands.

Sha'a: The title of the king of Azania.

shati: an overshirt worn by the men of the East Coast.

Shikaza: A remote tribe of the hinterlands known for the beauty of its women.

suruali: Cotton trousers worn by the men of the East Coast.

Tangwe: An Azanian border town, sacked by the *haramia*.

wa-nyanume: The highest rank a sorcerer can achieve in the East Coast kingdoms.

Zanj: A leading East Coast kingdom, and Azania's greatest rival.

Miscellaneous

Cloud Striders: Benign, extradimensional beings that oppose the Mashataan.

Isikukumadevu: A demonic creature aligned with the Mashataan that dwells in a fetid pool in the Black Hills

Jua: The sun of Nyumbani's world.

Mashataan: Demon Gods; extradimensional entities inimical to the people of Nyumbani.

Mwesu: The moon of Nyumbani's world.

Naama: Kingdom of the High Sorcerers of the Mashataan, located at the southernmost tip of Nyumbani.

Nyumbani: The continent on which Imaro's adventures take place; analogous to the Africa of the Earth we know.

AFTERWORD

BY BENJAMIN SZUMSKYJ

In 1958, a twelve-year-old African-American boy read *Star Man's Son, 2250 A.D.*, by Andre Norton. The book had a profound effect on its reader.

Years passed. In 1974, the young man, with aspirations of writing, made his way to the offices of Howard E. (Gene) Day, editor and publisher of *Dark Fantasy: The Magazine of Underground Creators*. In his hands was a short story titled "M'ji Ya Wazimu" (a.k.a. "The City of Madness"). The editor read the story and accepted it without a second thought. It appeared over two issues (4 and 5) of *Dark Fantasy* and was fantastically illustrated by the legendary Day.

The protagonist of the story was an African warrior named of Imaro. The young man's name? Charles R. Saunders.

Born in Pennsylvania 1946, Charles Robert Saunders was destined to write, which came from his youthful passion to read. From an early age, Saunders "read hard SF – Heinlein, Hal Clement, Murray Leinster, and so on – as well as the more adventuresome "planet stories," pulpish-type stuff, which was pure escapism… (as well as) Edgar Rice Burroughs's Tarzan and Mars books." In a May 2001 interview conducted by Amy Harlib, Saunders commented that:

"(F)antasy appealed to something deeper in me – the soul of the storyteller, perhaps. It was when I discovered fantasy that I also discovered that I wanted to be a storyteller – a *griot*, although I hadn't yet discovered that term. I soon would, though. I spent my university days at a historically-black college in Pennsylvania, Lincoln. Lincoln had a lot of students from Africa at the time, and I learned a great deal from them. I started reading more about the history and culture of Africa. And I began to realize that in the SF and fantasy genre, blacks were, with only few exceptions, either left out or depicted in racist and stereotypic ways. I had a choice: I could either stop reading SF and fantasy, or try to do something about my dissatisfaction with it by writing my own stories and trying to get them published. I chose the latter ..."

No sooner said than done. Saunders created Imaro and Day published the hero's first adventure in his fanzine. The fanzine found its way into the hands of Lin Carter, who just happened to be editing *The Year's Best Fantasy Stories*. Carter decided it was so good, that it would appear in the first volume of the ongoing series.

It was at this moment that Saunders's literary career began. During this time, his writing knew no bounds. He met and corresponded with fellow authors -- Karl Edward Wagner, Charles de Lint, L. Sprague de Camp, Andrew J. Offutt, Tanith Lee and Samuel R. Delany, to name but a few. Though the future wasn't certain at that point, the present for Saunders was a dream that had come true.

Imaro made Saunders's name known in the fantasy community. However, after three fine novels, the legend of the Ilyassai warrior was brought to a sad halt. Saunders, like Imaro, walked into the sunset. Years passed, and it was believed that Imaro would no longer leave any more footprints for his readers to follow.

It was then, that I came along, a twenty-one year old from Australia. I had learned of Imaro through my friend Dale R. Rippke, whose *Heroes of Dark Fantasy* remains one of the most resourceful websites on the Internet. Independent fantasy scholars Morgan Holmes and Joseph W. Marek also aided my quest to seek out as much as I could on Imaro and his creator, Charles R. Saunders. It took me some time to obtain the trilogy of novels, but it was worth it.

However, when I read the last page of *Imaro III: The Trail of Bohu* and realized there would be no more stories, my passion for the Ilyassai did not abate. I wanted *more* Imaro.

I've always had an interest and love for African and African-American history and culture, and Imaro was part of the reason for it. It's an interest I cannot explain, but one that continues strongly to this day. I wished there come a time when Imaro would be republished and his saga finished by the hand of his creator. I chose a star, made the wish, and hoped it would be heard.

It was.

Yet the resurrection of Imaro's adventures almost didn't occur. As Charles says in his preface, I sent an e-mail from the suburb of Melville, Western Australia, that reached his e-mailbox in Nova Scotia, eastern Canada.

His reply will forever be cherished. He began by thanking me for my appraisal and interest in his literary works, but was unable to accept my offer of bringing back Imaro to the field of fantasy literature. Throughout the letter he explained his reasons. As you can imagine, a sense of sadness came over me. After all, I loved the fantastical exploits of Imaro, not to mention the mesmerising style of Charles's prose.

Imaro, after all, was different. That is what made him unique and better than other fantasy heroes. Imaro deserved to be revived after so long an absence.

It was then that something magical happened. Yes, *magical* is the word. For, by the end of the letter, Charles had convinced himself that Imaro *could* come back – that his greatest creation *was* capable of breathing new life.

At that point, Charles began revising the Imaro stories. The moment he finished an instalment, I began to edit. It was a unique experience. As Charles states in his preface, his concerns over the story "Slaves of the Giant-Kings" was an issue that had to be addressed. As a result, "The Afua" was born.

Being the first to read "The Afua" was an experience I shall not forget. To me, it's a clear sign that Charles has not lost his touch as a fantasy author; that his craft was never one that was adopted in his life; rather, one he was born with.

Imaro is both an important and fascinating fantasy creation. He is an African warrior in a meticulously researched and detailed world, written by an African-American. Both author and character provide a beacon of true creativity in fantasy literature.

Thank you, reader, for joining me in witnessing the resurrection of Imaro.

Benjamin Szumskyj
Melville, Western Australia – 2005